CONQUEST OF PARADISE

Conquest Of Paradise

An End-times Nano-Thriller

Britt Gillette

Writers Club Press

New York Lincoln Shanghai

Conquest Of Paradise
An End-times Nano-Thriller

Writers Club Press
an imprint of iUniverse, Inc.

For information address:
iUniverse, Inc.
2021 Pine Lake Road, Suite 100
Lincoln, NE 68512
www.iuniverse.com

Artwork and Design by Greg Rolfes (enigma808.com)

ISBN: 0-595-26454-9

Printed in the United States of America

Dedicated to the billions of souls inhabiting Earth...

"His disciples came and asked him, 'Why do you always tell stories when you talk to the people?' Then he explained to them, 'You have been permitted to understand the secrets of the Kingdom of Heaven, but others have not. To those who are open to my teaching, more understanding will be given, and they will have an abundance of knowledge. But to those who are not listening, even what they have will be taken away from them. That is why I tell these stories, because people see what I do, but they don't really see. They hear what I say, but they don't really hear, and they don't understand."

—**Jesus Christ**
Matthew 12:10–13

"For all have sinned and fallen short of the glory of God…"

—**Paul**
Romans 3:23

CONTENTS

▼

PART III: MYTHIC ASCENT

PART IV: INFINITE JUSTICE FOR ALL MEN

PART V: THE ASSEMBLER BREAKTHROUGH

PART VI: IN THE NAMES OF PEACE AND SAFETY

Acknowledgements

Special thanks to God, my parents, my family, Ryan and Sara Farish, Patrick Kayulu, Greg Rolfes, Susan Andrews, and Rush Limbaugh...

P A R T I

▼

Remembering Courage

"The courage of many people will falter because of the fearful fate they see coming upon the earth, because the stability of the very heavens will be broken. So when all these things begin to happen, stand straight and look up, for your salvation is near!"

—Jesus Christ
Luke 21:26, 28

CHAPTER 1:

The Book Of Life

"And how do you benefit if you gain the whole world but lose your own soul in the process? Is anything worth more than your soul?"

—**Jesus Christ**
Mark 8:36–37

It was the fall. All the smells danced through the air—those brisk, sharp, prelude-to-winter smells that accompany football and Thanksgiving and the falling leaves. The leaves…they were always the part that stood out the most. Come every fall, they would exhibit their true colors, spiritedly transforming themselves into vivid, surrealist concoctions that even the most creative and artistic of minds would find hard to spawn. And as they fell from the trees, they fluttered across the lawn creating the sacred smells of seasonal passage. Hovering over the lawn, each seemed content to ride the strength of the cool and soothing wind, never wavering or rebelling or struggling to reach for another direction, another way.

And the grass…the grass was still a sprightly green this time of year, and the annual mud patches that would usually come in tandem had yet to show signs of arrival. The symmetrical buildings guiding its framework thrust themselves up the rolling hills toward the great Rotunda. And, yes, of course, the Rotunda…dazzling in its presentation, the Rotunda was the majestic centerpiece of the great lawn, anchoring all of the small residences that outlined the green, tree-lined pathway. These buildings had once composed the entire university, and the trees were firm pillars, staples in the ever-evolving campus—a witness to the greatness of modern Western history. It was a powerful sight igniting a flood of memories for anyone who had spent time there.

Signaling the coming winter, today levied a frosty chill to the air enveloping the lawn, one of those allowing a person to see his breath turn to smoke and curl away into the mist just as quickly as he could laugh it away. And as often was the case, there were several patches of couples, studious readers, and sportsman peppered among the trees and lying in the grass, enjoying the last glimmering rays of the warm sun as it ascended beneath the mountainous skyline. It was an awe-inspiring sight to be there, to smile beneath the blue and purple canopy that draped itself across the Charlottesville sky.

And the Doric porches…yes, the porches ran along the front of the student apartments, granting protection to their patrons from all the weathering elements of the unpredictable climate. And under the shelter of those porches, the lingering figure exuded his smile. It was a smile of contentment, of inner peace, of the thought of returning after so long to this grand and wonderful place and after the dim numbness of his experience.

The walk of the figure was firm, but not hurried—hammering its own mark and distinct sound upon the brooding concrete walkway, but not with the iron authority displayed by some of the ungrateful and arrogant walks that had passed through these chambers over the years. The figure that owned this walk took the time to enjoy the splendor of the moment. With polite study, it gracefully hugged the ground as it stopped before a single brown leaf. He lifted it by its stem and placed it in his open hand. Touching it with his finger, the brittle shell crushed into a thousand pieces.

The tiny bits were beyond repair, and the figure took the time to carefully brush them off into the cradle of the cool, soothing grass. It felt a depth of sorrow for the loss, reflecting on the days enjoyed by the leaf as it swung from its tree limb and the time that God must have spent on such a creation. Shaking away the remaining dust, the figure continued its walk, descending down the steep steps of the pathway—deeper and deeper into the cradle of its landscape. And once totally immersed, it took time to pause for a moment before a bronze and iron statue of Thomas Jefferson.

Its inscription read:

"I AM CLOSING THE LAST SCENE OF MY LIFE BY FASHIONING AND FOSTERING AN ESTABLISHMENT FOR THE INSTRUCTION OF THOSE WHO COME AFTER US. I HOPE THAT ITS INFLUENCE ON THEIR VIRTUE, FREEDOM, FAME, AND HAPPINESS WILL BE SALUTORY AND PERMANENT."

The head of the cold metal statue exacted its gaze upon the figure, while the figure set its mind to glorious mental images of a new and better world. With unhindered fantasy, the figure conjured up pictures of those who had passed in the shadow of the statue over the years, the decades, and the past two centuries. It remembered the multitudes slaughtered in the mechanized chaos of those times, and it dreamt of a better day. It reveled in the thought of a new world order, to see injustice eradicated, evil men destroyed, and disease and poverty utterly eliminated. The figure was bold enough to believe such a world possible, and it lingered in the notion of a world devoid of such war and conflict—a world of peace and of tolerance.

But he had come here to forget those things—at least for a while. Reaching into the bushes behind the statue, the figure picked up a flowery piece of hemlock wondering how it had ended up in the garden. He looked it over, immersed in its qualities and dreaming through its form. It was curved with a green stem and several white petals protruding from various angles. I will most certainly give this beautiful flower to the most beautiful of flowers, the figure thought to himself. To her…Yes, he would give it to her!

The hands of the figure gently rolled the stem of the budding flowers around as it glided through its flickering thoughts. Each hand was a sleek and dark hand, kind and forgiving…the type of hand you hope would lift you up if you ever fell or got knocked down or felt that all was lost or just, in general, you found you needed a hand. The head of the figure was tilted toward the sky, lost in its dreams and hooked on the subject of *her* and all that was good and wonderful and kind in the world. It had a handsome face with wavy black hair and short scraggly sideburns. Its nose was straight and firm, guarding a gracious smile that rose to the thoughts and dreams of great hopes and of good and oversaw the strong, sharp chin. Its eyes looked up past the statue, but they did not see anything in the sky or even in this world, but in the world of dreams that the figure was now immersed. The world in which he lived with *her*...

Suddenly, the concentrating, delusional gaze of the figure shattered and it dropped its flower on the cold stone throne that blazed in the setting sunlight just beneath the statue. The figure went running off toward the majestic Rotunda building and for the angel on its steps...

It was what he had been awaiting, *her*. She trotted out toward him, and as the figure approached, she called out to him,

"The good doctor put out his new book, and I got the last copy!"

"Let me see it," he said.

He extended his arms, but she pulled the book back toward her, wrapping it from his view.

"Its mine," she said.

He could hear the playfulness radiate from the depths of her voice. And as she reveled in amusement at his expense, she ran off toward the base of one of the giant oaks anchored in the middle of the lawn, and the figure chased after her. He followed her to the natural born seats chiseled by the meandering roots, and he sat down beside her so the two of them could open their new book—the book of life, the book explaining the mysteries of creation—*the good doctor's new book*. And as they turned the first pages, the final layers of the deep blackness of the night began to curl in around them...

CHAPTER 2:

Riddles In The Jungle

"But you, Daniel, keep this prophecy a secret; seal up the book until the time of the end. Many will rush here and there, and knowledge and travel will increase."

—**Daniel**
Daniel 12:4

The room was a sauna topped off by a massive cathedral ceiling. It had no windows, but multiple doors. The walls were brick, and cobblestones burrowed their way into the floor. The centerpiece of the room lodged itself into the floor, an empty black hole—a bottomless pit of darkness. Garrison's toes clenched the rounded edge of the pit, and he peered into its depths. It reminded him of an old brick well. One of those watering holes from ancient Samaria around which whole villages based their existence. He had seen one like it on a fieldtrip to Colonial Williamsburg years ago. His fourth grade class paraded past while the droning tour guide tried in vain to invoke an image of 17th Century life for a bunch of boys who only wanted to watch a luggie disappear into the dark chasm or see which one of them could spit to the far end of it. But this was no watering hole. It was a furnace. Burning air whistled from its far reaches, emanating a demonic vibration that struck fear into Garrison's heart. Beads of sweat trembled off the tips of his fingers, while he listened to the voices lurk far below, from 'the Void' as he called it.

The Void was infested with voices—soft-spoken voices, kindly voices, even laughing voices. They were infectious, their sweet beckons dancing through the hollow inner sanctums of every man's ear, hoping to draw him to the threshold of the dark pit. But in each voice, he detected a hint of something sinister—something he couldn't put his finger on. A faint trace of uneasiness melded with the siren calls, only serving to confirm that his fear was not misplaced. One by one, they called on him to plunge in and join them in the wonderful confines of the Void. *Come on, Garrison. Dive in and join us! What's wrong with you, Garrison? Come and take the Nestea plunge!*

That's the moment it always happened. It came from behind, a melodious, seductive voice, rapping on the edifice of his mind. Plodding along in meticulous fashion, the voice spun a quiet web of indoctrination. *"The Void is good,"* it whispered in his ear. Sweat ran off his face in rivers and droplets bounced through the air like hot firecrackers as they descended into the decaying cylinder. But with repetitious declaration, the voice droned forward: *"The Void is good"*. It prodded his inner-spirit, while the voices from the Void granted their own alluring welcomes. But he was certain it would lead to death if he followed their lead. Garrison sensed it. He always resisted, always—and that's when the voices changed their tone.

It was an abrupt change, sudden and deliberate. The hole that preached of tolerance and inclusiveness now found him abominably intolerable. The previously delicate voices bled into a cacophony of hate. They cursed him, screaming out blasphemous names. Fear convulsed his terrified body, enveloping his soul to the point he felt he could drop dead on the spot from shock. Beneath his feet, the Void belched out rings of fire and enraged sparks hurled upward, searing the tips of his toes. And all the while, the screaming moans rose louder and louder, weighing on his mind and driving him to the brink of outright insanity. But from behind, the whispering voice never relented. With a light softness, it scratched in his inner ear: *"The Void is good"*. With angelic beauty, it cradled his eardrum with that endless refrain—over and over in a horror of repetition, *"The Void is good…"*

Each and every time, before he opened his eyes and the nightmare fled, those were the last four words he heard—that eerie, raspy, quiet breath ripping at his soul,

"The Void is good..."

Garrison Nance leapt out of bed. His sheets dripped with sweat, and they felt ice-cold in the air-conditioned room. He was not before the Void. There was no hole before his feet, and no creepy voice to contend with.

It was midnight, and he was home. Home safe in the suburbs of Atlanta, Georgia in the same bedroom he had slept in since the day he was born. For months, the same recurring nightmare visited, and it was more frightening and lifelike each time. The screeching terror of the voices in the Void was beyond description, more horrible than gunpowder fingernails scraping over a flint chalkboard. He still heard them now, stalking his soul with their silent terror.

Walking to the window, he parted the curtains. The soft light of the moon poured out onto his shoulders, and he smiled. The sun would return soon. Only a week ago, he had graduated from high school, and rather than leave for college, he decided to spend a year working with Christian missionaries—teaching poor children to read and helping poor farmers to work their land. It was real work—worthwhile work. Something he could be proud of before he got lost in the party culture of a college campus. And once he was done, he would be able to feel good about that year of his life.

The minister at his church recommended several reputable missionary organizations and provided brochures on all of them. But Garrison wasn't your typical Sunday morning church type of guy. He pictured himself landing in a country club atmosphere, rubbing elbows with the same type of people he now saw every weekend. Such thoughts scared him almost as much as the Void. He didn't intend to travel to some unknown part of the world only to become another assembly-line worker in a sheltered, Disneyland organization—especially one with a political agenda. He wanted to get his hands dirty, and he craved the company of new people and the excitement of exotic experiences, maybe even a little danger.

In an attempt to broaden his options, he looked up "Christian Missionaries" on Prodigy. His grandmother had given him a Packard Bell when she thought he was going to college, and he loved to play around on it—especially the Internet. For this search, a single hit popped up, an organization titled "The Christian Brotherhood of San Cristobal".

He scoured the site for more information, but little appeared—a short list of the good deeds performed for the locals, a history of the area, and a handful of pictures. Most of the usual stuff, and none of it told him a thing about the place. It had a seal fixed at the bottom proclaiming it the "Best Mexican Website of 1993". Probably, the *only* Mexican website of 1993, he thought. But Garrison was impressed they even had a website, and something told him it would be different than the other destinations. The contact information gave an address for 'Cardinal Raul Ruiz". A link with the Catholic Church provided credibility to the venture, and Garrison decided then and there— sight unseen—to choose the "Christian Brotherhood" above all others. Besides, it would give him the opportunity to perfect his language skills. In five years of Spanish, he had never received less than an A minus.

Yes, tomorrow was the first day of a new life. Tomorrow, he would leave Atlanta for a rural village on the far outskirts of a lost, forgotten part of Mexico—Chiapas. He climbed back into bed, his sheets still soaked with buckets of cold sweat. It was over an hour before he fell back to sleep, the dark image of the Void still fresh in his mind.

*   *   *   *

Just short of 6'3" with a well-endowed frame, Garrison Nance was a sculpted athlete and brilliant academic. He graduated near the top of his high school class and was accepted by some of the top universities in the nation. But Garrison wasn't sure what he wanted to do with his life yet, and he certainly didn't know what he would study once he got to school, so he chose to take a year off instead. A lot of his friends did the same thing, although most of them went backpacking across Europe or skiing in Vail. The poorest province of Mexico was a far cry from both, and most of them considered him insane.

Walter Nance, Garrison's father, was a top executive of the Coca-Cola Company. He and his wife, Claire, met sophomore year at Georgia Tech. Claire was a professor of economics at Emory. After college, they settled in Atlanta and had three kids. Garrison was the youngest. His brother Ethan was two years older and attended Brown. Brenda was a few years older than Ethan, and she lived the typical stressed out life of a law student. She was always telling Garrison to take a year off—to run for it, before the world owned his life and forced him to spend eternity buried in a mountain of work in some claustrophobic cubicle. Naturally, Garrison shared her positive outlook on life. All together, they were an average upper-middle class black family, and they didn't want to see Garrison go.

One of the busiest airports in the nation, Hartsfield bustled with travelers, and the whole family came along to see Garrison off to what they felt was the farthest edge of the known universe. Walter Nance looked at his youngest son, holding a duffel bag in each hand and wondered why in the world he was sending him off to the back roads of a third world country, but he was sure Garrison could handle it. Claire broke the silence.

"Are you sure it's safe?"

"Of course it is," Garrison said.

"And you'll write as soon as you get there?"

"Yes," he said. They had been over this a hundred times before. "It's only a year. I'll be back before you know it."

Ethan couldn't resist the opportunity. He grabbed Garrison by the shoulders.

"You know there are no laws there. The police work for the local drug lords. I heard you have to bribe them to keep from being tortured."

"Ethan!"

Claire screamed while the rest of the family laughed.

"Look," Garrison said, "It's Mexico we're talking about, not Beirut. What's the worst that can happen?"

Walter lifted an eyebrow.

"Just watch yourself, okay. Ninety percent of staying out of trouble is being aware of what's around you. It is a foreign country."

His father was right.

"Yeah, no problem."

"I can't believe my little brother is going off to live in Mexico."

Brenda wrapped her arms around him. Looking over her shoulder, just for a moment, Garrison Nance couldn't believe it either. Never had he lived outside of Atlanta, or even in a different house. Now, he was moving to Mexico—another country, another language, and he didn't know a soul. But then again, would that really make it any different than college?

*   *   *   *

Sitting in the back of the passenger seat of an old tattered jeep, the hot sun beat with relentless fervor on Garrison's neck and shoulders. They hadn't passed a house, a person, or any sign of civilization for some time. He knew the area was underdeveloped. That's the main reason he decided to come, but it still surprised him to see nothing but row after row of trees flanking the dirt road.

A local from the airport, the driver didn't talk much. The air was saturated and its heavy burden weighed on Garrison. He had never endured such humidity, even at home. The Goodyear tires kicked up chunks of mud as they hugged the road to San Cristobal. As they disappeared further into the mountains, the jeep slowed to a creep, and Garrison sat up alert and rigid in his seat. An uneasy feeling soured his stomach.

"What is it?"

"Just routine," the driver said.

He curled his eyebrows and pressed his lips tight as if annoyed by the question. Garrison's eyes honed in on the men standing in the road ahead. Assault rifles dangled from their shoulders, and they didn't exhibit the least bit of concern as the jeep drew closer. Garrison cursed himself. He had been in Mexico less than a day, and already, he had screwed up. What had his father said? *Ninety percent of staying out of trouble is being aware.* Something like that. Then, he goes and gets right off the plane and the first thing he does is walk into some sort of a trap. At least, it appeared to be a trap. The driver picks up unsuspecting foreigners at the airport and drives them off into the jungle to be robbed, maybe even killed.

He braced himself for a fight, as the tiny men grew in size. The driver braked and shifted to park, bringing the vehicle to a complete stop before the two mysterious men. Each attended to a side of the jeep. They were dressed in regular clothing, not military uniforms. The one next to Garrison didn't say a word, but he eyed the knapsack sitting in the passenger side floor, while the driver chatted with his guy as if they were close friends and, as their hands crossed to shake, Garrison swore he saw something pass between them. Obviously, his suspicions confirmed, Garrison prepared to wrestle the rifle away and make a run for it.

"What's in the bag?"

The man jutted his rifle into Garrison's armpit.

"Clothes. My clothes."

Garrison wrapped his arms around the bag, but the first man pointed his rifle with a grimace, handing out a verbal lashing to Garrison's.

"No. Back off. These two are all right."

His command struck a chord, and the man withdrew his rifle from Garrison's side.

"Sorry campesino."

His words were sharp, a fake grin shining from his face. The gleam of his eye felt like a fang, boring into Garrison's veins. The first man gave a faint salute with a flick of his wrist, and at that, the driver accelerated. A dumbfounded expression overtook Garrison's face, and he turned to look over his shoulder.

"Who were they?"

"Just ranchers."

Just ranchers? The ease of the driver's reply left Garrison in total confusion. Just ranchers? Apparently, they weren't thieves or robbers after all. Part of him still waited for the driver to pull out a hidden gun and demand all of his possessions, but that didn't happen. He had never known ranchers to set up roadblocks, but maybe they wanted to keep poachers out, keep trespassers out, or maybe Ethan was right, and he was moving to a land with no laws. But those were all just myths and prejudices. Weren't they? Whatever the reason, it was clear to Garrison he wasn't in the Georgia suburbs anymore. And that's what really bothered him. He had no friends, no family, and no safe bedroom to run back to. He was at the mercy of the elements, just a kid alone in the jungle.

*   *   *   *

The city of San Cristobal should more adequately be referred to as a town, not a city. Though, it wasn't actually that bad. Garrison had pictured one of those mud-hut villages from National Geographic. But at first glance, it didn't look much different than a rural Georgia farming town. Of course, contrary to popular belief, the people of Georgia had indoor plumbing and the advanced tools of industry. Chiapas was a lot worse off than any place in Georgia.

In this area of the town, the buildings lacked any identifying numbers, and the streets remained absent of any signs to tell him if he was even hot or cold. All he had to go by was a picture of the mission headquarters and the driver's muddled directions. The air was dry in the noon heat, and dirt scattered in the wind as Garrison made his way on foot. Church steeples dotted the landscape, and barefoot children raced chickens over old sidewalks long ago overrun by weeds and crabgrass.

Garrison stopped in the middle of the road. Sandy particles of dust rode the breeze, polluting his hair and irritating his eyes. With its wide shadow lurking over him, he compared the building to the picture in his hand. The two matched. The same plain white structure with a flat roof, humble in its presentation. With everything he owned strapped over his shoulder, he lifted his arm and prepared to knock on the door. Before his knuckles struck the wood, it flung open on its hinges. A tall woman stepped out and came just short of running him over.

"Oh, excuse me!"

Her giggling voice echoed in his head, and he fell speechless for a moment. Just a shade above six feet tall, the wind whipped strands of light brown hair across her cheeks. From behind the veil of fluttering silk, a pair of emerald green eyes reflected her joy. They welcomed him without a word, and Garrison forgot for a moment he was alive at all, much less paralyzed and mute in the middle of a foreign land.

"You must be Garrison."

Her lips danced to the beautiful melody of her voice, and it took a few seconds for Garrison to re-enter the world of reality.

"Yes. Garrison Nance—from Atlanta, Georgia."

He extended his hand, and she shook it firmly. She couldn't have been much older than twenty-five.

"Poyner Vicente," she said. "You're going to love it here. You can just throw your bags over there."

She motioned toward a sofa on the far wall.

"I was just heading out to run some errands. Why don't you come with me, and I'll give you the grand tour of San Cristobal."

She darted off before he could answer one way or another, and after throwing his bags down, he fell in right behind her, following her down the gravel road. She was filled with energy, her feet moving at a rapid pace. Light blue jeans with frayed ends hugged her legs, and a solid white T-shirt rippled in the wind as they moved past ancient stone churches and cardboard houses. The edge of the city blended with the jungle, and Garrison could feel the smothering grip of poverty.

"Have you met anyone else yet?" she asked.

"No. I just got here when you opened the door."

"Well, you've met me, and there're only two people in the mission—me and Eduardo," she said. "I just have to pick up some groceries and send out the mail."

She pointed to the cardboard shacks lining the left hand side of the street.

"Those are all homes. Most of the residents make their living as farmers, but their 'estates' are probably no bigger than a backyard garden where you're from," she said.

Rounding the corner, a whole new world opened before Garrison's eyes. Street vendors lined the avenue. Dead chickens swung from string in the evening breeze. Boxes of vegetables and baskets of fruit were spread out before them, and the aroma of roasting nuts and mushrooms sprayed an aromatic mist into the air. It wasn't a dirty smell as he first imagined. Instead, it heightened his senses and provided him with a vivid feeling, an intensity of being alive.

"Senora Poyner...Poyner!"

The butterfly footsteps of a little girl came hurling toward them. Her hair was jet-black, and she had a dark complexion. When she reached Poyner, she latched her arms onto Poyner's leg.

"Maria, are you out shopping for the day?"

"No, Senora Poyner. You're silly! I don't have anything to buy with."

Her mouth hung open, and her eyes rolled back as if to say, 'Don't be preposterous'. Only, she was too young to know such a large word, so she just stood with her hands on her hips. Poyner cackled, and Maria didn't seem the least bit self-conscious.

"How would you like to meet my new friend?"

Maria looked over at Garrison, then nodded. Poyner introduced them. Garrison put his hands on his knees and said hello. Maria looked him up and down. She had never seen anyone so dark before.

"Is he going to teach us too, Poyner?"

"If you're nice, he will."

"Good. I like him."

Her look instantly transformed from doubtful to ecstatic like only a child's could.

By now, ten or twenty other children congregated around Poyner. Like waves on the ocean, they glided along with her as she hovered through the marketplace. The boys begged to carry her groceries, and the girls tore at her clothes for attention. Effortlessly, she navigated Garrison through the crowd while attending to each and every one of them.

"Going to the market and going to school are the only fun these children have," she said. "Most of them work alongside their parents in the fields, and all of them will by the age of twelve. Secondary education is rare. It's a shame. They live in a world that forces them to grow up so quickly with little time to just enjoy being children."

Garrison wasn't sure where to place her. Vicente was Spanish, but she didn't look Mexican.

"Where are you from?"

"Charlottesville, Virginia."

"What brought you all the way out here?"

She didn't have to think at all.

"Chiapas needs me more than Charlottesville. I'm a teacher, and the only trained teacher these children will probably ever meet."

The noise of the market began to dissipate as they approached its outer edge.

"How long have you been here?"

"Hmm…Three years, give or take a month."

"How often do you leave to see your family?" he asked.

Garrison couldn't imagine three years without returning home. Until now, he had never been gone more than a week.

"I don't have any family in the states. My father died when I was two, my mother eight years later. I stayed in a foster home for six years with a wonderful lady named Edna Stubbins until I went away to college, but she passed away a few years later."

"I'm sorry to hear that."

Poyner brushed it off.

"Don't be. I'm far from an orphan. I've got a lot of little admirers here in San Cristobal, and my husband works here as well."

"Your husband is a missionary too?"

"In a sense. He does all sorts of things, but it's basically the same work."

She pointed toward a towering ridge of trees that dwarfed even the church steeple.

"He spends most of his time over there. You'll learn in due time Garrison that we don't operate with a fixed schedule or a list of responsibilities around here. All work is the Lord's work, whether it's taking your morning to teach a child to read or spending the afternoon helping to fix a water pump. Trust me. You'll never be bored around here."

By now, they had left the market, but most of the children still orbited Poyner as if drawn by invisible forces. It was quiet in the residential streets and the children kept each other occupied, content only to be in the presence of their adopted older sister. She pointed up the road with a waving finger.

"When you want to write home. This is the route to the mail house."

*   *   *   *

Eduardo Ortiz sat on the wooden bench just outside of the mail house. It stretched out underneath a large tree, the leaves filtering the sunlight down to the ground in a thousand splintering rays. He studied the air. It was gritty and dirty. Particles floated through it, sparkling as beams of light struck each dimension of their exterior, and Eduardo thought about his primitive existence here in the jungle. He had traveled to posh hotels and luxurious houses of state all over the world, prestigious universities and institutions, but in relative terms, each was a primitive cave dwelling. Soon, the day would arrive when the air would be pure. It would be *perfectly* clean. Until that day arrived, he was condemned to live in the filth of the past, like a time traveler stuck in 18th Century London. In the future, he dreamed of a pristine existence with a wife, a house, two kids, and a white picket fence. He would grow old and play the role of kindly old grandfather. He and his wife would have matching rocking chairs that creaked on a wooden porch, and the Sunday morning breeze would flood over their souls.

It was a great dream and a comforting thought, but there wouldn't be a twenty years from now, much less forty or fifty, and it would be almost that long before he could be a grandpa. Although the rest of the world remained ignorant of the situation, that was the sad reality. He knew for certain. Maybe he was the only one on earth who knew, but that's why he had returned to the jungle. What else could he do? Put in years of sacrifice so his career would come to a crashing halt along with the rest of civilization? What was the point? No, he belonged here in the jungle, in the place where he had been born. This mission work was his penance, a payment of service for the God he loved.

Lost in his own thoughts, he didn't notice as Poyner and Garrison came to a stop directly in front of him.

"Hey, Eddie."

He looked up, shaking his head as if he had just rolled out of bed. Poyner stood before him, a congenial expression lighting her face. He studied the new man beside her. She introduced them. They exchanged pleasantries, and Poyner went inside to drop off the mail. Garrison put his hands into his pockets.

"Poyner tells me you just got back from the states. You went to school there?"

"Yes. I just finished some post-graduate work at Stanford. Prior to that, I attended MIT, studied materials science and engineering," Eduardo said.

Garrison gave off a look of respect, as if he had just been introduced to the Nobel Laureate or the President of the United States.

"And this is your hometown?"

Eduardo pointed just over the horizon.

"I grew up right over there in a little thatched hut made of mud and straw."

It was a slight exaggeration, but not much of one, and he was amused with the thought.

"So how long are you back for?" Garrison asked.

"I don't know. Things got stressful at work, so once I completed my projects, I shoved off for San Cristobal, and I don't know when I'll go back, if ever…Life is harder here, but a lot simpler."

Poyner returned.

"Lunch?"

She displayed her purchases from the market.

"Sounds good," Eduardo said.

The three of them embarked on the walk back to the mission. As Garrison got to know them, he looked down the street. The bitter sounds of a heated argument grabbed his attention. A pickup truck rested alongside the road, and three men sat in the back. A forth man stood on the dirt next to the road, arguing with a peasant farmer. Garrison recognized him immediately as the man from the roadblock. He screamed expletives while the town's people gathered around, and Eduardo took off running toward them. Poyner followed.

The three men in the back of the truck held bottles of tequila, and empty beer cans were scattered around their feet. They laughed up a storm as their friend waddled through the farmer's field sarcastically poking a stick in the ground. He jutted around, his head and body simulating the pecking motion of a grazing chicken. Then he kicked up the soil and uttered additional insults.

"I just kicked up your crops old man. Do something about it!"

The drunken man cackled with laughter and gave the old Indian farmer a shove to the chest. The farmer stood firm without a word.

"Come on peasant, defend your field…"

"Enough!"

The man cringed when he saw Eduardo.

"Back off, Eduardo. This isn't your fight."

"The hell it isn't! If this man will not defend his field, then I will. And don't doubt for a moment, Humberto, that I won't kick your drunk ass from here to Guaymas."

Humberto took several steps backward. The whole village surrounded him now. Several children locked onto Poyner's legs with fright. Humberto jumped in the back of the truck and stood on its tailgate, and as it pulled away, he yelled out.

"You can't protect them forever Eduardo!"

He wore a devious smile on his face, his friends intoxicated with laughter. The truck kicked up gravel and dust as it careened down the road.

"Who was that?" Garrison asked.

"Ranchers," Eduardo said.

And Garrison could hear the disdain in his voice.

CHAPTER 3:

Under The Masks

"You are good at reading the weather signs of the skies—red sky tonight means fair weather tomorrow; red sky in the morning means foul weather all day—but you can't read the obvious signs of the times!"

—Jesus Christ
Matthew 16:2–3

In the morning, Garrison awoke to the sharp heat of the blistering sun soaking through his window. He had slept well, and as best he could remember, he had escaped the wrath of the Void. It had been many nights since he had awakened without its haunting image roving through his mind. He threw both his feet on the floor and made his way into the kitchen. Eduardo was already seated at the table sipping on a cup of coffee.

"Want some?" he asked, raising the cup to his lips.

"What is it?"

"Coffee, the real stuff—not that instant junk you get back home. It's one of the few advantages of living out here."

Garrison rarely drank coffee, but the opportunity to try the genuine article appealed to him. He reached for his cup, but Eduardo held up his hand.

"Want it Spanish style?"

He held up a bottle of Tequila. Garrison winced at the thought.

"You put Tequila in your coffee?"

"Only a splash."

"Isn't it a little early in the morning?"

Eduardo shrugged his shoulders.

"You want it or not?"

Garrison pushed the cup toward Eduardo who tilted a splash of the bottle's contents into the small cup. Garrison stirred it with a spoon, then took a sip. As he did, the screen door creaked off its hinges and bent open. It was Poyner. She whistled a quick good morning, and sat down beside them.

"So what's on the agenda this morning?" Eduardo asked.

She sprinkled some sugar on a bowl of oatmeal and stirred it with a spoon.

"I thought the two of us would take Garrison on a tour of the jungle."

Garrison found it odd that they would take him into the jungle on his second day. He hoped he could meet Poyner's husband and some more of the locals, but it looked as if introductions would have to wait.

"What's out in the jungle?"

"The Lord's children," Poyner said.

Garrison tried to contemplate this strange world he had entered. The Lord's children? In the middle of the jungle? None of it made sense.

*   *   *   *

Poyner twirled a walking stick in her hand as the three of them hiked over the mountain ridge and down the narrow dirt pathway. The sun had been out for several hours, but one could barely tell it was day, the vegetation was so thick. With each careful step, Garrison inspected the ground and tree limbs for poisonous snakes. With each step, his mind glorified the exploits of men like Columbus and Magellan. He pretended to be from their ranks, a modern conquistador traversing uncharted waters, destined to stumble across mysterious creatures and unknown civilizations. It felt as if they had walked for hours by the time the weeds and underbrush started to thin. Finally, Poyner stopped.

"We're here."

"Where?" Garrison asked.

Their surroundings appeared to be no different than those of the past several hours.

"La selva Lacandona, Amigo…The Lacandon Jungle," she said.

Garrison studied the tree-lined hill. Little light escaped through the jungle canopy. As the area came into focus, Garrison witnessed the shadow of what appeared to be a child run over the crest of a hill, and the contours of other objects emerged as his eyes distinguished the dull colors. Bits and pieces twirled together and formed a sharper image so that he could make out the vague outlines of a jungle resort. His mouth dropped open at the sight.

"Wow."

"Not quite what you would expect is it?" Eduardo said.

Garrison didn't respond. Hidden behind the trunks of large trees, a third world metropolis sprung forth. From the corner of his eye, he noticed a flickering shadow dash behind a dead tree stump. He froze in his tracks, afraid it might reveal itself as a wild animal or some dangerous creature ready to pounce and tear him to shreds. But before he could warn Eduardo, it stepped into the dim light of the jungle.

It wore a black ski mask. Two fiery eyes and a red mouth protruded from the headgear, and the rest of its body was clothed in green military fatigues. Garrison motioned to Eduardo and Poyner, but they brushed off the encounter, not giving the man a passing thought. Continuing forward, the strange man darted in his own direction, as unconcerned with Garrison as Poyner and Eduardo were with him.

At the edge of the jungle town, children ran out in droves to greet them. Poyner patted them on the head.

"More of our children," she said.

Garrison spun his head in astonishment, amazed by the hidden village. The kids brimmed with life and excitement because of the arrival of their favorite person, and she seemed just as pleased to be with them. One by one, she introduced them, and each took pride in the individual recognition she gave them. She made no mention of the odd surroundings.

Like thousands of ants, hooded men crawled out of every crevice of the jungle. They looked alike, faceless and dressed the same. A boy tugged at Garrison's shirt.

"Yes?" Garrison asked.

"Do you know how to read?"

"Of course."

"I'm learning to read right now. Yesterday, I read an entire book all by myself."

The boy held his arms out wide so Garrison could visualize the true enormity of the task. Garrison encouraged him.

"That's amazing...!"

The rest of the children swarmed in, fascinated by Garrison's dark skin. They rarely had new visitors in the jungle.

"Looks like you've found some new friends," Poyner said. "I'll be right back. Don't get into trouble."

She left him with Eduardo while the children tugged at his shirt vying for attention. Trickling lines of the town's older residents came out to greet them. Garrison watched from afar as Poyner climbed the top of a rounded hill with a burlap tent perched on top. From its crest, a mysterious man emerged from the sea of twisted rain forest. His face hid behind the same black ski mask as the other men, and the same suit of green fatigues wrapped his body. In every way, he should have been the spitting image of the other men who crawled around the jungle, but something made this man stand out from the rest.

His right arm rested on his hip with an aura of confidence, and his left arm lurched outward as if poised to make some grand pronouncement. In the end of that same left hand burned a pipe that oozed out a gentle stream of rolling smoke. The smoke condensed in the atmosphere, blending into nothingness like soft waves brushing over a sandy shore. Out of his mouth ascended a billowing cloud of ash that curled away into the treetops as if to cast its own magic spell. Although he wore the same mask as every other man, somehow his face was different.

Mesmerized, Garrison trembled in the presence of the dark silhouette, the unnamed figure seemingly able to whisper in his ear, as though telling him not to be afraid. His posture, his walk, every manner in which he conducted himself, from the tiniest step to the emboldened way in which he waved his fingers, cried out with a supernatural authority, some sort of birthright deeming this man better than all others.

Poyner stood beside him, and Garrison saw them exchange a few brief words. Her face filled with life, as each of the strange figure's words penetrated their target. He rested his hand on her shoulder, and the two of them disappeared over the top of the hill. Garrison turned to Eduardo.

"Who are these men?"

Eduardo's eyes never met Garrison's, and it was obvious he had anticipated the question.

"It's probably best if men like us don't ask such questions."

"Well, don't you think it's a little odd?"

Eduardo gave an evasive answer.

"Yes, but I also think we have enough problems teaching illiterate children
and irrigating fields to be concerned with the affairs of a few odd men."

Garrison figured Eduardo knew more than he was telling, and that on
some level he didn't approve, but he didn't push the subject. He didn't want
Eduardo to get angry with him this early in their relationship, and it really
wasn't any of his business.

*   *   *   *

That night, the three of them slept in the jungle. Garrison checked his
sleeping bag for snakes before crawling in, and he used a dirt mound and
bundled straw for a pillow. Through a torn hole in the tent, and even further
through the holes between the leaves of the jungle canopy, he caught the light
of a handful of stars. He closed his eyes and began to dream.

Instantly, he found himself transported to the edge of the Void. The same
voices called up to him from its depths, and the same frigid heat blew
upward. He trembled in fear, the sweat pouring off his body measuring itself
in liters. Once again, he heard that eerie, quiet breath. *"The Void is good,"* it
said. A plume of smoke blew past his shoulder, and Garrison watched as it
inexplicably curled downward into the pit instead of ascending upward into
the air.

It was still just a whisper, but Garrison's blood turned to ice as it screeched
in his ear, *"The Void is good"*. A wealth of courage rose inside him. Slowly, he
turned to catch a glimpse of the voice. Smoke rode the air all around him in
tiny swirling mushrooms that raced toward the Void with excitement. His
eyes watered, and he batted the smoke away with his hands. Through the
thick haze, he could make out the remnant of a dark figure. It blended into
the pitch-black shadows, and it held a bath of fire in its hand—the source of
all the dark smoke whittling away into the Void. A pair of crimson red pupils
swirled like whirlpools in a black ocean. They jutted out from behind a mask,
and Garrison cringed in horror, his legs frozen in place.

The figure took a careful step toward him and opened its mouth.

"The Void is good," it said.

And as the voices from below laughed hysterically, the figure shoved him into the Void.

Garrison sprang back to life with sweat pouring off of his body. It was only a nightmare, and he had let his imagination run away with him. He reminded himself of how he couldn't sleep for days after seeing *Friday the 13th* as a kid, still realizing Jason wasn't real, but staying on guard just in case. He felt silly for feeling that way now.

*   *   *   *

The next morning came like any other, and Garrison was busy teaching some of the children to read. They thumbed through *Little House On The Prairie* books, a number of Spanish-translated Dr. Seuss works, and dozens of Bibles. Generations learned to read from the same books, their tattered covers still barely clinging to the bindings. Garrison was excited to see the quick progress made by the children. In America, a teacher could spend ninety percent of his time trying to get the kids to be quiet, much less pay attention. Here in the jungle, the kids were insatiable vacuums of learning, begging to be taught.

A little girl sat next to Garrison with an open copy of the Bible. While she read the words out loud, a sudden movement from the edge of the jungle caught Garrison's attention. He glanced up in time to see a dark figure slowly creep out of its depths. It rested at ease with its left hand gently propping its frame against a tall tree. Drawing its trademark pipe from a pocket with its other hand, it lit up and took a couple of puffs, all the while, listening intently to the words of the children.

In the light of day, it seemed to inspire a gentle tranquility of the soul and Garrison didn't feel the least bit uncomfortable. He certainly didn't feel the horror of the previous night's delusion. The gaze of the figure was gentle, and the smoky circles rising above its head like tiny hot air balloons seemed to call out with a soft whisper to the entire world. Its head bobbed slightly, with ears trying to catch the words of the children as if they were musical works of the highest genius. And the figure sprung to life with each utterance as if he derived his energy, his soul, and his reason for living from each radiant sound.

The girl continued reading, and Garrison detected a smile from beneath the mask of the figure as her gentle words stroked the air.

"But I tell you," she read. "Here at this table, sitting among us as a friend, is the man who will betray me. For I, the Son of Man, must die since it is part of God's plan. But how terrible it will be for my betrayer!"

"Good," Garrison told her. "Keep going…"

Garrison watched as the figure exhaled one final cloud of fiery ash and gingerly turned—expressionless—then melted back into the jungle, eaten alive by the simmering darkness to be lost forever in the wild adornment of tangled vegetation.

*   *   *   *

At dinner, Garrison broke bread with Eduardo. Poyner was off to some unknown destination, and most of the Indian people ate together as families.

"Do you still have family here?" Garrison asked.

"My father died when I was a child. My mother raised me by herself with only a small plot of land to work," Eduardo said.

Garrison's eyes lit up.

"And you rose from that to getting a degree at MIT?"

"Somewhat," he said. "My mother insisted I get an education. She sent me to the University of Mexico everyday as a child to sit on its steps. I begged the students to teach me anything. Then, one day, a rich landowner named Mr. Handro—my guardian angel—informed my mother he would pay for all of my schooling. He sent me off to a private school. I graduated at the top of the class, and at sixteen, I went off to MIT. My mother died that year, and Mr. Handro died soon thereafter. After MIT, I went to grad school at Stanford to study molecular engineering."

"Sounds like you have a bright future," he said.

Eduardo didn't reply.

"You said before," Garrison added. "That you didn't know when you might go back to the states if ever. I know you grew up here, but wouldn't your talents be better spent back in America or Europe or somewhere other than here?"

Eduardo took some time to respond.

"I'm a healer Garrison, not a destroyer. The people of Chiapas need men like myself and like you. They need to construct a better life for themselves. They're my people, and I would feel guilty if I abandoned them."

"I'm not saying you should abandon them. It just—seems curious that's all."

Eduardo could see that Garrison just wanted to learn more about him. He was a good man, and he wasn't being judgmental, nor was he insinuating that the people of Chiapas were insignificant.

"Things changed in the United States," he said. "I excelled in a field of study harboring great promise. In the world of academics, I had it made. Grants and fellowships called from around every corner, and it didn't hurt that I was a poor kid from the third world. That's a nice footnote for the universities. Gets them more funding."

He took a bite of bread.

"When I finished graduate school, I started work for the United States government—the Department of Defense to be more specific. At first, I was excited. The possibilities were endless. But it soon became clear that what I was doing posed a grave danger to life on earth. I couldn't sleep for weeks on end."

"What did you do?"

"I shared my fears with colleagues."

By now, Garrison hung on every word.

"What did they say?"

"They said I watched too much science-fiction, too much Jurassic Park and Frankenstein…They only concerned themselves with getting grants and getting to 'Point A'. What to do once they reached 'Point A' didn't concern them. They either didn't think it a problem, or simply didn't care. After a while, I couldn't handle it anymore. I had to get away—anywhere. The farthest place I could think of was where I had come from—Chiapas."

Garrison leaned forward, teetering on the edge of his seat.

"What could be that bad?"

"Garrison, I worked night and day laying the theoretical groundwork for a project I thought would heal the suffering of mankind. Then one day I awoke and realized I was working on a weapon so frightening I could no longer bear to carry myself through the day."

*   *   *   *

Alejandro was an indigenous Indian farmer on the edge of the jungle just east of Chiapas. He had cleared a considerable plot of land, and Garrison agreed to lend a hand in planting it. Farming in Chiapas meant a trip back to the Stone Age. Farmers built up mounds of dirt in long rows—all by hand. With the aid of crude tools, they tilled the area by poking holes into the mounds, one after another. Sometime after Garrison finished, Alejandro would make his way around and place the seeds into the holes. Garrison couldn't believe any farmer would endure such backbreaking work for a low crop yield.

As he poked the stick into the ground, a voice echoed in his ear. Garrison turned to see a tall man walking toward him from the place where Alejandro's field blended with the edge of the jungle. He wore the clothes of an Indian peasant and no mask, yet his walk remained unmistakable in appearance. He had a head of wavy black hair that glistened in the sunlight, sheltering his youthful features from the same blistering rays.

"I haven't yet had the pleasure of meeting you," he said.

His voice was sweet like honey with a raspy pitch complimentary to his Spanish accent. Garrison shook his hand, and the man smiled as if he were seeing his long lost brother for the first time. He introduced himself as Raphael Vicente, and Garrison told him his own name.

"Yes. Poyner's told me a lot about you," the man said.

"Good things I hope."

Raphael just lifted an eyebrow, a single eye peeking out at Garrison and a snickering smile that told him, 'of course,' without so much as a word, but only a wink.

"So you've joined us from America? It's been too long since I've been there. America is my favorite place on the face of the earth."

Garrison nodded his head as he discarded the crude farming implement.

"Atlanta. I decided to take a slight detour before I went away to college."

"Some detour," Raphael said.

His gaze wandered around in circles, tracing the edges of the sky. An aura surrounded him as though the birds talked down to him from their high perches in the circling treetops.

"Take a break," he said.

The two of them sat down in the middle of the field. Raphael leaned on the palms of his hands, his legs extended forward, and he let the sunlight bleed over him like a bucket of cool water.

"Is Madonna still popular? I really like Madonna…"

His thoughts seemed to fade away in mid-sentence, and Garrison hesitated, his tongue tied in response to such a question.

"Sure, I would say so."

He thought it to be an odd and amusing question for a man to ask another man he just met in the middle of the jungle. But it left him curious of the man, and the two of them began to reminisce about life in America. From pop culture to domestic politics, Raphael Vicente was a depository of knowledge on every subject. He spoke multiple languages, and he came across as the most intelligent and passionate person Garrison had ever met. They drifted through memories and laughed at recollections of old Saturday Night Live skits. Garrison felt at complete ease as if he had known this man forever. Eventually, he had to ask the question.

"Why do the men in Lacandon wear masks? And why do they live in the jungle?"

Garrison wanted the truth, and it was obvious Raphael anticipated the subject being broached.

"Garrison, what you see is a militia of sorts—a guerilla army."

Garrison nodded as if he now understood.

"For fighting the ranchers?"

Raphael hesitated for a moment as he weighed his response.

"No…To rise up against the entire government of Mexico."

Garrison wasn't sure he heard right, and it took all he had to keep from laughing.

"You think a band of jungle men can defeat the government of Mexico?"

Raphael endured the comment, unfazed by Garrison's disbelief.

"Not really, no…In fact, I'm fairly certain a band of jungle men could never do such a thing. Come on Garrison, you're a smart guy. Men with old, dilapidated rifles can not beat armies with tanks!"

His response left Garrison confused. Wasn't Raphael arguing against himself?

"Then I don't think I quite understand. What exactly is the point?"

"To cause a fracas!"

Raphael seemed happy with the word he had pulled out for just such an occasion.

"To cause a fracas?"

"Yes, to cause a fracas."

Then seriousness crept back into Raphael's face. He looked Garrison in the eyes without flinching. He pulled out a waving index finger, and with a stalwart confidence he told him.

"And then Garrison, you will see men with words defeat an entire world of tanks."

With those words, Garrison nearly concluded the man was insane, but he couldn't believe that to be true. He was normal only a moment ago, and Poyner had married the man.

"But why? What's wrong with the government of Mexico that you want to destroy it?"

Raphael stared out into the sky. He didn't face Garrison, but only the far-away clouds as if only they could hear his flowing pronouncements.

"You've seen the conditions here. The indigenous peoples—the Indians—they don't live like the rest of us. They can't run away to the United States. Their government has forgotten them. They have no schools, no paved roads, no clinics or hospitals. When they are born, the world does not take notice; And when they die, the world does not care."

His fingers frolicked in the air as if to caress each word, and his eyes turned to train themselves on Garrison as if to strike him down from a glare alone.

"The wealthy landowners and ranchers of Chiapas live like feudal lords, heaping their oppression onto modern-day serfs. They steal. They kill. They rape, and no one takes notice. Soon, they will take notice."

"Why don't you appeal to the federal government first?"

"We have. Our calls fall on deaf ears, Garrison. Mexico is not America. Here, the PRI rules everything. It's a corrupt system of one party rule with landowners and politicians exchanging bribes and influence. The indigenous people are not part of the equation."

Garrison tried to take it all in.

"Why not take on the landowners and the ranchers first?"

Raphael noticeably held back his laughter.

"Garrison," Raphael said. "People don't follow leaders who take half-measures."

He left his statement hanging in the air as if it was self-evident from its mere existence. He maintained the bold stare of a Roman warrior, one that instilled a quiet confidence in those who saw him, and Garrison had no doubt he would accomplish whatever he set his mind to. They went on to discuss the wide gap between the rich and poor, and Raphael exposed the illusion Garrison had formed in his mind of a democratic Mexico, friendly neighbor of the United States—modern, industrialized, and most of all, civilized. Parts of Mexico were moving forward rapidly, that much was true. But it was also true that parts were being left behind, perilously neglected, and Raphael had every intent to transform a nation.

*   *   *   *

New Year's Day, Garrison awoke to the crisp bite of the mountain air. He spent the previous night thinking of his family and what life was like back in Georgia. He phoned them from San Cristobal and chatted for a few minutes. They all missed him of course. Ethan and Brenda were both home from school, and they couldn't wait for him to come back. He told them everything was fine, failing to mention the small revolutionary movement unfolding around him.

But that was yesterday, and it was morning now. Emerging from his tent, he walked through the jungle, breathing in the clean, natural surroundings. After a few minutes of lingering in the forest, he stopped dead in his tracks. Raphael and Poyner stood a few feet away.

A heavy look of disappointment weighed upon Poyner's face. She wasn't the type to always be physically smiling, but her eyes always did. And on this morning, they did not. Raphael stood before her in such a way as if he didn't know what to tell her. His eyes only stared at the ground before her feet. Throwing her arms around his neck, she lifted herself up on her tiptoes and gave him a hug.

"Click."

The hammer knocked out a familiar sound. Garrison was used to hearing it in movies, but never in real life. He felt the cold metal lock onto the back of his head.

"Turn around real slow," a voice said.

Garrison turned around to find four men. They were masked men, and one held a gun to Garrison's head. He was the only one who spoke.

"Do you normally spy on people like this?" he asked.

The tone in his voice conveyed his unhappiness.

"N—"

Garrison tried to get the words out, but the gunman would have none of it.

"Shut up!" he said. "That was a rhetorical question. I'll do all the talking around here. We don't take kindly to spies in our jungle."

The other three men nodded their heads in agreement. Garrison wasn't sure what to do. Hadn't they seen him before? How could they miss him? He was the only unmasked black man in the entire state. The man with the gun squinted at him. Something started to register.

"You're that guy from America. The one I heard about. Aren't you...? Yeah, the one from Georgia."

Garrison froze in place.

"Answer me!"

Garrison jumped back.

"Yes...yes. I'm from Georgia."

The man looked at his friends, and they transcribed secret telepathic messages to each other, trading a series of sinister nods that Garrison couldn't understand.

"Answer me one thing," the man asked. "Do you know Bo and Luke Duke?"

The question caught him off guard.

"Bo and Luke Duke?"

"Yes," the man said. "Bo and Luke Duke—of Hazzard County. They drive an orange car."

He seemed serious, sifting his hand through the air to simulate the motion of a racecar. Garrison nervously mumbled an answer.

"Well, you see. They—Bo and Luke Duke aren't real..."

The four men burst out laughing, and Garrison still didn't understand what was going on. The man removed his gun from Garrison's head and smiled, his large teeth shining like sticks of ivory.

"Do you think you could get me a date with Daisy?" he asked.

Their laughter rose even louder. Finally, Garrison began laughing too. The man turned to his friends and motioned at his legs.

"She's the one, you know, with those short pants..."

Turning back, he seized Garrison's hand and shook it vigorously.

"We heard a man from the states had come to Chiapas. I figure either you are an honorable man or a damned crazy one. We have both types here. Welcome to Lacandon, friend."

The man smiled again, and Garrison wondered if indeed he was crazy—crazy to be standing in the middle of the jungle under this absurd set of circumstances with these ridiculous characters, all the while, hundreds of miles from his family and home. He did not know that it was the morning the masked men would launch an armed rebellion.

*   *   *   *

Garrison couldn't sleep. The night provided no refuge for his tired body, and his mind raced in circles. Overnight, his quiet corner of Mexico transformed into the focal point of the entire world as revolution spread across the countryside. He decided to take a walk. The only place in Lacandon one could walk at night was by the lakeside. It was the only place he could see. The reflection of the moon lit the night, and the crystal clear water harbored a sense of peace and solitude. In the hours of the night, the cool air welcomed him.

Stepping out into the reflected light of the lake, Garrison wasn't surprised to find Raphael resting in the sands that glued the edge of the jungle to the rippling waters. His hand was fixed to his chin, deep in thought. Garrison climbed onto a rock several feet above Raphael.

"Couldn't sleep either?"

"No," Raphael said. "I've just been staring at that mountain."

He nudged his head at the largest mountain in Lacandon. It was across the lake, several miles away.

"The indigenous people," he said. "Won't even approach it. The mountains are filled with magic, a place of good gods and bad gods, something sacred and ultimately terrible. Yet none of them have ever gone out to see for themselves. Do you ever wonder what makes us climb mountains?"

"Some people say just because they're there."

Raphael returned a smug look and shook his head.

"That's bad, Garrison…Sounds like a cliché. Do you really think that's why?"

Garrison's face curled in embarrassment. It was a corny line, but it was late at night, and he could be excused for saying such things.

"I don't know," Garrison said. "What makes us do anything?"

Raphael thought for a moment.

"Passion…" he said. "If I had to give one reason why I do anything, then it would be passion. That's what brought me here—a passion for the Mexican people, a passion to fight for justice."

Garrison wondered how Raphael and Poyner had ended up here. How did two people from Charlottesville end up living in Chiapas?

"How did you end up here of all places?"

"It was in my first year away from home. Home was here, Mexico. But not Chiapas, Tampico—a city on the shore of the Gulf. I was seventeen, and in my freshman year of college. My father owned a prosperous furniture business, and I was never in want of anything. I went to the best schools, played with the 'better' children, and vacationed in the premium settings, but something always stirred deep within, restless and unrelenting. I had an emptiness within my soul, and I tried to fill it with anything—philosophy, art, religion, drama—always searching for something that would ignite that spark and wake me from a slumber, no a prison—a prison of melancholy…"

CHAPTER 4:

Elevated Hero

"But as you watched, a rock was cut from a mountain by supernatural means. It struck the feet of iron and clay, smashing them to bits. The whole statue collapsed into a heap of iron, clay, bronze, silver, and gold. The pieces were crushed as small as chaff on a threshing floor, and the wind blew them all away without a trace. But the rock that knocked the statue down became a great mountain that covered the whole earth."

—Daniel
Daniel 2:34–35

Studious, earnest, and always early to class, the young man gently bounced his pencil's eraser on the foldout desk. Over and over, his hand jarred out a series of rapid percussive strokes. It was March in Charlottesville, and at least a few days every March the temperature would approach seventy degrees. Today was such a day. A voice drifted over his shoulder.

"Yo, man."

Raphael Vicente twisted his neck to find it. His friend Mark leaned over him.

"What 'cha doing here?" he asked.

Raphael measured his response to make sure he wasn't missing something.

"…waiting for class?"

"Class? It's like summer outside. Spring break, only without the beach. Check this out…"

He held out a Frisbee, dangling it beneath Raphael's chin.

"The lawn is calling."

The swinging Frisbee pendulum coaxed him into a trance-like state, but he fought it off.

"I don't think so. This is an important class."

"You always say that. Look, there'll be plenty of time to squeeze the fun out of your life once you have a real job. In the real world as they call it, you won't have any opportunities like this. You only get to be a kid once. Enjoy it."

Raphael tried to put up a viable defense.

"I'm not a kid."

"Can you even buy beer?"

"Yes."

"In the United States?"

His awkward pause killed any attempt for argument. Raphael was caught in a corner.

"Well…No. But I'm still not a kid."

"Fine. You're not a kid, but there's nothing wrong in pretending to be every now and then. Come on. The lawn beckons."

Raphael checked over each shoulder as if the professor would notice or someone—anyone—would actually care if he got up and left. He felt a jolt of life rush over his body as he snatched his notebook off the desk and hustled out the door.

*   *   *   *

The lawn stretched out beneath them like a giant green canvas, and the blades of grass generated a massaging pool of water for bare feet. Mark and Raphael danced across the lawn as they tossed the Frisbee back and forth in the springtime sun. The lawn burst at the seams with hundreds of students, and it occurred to Raphael that classes had emptied all across campus.

As they tossed the disc around, he observed the other students. Some lay reading on outstretched blankets. Others listened to music. A couple of guys grilled hamburgers, and a few girls walked past in skimpy shorts. Then, one particular girl passed. Not just any girl, but *her*. Raphael froze in place and just stared. As he did, something smacked upside his head, and in a daze, he attached his eyes to the Frisbee as it lay at his feet.

"Hey, retard!" Mark yelled. "What's wrong?"

He followed the path of Raphael's eyes, and put two and two together.

"Oh god," he said.

In a slow jog, he hurried his way over to Raphael who now held the Frisbee in his hands, looking to return the throw.

"Look, are you going to ask her out or what? One way or the other, I might as well have thrown that last one at a tree."

"Ask who?"

"Her."

Mark pointed over at the girl who now sat underneath a nearby tree. Elizabeth Poyner Addison was the most beautiful girl Raphael had ever laid eyes on. They shared a drama class together, and he loved everything about her— the sway of her hair, the grace of her walk.

"I don't know," Raphael said.

"You don't think she's hot?"

Mark tried his best to force something on the part of his friend.

"Of course, but what if she says no. I don't know if I could take that."

"So, you'd rather she never have a chance to say no, than she ever have a chance to say yes? Do I get that right?"

"Something like that."

"Whatever," Mark said. "Just pay attention, all right?"

He ran a few yards up the lawn and waited for his friend to return the Frisbee.

*   *   *   *

In brilliant character, Raphael enraptured the audience. His voice thundered through the air, his face alive and burning with disdain. His tongue quickly struck, each word clear and solid like a single keystroke on a grand piano vibrating through a luxurious concert hall. Raphael played the lead part in *Hamlet* to perfection, while Poyner, fittingly, played the part of Ophelia. On the stage, Raphael transformed into another being. Stepping into another person's shoes, he became a daring, enigmatic personality. As the curtain went down, he only wished he could summon the courage to speak to her in such a way off the stage as well.

Following the performance, he stepped out into the bleak darkness of the night. The air was pure and alive with the smell of grilling hamburgers and burning charcoal. Walking home, his eye caught hold of Poyner just ahead of him. Her brown hair lingered in the breeze as she strolled down the concrete sidewalk. Raphael stayed at a distance far behind her and scanned the neighborhood as she entered the old two-story house on Fountaine Road. The wooden house bordered itself with a large front porch, and the upstairs light flicked on within a few seconds. Raphael gazed up at the window. A weeping willow tree swayed in the wind just beneath it. It looked sad and lonely, jealous of the warmth and the light from inside. And Raphael identified with its sorrow.

*   *   *   *

An arduous history exam wreaked havoc on Raphael's brain as he stumbled down the brick steps toward campus. His books rumbled in his backpack and cement scuffed the bottoms of his shoes with each racing step. It was a bright morning. The trees glistened with a thin dew, and the sound of chirping birds littered the landscape.

Passing the Rotunda, his imagination played on its steps. A big fat "Z" painted itself across the stacked bricks. It was Greek, of course, but Raphael always imagined it stood for Zorro. Perhaps hundreds of years ago, Zorro rode his stallion through the streets of Charlottesville, vanquishing evil and saving the day for the innocent. Then as a sign to all enemies, his swashbuckling sword carved into the steps like lightening, creating the symbol as an eternal reminder to all evildoers. Or maybe the town's people painted it as a mural to the hero who had won their hearts. He knew it wasn't any of those things, but there had to be something more exciting than the world in which he lived, some grand cause larger than life itself to which he could devote everything. In his mind, he rode in on a white horse, and he carried his own large sword—one with a lightening quick reflex, able to slaughter evil and capable of branding its own eternal mark with a single brief stroke.

But the world did not create days for dreaming. He erased all thoughts of such things from his mind and pushed on the door of Newcomb Hall. It was time to study history, not useless fantasy.

Grabbing a seat in the front entrance lobby, Raphael emptied his backpack. He laid claim to a corner table where his books spread over the surface in measured piles of feet, not inches. But it didn't bother him. He loved to read about interesting places, and it came easily for him—straight A's so far. He poured over an outline of the test material, then splurged into his first textbook.

The history of Rome, grand and glorious Rome. A time of power and emperors. Flipping through the pages, he skimmed over the life and times of Julius Caesar. He read that at the age of twenty-five, Caesar fell into depression because he hadn't acquired the title of absolute ruler. Alexander the Great had conquerored the known world by his twenty-fifth birthday, so Caesar felt like a failure. How horrible a life that must be, to live with such discontent for things so far out of reach! Although, Caesar eventually reached his goal. Only it took him longer than he expected, but more people now remember his name than Alexander's. In a way, he admired Julius Caesar— not for conquering people and subjugating them, but for his sense of purpose. Actually, it was more of a jealousy than an admiration. Raphael wished some compelling force would drive him as well.

He tossed the book aside and braced his head with his hands. Lifting his notebook, he scribbled around with his pen and let the ink spill onto the page. The crafting of words gave him something to do, something of purpose. Not grand or perfect by any means, but perhaps, with a little work, maybe one day, he could present something worthwhile to future generations. His pen scratched across the paper as a torrent of thought pasting itself across the page. He couldn't muster a passion for history or calculus. He really had only two true passions. One was writing and the other was the subject of all writing—*her*. Poetry, paragraphs, gibberish, it was easy to flood a page with his mental images of her. He was hard at work on another poem, lost in a world of fantasy, when the unthinkable transpired.

"Hey."

He looked up with his mouth lurched open, astonished. It was *her*! Caught off guard and speechless, he was unable to do anything but sit and stare. She put her hand on the back of the chair directly across from him and pulled it out.

"What are you working on?" she asked.

He remained silent, in a near panic. His notebook lay open, filled with poem after poem about *her*! He moved his arm to cover up the page and leaned forward on his elbows. Finally, he called up the courage to respond.

"Just working on studying for a history exam."

Her eyes flickered between him and the table, and she slowly rocked back and forth in her chair. Her hair tied itself up in a ponytail, and it shadowed her head as she swayed from side to side.

"Those are always tough. You're taking a lot of notes, I see."

She angled forward, her eyes reaching at the page underneath his arms. He was so hanging on her every word, he almost forgot what she was talking about.

"Yeah. Notes. Observations really."

"Caesar?"

She motioned at the open book next to him, and he nodded back. All ability to speak had left him, and she carried the conversation herself.

"I think you did a great job in *Hamlet*. I've never seen anyone carry the part quite that way before."

He wished for once to act with that bold stage presence in real life. If only he could be Hamlet right now, he would tell her exactly what he thought. Instead, all he could fathom was a humble nod of the head.

"Thank you," he said. "It was easy with you out there. I think you're pretty good too."

"Thanks. Look…I'll let you finish your work."

Her arm reached across the table and stopped about halfway toward him. She stood up from the chair, and her fingers glossed the top of the table as she walked away.

"You should come by sometime. We could talk about Shakespeare. Maybe Julius Caesar."

He nodded in approval, and she left him with a parting smile.

*   *   *   *

After a long day of classes and gazing through books in Newcomb Hall, Raphael stretched out on the lawn. The sky faded into a navy blue, and the night moved in. His head rested on his backpack like a ready-made pillow, and his long legs fanned out on the ground before him. Stretching out his arms, he folded them behind his head and gazed into the sky. The stars were barely visible, but growing brighter by the moment.

"Boo!"

Raphael's skeleton nearly jumped out of its skin.

"Very funny…"

Mark stood above him, bent over with laughter. Raphael had almost forgotten about their late dinner. His mind had been playing out his chance meeting with Poyner. He and Mark had planned to hit the Corner, maybe The Deli. Raphael stood silent, shaking his head as Mark tried to control his hysterics.

"Very mature."

"Come on, man. It's just a joke."

His laugh sputtered away, and the smile drifted off his chin. By that point, Raphael decided it was funny after all. The two of them reversed roles until Raphael noticed Mark's change of emotion.

"Something wrong?"

Mark's eyes turned back. They were serious now.

"I got a phone call this afternoon."

His eyes averted away again, as if to look at any one thing for too long would cause them to burn in their sockets like balled up newspapers soaked in kerosene. Raphael stared at him, waiting.

"Ruben is dead."

A stunned shock painted over Raphael's face.

"My god, what happened?"

Mark couldn't look his friend in the eye. Instead, he clenched his eyebrows at the ground below. It wasn't a mien of hatred, so much as disgust, and Raphael knew exactly what had happened. Ruben was Mark's cousin, and the two of them grew up together in a town just outside of Managua. Raphael was aware of the underpinnings of their family's political philosophy well enough to know the Sandinistas killed his cousin.

"I'm sorry."

Mark shrugged.

"It's not your fault. Things like this happen, and that's why great men must rise up to stop them."

"What's that supposed to mean?"

Mark's eyes grew wider, and this time, they didn't look at the ground.

"I'm not coming back for the fall semester. I may not come back for a while, if ever."

"What? What are you talking about?"

"I'm going to fight with the Contras."

"What? You're crazy! That's insane."

Mark's cheeks changed to a bright red, and his hands tightened into fists.

"Why? Because I might fail?"

"That's exactly right, even worse, you could get killed."

"Maybe so, but I will not turn my back on my family. Do you know what's it like to be prancing around playing Frisbee and drinking beer while your country is trashed, family members killed and imprisoned? I can't stand it, and I can't stand to be here anymore—not in good conscience."

"But what about your education?"

The question melted a look of disgust onto Mark's face.

"Come on, Raphael. This isn't about education. You want me to stay in school, huh? I guess I'll have more earning power with a degree. Well, too bad! It won't do any damn good when I go home to a communist nation. This isn't about education. It's about what's right. It's about being a man."

"Being a man?"

"Yeah, being a man. Making a decision. Not being afraid if it's wrong and to hell with the consequences. You know, like asking a girl out instead of being scared shitless when she comes up talking to you and hitting on you."

Raphael felt a giant foot kick him in the teeth. He tried to mutter out some words.

"Look—"

"No, you look," Mark said. "I'm not going to apologize. You better wake up, before your whole life passes by. I'm going to Nicaragua. That's all there is to it, and I will not come back until Daniel Ortega is dead."

He didn't wait for a response before storming off into the night. Raphael stood in place for a few moments, unable to contemplate what had happened. Then, a bold look sparkled in his eye, and he raced off the lawn and into the darkness.

CHAPTER 5:

Poyner's Window

"And wars will break out near and far, but do not panic. Yes, these things must come, but the end won't follow immediately. The nations and kingdoms will proclaim war against each other, and there will be famines and earthquakes in many parts of the world. But all this will only be the beginning of sorrows."

—**Jesus Christ**
Matthew 24:6–8

A bit of crabgrass grew between the cracks of the sidewalk beneath his feet, and as he stepped onto the pillow-like surface of her front lawn, he shifted his head upward. The light from her window dripped down through the arms of the weeping willow, and he suddenly felt as never before. Darkness painted the rest of the house except for this one lone window. It was just after midnight and too late to ring the doorbell. He didn't want to wake up her roommates. For a brief time, a little voice from way down inside his stomach told him to leave—to just come back tomorrow. *What's one more day? Just turn and run!* But he refused to listen. He shut those voices out, and he moved himself forward.

But a greater challenge stood in his way. How would he get to her window? He could climb the tree, but it wasn't the kind of tree someone would normally climb, and anyway—that approach only worked in movies. For all he knew, she had a weapons permit, and she'd blow him away the second he tapped on her window. He could throw rocks at the window until she noticed, but that also was something that only worked in movies. With his luck and the window wrenched slightly open, he would probably smack her right the face. Or else end up throwing one right through the middle of her window and that wouldn't leave a very good impression either. For several minutes, he stood underneath the weeping willow, wondering and contemplating. Then, from the corner of his eye he saw her shadow.

Before he had a chance to move, Poyner placed her hands on the windowsill and stared back down at him. His instincts kicked in, and he flinched. His first inclination was to run. But he quickly squelched that thought and simply stood his ground. Running would be a disaster. Having seen him, she would have thought he was a peeping tom or a stalker or something. And he wasn't a stalker. *Was he?* Of course, not. By this time, he had no doubt she had spotted him. She poked her head out of the bottom part of the window and called out below.

"Raphael?"

It was an awkward moment, but it solved all his original problems. And it wasn't a big deal. He had a legitimate reason for being in her yard.

"Yeah."

She paused, waiting for him to say something else, like for instance, why he now stood in her front yard, staring into her window.

"What are you doing down there?"

He kept his voice low, as if he had a prayer of waking anyone in a college town.

"I was just wondering if you wanted to go out, maybe to the Corner, but I didn't want to ring the doorbell. I was just trying to figure out if I should throw a rock or something."

"Raphael, it's one-thirty in the morning."

"I know. Let's go out."

She shook her head, but he just held his arms out wide and shrugged back. He detected a guarded smile trying to break out as she held out all her fingers.

"Give me five minutes."

She pulled her upper body back into the window and slid the curtains closed. What in the world had he just done? She was actually coming down to meet him. A jolt of adrenaline rushed through his body. The most exhilarating feeling of his life poured over him. A few minutes later, her front door opened. Poyner stepped out onto the porch and locked the door behind her.

*   *   *   *

MacAdooes was a favorite hangout on the Corner. It had a nostalgic feel to its atmosphere. Carved names cluttered the wooden booths, and the walls had drawings strewn all over them like wallpaper. Memorabilia from Charlottesville, American sports icons, and rock and roll history decorated every nook and crevice. Raphael sat opposite Poyner. Her voice was sweet music as she lifted a glass of water to her lips.

"So, why did it take you all year to ask me out?"

He fiddled with his napkin and played with a crumpled up straw wrapper.

"I am a man of calculated and meticulous action."

She cocked her head back and laughed. He ran his hands through his hair, his elbows still on the table.

"I don't know, scared—frightened of my own shadow I guess. I was afraid you would say no."

She just looked up over her glass, her eyes picking him apart. But he didn't flinch this time.

"Don't worry. I won't let it happen again," he said.

A half-smile appeared while she traced the rim of her glass with her fingers.

"So are you going to make me wait another year to go out with you again?"

"Well, that depends on how well tonight goes."

"I guess we women have to be patient with men of such calculated and meticulous action."

"Well, of course. It's just one of my redeeming qualities. Let's see. I'm kind, generous, quite humorous, and of course, good looking..."

He relayed a confident look from across the table.

"Intelligent, bold, ambitious, yet meek—forgiving, athletic, studious, charming, well-accomplished, rich, brilliant, handsome. I have a sensual accent that drives women crazy. And let neither of us forget, I am very, very—humble..."

She burst out laughing, nearly unable to sit up straight.

"Well, you don't sound very humble to me, Raphael Vicente."

She leaned across the table, and he knew she was enjoying herself. It was the best night of his life.

*   *   *   *

That night, Raphael returned to his dorm room, brimming with excitement to tell Mark all about his date. He searched every room in the suite, but all of them were empty. Walking into his room, he tossed his keys and wallet on top of his desk. He sat down, and the phone rang. He picked it up, and a voice entered his ear.

"Raphael?"

He recognized it as that of his roommate.

"What's up?" Raphael asked.

His roommate was slow to speak and his voice cracked as he spoke.

"Man, you've got to get down here. Mark's been in an accident. It's really bad."

Raphael felt a shock lay siege to his entire body. All the good feelings from thirty seconds ago drained away, and the world turned into a numb jelly of pins and needles.

"Man, you still there?"

Raphael sat up straight in his chair.

"Yeah."

"The ICU at UVA…"

The roommate hung up, and it was as if a dagger had been plunged into Raphael's chest.

*   *   *   *

Raphael took the long way home from the medical center. He walked down the winding streets of Charlottesville with no particular destination in mind. After a mile or two, his head slumped down below his shoulders, and he stopped caring where he was. He just let his legs carry him to wherever. As he studied the cracks in the sidewalk, he somewhat hoped that a car would come along and hit him too. It would make things a lot easier, and a lot less painful.

Sprinkles of rain started to fall, and they glazed his body with a thin new skin. He lifted his head to see where he was, and the house towered before him. The weeping willow spread its leaves in all directions, its arms floating in the gentle wind. He followed them to a lighted second story window, and his despair drained away. He dwelt for a while on the warm feeling he received from the emergence of her window and the light that poured out. In his mind, the rain disappeared and the world fell away, and he set his course for that light.

CHAPTER 6:

A Faint Cry In The Dark

"But he said, 'Go now, Daniel, for what I have said is for the time of the end. Many will be purified, cleansed, and refined by these trials. But the wicked will continue in their wickedness, and none of them will understand. Only those who are wise will know what it means."

—Daniel
Daniel 12:9–10

The end of the school day approached, and the kids were finishing playtime. Poyner ran around the room trying to keep them from crayoning on walls, eating glue, and kicking at each other. Construction paper artwork and letters of the alphabet stuck to the walls with strange smelling glue, and the children formed a line at the door to wait for the final bell to ring. Raphael showed up and lightly rapped on the door's glass window.

Poyner opened the door, and he stepped inside.

"What a surprise," she said.

He smiled.

"Hello, children," he said.

They all sang in unison.

"Hello, Mr. Raphael!"

He waited for Poyner to usher the kids to the bus ramp. She disappeared for a couple of minutes, then re-entered the classroom, and the two of them sat down at a small circular table in the corner, half of it covered with books and crayons. Raphael still wore a look of sadness.

"I thought I'd drop by, see if you wanted to get ice cream or something."

It had been several weeks since Mark's death, and Raphael had been in a perpetual state of depression ever since. She slid her hand across the table and onto his.

"Are you going to be all right?"

Raphael hung his head low.

"I just can't forget about it."

"You're not supposed to forget about it."

She understood his suffering, and she wanted nothing more than to see his spirits lifted.

"I don't know…maybe I need to see a psychiatrist or something," he said.

Her face was expressionless, until she reached across the table and grabbed one of the books.

"How about this doctor?"

He looked at the book in her hand with a doubtful expression.

"Dr. Seuss is not a real doctor."

"I can't believe you would say such a thing. Of course, he's a real doctor. See, it says right here—Dr. Seuss."

She held the book up and pointed to his name.

"They couldn't write it on the cover of the book if he wasn't really a doctor!" she said.

A broad smile slowly crept across Raphael's face. He tried to hide it, but to no avail. She dashed in as if awaiting her cue, opening the book and reading the words out loud. A wild assortment of the craziest characters ever to traverse the depths of any imagination jumped to life. After a few pages, Raphael laughed uncontrollably.

"See. I told you he was a real doctor."

He braced himself against the table.

"I was just thinking that I remembered that one—that's all."

Poyner looked down at the books and ran her fingers over the covers.

"Before my mother died, she used to read me all of these books. She worked two jobs, but she was always around to tuck me in at night. We spent more time reading Dr. Seuss than doing anything else I can remember."

"What was your favorite?" he asked.

She thought for a moment.

"Green Eggs And Ham."

"I would not, could not in a tree. Not in a car! You let me be."

She placed her hand on his.

"You remember it?"

"I was a kid once too," he said.

*   *   *   *

Poyner sat in a booth at the corner deli, and the aroma of fresh cut peppers and baked bread permeated the stale air. Raphael walked in the door. His step had a spring to it, and his eyes were lit up like a kid at Christmas. He held a copy of *The Washington Post* in his left hand, and as soon as he spotted her, he bolted over to her table.

"Look at this!"

He tossed the paper down on the table. It was folded back to the Op/Ed page. Mid-way down was a pro-Contra editorial, *A Faint Cry In The Dark* by Raphael Vicente. A proud look donned her face as she studied the famous names that surrounded his.

"That's great Raphael."

He hurriedly pulled a number of items out of his backpack and stacked them on the table. His mouth moved as though he had been mute for seven years.

"There's more. I've organized a pro-Contra rally on the steps of the Rotunda on Friday, and I'm putting together a permanent student organization. Here's the poster I created. You're going to join, right?"

He slid the poster across the table so that it covered over the article.

"Of course," she said. "You know, I'm proud of you. You've done more here than most people will do in a lifetime. I believe you're going to change the world."

He leaned across the table and wrapped his hands around hers.

"I'm going to do more than change the world—I'm going to completely alter the course of human history, and when I die, people will look back and say, 'because he lived, we eat different, we breathe different, we live different, we think different'..."

*   *   *   *

"And that's the story of how we ended up here," Raphael said. "After graduation, I joined Radio Free America, authored a series of pro-democracy broadcasts, a number of things for Nicaragua. After the first free elections, I needed something bigger to do. When you experience something like that, you don't go back to a normal job in a factory. We moved back to Charlottesville for a while, but we had to move here to stay alive. I felt a moral obligation to do for Mexico what was done for Nicaragua."

PART II

▼

Outrage Within

"*He ordered the people of the world to make a great statue of the first beast, who was fatally wounded and then came back to life. He was permitted to give life to this statue so that it could speak. Then the statue commanded that anyone refusing to worship it must die.*"

—**John**
Revelation 13:14–15

CHAPTER 1:

Rivers Of Fear

"Whoever is thirsty, let him come, and whoever wishes, let him take the free gift of the water of life."

—Jesus Christ
Revelation 22:17

Inside, fear pierced the blood in his veins like an ice-cold twisting knife. Sweat drenched his body, and Eduardo opened his mouth to scream, but no sound rose from within. The humid breath touched his shoulder. Slowly, it drifted up his neck to his ear, and the eerie voice whispered.

Eduardo bent straight up in bed like a jack-in-the-box and screamed out into the darkness. His sheets dripped with sweat and a pair of wide-open eyes stared back at him through the darkness. Instinctively, he flinched in the face of the man standing over him.

"I heard you from outside."

Eduardo took a couple of breaths and relaxed.

"Garrison? You nearly scared me to death."

Garrison didn't react to the statement. He remained fixed like a stone statue, towering above Eduardo's bed. His eyes didn't blink. They only cut through the darkness.

"I heard you talk about it."

"Talk about what?"

Garrison's body maintained its frozen position, and the broad outline of his body entered into focus, forming a silhouette of light rising out from the night.

"It. The hole…The voices…"

"It was just a nightmare."

Garrison shook his head, yet his gaze never wandered.

"No, it's not just any nightmare. It was the Void."

Eduardo felt his body jump back at the sound of the word. A chill climbed its way up his spine.

"How did you know that?"

Garrison stayed mute for a few seconds, but it felt like hours on end as he hovered over Eduardo in the bleak darkness.

"Because the Void is real," Garrison said.

*   *   *   *

Barely old enough to drive, Derek Stevens sat in a small academic desk in the back of the auditorium at Marymount University. Several adult staffers from the Student World Affairs Conference encircled his desk, pouring over their notes. They wore gray suits with their ties fastened so close to their necks it was a miracle they could breathe. Derek studied their faces, ingesting every detail and committing them to memory. One of the men stepped forward from behind the table and addressed him.

"We're honored to have this time to spend one-on-one with you Derek. We like to meet with each student individually so we can learn how to improve the process for next year's attendees."

The Student World Affairs Conference gathered an annual collection of the nation's brightest high school students in the suburbs of DC to meet with national and international leaders. After a few lectures, they broke up the assembly to meet with each student on an individual basis.

"And now it's time to get down to business, to address the real reason we're all here, right?" Derek asked.

"Excuse me?" the man asked.

Derek sat in his chair with his fingers crossed and calmly resting in front of him.

"You're here on behalf of the government, right?"

"Why do say that?" the man asked.

Derek looked over the members of the panel a second time, then looked back at the man.

"Your name's Clayton, right?"

The man's mouth fell open, and he exchanged a sharp glance with the rest of the panel.

"Yeah, how'd you know that?"

Derek laughed with a slight smile.

"We've met before. You remember? I was in first grade and you came in to talk with me right after the class took a big test. You asked if I understood what I was doing and if I could do it again. You remember? And then in fourth grade you showed up again after our class took the standardized testing."

Clayton's eyes opened wide in exasperation, while the rest of the men on the panel shook their heads.

"And you remember that?" Clayton asked.

"Sure," Derek said. "The first time was a Thursday, and you wore a red tie with thin black stripes, not too much unlike the one you're wearing now. It rained that afternoon, and I remember it well because the art teacher helped us make baby chicks out of construction paper and egg cartons. I really liked that. The second time was a Wednesday morning, and you had a stain on your left collar. I remember thinking that was unusual for a grown man to spill food on himself before his day really even started."

Some of the men and women on the panel laughed out loud. Clayton took their jibes and returned to Derek's side. Kneeling next to the small desk, he looked him in the eye.

"Son, you're right. We brought you here for a reason. How would you like to work for the National Security Agency?"

CHAPTER 2:

Assembly Of God

"What is causing the quarrels and fights among you? Isn't it the whole army of evil desires at war within you? You want what you don't have, so you scheme and kill to get it. You are jealous for what others have, and you can't possess it, so you fight and quarrel to take it away from them. And yet the reason you don't have what you want is that you don't ask God for it."

—James
James 4:1–2

Memories of his past work for the department of defense tumbled through Eduardo's mind. Certain parts of him felt guilty for advancing it, even though it was only theoretical work. But it wasn't just theoretical. It was inevitable. He couldn't feel guilty knowing it would happen with or without his efforts. In fact, he now felt guilty for no longer being a part of it. Garrison reminded him of that.

"No problem ever gets solved by walking away from it," he had said.

At the time, Eduardo thought the comment was little more than a cliché, but being a cliché doesn't in and of itself make a statement untrue. He planned to go back, but perhaps Chiapas was the best place to rest his mind before doing so.

He wished Garrison was around to give more advice, but he had left for college two months earlier. Come summer, he would be back, but for the interim, the jungle was no longer the same. He couldn't stop thinking about his recurring nightmare and Garrison's intimate knowledge of it. It was as if Garrison had been in his head. He even called it by the same name, "the Void".

Eduardo wondered if he would have any dreams tonight, and if so, would the Void return? Pushing those thoughts from his mind, he said the Lord's prayer and crawled into bed for the evening. Closing his eyes, another world appeared.

A lifeless desert spread out beneath his feet, not a tree could be seen for miles around. Eduardo found himself standing in the middle of the endless sands, when from out of nowhere, an angry lion leapt in his path. Its mouth let out a ferocious roar, and saliva dripped from the razor sharp edges of its teeth. Eduardo's heart pounded in his chest. His entire body trembled. He turned and ran as fast as his legs would carry him. Only a few yards separated his flesh from the lion's needlepoint teeth, and he felt the breath of the beast huffing on his back.

Turning his head, he looked over his shoulder. Right before his eyes, one lion became two! Now both chased after him with single-minded purpose. Eduardo lifted his legs with every ounce of his energy and pounded them into the ground, but the furious sound of the lions only drew closer. Peering over his shoulder a second time, he found that the two lions were now four. Quickly, the four spawned four more, and then eight became sixteen, until finally—thousands and millions of lions chased after him. His blood turned cold, and Eduardo looked over his shoulder one last time. As he did, the first legion of mighty lions sprung into the air with unmitigated ferocity…

Eduardo sprung straight up in bed. His face gave off heat like a simmering cauldron and beads of sweat careened down his forehead. Frantically, he twisted his head in every direction. All the horrors had disappeared. It was a nightmare, one far more frightening than the Void—for he knew its true meaning. And it scared the life right out of him.

*   *   *   *

"You're going to knock 'em dead," Walter said.

His hand clamped down on Garrison's shoulder. The two of them occupied the end of the first pew at Ebenezer Baptist Church. Garrison wore a black robe that stretched down to just past his knees, and it rippled in the light as he rolled a copy of the Bible through his hands. Red, yellow, and blue post-it notes lunged out of the pages where he had marked certain passages for reference, and as the Reverend stepped up before the crowd, a hand tapped on Walter's shoulder with a gentle voice that whispered in his ear.

"Excuse me young man, I'm not as agile as I used to be."

Walter Nance twisted his head and found the smiling face staring back at him. The owner of the voice had bushy gray eyebrows and a pair of silver-rimmed glasses almost as thick as his head. He leaned forward with a hunched back. Walter and Garrison stood up and smiled out of respect as the man fingered his way past with a long wooden cane. Walter placed his left hand on the man's shoulder.

"You're going to miss the best part of the service, Mr. Jenkins."

Mr. Jenkins lifted his eyes to Walter's, his smile still omnipresent.

"I've been coming to this church for seventy years, son, and I haven't missed anything yet, but at my age, when the restroom calls, a man needs to listen."

His wobbly frame bobbed with laughter as his cane felt its way to the end of the pew and quietly disappeared down the aisle. The Reverend delivered his opening remarks.

"It is with great honor that Ebenezer Baptist Church announces our guest speaker for today. A young man well traveled and wise beyond his years. A man we've all known since before he could crawl...Ladies and gentlemen, Brother Garrison Nance."

The Reverend clutched his Bible in his right hand, holding it close to his body, while the open palm of his left hand extended out to welcome the young man in the first pew. Garrison stepped up onto the stage and walked to its center. The Reverend walked off to a chair positioned along the edge of the far wall and left Garrison alone on stage with the back wall's circular stained glass window lighting the floor beneath his feet.

He stood tall with no podium and no microphone and his eyes never left the audience. He flipped through the pages of scripture while the applause died to a silence, and then he opened his mouth to speak. When he did, his voice rumbled from the pulpit and throughout the chamber so that every splinter of every beam in the entire hall reverberated to his call. The hairs on the back of Walter's neck stood straight up as if to reach toward the heavens.

"Today I would like to speak on the topic of the spiritual emptiness so predominate in our modern world," Garrison said.

In the silence between Garrison's opening words and the rest of his sermon, Walter heard a frantic tapping echo through the church hall. He spun his head to see what it was. Mr. Jenkins raced down the aisle toward him. He skipped forward with his cane only touching the ground long enough to bang out the rudimentary beats, his posture firm and upright. His mouth hung wide open and his squinting eyes never left the man standing on the pulpit. He hobbled up to the seat next to Walter, a tear watering down his cheek. Walter draped his arm over Mr. Jenkins' shoulders.

"What's wrong?" he asked.

Mr. Jenkins glowed as he hung on Garrison's every word.

"I could have sworn that I heard Martin," he said.

Walter rubbed the man's shoulder and the two of them listened to the rest of the sermon. Garrison's voice was clear and concise and spoke with resounding authority.

"One day you will awake to find yourself stranded in a vast ocean of material prosperity and an emptiness will overtake your soul. Why should we think ourselves immune? For even the Lord was tempted by the devil."

"Amen!"

"In the coming days, the world will experience a great time of testing. Just as he tempted Jesus in desert, the devil will offer to throw the world at our feet if we only bow down and worship his name. He will shower us with astounding miracles and abundant wealth. He will grant power for the lame to walk and the blind to see, but the devil will not be able to fill the void in your heart. Only God can fill the void!"

"Amen!"

"It will be a time of great tribulation when those days come, but the Lord tells us not to forget his love."

"That's right!"

"Because those will be dark days, and he will not let us endure them alone. For what man alone can resist the temptations of the world? No man by himself, but with God anything is possible."

With his last words, he pounded a fist on the podium and pointed straight up to heaven.

"So don't be distraught when the coming days arrive, because the Lord is with you. As Jesus tells his people, 'Take heart, for I have overcome the world!'"

"Amen, Brother Garrison!"

The congregation rose to its feet and roared with applause as Garrison walked off the stage. Mr. Jenkins tapped his cane on the floor in elation.

"Today, I got to see Martin one last time," he said.

Walter shook his head and spoke loudly into the old man's ear.

"No, Mr. Jenkins. That's my son Garrison."

Mr. Jenkins shot a glance up at Walter along with a brief look of confusion. It harbored a fleeting look of anger that soon diminished.

"No," he said, correcting Walter. "Today I heard Martin Luther King, Jr."

*   *   *   *

The morning light poured through the open windows of the ramshackle hut, a small dwelling with nothing more than a frame of tree branches caked together with sun-baked mud and topped off with a cardboard roof. Raphael reached into the crib and ran his hand through the thin mat of hair on his infant son. Juan Diego Vicente smiled back.

Raphael blew a breath of air on Juan's face, and the baby giggled as it brushed past his eyelashes. He derived great joy from these rare moments alone with his child, and he reveled in the pleasure of unveiling the world to him. Raphael dug through a basket butted up against the wall. He fumbled around and pulled out one of the many children's books inside, but not just any book. A classic—one of the good doctor's books. Sitting beside the crib, he opened its pages.

"Now Juan, I will introduce you to the family doctor—Dr. Seuss. This one is a classic: *The Cat in the Hat*. This is one of your mother's favorites."

He thumbed through the pages, describing the crazy red and white hat and the wacky cat that toted it along. And as he turned the last page, Eduardo burst through the door. His feet scattered dust in every direction, his panted breathing drowning out all but his voice.

"Raphael! Raphael! You've got to come…Something terrible has happened!"

Raphael dropped the book and stood up. He could see the look covering Eduardo's face, so he hung his head out the window and called over to his neighbor. Quickly, she ran over.

"What's wrong?"

"I need you to look after Baby Juan," he said.

"Gladly."

Raphael dashed through the door and followed Eduardo down the path at a brisk and hurried pace. A crowd amassed around a small hut on the outer edge of the village. Small pockets of men pounded the palms of their hands with their fists and a furious chatter ravaged the atmosphere. The two of them navigated through the crowd. Inside the hut, a young Indian woman lay on the bed. Her face was black and blue, and scrapes ran across her forehead and arms. Her blouse was torn, and her dress was ripped along the seam. She kept her eyes closed and didn't murmur a word. Poyner attended her bedside, placing a cold rag on the woman's wounds. No words were exchanged, but it was enough for Raphael to know everything.

Poyner raised her eyes to meet Raphael's. A sudden panic entered her face.

"Where's Baby Juan?"

Raphael placed his hand on her head.

"Don't worry. He's with Pilar."

The shades of panic fled her face like water from a punctured bucket. Raphael tapped his hand on Eduardo's shoulder, and the two of them walked outside. Around the house, masked men gathered everywhere. Eduardo and Raphael stepped off by themselves to talk. Eduardo shook his head in frustration.

"What are we going to do? They want to storm the countryside."

"Who was it?"

Eduardo paused before speaking, the skin around his face shriveling into a clenched mass.

"Humberto."

Raphael did his best to hide his hatred. He could no longer stand to witness these conditions. The vandalism, the killings, the assaults…Living the lives of feudal lords, the ranchers now attacked women.

"We can't let this go unpunished."

The other men circled around them now. Their voices belted out, demanding justice. One shouted out high above the others.

"Burn his ranch to the ground! We'll kill every one of them!"

Raphael raised his hand, and the men fell silent.

"No. This is not a mob. We are above such things. But we will round up the one responsible and hold him accountable."

*   *   *   *

The ranch house projected its opulence from the top of a raised mound of earth closed in on all sides by a sea of corn just outside of San Cristobal. It stood three stories high with catwalks stretching parallel to the top floors and a huge wrap-around porch extending around all sides of the bottom floor. In many ways, it resembled a cross between a turn-of-the-century Iowa farm-house and a 19th Century Southern plantation. The hive of ranchers buzzed with activity. Armed guards covered every flank.

Raphael sifted through the corn on his hands and knees only a few feet from the dirt road leading into the compound. Eduardo was about four yards away resting on his stomach. From the right angle, they could view every one of the ranchers. Several feet from where the corn ended and the front edge of the lawn began, Humberto worked on the tire rim of a new pick-up. He crouched down on his knees, locking a ratchet onto the hub of one of the front wheels. Raphael turned his head in Eduardo's direction.

"Psst…There he is."

His pointing finger alerted Eduardo to their prey. Eduardo nodded, his eyes fixed on the ranch hand. With great patience, Raphael studied the ranch house. Seven men wielding semi-automatic weapons roved the lower floor. Two more, in addition to Humberto, milled around in the yard. The real question involved the number inside the compound. Twenty-seven rebels surrounded the ranch house along with Eduardo and himself. He hoped to get close enough to Humberto to grab him and flee before anyone noticed. The goal was to limit the bloodshed to the smallest degree possible. He believed the rebels should be above the methods of their oppressors.

While he assessed the situation, he noticed one of the guards on the porch froze in place and stared off into the cornfield. His head tilted to the side, and he motioned to one of his comrades. Raphael again whispered in Eduardo's direction.

"What's going on?"

Eduardo's head lurched forward, peering through the corn stalks.

"I think they spotted someone."

Raphael swallowed hard and trained his eyes on the porch. While he waited, a shot rang out. A bullet entered right above the guard's nose and slapped him to the floor. The other ranchers took cover and returned a spray of fire into the corn. They aimed their weapons randomly, spewing shells all over the field. Raphael held his position and watched as the other rebels stormed the compound.

"What's going on? They're supposed to stay back."

Eduardo looked his way.

"I know. They botched the whole operation, but hold your position."

"Hold my position? They're not doing what they're supposed to."

"Sometimes things don't go the way we plan. But we have to stay focused."

He pointed back toward the truck. Humberto remained silent in a crouched position, unseen by the rebels who rushed in from all sides and picked off the ranchers one by one. Seizing the perimeter, they entered the house through the windows and doors. Raphael kept his attention focused on Humberto.

The vile creature didn't make one effort to help his friends. Like a sniveling weasel, he popped his eyes over the hood of the pick-up and when all was clear, he took off running down the dirt road, ducking beside the rows of corn so no one could spot him. Raphael burrowed through the crops to the edge of the road in great stealth. Humberto ran straight toward him. Now, only fifteen yards separated them. Raphael stepped out into the road and pointed his rifle straight ahead. Humberto, looking over his shoulder, didn't yet notice him. As he turned to face the road ahead, Raphael saw the man's smile whither away. Humberto's feet stopped, his body went limp, and he slowly raised his hands above his head.

Raphael cocked the trigger and aimed at the man's face, then he lowered the gun and let out a deep breath. Unable to pull the trigger, he let the rifle fall to his side. Humberto formed an obnoxious smile, lowered his hands and took off running again, passing Raphael with a condescending smirk. Without hesitation, Raphael drew his rifle and aimed at the back of the man's head. He pulled the trigger and inserted a bullet dead center into the back of Humberto's skull. The dead body flopped to the ground, and the man's blood cut like a river through the hard dirt road.

Raphael strolled over to the body while the sounds of gunfire swallowed the compound behind him. He watched as the blood bubbled out of the man's skull and spread over the ground like a tentacled pattern of tiny streams. The blood gushed over the lifeless body, and Raphael didn't feel awful the way he thought he would. Instead, he felt wonderful, and more powerful than he had ever felt in his life.

CHAPTER 3:

Death Of The Innocent

"They called loudly to the Lord and said, 'O Sovereign Lord, holy and true, how long will it be before you judge the people who belong to this world for what they have done to us? When will you avenge our blood against these people."

—John
Revelation 6:10

Edging his way through the underbrush, Garrison carried a long stick in his hand that he used to smack away vines that had overtaken parts of the trail. The smell of the jungle was one he had never forgotten during his time away at school. He followed the progress of the revolution in the newspapers and kept in regular contact with Raphael via e-mail. Venturing past the last remnant of trees, he looked out over the village of Lacandon. It was still. No voices. No masked men, and no children running about.

"Garrison!"

He turned his head in time to see Poyner's smiling face running toward him. She rushed forward and slung her arms around his neck.

"I didn't know you were coming today," she said. "Raphael will be so happy."

"So where is this beautiful baby?"

Her face lit up, and she reached around her neck and grabbed hold of a gold chain. Dangling from the end, a heart-shaped locket sparkled in the dim light.

"He's playing with Pilar."

She stuck her fingernail into the side of the heart, and it hinged open. Inside was a miniature photo of Raphael and Poyner holding tiny Juan Diego. Her face brightened even further at sight of the picture.

"Do you want to go see him?" she asked.

"Of course."

He twisted his head. The village remained quiet with the exception of their lone conversation.

"Where is everyone?"

Poyner followed the path of his eyes and her face transformed from its previous state into a more strained contortion as if she were angry at something.

"They went off for a while."

"Went off for a while? A whole village?"

She never answered the question.

"Is Raphael with them?" he asked. "Is that where he is?"

She returned a graven look of disapproval.

"We'll talk about it later," she said. "Come on. Let's go."

She grabbed his arm and turned toward the village. The explosion knocked them both on all fours. Garrison lifted his chin. A fire burned through the dry leaves to his right. To his left, he could see Poyner was just as confused. He stumbled onto his feet in time to hear a whistle cutting through the sky. He jumped on Poyner and covered her with his body. The second shell blasted a hole in the ground thirty feet in front of them.

Dirt shot through the air as though flung from a lacrosse stick, whole clumps landing on his back in sprinkles. Poyner struggled from the jungle floor and pushed him away.

"Juan!"

She rushed forward into the village as a third shell rocketed into the clearing. Lines of fire burned up the trees like sparklers on the Fourth of July, and dirt rained down like heavy droplets of sleet.

For Garrison, it felt as though the whole earth shook in the grip of an earthquake as he chased through the jungle after her. She kept screaming out Juan's name as she flew through the village, the bombs falling with ever increasing frequency.

The wind filled her shirt like a sail as she sprinted forward, and her arms stretched out as her eyes caught hold of Pilar's small hut. The woman stood in the doorway, cradling Baby Juan in her arms and waiting for Poyner to arrive. With only forty yards separating mother from child, an artillery shell dropped from the sky and landed directly on top of the mud dwelling. The roof, the walls, the doorway, and the woman and baby in it, all turned to fire as if they were made of gunpowder glued together with kerosene.

Poyner screamed, still yelling out Juan's name, and Garrison struggled to catch up with her as she climbed into the fire, picking through the debris as though the fiery planks of wood and burning cinders were a pile of rag dolls to be tossed overhead. Garrison leapt into the flames, unaware that they crept up his body and set his own clothes ablaze. In total panic, Poyner threw away the pieces of flaming house, screaming with tears soaking her face. Garrison seized her arms and threw her over his shoulders. She kicked at the air and pounded his back with her fists as he carried her out of the burning rubble.

Lacandon turned into a hellish cauldron, and the screeching whistles still cut through the air. Poyner gave up her struggle, and Garrison felt her body go limp over his shoulders as he raced into the depths of the wild jungle. Repeatedly, she whispered the name in a muffled voice.

"Juan…Juan…"

Hundreds of yards from the village, he laid her down on the ground and checked her body for burns. Her face looked like a corpse, eyes frozen, but filled with water. Her skin was pasted with soot.

"Take me back," she said. "I want to die too."

He grabbed her hand and squeezed.

"No," he said, trying to cover her burns. "Some of us need you to live."

CHAPTER 4:

Intolerant Men

"During the reigns of those kings, the God of heaven will set up a kingdom that will never be destroyed; no one will ever conquer it. It will shatter all these kingdoms into nothingness, but it will stand forever. That is the meaning of the rock cut from the mountain by supernatural means, crushing to dust the statue of iron, bronze, clay, silver, and gold."

—Daniel
Daniel 2:44–45

"Of all things, an assembler is the key to your power, son."

Yang Hu Yafei let the utterance slip out, as he lay in bed in the sterile room. He had spent his entire life in adherence and commitment to the will of the state, sacrificing all of his personal ambitions in order to lay down his life for his homeland. The only self-interest he harbored was to see his only son, Jiang, rise to prominence in the Party and usher in the day when Imperial China would once again rule the world.

Yang Hu was proud of his own accomplishments. He had survived to a ripe age, successfully navigating the political waters of the Party, and ascending to a position of power giving him knowledge of things unknown to most citizens. Now, as he fought a battle against cancer, his only goal was to reinforce the teachings he had already ingrained in his son.

"I've gone to great lengths to secure your position, and you remain an unknown to the West. So never forget the words of Sun Tzu, 'no one is given rewards as rich as those given to spies'. You must follow this path with focus. The honor of our family rests on your shoulders."

Jiang crouched by his father's bedside. He was young, but a man quick to rise through the ranks of the Party.

"I will succeed in all of these things."

Yang Hu studied the facial expressions of his son.

"I believe you will. Do not forget the knowledge I have given you. Molecular nanotechnology. I can not emphasize in enough ways its central importance. No matter how long it takes, you must be patient. An assembler is the key to defeating the West. But don't forget to protect yourself from internal enemies as well."

Jiang nodded in compliance. He was prepared for this day. He spoke multiple languages and maintained a sharp intellect. He was well connected within the Chinese government, and he had just been promoted to an important position within the clandestine intelligence service.

Kneeling down on one knee by his father's bedside, he watched as Yang Hu took one last breath. And he could never forget the word his father repeated up until the very end, "nanotechnology, Jiang…nanotechnology…"

*   *   *   *

Raphael emerged at the edge of the smothering jungle. Lost in its shadows, he adjusted to the radiant sunlight that dominated the clearing of the wide-open field. A massive oak towered above the heads of grain as the breeze pushed them back like rolling waves in the ocean. Underneath, Raphael could see Poyner kneeling on the ground. She buried her head in her hands, while in front of her, a small tombstone jutted from the earth.

Raphael felt an icy sting of venom coursing through his veins, and a tear rolled out from the corner of his eye. He brushed it away, and began the long walk from the safety of the jungle to the exposed danger of the open field. As he approached his wife, he was overcome by the worst feeling of his entire life. It wasn't a normal pain or hurt, but a reckless lack of control—the hefty burden of powerlessness.

He bowed down before her and she collapsed in his arms.

*   *   *   *

Just past midnight, Raphael dug his bare feet into the sand by the lake's shore. His blank stare drifted off alone into the rippling waters. Garrison followed from behind and placed his hand on Raphael's shoulder. Then, he climbed atop a nearby rock. Raphael broke the silence and stood up.

"Why?"

He picked up a rock and hurled it into the air above the lake while screaming into the darkness.

"Why!"

His scream thundered across the lake to its far edge, then drowned in the vacant emptiness of the jungle. He kicked at the sands, the thought of Poyner's pained face still etched in his memory.

"I can't fight anymore, Garrison. All my energy has been sucked dry."

Garrison shuffled his position on the rock, but didn't say a word.

"When the idea of revolution first began, I believed in the power of words. I had a thirst for justice, and I believed the world would unite behind our cause. What cause could be more just than freedom for the poor and oppressed? Now, I don't believe the world cares."

"What are you going to do? Give up?"

"Poyner and I have only two things left in this world—our lives and the revolution. I can only give up one of them and still have a good conscience."

"You're going to stay?"

"Do I have another option? I arrived committed to an idea, the idea that men should be free. If I have to, I will die for that idea."

His fists clenched and pounded at the air as he spoke. Garrison remained perched on his rock.

"How are you going to fight tanks?"

"The only way I know how—with film and pictures and truth."

CHAPTER 5:

Sliver Of Hope

"If your enemies are hungry, feed them. If they are thirsty, give them something to drink, and they will be ashamed of what they have done to you. Don't let evil get the best of you, but conquer evil by doing good."

—**Paul**
Romans 12:20–21

Frustrated, Rincon paced the floor, wearing a hole in the carpet of his office.

"This is ridiculous," he said.

His top aide did his best to explain the situation.

"It's a public relations nightmare. They have pictures of dead women and children, and they've put them on the Internet. Supposedly, Vicente lost his own son, and they're turning him into a martyr. We've been under assault from every interest group in the world and the Secretary-General called personally to express his condemnation. You've got to do something to answer these charges."

Rincon took a deep breath. The whole Chiapas affair was making him look cruel and heartless, and it only added fuel to the accusations of corruption against his party. He shuffled through the pictures on his desk.

"Is all this true?"

He would face the wrath of world opinion no matter what, but Rincon wanted to know if the images of dead children were inventions of propaganda or fact. His aide seemed shocked.

"Of course it's true. You gave the order to put down this rebellion."

"I gave the order to put down a rebellion, not murder women and children."

"Well how did you expect we'd do that?"

"I didn't think this would be the result."

"The man's a terrorist trying to overthrow the government."

Rincon's secretary buzzed in.

"Mr. President?"

"Yes."

"The President of the United States is on the line."

Rincon shot an artful glance to his aide before reluctantly picking it up.

"Mr. President, what an honor."

"Would you mind telling me what the hell is going on down there?"

Rincon knew full well President Stanton would slam him in public. He had little choice given the images now circumnavigating the globe, but he believed he would act appropriately in private conversation. After all, quelling the rebellion was Stanton's idea. Actually, it was more of a command.

"Excuse me?" Rincon said.

"Look, I'm up here trying to keep the economy and the markets in good working order. I put my full reputation behind passage of NAFTA and forge a new openness between our countries, and in return, I get these images of dead women and children to contend with. What are you doing to me?"

Rincon's mouth fell open.

"Jack, I did this at your behest. You insisted I put down the rebellion or NAFTA was dead."

Stanton's voice cracked as if he were genuinely shocked by the accusation.

"Don't you dare try to push this on me."

He slammed down the phone, and Rincon held the receiver up to his ear speechless in the midst of the deafening silence. It took the aggravation of the sneering dial tone before he conjured the strength to finally put the phone down.

* * * *

Derek Stevens finished classes for the day. His final course was IDS 480, and as he left Zane Showker Hall, he put on a pair of dark sunglasses. The sun shined bright as his car pulled past the entrance sign to James Madison University and turned onto Port Republic Road. Harrisonburg was a city of few streets, a farming community with a university growing in the middle of it.

At age twenty-two, Derek Stevens was a senior finishing up a double major in political science and information security. He was an average student not as interested in studying as he should have been. He considered beer and dance music essential to a well-tuned mind.

Steering his car onto I-81, he headed toward work. It wasn't long before he veered onto Route 33 toward Elkton. The Appalachian Mountains rolled across the landscape on either side of the road, and the air remained cool with a slight breeze. All together, it was about a fifteen-minute drive.

In Elkton, Derek turned into the dirt gravel parking lot at Vitcor Pharmaceuticals. The Vitcor facility spread wide across the rolling meadow, looming in the shadow of one of the largest mountain ridges in the Shennandoah Valley. A chain link fence topped with barbed wire ran the length of the entire facility. Vitcor had only one main entrance, but multiple exit points. A single railroad gate guarded the entrance, reinforced by only a modest security booth, but all the guards were heavily armed.

New construction was an ongoing necessity at Vitcor with portable trailers taking up eighty percent of the grounds. But Vitcor only made one product, and very little of it. Built during the height of the Cold War, the Vitcor facility was the entrance to the true shadow government of the United States. Deep within the mountain ridge behind it were close to fourteen thousand acres of office space, complete with living quarters, an independent power and water supply, and all the necessary elements for running the federal government in the event that the unthinkable ever transpired.

Only an hour from Washington, a rock solid mountain ridge protected the facility from attack. By disguising the facility as a legitimate pharmaceutical plant, Russian intelligence never grew suspicious of the large parking lot, the barbed wire fence, and the increased security at the entrance as they studied satellite photos of the region. In Elkton, unsuspecting civilians arrived at work everyday and parked alongside government officials harboring top-level security clearances. Derek Stevens was one of those top-level officials.

Within the government, everyone just called the facility Elkton. Only two hundred of the thousands of acres available were in use. As the probability of a full-scale nuclear war dwindled, and Congress cut defense spending, the facility faded out of the minds of most in Washington. A few people from vital agencies in the government rotated in and out on a regular basis. One of the most feared jobs in public service, Derek was one of only two persons permanently stationed in Elkton. He would have been considered strange for seeking it out, but no one he worked with knew his position was permanent, nor did they know what he did.

He shared a workspace with only one other person, a military analyst named Phil who worked for the CIA. It was a relaxed atmosphere. When Derek arrived, Phil sat in his chair twirling a pencil and listening to old Sinatra CDs. *Jeopardy* was on a television in the corner.

"Here comes the man," Phil said.

Derek walked in smiling.

"What's up Phil?"

He went straight to the refrigerator and grabbed a Coors Light. Phil shook his head.

"You know, drinking on the job is frowned upon and just cause for dismissal."

He smiled at Derek.

"Out here, I'm willing to take that chance," Derek said.

"Good. Alcohol will dull your senses. We'll see how well you do today."

He turned off Sinatra and upped the volume of the television. Derek never bothered answering the regular questions. They weren't challenging enough. He preferred to guess the answer to Final Jeopardy from the category alone. Currently, his streak was seven episodes in a row, his all-time high being nineteen.

"All right, here it comes," Phil said.

Derek reclined with his beer as Alex Trebec appeared on the screen.

"Tonight's Final Jeopardy category is: WORLD LEADERS."

Phil began thinking out loud.

"Roosevelt…Stalin…Kofi Annan…I'm going with Churchill."

Derek cut into him immediately.

"You're wrong. The answer's Ho Chi Min."

"We'll see about that."

The show came back from commercial, and the answer was Ho Chi Min. Phil threw his hands up in the air.

"I swear you get the answers from somewhere. They have to show this early on satellite. But I even called *Jeopardy* and asked them."

Derek just laughed at him.

"How do you do it?" Phil asked.

"Basic math."

"How is that math?"

"Well, I figure Roosevelt, Stalin, Hitler, Churchill, Napoleon—all those names are too well known to be the answer. And they won't pick any leaders that are obscure or foreign to the audience. It's much more likely to be a leader from a small country, and someone recent, so the likely candidates are Ho Chi Min, Khaddafi, Hussein, Khomeini, or Milesovic. Khaddafi, Hussein, and Khomeini come from cultures so different from the US, the question would probably give them away. Milesovic is too recent. So Ho Chi Min is the most probable, and probability is math."

"You're so full of it."

Derek tossed his empty bottle across the room. It bounced off the wall and into the trashcan.

"Believe whatever you want, but being so full of it is why I quadrupled my money in the market this year. How'd you do?"

"Whatever."

Derek climbed behind his desk and dragged his mouse across the desktop to RUSH 24/7. A single click, and the EIB Network surged through his speakers. Phil rolled his eyes.

"Do you have to listen to that everyday?"

"Only fifteen hours a week," Derek said.

He pulled his chair closer to his desk, and as Rush Limbaugh's voice filtered through his ears, he delved into his work. It had been six years this month since he had joined the NSA. At the time, he thought that world war with radical Islam would begin at any moment. He self-taught himself Arabic and studied the culture and governments of the Middle East. He became an authority on the Koran, and set out to assess the security threats posed by Middle Eastern states and terror networks. Now, he began to doubt his conclusions.

The United States seemed all-powerful. The economy was booming, and although the prospect of biological or nuclear terrorism seemed to present an insurmountable threat to national security, America's enemies appeared incompetent. Perhaps for once he had been wrong. Maybe the critics were right, and Iraq did not pose the threat he had surmised. Maybe the future would be bright with no enemies in America's path. Maybe America would enjoy unchallenged technological superiority for several decades into the future.

But that probability was low. It was much more likely, he concluded, that America was experiencing a calm before the storm. Radical Islam declared war on the United States, but most Americans remained ignorant and oblivious. One day, reality would catch up with them. It was only a matter of when and how. Ironically, Derek longed for that day. He wanted the world to make sense again, and he wanted confirmation that he wasn't crazy for viewing the future the way he did. Most of all, he wanted the opportunity to take advantage. He wanted to destroy America's enemies. Because while America's enemies plotted against her, Derek Stevens spent his days plotting against them. Convinced of the inevitability of his world view, Derek continued his work crafting a war plan against terrorism. Certain it would lead to absolute victory, he gave it a new subtitle—"The White Horse Plan".

CHAPTER 6:

Endless Cavern

"Then if anyone tells you, 'Look, here is the Messiah,' or 'There he is,' do not pay attention. For false messiahs and false prophets will rise up and perform great miraculous signs and wonders so as to deceive, if possible, even God's chosen ones."

—Jesus Christ
Matthew 24:23–24

Gritty flakes of paint pealed off the walls of the concrete tunnel underneath National Stadium. Cold and damp, a combination of mold and mildew climbed the walls like vines at Wrigley Field. Outside, in the facility's arena, a giant stage had been erected as part of the festivities and celebration surrounding President Ordonez's inauguration. A contagious feeling of possibility floated through the air of Mexico City, and Raphael's feet clanked on the floor of the concrete hallway until they came to rest in front of Garrison.

"We're going to miss you, Garrison."

Garrison patted his friend's shoulder.

"You'll be too busy keeping the new administration in line."

Raphael shook his head.

"I turned down the position."

"Oh…"

Garrison's surprise was apparent from the expression he let slip.

"I can hardly stand it here anymore," Raphael said. "Looking around, I'm reminded of so much that has been accomplished, so much the Mexican people and the nation have won. But I'm also reminded of what has been lost."

Garrison hung his head.

"Juan…"

"His loss has taken a toll on Poyner."

Down the hallway, the crowded stadium rumbled with calls for the masked man of revolution. Garrison worked up a parting smile and tossed his backpack over his shoulder, holding on by only one strap.

"Back to Atlanta?"

"No. Jerusalem…the Lord has work for me there."

Raphael nodded, and the two shook hands. Garrison watched as he climbed up the back steps to the stage, and he heard the mouths erupt in cheer when the figure disappeared to the other side. His voice calmed the crowd, and Garrison marveled that the world still played habitat to men who would deny power. He turned and walked down the long corridor. It was only a universe of blackness with a pinpoint of light at its far end. Inside its walls, Raphael's voice vibrated alongside the electrifying madness of the crowded stadium. The two intertwined as one, and Garrison listened as he moved forward, never removing his eyes from that distant light. His ear eked out the biggest applause line of the speech, and it echoed through his head.

"Freedom, liberty, democracy—these are inalienable rights—and no man, no government, has the right to take them away…"

*　　*　　*　　*

"Alfred Nobel, by way of the will he made in 1895, was inspired and driven by a belief in the community of man".

The Chairman of the Norwegian Nobel Committee delivered the opening speech of the annual awarding of the Nobel Prize for Peace in Oslo, Norway. It was a frigid December day, and the chamber of Oslo City Hall overflowed with people from all over the world. The king and queen of Norway were present, as were several government officials. The entire Norwegian Nobel

Committee was present, and so were the friends and guests of Raphael Vicente.

The efforts of Raphael Vicente to draw attention to the plight of Indian peasants in the forgotten backroads of Mexico won him international praise. His work to secure the basic rights of all people, to ensure each secured a voice, and to bring about an end to one party rule in Mexico, helped lead the Mexican people to a more democratic form of government in the summer of 2000. The humility of a rich man who volunteered to live among the poor, coupled with the non-violence of a movement beaten down by tanks and guns, symbolized the growing problem of the wide chasm between the world's rich and poor. Raphael's role won him international standing and based upon that work he was being awarded the Nobel Prize for Peace.

Tradition demanded that he deliver a "lecture" to the assembled hall, not a gracious acceptance speech or a humble sermon, but a lecture—a distinction Raphael Vicente made note of and was determined to abide by. As he rose to the podium, the crowd fell silent.

He towered high above them, a commanding presence with shiny black hair that waved through the air as he bucked his head. The folds of his wavy locks swayed like hypnotic beings, dancing between his words and lulling the audience into a trance, and his eyes took hold of each spectator as if in a private conversation, never wavering in their persuasion. Each member of the audience could be forgiven for believing he talked only to them as his eyes penetrated deep within—neither weak, nor threatening.

"Your Majesties, Your Royal Highnesses, Excellencies, Members of the Norwegian Nobel Committee, Ladies and Gentleman...

It is with the utmost humility that I speak on behalf of an award that bestows accolades for a job we should all be doing anyway.

As a boy growing up in Mexico, I was confronted on a daily basis with man's inhumanity to man. The rich and powerful ensured that the political voices of the poor never rose loud enough to be heard, and a single party exerted its rule over an entire nation. As a young man, I had the opportunity to live amid the freedom of the United States, and it was that experience which exacerbated my feelings of injustice toward Mexico. From then on, I set my mind to joining those bent on destroying the institutions and one party rule that drowned out the voices of an entire people. The American system was morally superior, and I realized democracy was essential to our nation's future. Men were created to be free, to share ideas, to live together in peace, and to have dominion over their own lives. Many Mexicans learned there are many roads, many ideas, and many can be simultaneously valid and right. It is this realization that makes men free.

The idea there is one people in possession of the truth, one answer for the world's ills, or one solution to humanity's needs, has done untold harm throughout history—especially in the twentieth century. However, an assertion just as flawed, is that all paths are equal, that no one culture, government, or people is superior to another. Such an assertion is utterly false, and the moral relativism that has permeated the international scene threatens to corrode any hope for humanity in the coming century. The idea that non-democratic nations and leaders can maintain an equal and valid moral standing in relation to their democratic counterparts is one that over time will decay and erode the foundations of peace and catapult the world into all out war.

It is this agenda of moral relativism, and its proponents, who pose the greatest threat to life, liberty, and individual rights...

In 1994, this prize was awarded to a man history will remember as a bloodthirsty tyrant. Operating under the false premise of moral relativism, Yasser Arafat—a man who invented the modern definition of terrorism—was given equal standing with two men who sacrificed the security and existence of their nation because of an overwhelming thirst for peace. Hungry for any promise of peace, those men resurrected an irrelevant despot and gave him validity in the eyes of statesmen around the world. By awarding this prize to him, this committee participated in propping up the regime of a man whose sole purpose for existence has been the extermination of a people—not peace.

Earlier in this century, our world was faced with a mad dictator bent on dreams of world conquest and mass genocide. Collectively, we joined together to defeat him and swore to ourselves, "Never again". But today's irrational politics demands that we attribute special moral authority to this century's third most infamous Jew-killer—simply because he is weak, simply because he lacks the ability to carry out his grand designs of conquest and genocide. Weakness is not courage, and weakness alone does not bestow honorability.

When Alfred Nobel created this prize, he stated in his will that his intentions were for it to be given to those who "shall have conferred the greatest benefit on mankind" and "shall have done the most or the best work for fraternity between nations, for the abolition or reduction of standing armies and for the holding and promotion of peace congresses." The best way that I can illustrate these criteria is to turn down the Nobel Peace Prize with which you have awarded me.

My reason for so doing is not based on Arafat's awarding alone. Everyone makes mistakes, but men of honor correct them. This committee's inability to rescind the title of 'peacemaker' from a man who spent decades in the public eye draped in scarves of bullets, a man who has continually called for the destruction of an entire race and nation, a man who to this day lies and fails to live up to his obligations—their inaction in the face of his deeds is what leads me to my action today.

The refusal of the world to recognize evil, to play instead a game of moral relativism, is what compels me today to turn down this award.

I hope that my actions today will cause the committee to reexamine and redefine its notions of 'peace'. The goal of peace is not furthered when evil dictators capitulate in a moment of weakness. Peace is furthered when we single out such men and such governments, then set our hearts and minds to destroying them forever. This is a valid road to peace—the liberation of peoples via the elimination of their oppressors. Out of the ashes of this destruction rise the morally righteous principles of justice—individual rights, freedom of thought, freedom of speech, and the moral preeminence of self-rule. Our willingness to embrace these principles will determine whether our generation's legacy will be one of righteous warriors or one of a legacy of fools...

May God bless us in our quest to spread the principles of righteous warriors."

As he stepped down from the podium, the crowd remained in stunned silence. A few members of the committee noticeably stormed out in protest, but then, others rose from their seats and began to applaud. One after another, the entire room was brought to its feet in a standing ovation for Raphael Vicente—the man who turned down the Nobel Peace Prize.

*   *   *   *

Following what was to be the awarding of the prize, the traditional banquet was held for the man who was supposed to be Nobel Laureate. The same people from Oslo City Hall flooded the room, absent the press. Media personnel fought with door security to catch a glimpse of a celebrity or capture a stray picture. The room hummed with the controversy of Raphael's remarks.

"Wonderful speech."

Raphael looked up and extended his hand. When the man caught it, a jarring chill ran up Raphael's arm. A French national with curly blonde hair, the man's unblinking eyes bored into Raphael without mercy, and the man's young hand felt slimy wet like a much older politician's. He never once broke eye contact.

"It's my honor to meet only the second man ever to turn down the Nobel Peace Prize."

"Thank you," Raphael said. "And you are?"

"Jean Riguad Prieur, Commissioner of Justice and Home Affairs for the European Commission."

A grin rolled over his face, and the two men chatted about Continental politics and international policy for several minutes. Jean projected an appearance of jubilation akin to an older child who found yet another toy hidden under the Christmas tree.

"You know, we could use a man like you in Parliament, especially on the Commission," Jean said.

"I moved to the United Kingdom to lecture and write."

A faint trace of disappointment painted over the man's face, particularly in the dark bags beneath his eyes, but it soon disappeared. The rejection only made him more determined.

"Well you don't have to hold political office, but you could join the formal integration movement. We could always use an extra voice to help persuade public opinion."

Before Raphael offered a response, Poyner emerged from the crowd and tugged at his sleeve.

"What's wrong?"

"I'm ready to leave," she said.

Raphael turned toward Jean and shook his hand.

"It was nice meeting you."

Jean nodded, noticeably upset that his sales pitch was cut short. Raphael whispered in his wife's ear.

"Everyone in here wants something."

"I know," she said. "That's why I want to leave."

PART III

▼

Mythic Ascent

"And now in my vision I saw a beast rising up out of the sea. It had seven heads and ten horns, with ten crowns on its horns and written on each head were names that blasphemed God. This beast looked like a leopard, but it had bear's feet and a lion's mouth! And the dragon gave him his own power and throne and great authority."

—John
Revelation 13:1–2

CHAPTER 1:

Coming Testing

"Does a lion ever roar in a thicket without first finding a victim? When the war trumpet blares, shouldn't the people be alarmed? When disaster comes to a city, isn't it because the Lord planned it? But always, first of all, I warn you through my servants the prophets that I, the Sovereign Lord, have now done this."

—Amos
Amos 3:4, 6–7

"Repent, for the kingdom of heaven is near!"

Garrison's voice carried through the streets of Jerusalem with a piercing resonance. Standing tall on an iron table in a corner sidewalk café, he conducted his speech into the farthest corners of the busy street.

Pedestrians stopped dead in their tracks and looked up at him with skeptical faces. Most of them shrugged him off with a quick wave of the hand and a shake of the head, but several men and women rested their hands on the café railing and listened in earnest. With forceful confidence, he spoke to anyone who would listen.

"The coming days will be a time of great testing. The world will be seized by an era of tribulation, but the Lord wants his people to know that he will never leave them. He only allows these things to happen so that those asleep will awake from their slumber and come back to him. So when these things begin to take place, stand straight and look up, for your salvation is near!"

As Garrison finished his words, he felt a strong tug on the edge of his ankle. He peered down to find the café manager waving him down with an angry glare. Garrison climbed down from the table. When he stepped on the ground, he expected the manager to kick him out, but the man was now distracted by something of greater concern. He stared intently over Garrison's shoulder.

A loud furor rumbled in the street behind him. Garrison turned around to find a large group of Arab men marching in the street. Palestinian flags waved through the air like butterflies, and American flags burned on the ground beneath their feet. The disorganized chant slowly became unified until it was loud enough for him to understand.

"Death to America! Death to America!"

Tattered remnants of the star spangled banner danced through the air like fluttering seagulls then disintegrated into ash and fell back to the earth. The forces of evil advanced upon the world.

*   *   *   *

Eduardo still marveled at its size. He had visited the Pentagon several times before, years ago. Since his youth, he had been subjected to the myths surrounding this famous building, the epicenter of world military power, but they did not do justice in the eyes of those with the privilege to see it first hand. One could literally drive a train—maybe several trains—through the hallway, it was so massive.

Eduardo followed Dr. Jonathan Alexander who was, in essence, the procurement officer for DARPA, the Defense Advanced Research Projects Agency. As Deputy Director, Alexander could rubber stamp whatever he wished, and Eduardo hoped to acquire an R&D grant for his newest materials research project. Alexander motioned toward an empty conference room just off the hallway. The two entered, and he closed the door behind them.

"I'm glad to see you're back," he said. "I've heard a lot of great things about Eduardo Ortiz, most of it from those who don't hand out praise so readily."

Eduardo returned a humble nod.

"So now you're back on the payroll with DOD?"

"Hopefully."

"Well, let me see what you've got."

Eduardo handed him the proposal. Alexander thumbed through it with a heightened interest. Eduardo stretched back in his chair, folding his hands in his lap.

"I assume you're still interested in carbon nanotubes," he said.

It was an unnecessary question. Of course they were. The lifeblood and primary structural element in the future era of nanotechnology, carbon nano-tubes were subjects of great interest in the DOD. Ten thousand times smaller than a human hair, they boasted properties a thousand times stronger than steel and over a hundred times lighter. Constructed of perfectly positioned carbon atoms, they promised to revolutionize the semiconductor field, increasing computing power exponentially. The possible military applications seemed endless, and he was offering a plan to make them prevalent and inexpensive.

"This is impressive. We're very interested."

Alexander hovered over the proposal, flipping through each page and soaking up every word. Somewhere midway through, he raised his eyebrows.

"True self-replication?"

He uttered the words under his breath and shook his head as if capturing a glimpse into a grand revolutionary document.

"They need to see this at our office downtown. Follow me down the hall. There's somebody you need to meet who would be very interested in this."

The two of them stepped into the hallway, and closed the door behind them. The explosion nearly burst their eardrums. The walls shook as though a train approached from the far corridor. Several yards to Eduardo's right, a yellowish-red ball of fire revolved on an invisible axis, advancing a scourge of billowing smoke through the hallway.

Dr. Alexander grabbed Eduardo and raced toward the nearest stairwell. Inside, arms and legs slammed together and converged in a bottleneck as everyone tried at once to stuff themselves out of the building. As the barrage of people streamed out of the door and onto the lawn outside the Pentagon, rumors flew through the air. One man jabbered in a loud and frantic voice, while driving his hands through the air in an attempt to explain.

"I swear. I saw a plane fly right into it!"

Crews of rescue workers circled the broken wall, the heat so vicious, it burned those who dared to approach. Voices bandied about—some calm, some angry, some silent. They argued over the cause of the accident. But regardless of the true cause, Eduardo knew who was responsible. Terrorists had attacked the Pentagon, and any doubts in regard to continuing his work faded away forever. Watching the tear-drenched faces of those who had lost friends and co-workers, he vowed to create a weapon so powerful, so all-encompassing in its ability to dominate the theater of battle that it would eliminate all the world's terrorists in a single stroke.

CHAPTER 2:

A Day Which Changed Our World

"Then there will be a time of anguish greater than any since nations first came into existence."

—Daniel
Daniel 12:1

Engulfed by the day's events, the White House never slept. No more than a couple of yards down the hallway from the Oval Office, Dr. Elmore threw a couple of folders into a briefcase, clicked it shut, and exited her office. As National Security Advisor, she enjoyed unhindered access to the president, making her influence far greater than most within the president's inner-circle. Cabinet secretaries found themselves randomly strewn in bureaucratic buildings all over the District. Some benefited from closer proximity than others, but few other than the president's chief-of-staff possessed the level of access enjoyed by Dr. Elmore. Today, she managed to garner fifteen minutes on the president's calendar for a private meeting between herself, President Burton, and Secretary Lukin. It was a meeting she knew with certainty would change the course of human events forever.

Entering the Oval Office, she settled into the white Ottoman perpendicular to the president's desk. The thought entered her mind of the importance of this meeting, its place in history, and her mind reflected over all the drama played out in this office over the past two centuries. From Lincoln's planning of the Civil War to Kennedy's handling of the Cuban Missile Crisis, it all happened here, and it happened in the defense of freedom and liberty. It was in this room where Roosevelt read Einstein's letter about a theoretical bomb capable of winning the Allied forces final victory, and it was here where Truman decided to secure that victory once and for all.

The door opened, and Secretary Lukin strode across the elegant carpet. Taking a seat next to Dr. Elmore, he let out a prolonged breath and closed his eyelids so they could steal at least a second's worth of sleep. A man of vast experience in both Washington and in the private sector, Ronald Lukin accepted the job of Secretary of Defense because of the mere challenge, the challenge to move the Armed Forces into a new era of combat readiness with reliance on highly sophisticated technology and highly trained, dynamic individuals.

"You ready?" he asked.

His cheeks emitted a look of slight amusement, and his eyes relayed a comic charm from behind a rigid pair of wire-rimmed glasses. His voice relayed his optimism.

"The president's going to go for this. You've got our full cooperation. In fact, it was my intention to propose this anyway after next year's budget analysis—although not on such a massive scale. Yesterday's events obviously change our timetable."

A door slammed shut.

"I'll be right with you."

The president smiled as he walked past them with a hurried step. He dumped a pile of papers on his desk and sorted through some others. After a moment, his eye caught hold of something. He packed it under his arm and moved around his desk to a gold upholstered chair facing Lukin and Elmore. Sitting down, he leaned back with both his hands cradling the armrests. His eyes darted back and forth between the two of them, and he let out a deep breath as he spoke to them.

"Both of you give your people a pat on the back for that Afghan proposal. It was a knockout. I have a few questions and concerns, but we'll get to those this afternoon. What have you got?"

The president studied Dr. Elmore, his chin pressed into the palm of his hand. He had bags under his eyes and drooping eyelids, but his attention was firmly locked onto the national security advisor.

"I wanted to make sure you're aware of a second policy option at your disposal. We will win the war on terror decisively, and without a single casualty, once we accomplish this effort. But it will take time…we're not sure how much time, and in the interim, we're forced to rely on conventional war plans."

The president lurched forward in his chair, his elbows resting on both knees. He was totally awake now.

"And why wasn't this brought up in our last meeting?"

"It's not a viable option for the near-term. It's contingent on several factors, and more importantly, work on it needs to retain a veil of secrecy from day one."

"Good enough," the president said. "So, you mean to sit here and tell me a worldwide war on terror against multiple states and hidden networks of criminals spaced in every corner of every country in the world—criminals possibly numbering in the hundreds of thousands,…we can defeat them forever in a matter of days?"

His mouth fell open in disbelief. Secretary Lukin leaned forward and looked him straight in the eye.

"Yes, Mr. President."

He paused while the news sank in.

"This plan is reliant on our creation of a new class of weaponry—actually an entirely new technology, based on the molecular stealth technology we outfitted the B-2s with earlier in the year," Lukin said.

"Mr. President," Dr. Elmore said. "We will lose the war on terror if we fail to create an assembler."

The president's ears perked up. He was well aware of the concept of an assembler. As the former governor of Texas, his state was home to the first and only private company actively committed to building one.

"And you think it's possible?" he asked.

Her response was quick and decisive.

"Yes. I've consulted numerous experts in the field, and they all say its creation is inevitable. No one yet has refuted them. The concept of a controlled nuclear reaction was still theoretical prior to the Second World War. I believe we face the same circumstances with assembler-based molecular nanotechnology today."

By now, the president paced the room in small circles.

"Okay, let's say we can build an assembler, to the exact specifications you believe we can. How do we go about organizing this?"

Secretary Lukin jumped on the question.

"A young man from NSA has taken the time to prepare a brief that explains in great detail the fastest route to implementation of a federal project for the construction of an assembler. In addition, it maps out a plan of victory for the war and what to expect in a post-assembler breakthrough era."

Lukin handed the brief to the president. The title dominated its cover, "Defeating Evil In The Nanotechnic Era". Peeling through the pages, the enormity of the moment became clear. The face of humanity would inexorably be changed forever. The president ran the palm of his free hand through his hair.

"What sort of time horizon are we dealing with?" he asked.

Dr. Elmore remained calm and poised.

"I get answers ranging from one decade to three, but new discoveries have been uncovered at breakneck speed. A couple of years ago, all the experts said it would be 2005 at the earliest before the human genome would be mapped, but competition with Celera provided the necessary stimulus to accelerate that process. Eighteen months later, we had a working map of the human genome. In this case, war provides us with the greatest incentive. With the full backing of the federal government, three to five years is a fair estimate. Five years being the max."

The president wore a faraway look with thick wrinkles embroidered across his forehead. Years could be cut off the current estimates for the war on terror, saving countless American lives, as well as innocent civilians abroad.

"And the guy who wrote this works for you?" he asked.

"Yes."

"In what capacity?"

"Currently, his official title is Information Security Systems Analyst and he works out of Elkton, but his responsibilities aren't narrowly defined. He reports directly to me as he did Samuel Bergman in the previous administration. Prior to that, he was a military analyst in the CIA."

"And he reports directly to you?" Burton asked.

"Apparently, the last administration thought him to be indispensable enough to work on his own projects and report directly to the National Security Advisor. To be honest, I had actually forgotten about him."

"And he works in Elkton?" the president asked.

"Yes."

"Why? Why would they put a guy with this skill in Elkton?"

"It was a personal request. His stated reason was he didn't want to work in a city that was such a wide-open target for international terrorism," she said.

The president stood by the window just behind his desk. He couldn't help but snicker under his breath. Turning, he walked over to the two of them.

"Thanks for calling this meeting. I've got a lot on the plate right now, but I'll read this brief cover-to-cover tonight. I want to meet this guy. Tell him to be prepared to defend this brief first thing tomorrow morning. I'll fill in Card, Picker, and the Vice President. Nobody else is to be talked to or have knowledge of any of this."

And with those words, Lukin, Elmore, and the president left the Oval Office.

CHAPTER 3:

No Place To Hide

"Following that kingdom, there will be a fourth great kingdom, as strong as iron. That kingdom will smash and crush all previous empires, just as iron smashes and crushes everything it strikes. Some parts of it will be as strong as iron, and others as weak as clay. This mixture of iron and clay also shows that these kingdoms will try to strengthen themselves by forming alliances with each other through intermarriage. But this will not succeed, just as iron and clay do not mix."

—Daniel
Daniel 2:40, 42–43

A later hour would have been preferable. It was far too early in the morning for Derek Stevens. He did his best work in the later hours of the evening. But for such an occasion he made an exception. It had been sometime since he last visited the West Wing and the first time during this administration. He stared at the door to the Oval Office and his mind began racing—the history of the office, its significance, its occupants. He thought about the World

Trade Center and the war now underway. Finally, America would wake up and recognize the threat posed by its enemies. Finally, he was not alone in viewing the world the way he did. The president's secretary broke his concentration.

"The President will see you now."

She ushered him to the door. It blended into the wall, and her hands magically opened it to reveal a whole new world. Derek walked in with a subdued look of confidence. All the top officials in the administration were present, and the president extended his hand.

"It's nice to meet you Derek. You've done some good work," he said.

Derek acknowledged the compliment. The others remained seated.

"Derek," the president said. "You know Dr. Elmore and Vice President Thomas Price."

The president's chief of staff and Secretary of State also were in attendance. Derek sat down in a wooden chair. The six of them formed a circle, and the president seated himself at the helm. His face parlayed a look of the utmost seriousness.

"Yesterday, I had a brief discussion with Dr. Elmore and Secretary Lukin. They tried to convince me to open a new phase in the war on terror. I told them I would listen to the proposal. Derek, here, is going to brief the rest of us on what that would entail."

The president yielded the floor to Derek. The young man opened his briefcase and handed each person a copy of the brief he had produced for the president.

"In order to bring the war on terror to a swift and decisive conclusion, the federal government will muster its full resources in an effort to create assembler-based molecular nanotechnology. Employing rooms of engineers, the government will pre-design the next generation of military hardware. On the day of the assembler breakthrough, the newly deployed Armed Forces of the United States will be capable of defeating any enemy now imagined."

The sound of turning pages bit into his silent pause as the room's occupants thumbed through the proposal.

"Following the creation of this new weapon, I suggest the United States implement what I call the White Horse Plan. Under that plan, America will take advantage of the omnipotent power of an assembler to build an overwhelming military force for conquering rogue states and totalitarian regimes.

The White Horse Plan can be implemented within days, perhaps hours, of the assembler breakthrough with one hundred percent effectiveness."

He pointed to the bottom of the page in his hand.

"From a defensive standpoint, an assembler will make our borders impenetrable, and we will become immune to today's unconventional threats. Nuclear threats will be rendered useless, and even the most imaginative, elaborately planned biological or chemical terror attacks will be limited to the immediate vicinity of the attack. In effect, the threat will come from the force of a bomb itself and not its associated chemical or biological elements."

He took several steps around the room, animating his words with the movement of his hands.

"The proposal calls for all current research on assembler-based technologies to be placed under one umbrella in the Elkton facility. Currently, over one hundred seventy-nine different grants and projects carry on similar research, and they do so under seventeen different cabinet level departments and independent agencies."

Derek pointed out the bureaucracy, as well as his own ability to weed through it, and he looked at the president.

"As a businessman, you know how inefficient this is."

"I've already decided on the project, Derek. We need only to hammer out the details," Burton said.

Derek did not express outwardly the jubilation he felt rush over him following the president's decision. His proposal called for a single director answering only to the president. He planned on being that director. It had been his ambition since he first read *Engines of Creation* four years earlier. Price weighed in.

"What about additional funding? At the very least, we'll have to incur transition costs for moving these programs to a new location and tying them together," he said.

This was the only part where Derek anticipated a serious objection.

"The project requires an additional forty billion dollars annually," he said.

Price remained calm, but didn't hide his silence long.

"Forty billion dollars a year? That's a tall order for a classified project. It'll be nearly impossible to hide that kind of money in the budget."

"But not impossible," Derek said.

"Tell them your idea," Burton said.

Derek rubbed his chin with his right hand as he spoke.

"Last year, our nation spent close to seventy billion dollars just to maintain our nuclear arsenal. With the Cold War over, most of our stockpile is unnecessary. If we put somewhere between half to two-thirds in storage, we could divert those funds to an assembler project."

"And you don't think that will place us in a position of vulnerability?" Price asked.

"The Cold War is over. We won. If we want to win this war, we must do so with assemblers, not ICBMs."

"It would certainly look good in the eyes of the world, and it would be a show of good faith to the Russians, given our work to end the ABM Treaty," Price said.

The president clapped his hands together.

"We can piddle over details in the coming days, but we're going to do this. We have to. As the occupant of this office, I swore on oath to protect this nation, and I will."

He motioned as if to call the meeting to an end, but then quickly remembered one remaining point.

"I'll be meeting with Prime Minister Hume tonight. I believe our actions should be part of a greater effort, an ongoing shared development of molecular assembler technology between Europe, Japan, and ourselves. We need to work together with our allies, and we need to find someone we can all trust to build a team to work with each project. That way, each nation can benefit from major breakthroughs and developments. The less people involved, the less likely valuable information will fall into the hands of our enemies."

*   *   *   *

The usher guided Eduardo through the west wing of the White House. He swung the door open at the end of the hallway. The president's secretary made note of their arrival and buzzed the president in his office. Putting down the phone, she addressed Eduardo.

"The President will see you now."

She escorted him to the door of the Oval Office. Her touch opened it effortlessly without a sound. The president was at work behind his desk. He peered up over his reading glasses.

"Mr. Ortiz, make yourself comfortable."

Eduardo sat down directly across from the president. The Oval Office was much bigger than he imagined. The entire White House was. On television, it looked so small. Unlike most offices, there was no clutter. The rug underneath his feet displayed a branded image of the presidential seal. Its fierce eagle stared back at him.

"Would you like something to eat, something to drink?"

Eduardo shook his head. The president walked over to the bar and poured himself a Coke, floating three pieces of ice in it.

"Thanks for coming," he said. "Do you have any idea why I wanted to see you?"

Eduardo shrugged.

"Given the signs of the times, I figure it probably has something to do with renewed interest in the viability of an assembler project," Eduardo said.

The president nodded.

"That's right, although I already know it's viable. I wanted to talk to you for a different reason," he said.

The president told him of the massive effort now underway to construct the world's first assembler. Eduardo sat back in his chair, amazed that with everything going on, the administration had the time to pull together such a plan, raise the money for it, and already begin its execution. Less than three days had passed since September 11th. And the president kicked around billions as if it were small change, while Eduardo begged for scraps and small grants from the Department of Defense and a myriad of bureaucratic wastelands.

The additional revelation of a secret compound hiding thousands of acres of the federal government somewhere in the Blue Ridge Mountains blew him away. He had heard rumors about two other government fallout shelters, but nothing of this magnitude. The president offered him a job working for the allied projects, pending the approval of Japan and Europe.

"What do you think?" Burton asked.

It was obvious the president expected greater excitement. Eduardo's morose expression remained unchanged, and the president, his curiosity heightened, listened to and weighed Eduardo's every word.

"I have serious reservations about this project and its new operating conditions. I don't think you've been provided all the information."

The president shifted in his chair, his discomfort apparent.

"Talk to me," he said.

"All the things you've said about winning the war on terror are true. The maturation of assembler-based nanotechnology will shower tremendous benefits on America and humanity, but those benefits come with a price. Serious dangers lurk around the corner."

He went on to tell the president everything he knew of the possible dangers of assembler development. One, he believed nearly insurmountable. He labeled it "The Terror Conundrum", and he relayed his fears to the president.

"The first weeks and months are most crucial. Whoever breaks out with the assembler lead, whether it's a several hour lead or several year lead—that state will have the rest of the world at its mercy."

"I can handle it," the president said.

Eduardo nodded. He believed the president to be an honest man.

"Irrespective of whether you or the people around you can be trusted with this type of power, you can not ignore the possibility America might lose the assembler race to an ally, or a leak might somehow place frightening powers in the hands of one of America's enemies."

"We're taking every precaution for secrecy," Burton said. "Any recommendations you have will be considered."

That was part of the problem in Eduardo's mind. September 11th was on its way to ensuring the premature development of an assembler. Most Americans didn't know what one was, much less that plans were now underway to construct one. Confining its development to a small circle of people enhanced the probability of unleashing its powers on an unprepared world. Ironically, it threatened to create a world far worse than the one in which they now lived.

"My recommendation is to surround yourself with the smartest people you can find. Men and women who can help you prepare a policy for the period following the assembler breakthrough. Because when that day comes, it will be the single greatest threat to international stability and world security since the day the human race began."

Burton nodded in agreement.

"Actually, I've already been presented with a plan. My people tell me it's the best policy option available, but I want to know what you think about it."

Burton tossed the brief across the table. It was titled: "The White Horse Plan". Eduardo scanned its pages with great interest.

"No, it's not the best option," he said.

Eduardo shook his head, and the president made no attempt to hide his look of surprise.

"It's the only option."

Burton appeared relieved.

"Why?" he asked.

"You have no other realistic option. If you sit on your lead while nations like China and North Korea develop assemblers independently, you'll launch an unprecedented nanotechnic arms race that, by its very nature, will lead the world to the threshold of final holocaust. Bilateral assembler development, without an active shield, is inherently confrontational and destructive."

He tossed the brief back onto the president's desk.

"Eventually, one side will feel the need to strike before its technology falls behind, and the result will be devastation on an unimagined scale. Therefore, your only option is to guarantee you remain the leading force by eliminating potential competitors as early as possible. From a moral standpoint, you have an obligation to liberate the oppressed peoples of the world and spread the material benefits of assemblers."

The president smiled.

"The good guys always wear white, don't they?"

Eduardo didn't laugh.

"I'd like to think so, but I advise you to implement this White Horse Plan in parallel with the effort to construct an active shield. Don't fall into the trap of thinking a good offense alone will make the world safe."

Burton twirled a ballpoint pen through his fingers. Its gold embroidered seal sparkled in the light.

"Because we need to defend against individuals too," he said.

"Such a level of concentrated power has never existed before, except in the hands of God. And terrorists will be salivating. For Osama Bin Laden to destroy the world with nuclear weapons, he needs sophisticated hardware and rare isotopes. But if he wants to enslave humanity forever with an assembler, he only needs a speck of simple ordinary dust."

*   *   *   *

The Lord Mayor of London's annual banquet at Guildhall was a vast collection of the social-elite of British society. Tradition dictated that the Prime Minister always attend, and over time, that meant politicians, prospective politicians, and interest groups also made it tradition to attend. As an invited guest of the Lord Mayor, Raphael felt obligated to attend.

Wineglasses traversed the room as if by their own volition, refracting the light of the hall through their fine crystal prisms.

Centered in the storm of faces, Jean Riguad Prieur held a full glass in his left hand while patting an older gentleman on the shoulder. The man's face gleamed with each stroke of the shoulder blade, and Jean captured his full attention. The largest circle in the room formed itself around the young Frenchman, and Raphael tried to ignore it.

As if by a sixth sense, Jean became aware of Raphael's presence, leaving his audience with a parting joke and diverting his path to Raphael's side of the room. Still holding his full glass, he charged through the crowd and placed his free hand on Raphael's shoulder, moving his face in close. His voice whispered.

"Interesting rumors have been circulating."

Raphael's eyes grew wide.

"I was young. I needed the money."

Jean relayed an amused smile.

"No, nothing like that. I'm talking about integration. I have advance information the Prime Minister's placing his full support behind it."

Raphael lurched backward.

"Political suicide."

"Perhaps not. The war has changed a lot of things. The prospect of American unilateralism has a lot of Continentals upset. They fear irrelevance more than death itself, and the terror war threatens our economic system just as much as America's. A blueprint for a new constitution for Europe will be unveiled tomorrow."

Raphael probed the room.

"What kind of hierarchy?"

"There's at least forty-six articles. But it includes the creation of an appointed president to run the European Council. He'll direct foreign policy and military affairs."

Jean took a sip of wine and reveled in the excitement.

"And the way I see it," he said. "No one is a better candidate."

Instinctively, Raphael pulled away from the man.

"Me? I couldn't be president."

"You have a natural way with people I've never seen before. They hang on your every word."

"I haven't lived here but a few years."

"That's a selling point, part of your appeal. It makes you less likely to be partial to your home nation's interests."

Behind them, the crowd broke into a steady applause that rained on their conversation. Across the hall, a long table draped with a white cloth covered the stage. Everyone seated behind it stood up as Prime Minister Hume made his way to the rostrum for the keynote address. He shifted the microphone and sunk his fingers into the wood grain edges of the podium.

"It has been echoed throughout the world that the events of eleven September transformed our world. A relatively peaceful period at the end of a tumultuous century came crashing down to earth on that day. For the United Kingdom, the objective is clear. We must rise to the challenge of this showdown with international terrorism. We must be willing to destroy it, or else risk being destroyed by it."

The palm of his hand smacked the podium as he spoke, and the sound of clapping hands caused him to pause.

"Each of these terrible individuals displays the iron will and fierce hatred of a thousand Adolf Hitlers. They number in the hundreds of thousands, if not millions, and they believe that by killing innocent women and children, they carry out the work of their deranged god."

Jean nudged Raphael in the ribcage and transferred a glaring smile. The two listened in silence as Hume continued.

"Confronted by such an enemy, the United Kingdom must reevaluate its place among nations. The idea that the interests of Continental Europe are in conflict with the interests of Britain is no longer valid. The recent terrorist attacks illustrate clearly how a nation lacking conventional military capability can export terror over oceans, destroying forever the illusion that we can live our lives irrespective of the rest of the world."

The Prime Minister paused for effect so that he could ensure every ear in the room was attentive to his message.

"To preserve our way of life, we must protect our borders. Security and safety come from active intelligence and preventative measures, but they also come from strong foreign policy and determined use of military force. The greater interests of Britain are best served when used in cooperation with America and Europe. I urge this nation to make a greater commitment to the European Union and to forge forward to bring America and Continental Europe closer together in this war to end all wars. Our very survival is at stake. The safety of our children, the security of our families, all that's precious—it rests on our ability to work together."

The hundreds of hands gathered in applause, and the mass of guests erupted into a low chatter. Was the Prime Minister advocating the United Kingdom's full entry into the European Union? No Prime Minister had ever advocated adoption of the Euro, much less political integration. Jean snaked his arm over Raphael's shoulders.

"The world is falling apart," he said. "And if you want, I can make you president of its newest and greatest superpower."

*   *   *   *

The 741st MI Battalion sped through the streets of Kabul. The whole city was no more than a pile of concrete and rusted metal, most of it the legacy of the Russian war against the Afghans. The multi-story buildings lining the streets were a rare sight given the rest of the nation's standard of living. In the streets, people walked around freely—men with shaved beards, women without burqas. Music floated high above the mixed sounds of transistor radios, and a number of Afghans danced to the melodies.

From this perspective, Lt. Col. Sandy Levin directed the men of the 741st.

"Take a left here," he said. "Over there on the right."

He pointed to a two-story building that in the United States would have been nothing more than a rundown apartment building in the ghetto. In Afghanistan, it was the pinnacle of luxury. The place had been marked as a former safehouse for al-Qaeda operatives. Sources speculated Bin Laden himself had visited the house in the recent past.

They pulled alongside the house and parked. From inside the safehouse, a man dressed in US Army fatigues walked toward them. Levin stepped in the man's path.

"Soldier this perimeter is the sole domain of the 741st. I'm Lt. Col. Sandy Levin, my team can take over from here."

The man extended his hand to Levin.

"Nice to meet you Levin. I'm Lt. Col. John Gruman—Task Force 157. And my people have sole jurisdiction over this house until they complete their mission," he said.

Levin looked confused.

"Task Force 157? I've never even heard of it," Levin said.

He walked past Gruman and surveyed the foyer. Half-burned boxes of paper and overturned bookcases covered the floor. Stacks of al-Qaeda documents lay untouched on a table. A team of soldiers, dressed in plastic suits, combed the floor in meticulous fashion with tweezers and other instruments.

"I don't know what's going on here Gruman, but my team has direct orders to lockdown this perimeter and gather all relevant intelligence," Levin said.

Gruman nodded.

"And your team will be able to do just that once my team has finished."

Disgusted, Levin radioed back to base and received an unexpected reply.

"Gruman's right—Task Force 157 was sent ahead of you. The order came from the president himself."

Gruman didn't express an outward reaction to the news.

"We'll only be a few more moments. You're welcome to follow me in and assess the area if you wish."

The two of them stepped inside. Levin walked through the room making mental notes. Lifting a file from one of the tables, it was clear a treasure trove of al-Qaeda documents had been uncovered. The strange part was that not one member of Task Force 157 touched any of them. Instead, they reacted like forensic scientists at a murder scene, perched over the floor with gloved hands.

*   *   *   *

The United States Deputy Secretary of State sat in a chair facing a white wall. His eyes followed the intricate pattern on the Persian rug sprawled across the floor, and his monochromatic suit stood in stark contrast to the surroundings. Given his position, it was his responsibility to work on these seemingly lesser important matters, and that was one of the more annoying aspects of his career. The Secretary, the president, and his advisors defined the broad policy details while he carried them out. Today, his duties required an important request of the royal family.

Prince Fahd Abd al-Rahman, the Saudi Foreign Minister, entered the room. The two men exchanged the formal greetings familiar to the region, then took seats across from each other.

"So what is our topic of discussion this evening?" the Prince asked.

The young man uncrossed his legs and leaned forward in his chair.

"My government would like to request your permission to meet with the Bin Laden family."

An unbroken silence filtered over the room for a brief moment before the prince responded.

"And for what purpose would this meeting take place? The Bin Ladens have made it clear that they cut off contact with Osama some years ago, and we know for certain they know nothing of his activities or whereabouts."

"We don't wish to interrogate them. We only wish to propose a request. A request to obtain a genetic sample from the family, one we could use to verify Osama's body upon his death."

The Prince looked at the man with suspicion.

"And this is all?"

"That is all."

"Then this is the answer. The royal family will relay your request to the Bin Ladens personally. It will be their decision as to whether or not cooperation will take place."

The Prince rose to his feet. The Deputy Secretary followed suit out of respect and bowed to the prince.

"Peace be with you."

"And on you, peace," the Prince answered.

With those parting words, the two of them left the room—but the young man knew that it would not be the decision of the Bin Laden family as to whether or not they would cooperate. Though, he wondered why it mattered. Why was the president making such a big deal over obtaining this sample? Who cared if they could confirm Bin Laden's death? As long as he never shows up again, that's all that should matter.

CHAPTER 4:

Overthrowing Nazi Fascists

"I will make Jerusalem and Judah like an intoxicating drink to all the nearby nations that send their armies to besiege her. In that day I will make Jerusalem a heavy stone, a burden for the world. None of the nations who try to lift her will escape unscathed...For my plan is to destroy all the nations that come against Jerusalem!"

—**Zechariah**
Zechariah 12:2–3, 9

The long ride as smuggled cargo in a caravan from Turbat to Dehak took its toll on Jiang Yafei. The flight into Karachi, followed by the drive to Turbat, didn't help either. He was exhausted almost to the point that it would hinder his abilities. But the extra precaution was necessary. A lone Chinese man traveling through Iranian Baluchistan would not only be noticed, but remembered. The last thing Jiang wanted was to be remembered. It was crucial that no one ever find out about his trip.

When the caravan arrived in the city of Dehak, the driver unloaded Jiang under cover of darkness. He paid handsomely for the smuggling of human cargo as well as the driver's continued silence. Although if the caravan driver ever talked, it would be such a weak link it wouldn't matter.

Standing in the alleyway where the driver had dropped him off, Jiang listened to the rustling sound of rats digging through the trash. They gave a crackling voice to the darkness. The entire area surrounding the border of Iran and Pakistan had its own system of laws, the central concept being survival of the fittest. Jiang walked down the alley several yards before reaching the correct door, then gave it a soft knock. For a moment, no one answered. After a few seconds, the door cracked. A voice leaked out.

"Who is it?"

"Li Ming Hu," Jiang said.

The door swiveled, and the brief light that spread into the alley blinded Jiang as he stepped forward. Inside, a dim light fell over the room. Several Arabic tapestries wallpapered the single room apartment and a solitary table jutted up against the center wall. An ashtray sat on top of it with a single lit cigarette burning within.

"Have a seat," the voice said.

Jiang pulled a chair out from the table. The man across from him had a darkened complexion and sported a thin black mustache. He had an air about him that made others look upon him with subdued fear, coupled with an admiring curiosity. His eyes cut through the darkness, lighting his dark silhouette.

"I was just about to have a drink. Would you like to join me?" he asked.

"I'll have whatever you're having," Jiang said.

The man poured what looked like scotch into two old-fashioned glasses, and he sat one of them on the table. Jiang lifted the glass, inhaling its aroma. It was scotch for sure. Moving out from the shadows, the man sat in the chair opposite Jiang. The table rested between them, the cigarette still burning, and a glimmer of light fell onto his face. The man spoke.

"I could've come to see you. I'm not an amateur. I wouldn't have been followed."

"Extra precaution," Jiang said. "I'm well aware you're no amateur. That's why you were contacted."

"And I'm well aware of yours reputation, or else I might well have been offended."

Jiang wondered what this man knew, if his contacts ran as deep as he believed they did. Muhammad Jumma Marri was a Baluch born in southwestern Pakistan. Highly intelligent, he maintained a lucrative career working for the Iraqi Mukhabarat. But that career would soon come to an end, and Jiang made sure to underline that fact.

"The United States is certain to invade Iraq by the end of the year," he said.

"I'm well aware. It's the only reason I'm willing to entertain your country as a client. So tell me, what is your proposition?"

Jiang explained in detail a lengthy operation involving two targets. No trail could be left, no sign linking Jiang or his country to the plotting. Muhammad ingested the details, unfazed by any of the conditions.

"As the third foreign conspirator in the original World Trade Center bombing, I command a high price."

"Saddam only sent two agents to plan and execute that plot—Yousef and Yasin," Jiang said.

By dropping such bits of detail, he hoped to make a positive impression. He didn't want to be viewed as someone to be taken lightly. His words did not have the desired affect.

"No, Saddam sent two agents who were caught. The third was a professional in his trade, and thus, he left without the slightest detection."

The man's eyes burned with pride, and Jiang no longer doubted Muhammad told the truth. That is, after all, why he had contacted him.

"Here is my price."

Muhammad slid a folded piece of paper across the table.

"I want half in Zurich by tomorrow evening. The other half I do not expect until I finish the job, but when I do, I want it hand delivered by you—all of it in Euros."

"You don't want dollars?" Jiang asked.

Muhammad shook his head.

"I plan on doing my job."

The creases of a smile lurked up his face, and Muhammad reclined in his chair to await Jiang's reply. It came quickly.

"Your offer is accepted. The desired funds will be in Zurich six p.m. tomorrow, Swiss time," Jiang said.

Noticeably shocked, Muhammad tried to hide his surprise. He lifted his glass and held it in Jiang's direction.

"To a new partnership between businessmen."

Jiang held up his glass and drank the scotch. It washed over his palette with the sweetest aftertaste.

*   *   *   *

The horde of screaming mouths pressed against the stage while Prime Minister Hume stood high above them as though he were a famous conductor and they were his symphony. The assembly of faces, packed shoulder to shoulder, waved signs in the air that read 'Yes To Integration' and 'United We Stand'. A row of European politicians supporting passage of the new constitution stood on both sides of Hume as he spoke. Raphael stood in the far corner of the gathering, several feet from the proscenium. Jean Riguad Prieur emerged from the darkest recesses of the backstage area and pressed his hand against Raphael's shoulder.

"The polls show an eighty-two percent favorable rating among UK voters on the issue of integration. Even better, they show an eighty-six percent favorable rating for Raphael Vicente."

Raphael kept his eyes trained on the event's speaker.

"So what."

Jean moved his own face close to Raphael's, forcing him to make eye contact.

"Popularity can be very useful."

Raphael's brief display of irritation transmitted his dislike for the conversation, but Jean kept talking anyway.

"Someone so popular is a definite front-runner for the presidential slot."

"Europe doesn't have a president."

Jean's voice took on a more confrontational and authoritative tone.

"But it will."

"I've never served in political office. Why would anyone want me to be president?"

Jean smiled, an excitement entering the motions of his head and hands as he spoke.

"But that's your greatest strength. You're not a politician. People trust you. Their minds foster images of a romantic poet warrior, lifting his pen instead of his sword to fight against evil and injustice."

Raphael's eyes rolled, annoyed by the man's overtures, as he tried to listen to Prime Minister Hume.

"Well, there's a reason I've never held office. Democratic politics is weak. One has far more power to affect change from the outside, in the private sector."

"This isn't an appointment to the Mexican government we're talking about. This is United Europe, the greatest economic power on earth. This office is being created for a reason. To fight a war on terror. To integrate and improve our military capability. What office could be more powerful?"

The crowd let out a roar, and Raphael turned his head to face Jean. His eyes branded the man's skull with their loathing.

"I told you before, and I'll tell you again. No."

His answer was firm, but Jean continued to push.

"Imagine the influence. The ability to send foreign aid to poor nations. To build schools and roads and hospitals."

"No."

"If you don't care about the suffering of the poor, at least have some regard for their lives. Terrorism threatens our global economic order. A direct hit, and the third world will starve. Millions could die if the war isn't handled properly."

"Look, I said no!"

The heightened volume of Raphael's voice silenced Jean for a brief moment before his appeals took on a softer, more measured tone.

"I only bring it up because I care about Europe. I don't want to see it crumble, and I know you're the best man for the job."

Raphael returned a look of unbelief.

"Best man for the job, huh?"

"That's right."

"Then why don't you throw your own name in the ring? You don't think you can do a better job?"

A devilish smile rose from Jean's lips as though he had been caught in a sinister act.

"As a sitting member of the European Commission, it would be a conflict of interest to lobby for my own appointment."

"You're a liar. You aren't vying for the job, because even your own mother wouldn't trust you with it."

Jean laughed out loud.

"I have one of the seventeen votes myself. I can get you the other eight. All I ask is an appointment once you're in."

A multitude of cheers swelled into the air as the Prime Minister announced Raphael's name to the crowd. Raphael buttoned his coat and prepared to step onto the stage.

"What appointment?" he asked.

"Head of United Europe Intelligence."

This time it was Raphael who laughed. Jean did not.

"I have powerful allies and influential friends. If you change your mind, I can make you the most powerful man on earth."

Raphael looked him up and down before responding.

"I'm already the most powerful man on earth."

He stepped forward, parting the curtain, and at the sight of his face, thousands of screaming people called out to him.

CHAPTER 5:

Nations Arise Against Nations

"Since everything around us is going to melt away, what holy, godly lives you should be living! You should look forward to that day and hurry it along—the day when God will set the heavens on fire and the elements will melt away in the flames."

—Peter
2 Peter 3:11–12

The man's voice was the sound of music.

"Yousef Abdullah Al-Rahman," Muhammad said.

Azan Aji shook his hand. He could use a friend right now. He was always getting himself into trouble. As a forgery expert and gunrunner for the PLO, or at least that's how he viewed himself, he wasn't an expert in either field. But that fact didn't stop various groups from exploiting him—al-Fatah, Western Sector, al-Aqsa, even Islamic Jihad and Hamas. Currency, passports, driver's licenses, any and all documents—he had counterfeited them all. At the age of twenty-four, he had already been arrested in four different coun-tries for various such offenses, but it had been gunrunning for the PLO that finally nailed him. Two Israeli soldiers caught him trying to smuggle a truck-load of small arms into the West Bank. Israel promptly deported him back to Jordan.

Tired of being led around, and wanting to create a better life for himself, Azan flew to the United States in March of 2000. He landed in New York and claimed political asylum. Moving in with his uncle, he drove a cab in New York City and lived a fairly normal life. Then came September 11th. When the war in Afghanistan began, it re-ignited his political views, and he decided to lend his services to his brothers once again. A man at a local mosque had a non-refundable one-way ticket to Pakistan that he couldn't use. Azan bought it, and using the man's passport, he flew to Pakistan. Within a week, he mailed the passport back, figuring he would never need it again.

With the war in Afghanistan not lasting as long as he had originally planned, Azan tried to return to the United States. In June, he went to the US embassy in Islamabad seeking a visa to return. The embassy refused. Azan was in Pakistan illegally. His own passport lacked an entry stamp, and with his asylum application pending, he had failed to obtain permission to leave the country. Without a visa or an entry stamp, he couldn't leave Pakistan under his own name. Azan turned to the same place and the same people he always turned to for help. He visited the local mosque.

It was in the mosque that a friend introduced him to Yousef Abdullah Al-Rahman, the name Muhammad Jumma Marri had assumed.

"I heard about your situation," Muhammad told him. "I think I might be able to help. I'm on my way to the United States as well."

Azan looked over this new Yousef character. When it came to Muslim brothers, he gave them only loyalty and trust. The man that Azan knew as Al-Rahman was charming and sophisticated. He had all the answers. He had a catalogue of stolen identity papers. He let Azan pick out his own and the two of them pasted his picture into place on a European passport and a Paki-stani visa. Muhammad's portfolio of stolen documents left a lasting impres-sion on Azan.

"Keep them," Muhammad said.

Azan couldn't believe it. He shoved the documents into his suitcase.

"Now, wait here," Muhammad said.

He went to get their tickets. After waiting in line for a few minutes, he purchased two one-way tickets from Islamabad to New York, paying by voucher.

"This one's yours," he said.

He handed the ticket to Azan, and the man looked him in the face with infinite gratitude.

"You're a true friend, Yousef."

*   *   *   *

The stopover flight from London landed in JFK at 9:30am. Muhammad took hold of the small bag he had placed between his legs and made his way down the aisle. Azan struggled to carry his own heavy luggage. He brought a massive carry-on with two suitcases underneath the plane.

Muhammad was tall and well dressed. He wore a pair of gray-lens sunglasses, and his clothes looked expensive. Stepping off the plane, he walked over to the nearest INS official. She was a woman in her mid-twenties. He removed his glasses before speaking.

"I seek political asylum," he said.

He placed his passport and identity papers on the counter.

"One moment," she said.

Within seconds, three agents moved in beside her. He had figured border security would tighten after September 11th. Before any of them said a word, the phone rang on the counter. One of the agents picked it up. He listened for a moment before turning to the woman.

"We've got a situation. Can you handle this?" he asked, nodding his head at Muhammad.

"I've got him," she said.

Suddenly, Muhammad had only one official with which to contend. He watched as the agents moved in around Azan. Muhammad had been all but forgotten as the agent led him into a small room off the main corridor.

"Agent Brackins," she said, closing the door.

"Nice to meet you Ms. Brackins."

He relayed a charming smile.

"This might take a while," she said.

"That's certainly understandable, given the circumstances."

"And what exactly do you think of the recent circumstances, Mr. Al-Rahman?"

"Disgusted. Angry. I was schooled at NYU. Got my Masters at Columbia. I took the cowardly attacks on America personally," he said.

She looked him over. He was eloquent and convincing.

"We'll have to run a background check and take your fingerprints. If everything is in order, you might be released by the end of the day."

With a gracious smile, Muhammad nodded his head in appreciation.

Outside, the INS placed Azan in detention. They easily unveiled his crude passport as a fraud. Searching his luggage, they uncovered multiple counterfeit identity documents, along with several bomb-making manuals. They arrested Azan and transported him to a detention facility where he would stay until long after Muhammad would leave the country. Several months later, he was deported back to Pakistan, never realizing that the man who called himself Yousef Al-Rahman was not his friend.

*   *   *   *

Lt. Commander Richard Heighton had been expecting him. His commanding officer had called the day before, telling him to be on the lookout for a Task Force 157. "Give them anything they want," he had said.

Tora Bora remained crowded with activity, and Heighton wanted to get this new team in and out as quickly as possible. Lt. Col. John Gruman now requested a personal meeting to discuss the network of caves under Heighton's control. Heighton invited him into his quarters.

"Gruman, we've got a lot going on. You and your team are welcome to poke around in any cave you want, but I assure you you're not going to find anything. We swept those caves at least fives times already. They're picked clean," he said.

Gruman seemed unfazed.

"I understand, but we'd still like to take a look," he said.

Heighton didn't hide his disapproval, but he remembered what his commanding officer had told him. The order came down from the President of the United States himself. But why? Did the president not trust his unit to get the job done? Did he feel they were incompetent? The whole thing irritated him.

"Do what you have to do."

Gruman nodded his head in gratitude.

"Just one more thing," he said. "My team will need a list of every member of the coalition forces to set foot in those caves. We need to know who's been there so we can reconcile their presence with any evidence we find."

Heighton shook his head. He felt this to be a tremendous waste of resources, but by now he just wanted to get Gruman out of his hair.

"We'll also need tissue samples from each of those persons," Gruman said.

Heighton had been trying to dig up a list on his laptop when Gruman's latest request came flying at him. On this, he was determined to draw the line.

"Tissue samples?"

His face conveyed outright disgust.

"If it makes you uncomfortable, I can secure an executive order," Gruman said.

The absurdity of the exchange caused Heighton's blood pressure to rise so far skyward he thought blood might pour through his hair follicles. Gruman and his task force ran around checking cholesterol counts, while his men put their lives on the line every minute. His patience was wearing thin when he decided the best way to get rid of Gruman was to give him what he wanted.

"No. That won't be necessary. You'll have your tissue samples by the end of the day."

Gruman extended his gratitude and left the makeshift office. Then, he and the men of Task Force 157 scoured the caves of Tora Bora for additional tissue samples, specifically dead skin and hair.

*   *   *   *

The laptop hummed with silence except for the brute hammering of its keys as Raphael worked on the manuscript of his upcoming book. After finishing the sixth paragraph, he paused with his fingers frozen on the keys. He cast a blank stare onto the oak door and nervously fidgeted while the four walls closed in on him.

Who are these people that they would hurl themselves and the world toward utter destruction? Religious fanatics? Fascists? Religious fascists.

Raphael took out a scrap of paper and scrawled ink all over it. It read, "The power of words is the power to create and destroy. I will create a book to destroy intolerance". He shoved the paper into his pocket as a motivational reminder and placed his fingers back on the keyboard. A knock pounded at the door of his office, and he turned in his chair.

"Come in."

The doorknob twisted, and Jean walked in, waving a silver disk in his hand.

"A friend of mine from Mossad sent me this video footage, and I think you ought to see it."

He stopped in front of the television and popped open the DVD player. Turning on the television, he pressed play.

A burning building appeared on the screen. The screams of women and children nearly drowned out the blaring sirens, and men ran in every direction. The building stood three stories tall, and a fire truck parked in front lifted its latter up to the top floor. Women and children stretched out from the open windows, their lurching arms and fearful faces barely visible from the black smoke puffing around them. The camera angled down to the first floor, where firemen helped children climb through the broken windows, but then several men appeared and turned them away. The camera focused in. The men held sticks in their hands, and they approached the smoke-filled windows.

Screaming epithets, they beat the children unmercifully. Their violent lashes corralled the small girls back into the burning building. The firemen protested, but a new legion of armed men arrived on the scene and drove them back.

Jean took a step forward. His pockets hid both of his hands, and his demeanor remained morbidly unchanged by the rolling footage. His blank expression glanced at Raphael, then back at the video, then back at Raphael again.

"Mecca," he said. "The building is a school that caters to little girls between the ages of five and nine. They forgot their burqas while trying to escape the fire. The men reminding them are religious police from the Ministry for the Propagation of Virtue and the Prevention of Vice."

He shook his head.

"Reminds me of something out of Orwell," he said.

His hands still buried in his pockets, he jingled some loose change while he waited for a reaction from Raphael. Not getting one, he politely removed his right hand to cover his yawning mouth.

"I'll just leave this here for your further review."

Raphael remained silent, a frown and clinched eyebrows stenciled into his face. Jean turned to leave, but stopped at the door, his hand on a half-turned doorknob.

"Oh yes, one more thing. My friend also reminded me that twenty-six portable nuclear devices, ranging in potency from one-kiloton to ten, are still unaccounted for since the break up of the Soviet Union. He seems convinced these men and their friends have them, but what does he know?"

The undercurrent of his voice harbored a slight twinge of sarcasm. Quickly, his tone went cold again as he turned the knob and opened the door.

"You have my number," he said. "Call me if you change your mind about the presidency."

He latched the door shut behind him, and Raphael sat alone, the video still rolling. The screams of the children had been snuffed out as if they were the last smoldering ashes of a campfire doused by buckets of water.

Gone was the playful ring of tiny voices, innocent and pure. Left was a spirit of evil that rejoiced in the silence as the towering flames reduced the desolate school building to a burnt and twisted ruin.

Deep within his soul, Raphael hosted a fire of his own. Images of Poyner and Juan Diego flipped through his head. He pressed a key on his laptop and the cursor advanced to the first page of his Word document. He deleted the title of his manuscript and replaced it with a new one. In bold typeface, he wrote "Blood Brothers". Then, he picked up his cell phone and hit the speed dial. The voice mail beeped.

"Jean, it's Raphael. Give me a call when you get this message."

*   *   *   *

Henri Claudel picked a copy of *The Daily Telegraph* off the newsstand shelf. All around him, the streets of Paris bustled with early morning rush hour traffic. Standing next to an iron lamppost on the corner, he read the headline: "Vicente Considers Presidency". The same information, packaged in different phrases, plastered itself across the front page of every other publication as well.

Claudel shook his head. Vicente could garner the appointment, but he had made up his mind to move ahead regardless of the policy decisions of United Europe, whether made by Prime Ministers or some future president of United Europe. Because, in the end, only a policy of equilibrium could prevail. A unilateralist policy would be immoral and destructive. He wondered how a Vicente administration would govern.

In fact, it was humorous, if not outright ridiculous, that a man who had only been a citizen of the United Kingdom for a few years could be appointed to the highest office in a new United Europe. The man did not know what he was getting into. The world teetered on the brink of catastrophic change and only a handful of people knew the truth.

He scoffed as he tossed the paper back on the rack and snatched a copy of *The Guardian Weekly* instead. Politics! That's what he was trying to avoid at all costs. Too many good men ruined their lives and the lives of others by allowing themselves to be consumed by petty politics. He cursed them under his breath as he entered a nearby café.

Taking a seat in a secluded corner booth in the back, he ordered his coffee black and waited. He double-checked to make sure nothing looked out of the ordinary, then scanned the paper. He kept one eye on the door and found himself staring at the people out on the sidewalk, sitting at iron tables and sipping on designer beverages. Did they have any idea what was about to happen to their world? In a way, he found the thought somewhat humorous. A devilish smile wrapped itself over his face.

His stare was broken when a clean-shaven man entered from the same sidewalk he had been so intent on observing. The man looked to be in his early thirties and of average height. His eyes took time to adjust after stepping inside, but once they did, they immediately trained themselves on Henri Claudel. Henri pretended not to notice and shielded his face with the newspaper, but the man walked over to his table and sat down directly across from him.

"You can put the paper down. No one is looking," Jiang said.

Henri lowered the paper, and his eyes darted around the room. He kept his voice at a whisper.

"Easy for you to say. If someone recognizes me, then starts asking who you are—"

Jiang laughed out loud.

"If so, I'll just make up a story. I'm your old friend," he said.

The whites of Jiang's teeth sparkled like the fangs of a tiger.

"Now, let's talk business," he said. "You called me, remember?"

CHAPTER 6:

Life As Coding

"For the time is near when all these things will happen."

—John
Revelation 1:3

Immersed in paperwork, Raphael hunkered into position behind his desk, nearly overwhelmed by it all. How could the Union generate so much bureaucratic waste for a job that had only existed for twenty-four hours or so? It was mindboggling, but a small price to pay for the opportunity to serve in these historic times. The phone rang, and Raphael picked it up.

"Yes?"

"Mr. President, Prime Minister Hume is here to see you," the voice said.

"Did I forget an appointment?"

He didn't remember making arrangements for a meeting with the Prime Minister.

"No, sir. Should I send him in?"

"Of course."

Raphael rearranged the papers on his desk and climbed out of his chair as the door opened. Prime Minister Hume greeted Raphael warmly as he entered, and two more men followed behind him. The first man was French President Gehan. The second was German Chancellor Scharping. Raphael didn't know what to say. None of them looked distressed, so it couldn't be some sort of breaking international incident. Perhaps it was just a welcoming party.

"Have a seat gentlemen. To what do I owe this honor?" he asked.

Each man took a seat, and the four of them formed a sort of disorganized circle.

"We came here to initiate you," Scharping said.

"Well, I hope you're not too rough," Raphael said.

He was trying to break the ice. But a serious look hung over Hume's face, and his eyes never left Raphael's.

"Raphael, the four of us have not always agreed on policy, but that no longer matters. Your record demonstrates that you put good policy ahead of personal ambition, and in my personal dealings with you, I have become convinced that the four of us share the same vision—that you are a man who can be trusted."

"Of course," Raphael said. "But what's your point?"

President Gehan shifted in his chair and entered the conversation.

"The point is your ability to be trusted with such power," he said.

Raphael laughed out loud, but no one else joined him.

"I don't think you have to worry about that. I don't have but so much power, and Parliament, the courts, the European Council—they all work to keep the power of the president in check."

The three men looked at each other in apprehension.

"Raphael, this office will become more powerful than you can possibly imagine," Scharping said.

Hume waved the man off in such a way as to let him know he would finish.

"The war on terror," Hume said. "Is the greatest threat Europe has ever faced. The longer this war continues, the more likely we will lose. In the days following the eleventh of September, I talked at great length with President Burton. We discussed a plan to create a modern-day Manhattan Project. A top priority of his administration, his hope was that Britain and Europe would join in the effort."

He shifted his eyes toward Scharping and Gehan.

"Within a few days, I met with Chancellor Scharping and President Gehan. We agreed to devote our full energies and resources toward the creation of a comprehensive project of our own, Project Mercury. Since that day, the most brilliant minds in Europe have been working non-stop, twenty-four-seven to complete a finished prototype of a weapon that will forever end the war on terror."

Raphael's eyes grew wide as Hume continued.

"The United States and Japan are conducting identical research independently. Our intelligence gives us good reason to believe we are in the lead. If we maintain that lead, United Europe will one day become the undisputed, preeminent world military power. No nation will be able to oppose us, and this office will become the most powerful the world has ever witnessed."

"And that is the point of this meeting," Gehan said.

Raphael was speechless. What single weapon could be that powerful?

"Why wasn't this disclosed in my inaugural briefing?" he asked.

Again, all three men looked at each other. Raphael waited patiently. He was angry that something so important had been hidden from him, but he was glad to be learning of it on the first day from men he could trust.

"United Europe knows nothing about this," Hume said.

"What?" Raphael asked.

Scharping put his hand on Raphael's shoulder.

"The Union is a massive political bureaucracy. Had we tried to pull something like this together under Union cooperation, every petty interest would've wanted to push a political agenda. We'd be so bogged down in regulation and indecision, not an inch of progress would be made. Just ask the Americans. That's why we're in the lead, and they aren't," Scharping said.

"Then who knows about this?" Raphael asked.

"Just the three of us, the people working on the project, and now, you," Gehan said.

"But I don't know anything."

"You will very shortly," Hume said.

Every aspect of the appearance of these three men told Raphael that they were dead serious. This was something larger than their personal careers, and it was obvious they were not exaggerating when they said only they and the people on the project knew.

"And you trust me enough to put such a weapon in my hands?" Raphael asked.

"You received the answer to that question when we pushed for integration and lobbied for your appointment. Lord Becton is the man in charge of Project Mercury. Later today, he'll give you a personal tour of the project facility and an overview of its goals. I advise you to clear your schedule," Hume said.

As he finished his comments, the Prime Minister made his way to the door. Gehan and Scharping followed. Scharping bit his lower lip.

"We won't be in power forever. Project Mercury is yours now. We'll be available for advice, but the fate of United Europe now rests in your hands."

The three of them stepped into the hallway. As they disappeared into its darkness, Raphael's trailing words echoed through the dank chasm.

"That's why I accepted this job."

*   *   *   *

The unmarked Ford Explorer rushed the president to an undisclosed location in the French Alps. Armed guards stationed themselves in pairs along the side of the road, accompanied by signs that read 'Restricted Area', and the president's escort followed a narrow pathway into the side of a mountain ridge. Pulling into an underground garage, the motorcade stopped. A door on the Explorer popped open, and Raphael jumped out. Lord Becton waited by a pair of glass doors.

"Mr. President, welcome to Assembly Hall," he said.

The two shook hands and acknowledged each other, then walked side-by-side into the depths of the compound. Becton towered in height, a true Lord from the House of Commons and a man of impeccable character. His peers saluted him even when unnecessary, sometimes when his back faced them. Few men garnered greater respect within United Europe.

Inside, a mountain facility thousands of acres in size hummed with activity. Most of the facility's space remained vacant, and they now walked along a wide hallway flanked by rows of internal windows. Behind one of the Plexiglas panels, men and women worked with sophisticated equipment and high-powered computers. Becton pointed at them through the glass.

"If all goes well, the assembler breakthrough will transpire within this room," he said.

"Assembler breakthrough?"

Raphael lifted his eyebrows in confusion. Becton reacted to the question with genuine surprise.

"Well yes, that's what we're working on. It's the entire basis for Project Mercury. With a little luck, it will all happen here."

Raphael's head roved in all directions, taking in everything he could lay eyes on.

"And what's an assembler?"

"You mean they never told you?"

"They told me you would explain everything."

"Oh..."

Becton submerged his face in his hands for a few moments, then reappeared fresh with life.

"I'm not sure where to start," he said. "So I'll just jump in. The purpose of Project Mercury is to create an assembler, an atom stacking device that will allow us to maintain complete and total control of the precision placement of all molecules in the structure of matter."

Raphael seemed to drift off into a daydream before responding. His skeptical eye probed over Becton.

"And you believe this is possible?"

His doubt failed to dent Becton's outer appearance, and the man injected his reply with a tone of complete confidence.

"I don't believe so. I know so. Very soon, we will have an assembler—a submicroscopic robotic arm capable of securing and positioning compounds in the precise locations at which chemical reactions occur."

"But if you can do that, then—"

"Then United Europe will possess a manufacturing technology able to build any structure allowed by the physical laws of the universe—in effect, a thorough and inexpensive system for controlling all matter."

Raphael stood in silence, unable to say a word. Becton pointed to different parts of the facility.

"Over there, we're perfecting techniques for storing atom inventory...That wing specializes in methods for delivering an atom or molecule from inventory to the manufacturing floor...And development of a computer for receiving and sending sets of instructions to dictate assembler actions..."

Becton's voice withered away inside Raphael's mind. Was this really possible? A machine to process matter? Capable of creating anything?

As he thought, a man walked by, and Becton called out to him. He put his hand on the man's arm and presented him to Raphael.

"Mr. President, I'd like you to meet one of the project's top engineers—Dr. Henri Claudel."

Raphael shook the man's hand. Claudel looked deep into the president's eyes.

"We're glad to have you on board, Mr. President. It's a pleasure to meet you."

The three of them made small talk for sometime before Claudel interjected.

"I was wondering, Mr. President, have you discussed post-assembler breakthrough policies with your advisors?"

Becton nudged an elbow in Claudel's ribcage, but the man did not back away from his question. Raphael resented the question coming from a subordinate and pretended to be deeply ensconced in the project's planning.

"Of course I have," he said.

Claudel appeared to be waiting for more, but nothing came.

"Well?"

"Well what?" Raphael asked.

"What do you plan to do?"

"That information is classified."

Becton yanked Claudel's arm.

"Come on Henri," he said. "The president is a very busy man."

Raphael watched as Becton dragged Claudel away. The man signaled a look of utter disdain as if being carried off in handcuffs, and Raphael couldn't help but feel he was the intended target of the angry glare.

As Becton returned, Raphael purged his memory of Claudel's unprofessional behavior and refocused his thoughts on the assembler project. The implications were staggering. Not only would an assembler end the war on terror, it would change the way humanity lived forever.

"And all this can be accomplished with an assembler?" he asked.

Becton shrugged.

"Not by itself. It would take a single assembler arm a million years to build something the size of your little finger, but once we have one, it can be ordered to build a duplicate copy of itself. Then those two can be directed to build two more. If the process of self-replication is fifteen minutes—a conservative estimate—then by the end of one day, the first assembler can self-replicate into two to the ninety-fifth power assemblers. And that many assemblers can build anything we wish."

"Such as tanks and airplanes?" Raphael asked.

"If that's what United Europe wants. But the industrial revolution didn't lead to armored horses, it led to armored tanks."

"And how long before we have this?"

"A few years at the most. We really don't know."

Raphael's jaw landed on the floor as he considered the work that lay ahead.

"I don't know if I'm ready for this. What if it comes tomorrow? What do I do then?"

"I don't know, but I pray to God you figure it out, because on that day all hell is going to break loose."

PART IV

▼

Infinite Justice For All Men

"His ten horns are ten kings who have not yet risen to power; they will be appointed to their kingdoms for one brief moment to reign with the beast. They will all agree to give their power and authority to him."

—**John**
Revelation 17:12–13

CHAPTER I:

Years Of Tribulation

"In fact, unless that time of calamity is shortened, the entire human race will be destroyed. But it will be shortened for the sake of God's chosen ones."

—Jesus Christ
Matthew 24:22

Standing on the rooftop of his Jerusalem apartment, Daniel Heron allowed the morning light to drench his shoulders. Inhaling a deep breath of the crisp air, the gravity of the moment became fully apparent. Truly, it was the appointed time. Israel was once again a nation. Jerusalem was once again in the hands of God's chosen people. A man approached from behind, and Daniel turned. With a rigid finger, he pointed across the landscape. The appointed time had arrived for rebuilding the Temple.

"Restoring the Temple will surely pave the way for the coming Messiah to vanquish Israel's enemies and set up his godly kingdom on earth."

The man nodded in silent agreement, and the two of them looked out at the protrusion. Daniel grit his teeth, his lower lip quivering.

"Look at it. It's nothing more than a cancerous growth, a scar on Jerusalem's beautiful skyline."

The golden dome stood out like a blot of ink on a fine painting, its twisted architecture symbolic in his mind of a clump of ugly vines winding through god's well-pruned garden. The abomination filled his stomach with a sour feeling. And its inevitable destruction remained his sole reason for living. Surely, god chose him as a servant, a tool to carry out this grand design.

Tapping Daniel's shoulder, the other man pointed down at the shrine.

"They say they're brothers of the Jew, but they're pagans who worship a rock god. And they seek nothing but the destruction of this nation."

The two scanned the outer courtyard filled with exotic robes, robes that cloaked the pagan men who trod their dirty feet upon the foundations of God's beloved Temple. Bowing down to their rock five-times a day, they were an infection surrounding God's chosen people on all sides, outnumbering the Jews forty-to-one. Daniel presented his friend with an arrogant smirk. In Daniel's mind, all the institutions of man gathered together could never halt God's will. In his eyes, the absurdity of such a plot was enough reason to believe it divine. Where others saw obstacles, Daniel saw proof his god would overcome all of Israel's enemies.

As his eyes surveyed the city, he obtained blissful delight from the thought that the Messiah was out there, walking among the crowds, traveling the streets and anxiously awaiting the appointed moment when the plans of his god would come into being. He ached for the next world, unable to look at the godless people who polluted the world around him. He was better than all of them. He was the messenger of his god.

*   *   *   *

"This is absurd. It's suicidal. We need to turn back now!"

The special assistant to the Prime Minister unleashed a barrage of declarations at his boss. Prime Minister Vajpee's limousine bounced over the potholes inlaid in the pavement like gaping wounds. Vajpee listened to the man's ravings, but sat with his hands neatly folded, his mind firm and resolved.

"I must do this. I will do this," he said.

His assistant shifted position as though poison ivy wrapped around his legs.

"It's much too dangerous. We can't ensure your safety."

Vajpee drew his hand up to his chin, his eyes lost outside the window.

"I don't care. No one ensures the safety of our troops either."

The possibility of India's involvement in a nuclear war heightened with each passing hour, and the soldiers stationed on the border in Kashmir remained the most likely recipients of Pakistan's first launch. His assistant seemed to be silenced by the comment, and he retracted into the leather cushions.

Vajpee let his mind wander outside the window, gliding over the passing landscape of houses and people. Three nights had passed without sleep. It started when masked gunmen ambushed Majun Lahiri, the lone voice of reason in Kashmir. The leader's followers blamed Pakistan; Pakistan blamed India. Less than a day later, Islamic separatists assassinated twelve members of the Indian Parliament, spraying bullets at the Parliament building steps before being gunned down by security.

Direct diplomatic ties between the two countries had been severed, and now he found himself personally making the trip to address the troops in Kashmir. Through the bulletproof windows, row after row of distraught citizens stood alongside the road. Some cheered, some waved, and others held up signs such as "Remember Kargil". How could he forget? Kargil had once placed his country on the brink of a war that now seemed imminent.

"All right, we're here," the assistant said.

The limousine and its caravan rolled to a stop at an Indian military base near Jammu. Vajpee peered out from his window. He could see Pakistan from where he sat. A hand clicked the door open, and he stepped outside. Planting his feet on the ground, he shook hands with the commanding officers as the sound of beating drums and blaring trumpets announced his arrival. Walking forward, a group of armed guards instantly formed a protective shell around the leader. The base erected a makeshift platform for his address, and Vajpee climbed its steps with the guards in tow.

From high above, he saw hundreds upon hundreds of troops in perfect formation, all saluting his presence. They stood alert and disciplined, their clean uniforms and trim bodies a testament to their unmatched preparation. Vajpee darted straight for the microphone, his fist pounding the air at an unseen enemy.

"The day of reckoning has come, a monumental battle has yet to be fought, and we will not lose."

The soldiers hollered their approval. The car bomb knocked a quarter of them flat on their backs. Twisting through the air in a double somersault, the car itself landed on seven men crushing them instantly. The doors hinged open, and the car let go of another fiery explosion.

Before the Prime Minister's guard had time to react, two soldiers in the front row lurched forward and raised their guns, hurling a flurry of bullets on Vajpee's position. A second car exploded, and the ranks of the army fell into disarray with men running in every direction looking in vain for an unseen enemy. The Prime Minister's bodyguards leapt onto his back, tackling him to the stage and covering his body from the rain of bullets. Two of them returned fire and killed the terrorist gunmen. Weapons raised, they turned their heads, the situation now under control. Lifeless, Prime Minister Vajpee lay on the bloody stage.

*   *   *   *

Hector Salzburg's smooth voice meandered through the air. He had a scraggly black beard and a receding hairline. His suits were always well pressed and of the finest quality. Born into money, he spent most of his college years protesting Vietnam and after a few years in the Peace Corps, he moved back to New York City to acquire a law degree. Money was of secondary concern, and his latest client now sat across from him.

"You let me handle this Saeed. You have rights. This is racial profiling, plain and simple, and we can nail them to the wall. At the very least, I can buy you a year or two. There's nothing to worry about," Salzburg said.

Saeed nodded his head in agreement. He didn't understand most of it. It seemed to him that if a person was in the country illegally, the authorities would just pick him up and take him back to where he came from. That's what they did in Jordan. It all served to confirm his belief America was an inferior society. Salzburg stood up from the small table, his hands lurching up and down in a reassuring posture.

"Look, I've got to get out of here. I've got another appointment down the street, but don't worry about anything. If you need me, just give me a call," Salzburg said.

His face wore a pasty grin, and he shook Saeed's hand as if Saeed was his best friend in the whole world. Saeed returned the gesture, but his smile was more out of disbelief than sincerity. As he pondered the idiocy of America, the small apartment's door burst open. His roommate, Ali Fatal, walked into the room, another man in tow.

"Saeed, we have a new neighbor, Yousef Abdullah Al-Rahman. He just moved in from Iran," Ali said.

Muhammad held out his hand, and Saeed shook it. It didn't take long for Salzburg to move in. His hand quickly attached itself to Muhammad's shoulder.

"Iran, huh? You here permanently or temporarily?" Salzburg asked.

"Hopefully, permanently. I posted an application for political asylum."

Salzburg let out a boisterous laugh.

"If you want to be here permanently, I can arrange it—no matter what happens to your application. Here's my card. Give me a call."

He shoved the card into Muhammad's hand, then turned to Ali and Saeed.

"I'll see you guys later."

He bolted for the door and was gone. Ali locked it, while Muhammad looked down at the card. It read, "Hector Salzburg, Immigration Attorney, ACLU". He shook his head before cramming the card into the bottom dredges of his pocket. Only in America would men actually fight for the rights of lawbreakers and enemies of their own state.

Ali and Saeed invited Muhammad in, and the three of them discussed Islam and the monumental worldwide struggle.

*   *   *   *

"For God's sake, they just killed the Prime Minister, and you think I should back down!"

The phone slammed down, and all Raphael could hear was the mocking dial tone. He paced the office revisiting every scenario over and over again in his head. A team of advisors waited down the hall discussing alternatives, hoping for some loophole concession to put an end to the current escalation. For too long, the world focused its efforts on the Arab-Israeli conflict, but only at the expense of this now greater problem. Billions of people, hundreds of languages, countless religions with their multiple sects—all of them now stewing together in a dangerous cauldron of random colonial borders and nuclear weapons.

Gilder stepped forward and placed his hands on the president's desk, a worried frown angling downward. Raphael shared his frustration.

"Under normal circumstances, my support for India would be without compromise, but the terror war complicates the picture."

"I'm sure the Americans are prodding them. Pakistan is a valuable ally in the Afghan war."

Raphael nodded his head in agreement, while his fingers dug into a stack of papers and crumpled them into mangled balls.

"I feel like a hypocrite!" he said. "Why can't India be our ally, and we'll fight Pakistan too?"

He stood up from his chair and paced around the desk. Gilder straightened his back.

"The Americans call the shots. That's the reality, and right now, they feel if they sanction the invasion of a third Muslim country, it'll embolden the Arab street and ignite a holy war against the West."

"A holy war? Aren't they already fighting a holy war? Everywhere I turn, it's Muslims killing people—Kashmir, Chechnya, the Philippines, Palestine, Sudan, Indonesia! And what the hell is the Arab street anyway? That's a fictional conception."

Gilder bit down on his lower lip.

"What do you think we should do?"

Raphael sat back down, bouncing his leg on the floor, and drawing his interlocked fingers up to his face so that the clenched hands masked all but his eyes.

"We have only two options. We can refuse to recognize reality, that Muslims want to kill us, or we can face the problem head on and defeat it."

"But America…"

"To hell with America. If it weren't for the millions of innocent people, I'd nuke all the Muslim terrorists myself."

Gilder waited for the blood tint to lower from the president's cheeks, then chased after him with a more subdued tone.

"The citizens in these countries—most of them don't know anything but what the government tells them. They live in abject poverty with no concept of nuclear warfare. They have no clue what they're playing with."

Raphael ran his fingers through his hair, his leg still bouncing on the floor.

"I know. That's why we're going to save them from themselves. I want you to find out what I have to do to end this escalation—whatever it is, whatever the cost."

Gilder stroked his chin, a confused expression on his face.

"Why?"

Raphael rolled his tapping fingers over the surface of the desk.

"Because the long-term effect is irrelevant. We're going to pursue a new policy of war avoidance at any cost, saving time until the day of the assembler breakthrough."

"You'd risk making the situation worse based on the hope of this 'magic weapon?"

Raphael shook his head, a smile covering his face.

"No. I'd risk anything, anywhere—knowing the imminence of the assembler breakthrough."

"But I thought you wanted to face the problem head on?"

"I will. With an assembler in hand."

Gilder let out a deep breath and his body calmed as though all the tension had drained away.

"You must have a lot of faith in Becton and his theories."

Raphael smiled and placed his hand on Gilder's shoulder.

"I have a lot of faith in both of you. Now, can you keep these nations from going to war?"

*   *   *   *

In Jerusalem, Garrison climbed onto a stone bench outside of a local synagogue and spoke to a large crowd. A great number of Israelis who followed him night and day gathered around, and a much larger crowd formed in a circle around them. Garrison's voice was soft and gracious, yet it filled the entire street.

"The people of this world mock God. They turn him away, because they don't want to hear what he has to say."

When the crowd heard him, they accepted his words, but they were confused.

"Is this why God has sent this plague of terror against us?"

Garrison shook his head.

"God has not poured out these tribulations as punishment for the world. God is not acting in anger, but in love. The terrible things that have happened, and will soon happen, are God's way of waking the world from its slumber. God is telling you he is here, that you should not put your faith in the things of this world, because the things of this world will soon pass away."

The crowd stood in amazement at the words that fell from his lips. Then he said,

"In the coming days, far greater horrors will beset this world, but this is not God persecuting you. It is not God's judgement. Rather, it is God's way of shaking the world from its false sense of security. Through this effort, an incalculable number of individuals will come to have faith in the Lord Jesus Christ."

Those who were hearing these words for the first time spoke among themselves and asked many questions.

"What does God want? How do we avoid these things?"

The authority of Garrison's voice echoed off the buildings in the street.

"This is what God wants—believe in the one he has sent. He who makes Jesus Christ his foundation will find that when the tribulations of this world rock his life, he will stand firm. But anyone who does not make Christ the foundation of his life will find himself ruined. For the Father first sent the Son to save the world before he sent him to judge it."

*   *   *   *

"Get me Marharti."

Raphael lifted his finger from the intercom, then picked up the phone. The Prime Minister of India, Kasol Marharti, had accepted the peace proposal put forth by United Europe, as had Pakistan. Gilder came through, and the road to peace repaired itself for the short-term until the benefits of the assembler breakthrough could be leveraged.

"Kasol?"

The Prime Minister's voice arrived on the other end.

"Mr. Raphael, you have saved us all from a great horror."

He went on to praise the work of United Europe, especially the president's personal efforts to disengage the conflict. While Raphael took it all in, Gilder rushed into the office with a pile of files under one arm and a cell-phone glued to his ear with the other. He jabbered into the phone, while motioning for the president's attention. Raphael waved him off and kept talking.

Still whispering into his cell phone, Gilder threw a clump of photos on Raphael's desk and smacked him on the shoulder. Marharti's voice emanated from the receiver next to his head, and Raphael spread the photos over his desktop. They indicated a massive build up of Pakistani ground troops on the Kashmir border.

"Excuse me for just a moment Kasol."

He put his hand over the mouthpiece, and pointed at the pictures.

"What the hell is this?"

Gilder kept the cell-phone nestled to his ear. He whispered back in a worried tone.

"Pakistan's broken the agreement. They've moved a massive conventional force into the area over the past half hour."

Raphael said nothing for a moment, but just stared at the photos.

"This isn't an exercise?"

"Not of this magnitude. Our analysts believe it's a precursor to an invasion."

Raphael traced over the pictures with his fingers. He drew the phone back to his mouth.

"Sorry about that, Kasol. What was it you were saying?"

He received only silence.

"Kasol?...Kasol?"

Raphael pounded the receiver on his walnut desk several times, then hurled it at the wall. It shattered into several pieces, and his feet became tangled in the winding cord as he stormed across the room. It almost tripped him before he ripped it from the wall. Gilder looked at him.

"No doubt he knows the same things we do..."

Raphael could only manage a slight tilt of his head in acknowledgement. The blood in his veins elevated into his face, his emotions glazed with anger, and he ached to strike out at them—those who had destroyed his ingenious balancing act. His stewardship remained superior, and he knew what was best for the world. Yet, they refused to listen.

*   *   *   *

Just east of the center of Kargil, two children kicked a soccer ball through the narrow streets—completely unaware that they shouldn't be playing together. One was Hindu; one was Muslim. Both stopped kicking the ball and let it roll away as they gazed in amazement at the large object now eclipsing the sun. They weren't sure what to make of it, but people in the street pointed upward, frightened and upset. The rest of Kargil stood in silent terror as the sun reflected off the cold metal hull of the object now dropping rapidly to the earth.

It disappeared over the horizon with deafening silence. The two boys watched out of curiosity. For a few seconds, nothing happened. Then, a terrible piercing flash of light burst forward nearly blinding them. The sky above turned to fire for miles, and within seconds, a rolling wave of white fire covered over them. In a four-mile radius around the missile landing—houses, farms, trees, animals, and people—anything in the grasp of the pulse was instantly turned to dust. Right behind it was a powerful shockwave that scattered the leftover dust particles in every direction. On the outer edges of the blast, the secondary shockwaves lifted every object not yet destroyed and tossed them thousands of yards away like a vicious tornado.

From a hundred miles away, people could see the blast mushroom miles into the air, fire turning over inside of it. And all around them, everywhere they looked, mushrooms terrorized the landscape, creating hell on earth.

From a monitor in his office, Raphael watched in horror as tiny white pulsars lit up Bombay, New Delhi, and Calcutta. Like fireflies in the jungles of Chiapas, the light briefly swallowed Islamabad, Quetta, and Peshawar. Gilder looked at the president, unable to summon a single word.

Raphael paced the room like a rabid lunatic. One by one, he lifted objects from around the office and slammed them to the ground. Glass vases smashed. His hands ripped through works of art, and with all his weight, he flipped his desk on its side, papers flying in all directions. With little left to destroy, he plopped down onto his overturned desk, his breath prolonged and heavy.

Placing a clenched fist next to the wooden surface, his stare tunneled a hole into Gilder's head.

"I will never—never, allow this to happen again…Never!"

He jumped up and kicked his desk, trying to regain his composure, but the images warped his mind. The voices of children cried out, just as Juan Diego had cried out. And he was unable to save them. He thought of the innocent people who had no hand in this war, who didn't know any better. And he burned with hatred for all he viewed as intolerant—Muslim and Hindu alike.

CHAPTER 2:

Butter Battles

"Let the children come to me. Do not stop them! For the King-dom of God belongs to such as these. I assure you, anyone who doesn't have their kind of faith will never get into the Kingdom of God."

—Jesus Christ
Luke 18:16–17

"This is a horror to the whole world, and United Europe continues to stand in unison with the United States."

A barrage of questions battered the podium along with the bright flashes of the camera as Raphael turned from the microphone and hurried into the hospital. Poyner walked beside him.

Down the hall, Jose Vicente fought a losing battle with cancer. Poyner held Raphael's hand as they made their way down the corridor and into Jose's room. When the door swung open, the old man's face wore a radiant glow. Always in good spirits, no one could tell he was in his last days, but his only concern was for his son and daughter-in-law. He turned off the television and looked at them.

"After your mother died last year, I lost any extra time I had in reserve. I guess I didn't realize how much of my own strength was hers."

Raphael didn't let him continue.

"You'll be just fine."

Jose acted unconvinced. He let out a soft breath and let his head fall onto the pillow.

"With things the way they are in the world today, maybe it's best if I left it."

"Don't say such things. This is all an aberration. Soon, the world will be at peace."

Jose lifted his head quickly.

"And how can you be so certain?"

A sharp anger simmered from behind Raphael's eyes.

"If I have to, I will force peace."

His statement caught Poyner off guard. She flinched at the statement, but Jose laughed.

"You were always Mr. Law & Order," he said.

His dreaming eyes scanned Poyner from head to toe.

"That's what we used to call him, Mr. Law & Order..."

For Raphael, the name brought back a flood of memories. What he wouldn't give to be back in the comfort of those days. Those days when a sense of law and order existed, a black and white, a right and wrong.

*   *   *   *

"A boy in class today took a pencil off the teacher's desk, and she sent him to the principal's office!"

Jose Vicente sat on the edge of his son's bed, tucking the sheets under the young boy's chin.

"And what do you think should've happened to him?"

Raphael balled his hand into a knotted fist.

"They should've sent him to jail. That's stealing!"

Jose laughed out loud.

"Mr. Law and Order...Well, maybe they should have."

"Daddy, what's a mestizo?"

Jose displayed no look of shock or disdain at the question, only a tentative curiosity.

"And where did you hear that word?" he asked.

"Ernesto Guerva said that I shouldn't play with Roddy because he's a mestizo."

"And what do you think?"

Raphael held his head back for a moment, deep in thought.

"I don't care what he is. I like playing with him."

"Then don't feel bad for doing so."

He patted Raphael on the head and walked toward the door.

"So what's a mestizo?" Raphael asked.

Jose sat back down.

"A mestizo is someone of mixed race, an Indian, a mix between the original Spanish explorers and the indigenous Aztecs. Sometimes people like Ernesto are scared when they don't understand someone different. Do you understand now?"

The boy remained quiet, and Jose could see the gears turning in his head.

"I think so."

Jose could have left it at that, but he didn't.

"Do you remember what I told you about yourself, Raphael?"

"That I'm adopted."

"That's right. And what else?"

"I'm half Muslim and half Jew."

Jose nodded his head.

"And do you understand what that means."

Raphael shook his head. No two words could be more foreign in concept. Jose walked over to his bookcase and ran his index finger across the spines of the many titles. Stopping at one in particular, he plucked it from the shelf and opened it up. From cover to cover, he proceeded to read the contents of *The Butter Battle Book* by Dr. Seuss. When it was finished, he looked his son in the eyes.

"You see, son, in another part of the world, the Jews are like those who butter their bread on the top and the Muslims are like those who butter their bread on the bottom. And for this reason, they are constantly fighting."

A puzzled expression festered on the boy's face.

"That's silly," he said.

"I think so too, son."

At this, the boy's eyes became defiant, and he bit his lower lip.
"One day when I grow up, I'll stop them from fighting. It's wrong!"
Jose laughed and patted Raphael on the head.
"That's quite a dream. If anyone could do it son, it would be you."
And he flipped off the lights.

CHAPTER 3:

Eagerly Awaiting The Savior

"Stop putting your trust in mere humans. They are as frail as breath. How can they be of help to anyone?"

—**Isaiah**
Isaiah 2:22

Idle thoughts of the horrible images branded themselves upon his memory. Children covered from head to toe with a thick film of dust. Men so bludgeoned by debris that they became zombies walking down the street. Trees flattened to the ground like toothpicks. And miles of indiscernible space of nothing but blackness. That was the most haunting image of all, that empty blackness. It all became his unreal nightmare, except that it was real. Hundreds of millions of people dead—murdered, butchered, liquidated.

Raphael couldn't let go of those images as he sat by his father's bedside. Jose was asleep, and Poyner sat down beside Raphael. She didn't say a word, but wrapped her hands around his head and massaged his temple. The forlorn look on his face remained as if he were ignorant of her presence.

"The worst part is...I don't feel any different. This day goes by just the same as the last," he said.

Poyner moved her hands down his shoulders.

"That's not true. The world is horrified."

"I wish you were right. I wish the whole world was filled with empathetic hearts like yours, but that's not reality. Reality is that it's the economy stupid."

His head fell into his hands to grapple with a pounding headache.

"That phrase keeps running through my brain. It's the economy stupid. That's all the world cares about anymore. Four hundred million people are dead, but it doesn't matter, because they didn't produce oil. They didn't manufacture automobiles or computers. They didn't make video games or Hollywood movies or mail out government checks. So nobody cares. Life goes on as usual."

He stood up, and Poyner cradled his hand in hers.

"I hate to see you so pessimistic," she said.

"And how am I supposed to be? The world cannot be allowed to continue down this road. Again, this was a direct result of the ongoing Muslim holy war. These religious fanatics will be the downfall of all humanity."

*   *   *   *

"Welcome, Mr. President."

Lord Becton stood alone in the front hallway. His hands jingled loose change in the pockets of his tailored pants, and his right hand darted out to shake Raphael's. With his free hand, he directed the president down the corridor. Darkness enveloped the hallway except for the scattered remnants of light pouring in from the laboratories on either side.

"I want an assessment of progress, and whatever it is, I want our efforts redoubled. Our world is in shambles. If it weren't for the hope of this project, I'd be driven to the brink of madness."

"That's what I'm here for. Just step this way," Becton said.

He guided Raphael's step with a well-placed prod from his right hand, and the two of them entered a laboratory down a side hall. Inside the room, Raphael's eyes adjusted to the brightness of the clean white interior. A young woman sat at a computer terminal swirling a mouse around on the desktop as

Becton approached. Raphael looked around the room. It played home to an incalculable number of individuals involved in similar activities. Becton motioned for Raphael to walk over, and every head in the room hinged up to catch a glimpse of him as he joined Becton and the girl in her workspace.

"With the aid of this CAD," Becton said. "We're able to test the components, materials, and operational conditions of the next generation of military hardware from a pre-design stage—not just before we build it, but before we're capable of building it."

Raphael bent over and studied the monitor. It displayed a number of spheres representing atoms, and the perspective viewpoint periodically changed so that the end user could see the object from every dimension. The spheres joined together in a rather crude graphical representation of an actual spider.

"What you're looking at is the key component in the future land forces of United Europe. We call it SPIDERS—Self-Propelled Individual Device for Exploration, Reconnaissance, and Surveillance. It can use its legs for crawling in any direction—forward, backward, left, right—or to re-position atoms for self-replication."

Becton pushed a button on the keyboard, and the computer image began to move. The animated SPIDERS reminded Raphael of the early Atari video game graphics. He could count each individual atom in its structure—in total, he estimated less than a couple thousand. Becton traced his finger over the screen.

"In this part, where the abdomen would be on nature's version, we've inserted an onboard nanocomputer—or at least a molecular hard drive for storing information. Each one is capable of sending signals back and forth, enabling us to network entire legions of SPIDERS on the battlefield."

Becton bent down to the girl and whispered a series of statements in her ear. Raphael missed what was said, his eyes were so fixated on the computer-generated image. Becton touched another key and the screen refreshed itself.

"What you're looking at now is the backbone of our future Air Force. We call them MFIs—Micro-mechanical Flying Insects. We call this particular design a LOCUSTS because of its operational behavior on the battlefield. Like a real locust, a single MFI is harmless, but a whole group of them can be devastating. MFIs and SPIDERS will operate in blanket waves in order to exact optimum dominion over a territory. Both devices operate in a technological category called swarm robotics."

Again, Becton put the computer-generated image into motion on the screen. Raphael stood mesmerized. Becton pointed at the interior window.

"Across the hall, software engineers are working double shifts to improve artificial intelligence programs that will speed up this entire design process. By the time the assembler breakthrough occurs, we'll be able to use AI systems to improve upon these designs. Within a couple of weeks of the breakthrough, we'll have LOCUSTS and SPIDERS of such refined quality they'll dwarf the ability of these prototypes by several orders of magnitude."

Raphael rubbed his chin with the palm of his left hand, his elbow nestled in his right hand. He let out a muted laugh and shook his head before directing his gaze at Becton.

"And when that day comes, what capability will we be lacking?" he asked.

Becton took a few seconds to reflect on the question.

"Terrorists have weaponized anthrax. But within hours of the assembler breakthrough, United Europe will construct a force like weaponized rain, or better yet, weaponized oxygen. It will fall on our enemies from high above. Spring forth from the ground under their feet like gushing wells. We'll surround them from every direction, and there will be no escape. All the combined armies of human history would be defenseless against this force."

CHAPTER 4:

Rider With A Bow

"Say to those who are afraid, 'Be strong, and do not fear, for your God is coming to destroy your enemies. He is coming to save you.' And when he comes, he will open the eyes of the blind and unstop the ears of the deaf. The lame will leap like a deer, and those who cannot speak will shout and sing!"

—**Isaiah**
Isaiah 35:4–6

Numerous rows of hardcover books lined a wooden display behind United Europe's president, while cameras snapped and flashed. A lone microphone stood in front of the shelves, just inches above the pack of hungry journalists. Raphael scanned over their faces. Could they even vaguely imagine what he had to deal with or what he knew? Did they have any idea how difficult it was to juggle so many potential fuses in the international arena, while awaiting the assembler breakthrough? Could they even fathom something as monumental as the assembler breakthrough? Regardless, he alone shouldered the responsibility of bringing the world together.

He placed his hand on the edge of the microphone as a signal that he was prepared to speak. The frenzy of media grew quiet and pulled out their recorders and notepads, hanging on his every word.

"I've written this book as a way of accentuating the common ground shared by the world's three largest monotheistic religions. It is my hope that *Blood Brothers* will lead Christians, Jews, and Muslims to unite on behalf of their common ancestor Abraham as well as their common home in the world of today."

The journalists bombarded him with tough questions.

"Don't you think this will only serve to anger the Arab street?"

He looked over their faces. Didn't they understand? He had to do what was right, and he spoke with a determined voice.

"My goal is not to divide people, but to unite them."

*   *   *   *

The day was overcast with dark clouds stretching over the horizon. In the open courtyard in front of the Wailing Wall, people from all over the globe gathered to worship God. Fingers brushed over the stone ediface and lips kissed at the dust and mortar. Prayers rose to the heavens while tears fell to the earth. It was the Sabbath, and Garrison walked across the Temple Mount and came to rest in front of the wall.

He wore brown robes that draped over his arms and legs like curtains. He carried only one possession—a single copy of the Bible, which he gripped tightly under his left arm. Several people instantly recognized him and rushed forward to hear what he had to say. He let them gather around before raising his voice to speak.

"The assembler breakthrough is the first seal of the Book of Revelation, and the white horse will soon follow!"

Without the aid of any sound equipment, his voice thundered through the courtyard with relative ease. The ears of those in prayer lifted up, and the large crowd around him grew larger. He made additional prophecies and delivered his pronouncements with a confident sense of authority that left many in the crowd uneasy. They confronted him.

"Who are you to make such claims? This is blasphemy!"

"If these things do not come to pass," he said. "Then you know they are of my own words. But when they do come to pass, then you will know that my words are not my own, but a message from God to his people."

He raised his right arm and pointed into the sky. The clouds drifted apart so that a number of streaking rays of light shined down from the heavens.

"God is soon returning to his people, and so it will be that when he returns, the earth will be like it was in the days of Noah. For although they were warned, the people continued to throw parties and weddings and banquets right up until the time Noah entered his boat. They did not realize what was going to happen until the Flood came and swept them all away. That is the way it will be on the last day."

He continued to wave his finger through the air as he spoke.

"Yet up until the last moment of their lives, people will maintain faith in their ability to put the earth back together—to overcome the horrors of their own making. They will fail. For it is this generation the Lord spoke of when he said, 'they are deeply guilty, for their power is their own god!'"

His words caused a great stir and a loud buzz of voices in the courtyard as the people tried to figure out what he was saying.

"What's the assembler breakthrough?"

"What does he mean that we will try to put the earth back together?"

They considered him a madman, but a number of their neighbors considered him a prophet, so they decided to test him.

"Brother Garrison," they said. "You have professed in the past that the only path to heaven is through Jesus Christ. If this is true, then we must believe that many good men are turned away from heaven. For Ghandi was a Hindu, yet the entire world acknowledges his greatness. Is Ghandi in hell?"

They crossed their arms and waited for his answer. Garrison smiled at their question, then he looked into the eyes of his audience and told them the truth.

"There are many paths to heaven, but all must pass through God's Son. For it is the blood of Jesus Christ that cleanses the world of sin. So here is the answer to your question: This is what the Sovereign Lord says, 'A tree is identified by its fruit. A good tree will bear good fruit; A bad tree will bear bad fruit. For whatever is in your heart determines what you say, and on the day of judgement, all must give an account of every idle word they speak!'"

The men who asked the question huddled together and asked themselves, "Who is this man that he believes he speaks on behalf of God?" And they left the courtyard, but their neighbors in the crowd stayed and listened to what Garrison had to say.

"Don't let the false prophet lead you to place your faith in the things of this world," he said. "For all the heavens and the earth will pass away, and everything here before you for as far as your eyes can see will be destroyed, but the word of God will be with you forever."

He warned them to be alert because the coming days would be a time of great testing for all humanity, but those who endure the coming days will be blessed doubly in the eyes of God.

"Throughout history, Satan has never possessed the true power to create, only the ability to manipulate what God has created already. Don't let the devil fool you!"

*   *   *   *

Muhammad had been driving all morning when his car came to a stop in the parking lot of the Al-Saahib Mosque in Reston, Virginia. He shifted into park and studied the people as they walked in and out. Reaching underneath the passenger side seat, he pulled out a brown envelope, then walked into the building.

Inside, the mosque resembled any other. Men on their knees covered the floors like carpet, and demarcations on the walls pointed them in the proper direction of Mecca. A man with a jet-black mustache leaned against one of the far walls of the front hallway. When he saw Muhammad, he motioned for another man to come join him. Muhammad approached and the three of them formed a huddle in the hallway. The newest man introduced himself. Motioning to the man with the jet-black mustache, he spoke to Muhammad in broken English.

"Fareed tells me you have a ticket to Tehran?"

Muhammad nodded.

"Yes, I bought it, then some things came up at work. Now I am unable to use it."

The man acted very interested.

"How much?"

"For a Muslim brother, I'll give you a discount. Fifty cents on the dollar."

The man's eyes lit up.

"I'll take it."

Muhammad expected as much.

"Just one thing. You'll have to use my passport, but I know I can trust you as a brother. Here is an envelope with my address. Promise to mail it back to me once you get to Tehran, and I will sell you the ticket," Muhammad said.

The man took the envelope and the ticket and agreed to mail back the passport. After paying Muhammad with cash, he bolted for the door, leaving Muhammad and Fareed alone in the hallway. Muhammad's voice fell to a whisper.

"How is the DC project coming?" he asked.

Fareed nodded.

"As well as expected. Men like the one you just encountered are abundant. It should unravel perfectly."

"I expect nothing but perfection, so it better," Muhammad said.

He pulled the brown envelope from his jacket and handed it to Fareed. Opening one end, Fareed peered in and nodded his approval.

"I'm impressed," he said.

Muhammad didn't respond directly.

"I am not concerned with impressions. That should be more than enough to see the DC project through to conclusion. I'll contact you in two days," he said.

Fareed relayed his understanding, and Muhammad's footsteps hammered down on the black asphalt as he left the mosque and was swallowed whole by the impending darkness.

*   *   *   *

The weight of the world bore down on Raphael as he pushed open the door to his office and walked in. Noise from the television filled the room, and Jean waited for him. He wore a look of extreme disapproval, while the television parlayed image after image of the broken Dome of the Rock minaret topping a heap of rubble.

"What the hell were you thinking?" Jean said.

Not in the mood for criticism, Raphael's tone turned angry.

"You're going to lay the blame for this at my feet?"

Jean folded his arms and returned Raphael's angry stare.

"Yes. They found copies of *Blood Brothers* in the apartment of this man Daniel Heron, leader of the group. They call themselves the Temple Seven, and one of the primary targets of their hatred is your heretical writings."

Raphael let the news sink in. He refrained from speaking further. Jean filled in the void of the conversation.

"You're a great leader," he said. "But you've got to forget this noble idealism. These religious fanatics can't be dealt with on an intellectual level. They're theological fascists worse than the Nazis, and that's saying a lot. The world defeated Hitler with overwhelming force. The day you realize overwhelming force is the way to stop these fanatics is the day the world will live in true peace."

CHAPTER 5:

Enemies Of God

"True, many nations have gathered together against you, calling for your blood, eager to gloat over your destruction. But they do not know the Lord's thoughts or understand his plan. These nations don't know that he is gathering them together to be beaten and trampled like bundles of grain on a threshing floor."

—Micah
Micah 4:11–12

Gravel scattered underneath his shoes as Muhammad stepped into the new Chevy Blazer and drove toward his apartment building. The middle row of seats had been removed, and a blanket covered the cargo placed in the vacant cavity.

As he pulled into the building's parking lot, Fahd and Ali waited to meet him. Muhammad parked the Blazer and got out. Handing the keys to Fahd, he placed his hand on the hood.

"Remember, park as close to the corner of Wall and Broad as you can. Wait for me there. If I don't show up by eleven-thirty, proceed without me.

The government will have NEST teams all over the place, so don't deviate from the route I gave you."

They each shook hands and traded brotherly hugs. Fahd and Ali climbed into the Blazer and drove off, headed toward Manhattan. They wanted to arrive early, before the police cordoned off the roads around Times Square.

Back at the apartment complex, Muhammad packed his bag and called a taxi. While his friends fought the traffic in the Lincoln Tunnel, he drove to JFK and nestled into a first-class seat bound for Paris.

*   *   *   *

The lawn was a lush green, the blades of grass perfectly trimmed and sharp like unsheathed swords preparing for battle. The feet of Jiang Yafei strolled across the sculpted surface until they came to rest in front of Muhammad Jumma Marri. The Eiffel Tower dominated the skyline, and Muhammad was dressed in his usual designer clothes, the clothes he wore when being himself and not some alternate identity. He stood erect, his eyes hidden behind the gray lenses of his sunglasses.

Jiang was alone as always, and he carried a black briefcase in his right hand. Without speaking, the two men strolled together to a secluded spot underneath a nearby tree. Jiang tossed the briefcase on top of a trashcan and popped the locks. He opened it just enough for Muhammad to run his hand through and check it. A nod of his head acknowledged approval of the transaction, and Jiang closed the briefcase and handed it over to his accomplice.

"So where are you staying?" Jiang asked.

Muhammad scanned the landscape as he responded.

"Waldorf Madeleine."

Jiang smiled, his hands jingling in the pockets of his beige khakis. He never once made eye contact.

"You'll have to visit Salvador Farrago and Gucci. Buy yourself some special treats for a job well done."

Muhammad reacted favorably to the suggestion.

"What a marvelous idea. I might just have to do that."

And with his reply, Muhammad casually walked away. Jiang gazed at the highly skilled laborer as he blended into the crowded streets and disappeared into its ocean of people. Really that's all the man was—highly skilled labor. And if everything went according to plan, Jiang would no longer have a need for highly skilled laborers. He scoffed at the idea of wasting anymore thought on the man. His parting words were only a sarcastic whisper.

"Happy New Year's," he said.

*   *   *   *

The Chevy Blazer circled the street several times before a space opened a block and a half from the corner of Wall and Broad. Fahd Al-Shehhi pulled into the spot headfirst, bringing the vehicle parallel to the curb, then he stabbed at the emergency brake and threw it into park. He released a deep breath and pulled his hands off the wheel. Ali sat in the passenger seat.

"Where are we meeting Yousef?" he asked.

Fahd turned his head to face his friend.

"The corner."

Grabbing the door handle, he sprung the door open and stepped out into the street. The sound of Ali's door slamming shut left a blunt echo in his ear. Fahd ran his hand over the hood of the Blazer as he walked around it and hopped onto the sidewalk. Hands in their pockets, the two of them walked in silence to the corner and stopped to wait. Ali pulled out a cigarette and lit it up as Fahd nervously traced over the faces walking through the intersecting streets.

"Hey guys. Over here!"

A voice yelled out from several yards away, and the clacking of shoes on concrete followed the call. Fahd spun around in anticipation, but Yousef wasn't there. Just a suit, a designer suit, and the irritating bellow of that mouth that never knew when to close.

"What are you two doing out here? Come to join the party?"

Ali continued to blow smoke from his mouth, completely ignoring the man. Fahd studied this man for whom he harbored the utmost contempt. Hector Salzburg invaded their space and his mouth gushed forward as usual.

"We're meeting a friend," Fahd said.

An instant light flared up in Salzburg's eye.

"Is it your friend Yousef? How's his case working out? You tell him to give me a call. Worst case scenario, I can extend his stay four years."

"It's someone else. What are you doing here?"

Salzburg pointed up at the tall building behind them.

"That's my office. Up there on the top floor. Ain't America great?"

"You're working on New Year's Eve?"

Salzburg punched Fahd in the arm as if they were long lost buddies.

"Every night, friend. Every night. I never sleep. This is my life."

Fahd wrinkled the toes in his shoes and twitched his lips waiting for the man to leave his presence. After a few more minutes of having Ali blow smoke in his face, Salzburg finally excused himself and climbed upstairs to his office. Fahd turned his attention back to the streets, jingling change in his pocket, and wondering how much longer Yousef would take.

*   *   *   *

Henri Claudel strolled down the ancient side street, his feet brushing along its cobblestone surface. Slipping in between two tall apartment buildings, he leaned over his shoulder to make sure he was alone. No one was following, and reaching the end of the dim alleyway, he stopped in its far corner and waited. Steam condensed in the air, filtering from the sewers beneath the street. The alley itself was filled with garbage and refuse.

Jiang appeared from the shadows and walked toward him. The man's sudden appearance made Claudel flinch.

"Jesus, man. You caught me off guard. I thought this place was empty," he said.

Jiang now stood right in front of his face.

"And I thought scientists were supposed to be practitioners of acute observation," Jiang said.

His tone was indignant, and Claudel did not take pleasure in the criticism.

"I was good enough to get this far. Was I not?"

Jiang didn't respond, but only nudged his own head in half-hearted acknowledgement. Claudel reached in his pocket and pulled out a CD. He handed it over to Jiang, while taking off his watch.

"Just pop that in any hard-drive. It's a software program I drummed up. Sort of an 'Assembler-Setup Program'."

Claudel amused himself with his own comment, while Jiang waited for the rest.

"And the device?" he asked.

Claudel pointed to the face of his Time-X watch.

"It's inside. Detachable face with a USB on the back."

He took it apart to demonstrate, then reassembled the parts and handed it over to Jiang who was enamored by the man's handiwork.

"That's impressive."

Claudel held his chin up high.

"Thank you."

"Just one thing," Jiang asked. "Why did you do it?"

An arrogant expression appeared on the Frenchman's face as he began to drone on about his grand utopian dreams and the immorality of a unilateral nanotechnic power.

"Well, I first thought about the inadequate balance of power between the United States and Russia in post-World War…"

Jiang pulled out a .35 and lodged two bullets in Claudel's temple.

"I don't care why you did it idiot."

And with those words, Jiang gave Henri Claudel's body a swift kick to the groin. He replaced the .35 in his belt and left Claudel's body lying in the back alley in a heap of trash.

*   *   *   *

Antonio Porfiri wore the clothes of a common tourist and snapped pictures of the Church of Santa Susanna. President Vicente and his wife were guests at the Bernini Bristol just a few blocks away, and Rome crawled with double its normal New Year's Eve security. Antonio had snapped a third picture in as many minutes when his instruments started to move. Calmly, he lowered his camera, turned to face the streets, and scanned the crowd from behind his dark sunglasses. Nothing out of the ordinary as far as he could see, but that in and of itself meant nothing. Observing the instruments closely, he meandered his way through the crowd of tourists and stepped off the curb into the street. The signal only grew stronger.

Without hesitation, he radioed his team.

"NEST Team 5, I have a strong signal in my area. Probable WMD."

Within two minutes, three additional members of the team had arrived. Crossing the street, all of their instruments went haywire. Frantically, they spread out along the street, trying not to raise suspicion. Finally, one of the members spotted the problem. She radioed the other three, and they all converged at once around the vehicle.

It was a metallic green Ford Explorer parked alongside the curb. Two men sat in the driver and passenger side seats. With the large crowd buzzing around them, they had little time to notice the four agents closing in. The two were sharing a laugh when a .35 was thrust in the face of the driver.

"Raise your hands high and place them in back of your head," the voice said.

The voice was loud and forceful, but ineffective. The driver lunged for something between the seats. Without hesitation, the agent pumped multiple rounds into both men's temples. Instantly, the crowded street erupted with screams as people clamored to get away from the shots. The blood of the men trickled down the passenger side window as the other three agents climbed into the vehicle. The back seat of the Explorer concealed a large cargo load covered with a sheet. Antonio reached inside and folded it back with his hand.

"Jesus Christ," he said.

Immediately, he radioed for backup.

"There's a package in the city. I repeat. There's a package in the city."

For a moment, his mind slowed to a halt and went vacant as he stared at the silver contraption. It was at least a ten-kiloton nuclear device, one of the oft-referenced Soviet "suitcase" bombs that weren't really the size of suitcases, but rather small refrigerators. He hoped this was the only one, that the president would be able to escape if the facts proved otherwise.

*   *   *   *

Jiang rested comfortably in the leather-covered seat with his laptop humming as the plane drifted through the air toward Switzerland. He had chartered a plane months in advance so he wouldn't have to run the risk of being stuck in de Gaulle with a cancelled flight or any other unforeseen circumstance. Tonight was not a night he wished to watch the fireworks in Paris. He thought about Muhammad and the irony of his visit to the beautiful city. He hoped the man was enjoying his last night there.

On the screen of his Apple powerbook, Jiang pulled up a map of the world as he sipped on a glass of Bourbon. As far as he knew, everything had fallen into place. The operation was compartmentalized and all the witnesses except himself would meet with an unfortunate demise within the hour. He looked over the blots in America, Europe, and Israel. All he could do was take another measured sip of his drink and smile.

China would soon be restored to its rightful glory. He glimpsed at his watch. It was 11:30pm in Rome. Only a half-hour left to go, and the power of god—an assembler—was attached to his left arm. He wished his father had lived to see this moment of triumph. Within a couple of days at the very least, he would return to Beijing in glorious victory. Which reminded him of one additional matter now that he had accomplished his mission.

He double-clicked on the world map and pulled up a shipping schedule. The arrival time was listed in Eastern Standard Time. He added and subtracted to make sure it was still in port. Arrived just a little under three hours ago he figured. Returning to the map, he added the Port of Charleston in South Carolina to his list of cities on the Jiang Yafei world tour. Within a few hours, it too would be gone, and along with it, all world trade.

It would have been on his original list of targets, but if Claudel hadn't have come through, the hit on Charleston would've hurt the People's Republic almost as much as the West. Now, with an assembler in hand, China would no longer have a need for imports and exports. Taking out Charleston would just be the icing on the cake in terms of crippling western power. By the end of the week, China would be the undisputed ruling power of the world. For the interim, it would be pure entertainment to watch the Western nations fall in agony.

CHAPTER 6:

Attack To End All Other Attacks

"Rejoice, O heavens! And you who live in the heavens, rejoice! But terror will come on the earth and the sea. For the Devil has come down to you in great anger, and he knows that he has little time."

—John
Revelation 12:12

Firmly, Poyner held onto Raphael's arm out of support as Offen Gilder briefed them of the situation in the lobby of the Bernini Bristol.

"Just walk out to the limousine casually. Take some time to wave and greet people. We don't want to cause a riot."

The words hit Raphael with the weight of the world. First, Pakistan and India—now, Rome facing a nuclear assault. But Gilder assured him they had the bomb in their possession. Fleeing the city was only a precaution, and they had no reason to expect a wider conspiracy. Raphael squeezed Poyner's arm.

"I love you," he said.

She smiled and kissed him on the forehead. Then, she wrapped her arm in his, and they walked out of the hotel.

A wide sidewalk stretched from the front door of the lobby to the edge of the curb where their limousine waited. On either side of the walkway, a line of ropes and the presidential guard pushed back an anxious crowd. Smiling faces waved at the couple as they paused before entering the limousine. Cameras flashed and supporters screamed out. Raphael shook a few hands and signed several autographs.

As he rejoined his arm in Poyner's, a man from the crowd lunged forward and pulled out a weapon. Within a brief second, a member of the presidential guard jumped on Raphael's back and pushed him to the ground. As the man's gun fired, three bullets shot forward, two of them striking Poyner and the third disappearing into the crowd. Before the final shot unloaded, a member of the presidential guard threw Raphael into the back of the limousine, and it squealed away at a high rate of speed.

Raphael picked himself up from the floor of the vehicle and grabbed for the door, but the agent wrestled him back down.

"Poyner! My god, they hit Poyner!"

Raphael clawed his way up the back of the seat and pounded on the rear windshield, but it was useless. The hotel's image dwindled in the distance, and Raphael no longer remained in control.

*   *   *   *

"What is this place? I demand to know where I am!"

Visibly agitated, Jean shook off the uniformed men surrounding him. He lurched forward to strike one of them when a voice called out.

"You can release him. I'll take care of it."

The men scattered like marbles on a ceramic floor, and Jean stood by himself, appearing totally lost. He studied the man in front of him from head to toe.

"Becton," he said. "What are you doing here?"

Becton walked over to Jean's side.

"I'm in charge of this facility."

Jean angled his head in every imaginable direction as Becton led him down the hallway of the monstrous complex.

"What facility? What is this? Why was I brought here?"

"This is Assembly Hall, and you were brought here because you're the highest ranking member of the Cabinet Ministry, and there's been a security breach concerning the president."

Jean stopped in the hallway, his eyes bulging wide.

"What breach? What happened?"

"Nothing yet," Becton said. "But a potential nuclear event was averted in Rome less than an hour ago. The president is being evacuated as we speak."

Jean began walking once again.

"So what is this facility's function, and why has my knowledge of its existence been suppressed?"

"That's not of your concern," Becton said. "And you lack proper clearance."

"Lack proper clearance? I'm the head of European Intelligence!"

Becton acted unconcerned. Jean continued to argue and demand answers as Becton brought him to a pair of double doors with solid brass handles.

Grabbing a handle, he flung the doors open. Jean felt his voice abandon him as he took in the sight. Decadent in its size, hundreds of lighted screens acted as portals to destinations all over the world, and hundreds of officials manned the massive command center.

The mood of its occupants soon diverted Jean's interest in the room. He now noticed its occupants frantically racing in every direction, panic enveloping every face. Becton ran over to one of the officials and left Jean alone in the back of the room. The worried faces rushing through the aisles left him with a nervous feeling. Reclining in a chair, he listened to the fragmented conversations.

The rumors he heard frightened him, and Jean picked at his fingernails, swaying back and forth in his chair. One of the televisions stayed permanently tuned to CNN and the pictures arrived of hazy landscapes. Their images conveyed nothing but smoke and blackness with scattered points of light.

Underneath, the caption read: "Live—Paris, France". A commentator's voice grew increasingly louder as it flooded the chamber. Everyone in the room froze as they listened.

"...Paris, when six minutes earlier, all outbound communications were lost. Witnesses claim an explosion ripped through the city, heard as far as fifty miles away in Compiegne. Unconfirmed reports are rolling in describing similar events in London and Frankfurt..."

Jean scanned the wall of images. Satellite footage of the three cities dominated the largest screens. Massive plumes of smoke smudged the pictures like inkblots from a broken fountain pen. He tried to remain calm and poised. His instincts told him to do something, anything. He rushed over to Becton's side.

"What the hell is going on?"

"Your guess is as good as mine," Becton said.

Jean's face turned red.

"Damn it, Becton. I know you know, and I demand to know what's going on."

Becton looked directly into the man's face.

"I take orders only from the president, and as long as he's alive, I answer to no one but him."

Jean engaged him with an angry stare, but the voice of the commentator diverted his attention.

"*...And we have breaking news. CNN will now cut live to the White House Press Room where President Burton's Press Secretary is poised to deliver a statement on the events in Europe...*"

The broadcast image cut from Paris to Washington, with the face of the Press Secretary centered on the screen. He stood at the podium with a raised hand as the White House Press Corps screamed out questions and shoved microphones in his face. The Press Secretary shouted back, trying to quiet them, his face noticeably pale. When they finally quieted, he opened his mouth to speak.

"*First off, let me say the president is safely...*"

The feed went dead, cutting him off in mid-sentence. Snow battered the screen for several seconds, before the anchor cut back in with his apologies for the technical difficulties. But technical difficulties didn't end the White House feed. Detonation of a nuclear bomb did. Jean watched it explode in real-time from a satellite image broadcast on the larger screen next to the CNN feed. It hosted a map of the entire globe with geographic markers denoting all the important locations. The piercing white pulse arrived in a quick burst of light, then vanished. Almost simultaneously, two additional white dots flashed over the screen. One in New York City and the other in Charleston, South Carolina.

*   *   *   *

Hidden in a United Europe compound in the eastern mountains of Switzerland, Raphael fumed while his advisors attempted to gather up-to-date information.

"I will not leave until I speak to my wife," he said.

Gilder handed him a mobile phone.

"It's the hospital," he said.

Raphael looked down at it suspiciously, then lifted the phone to his head. He demanded to speak to his wife, then fell completely silent. Gilder and a few of the other advisors studied the president's face as he listened. His hands fell to his side in a look of disbelief. His mouth hung wide open, his eyes frozen, and he took a few stumbling steps toward the wall. Gilder rushed forward to brace him.

"Mr. President, what is it?"

Raphael returned nothing but silence. Just short of the wall, his knees buckled, and he collapsed to the floor. He buried his head in his hands and wept. His fists clenched together, and he made erratic sweeps of the air with his arms. His advisors could only watch. Paralyzed, they were at a loss for words, wondering if anything they could say or do would make a difference. They just stood aloof like cold statues and watched as their president lay on the floor.

Gilder stepped forward, kneeling next to Raphael. He rested his arm on the president's shoulder and gently whispered in his ear.

"Mr. President, perhaps it would be best to temporarily transfer your powers and authority to someone else. At least until the proper time for mourning has passed."

Raphael rose to his feet and lashed out with his tongue. His elbow angling downward like a jagged spear, he held his angry fist before his eyes as though it were Yorick's skull.

"No! Now is the time when I'm needed most, and I will not let my people down. These men will pay. As surely as I'm alive, I'll kill every last one of them."

PART V

▼

The Assembler Breakthrough

"Then locusts came from the smoke and descended upon the earth, and they were given power to sting like scorpions. They were told not to hurt the grass or plants or trees but to attack all the people who did not have the seal of God on their foreheads."

—John
Revelation 9:3–4

CHAPTER 1:

Leading Forces

"I saw that one of the heads of the beast seemed wounded beyond recovery—but the fatal wound was healed! All the world marveled at this miracle and followed the beast in awe. They worshiped the dragon for giving the beast such power, and they worshiped the beast. 'Is there anyone as great as the beast?' they exclaimed. 'Who is able to make war against him?'"

—John
Revelation 13:3–4

On an ordinary evening, Dr. Jeremiah Dolev would walk out the door of Assaf Harofeh Medical Center and spend the evening with his family. But this night was different from the others. Large explosions in Paris, Frankfurt, and London cut off all communications with everyone in the center of those cities. Minutes afterward, grim pictures filtered over the television. They were like nothing he had ever seen before. The smoke still hovered in a cloud high above every one of the cities, masking the true extent of the damage as he watched President Burton's press secretary step out and issue a statement to the White House Press Corps. Around the same time the feed went dead, a one-kiloton nuclear device detonated in Tel Aviv. The blast leveled large sections of the city, and Dr. Dolev stayed in the emergency room to care for the victims sure to come pouring in.

After a quick call home, he walked into the trauma ward and waited. He didn't have to wait long. Patients with third degree burns, shrapnel wounds, and respiratory problems swamped the hospital. The first hour was so overwhelming that the IDF and Tel Aviv Police Department turned people away. In the first minutes, Dr. Dolev ran across Richie Weismann.

Only nine years old, Richie and his parents were on their way to Tel Aviv when they caught the brunt of the fallout. Cuts and slashes covered the boy's body as he lay on the foldout bed. He had been complaining of respiratory problems and Dr. Dolev was tasked with checking him for radiation poisoning.

"So I hear you're not feeling well, Richie. Could you describe your symptoms?"

The young boy's hands shook, and his glowing forehead was hot to the touch. His mother sat by his side with lots of water.

"My head really hurts bad, and my body aches all over. I feel really tired, but I don't want to go to sleep. I'm starting to feel like I want to throw up."

Dr. Dolev looked into the boy's ears and checked his pulse. On the boy's chest, a small aberration caught his attention. He turned to the boy's mother.

"Has Richie ever had the chicken pox?"

"Yes, he had them last year. Why? What is it?"

"Just wondering. It's probably a routine virus, but I'd like to run some tests to make sure. Given the circumstances, it could be radiation poisoning, so I'd like to make sure."

He assured her the hospital had a decent size stockpile of Potassium Iodide if it was indeed radiation related. As he prepared to draw blood from Richie, a piercing fear struck deep inside his stomach, but he didn't relay one bit of it to Richie or his mother. Placing the syringe on the table next to Richie's bed, Dr. Dolev put on a pair of rubber gloves, doubling up on them. With great care, he withdrew a vile of blood and taped a bandage onto the boy's arm. With the specimen in hand, he turned to Richie's mother.

"It'll be just one minute, and then we'll know for sure."

She nodded her head and held her son's hand. Dr. Dolev carried the vile of blood into the adjacent room and sat down in front of a large semi-circular desk. A Compaq computer rested on top, flanked by a brand-new NanoChip Molecular Biology Workstation. Grabbing a syringe, he withdrew a few droplets of Richie's blood from the vile and injected them onto the surface of a microarray. The microarray was encased in a plastic cartridge the doctor then plugged into the workstation. With a click of the mouse, an electric charge ran through it, and the hybridization process aligned Richie's blood on the surface with that of the pre-printed pattern.

On the screen before him, the results filtered back. Variations in the genetic code of Richie's blood matched that indicative of smallpox. Dr. Dolev's heart sank. As he scrolled through the data, it got worse. What Ricky had was some sort of mutation of the smallpox virus. The database didn't have a record of it. As it became apparent how much worse the situation was, Dr. Dolev's eyes reverted back to Richie in the adjacent room. The boy did not look well.

His mother held a plastic vomit tray underneath his chin because his nausea had gotten worse. A tear sprung forth from Dr. Dolev's eye as he watched, not just for Richie, but for everyone in Israel. As it did, Richie's mother let out a piercing scream. Richie threw up, and blood splattered everywhere.

*   *   *   *

The president's plane had landed in Geneva fifteen minutes earlier. His motorcade met him at the landing strip, anxious to whisk him off to the rock solid safety of Assembly Hall. Speeding into the mountains, it crossed the border into France. RAF fighter pilots practiced figure eights overhead, and the vehicles were armed for engagement. The threat of additional attacks remained imminent, and every precaution was taken. The president's limousine itself was empty, but two cars back, he sat inside a heavily armored SUV. On either side of him, members of the presidential guard cradled assault rifles in their hands, their eyes directed outside the vehicle. Offen Gilder sat directly across from Raphael, along with a top aide and two additional presidential guards.

The tire treads hugged the road, smooth and silent, and Raphael's mind raced in ten different directions at once. Gilder held his cell phone tight against his head and plugged his open ear with the other hand.

"Tell me again," Raphael said.

Gilder lifted his eyes to meet the president's.

"Six nuclear devices detonated inside the United States and United Europe. London, Paris, Frankfurt, New York City, DC, and Charleston. All followed minutes later by a seventh in Tel Aviv."

"So what are we dealing with?"

"Burton's dead. And most of Congress. Most of the agencies and bureaucracies running the federal government of the United States were wiped out."

"Christ."

The initial loss of Burton and the US leadership hurt, but the prospective aftershocks were far more frightening. Wall Street was gone, and with it, the headquarters and leadership of most of the world's leading financial institutions. The London Exchange and the Frankfurt markets—gone. The Port of Charleston, the hub of international trade, decimated.

"How long before Charleston can reopen?"

"Months, maybe years...Every port in the world is closed."

Insurance losses calculated in the incomprehensible sum of the multiple trillions. Airlines all over the world grounded indefinitely. Businessmen scattered across the globe, stranded in airports. Embassies closed, roads jammed with traffic, and mass exodus from the world's major cities.

The attacks were certain to cause a chain reaction of apocalyptic anarchy. Bankruptcies and layoffs. Inflation. Rampant shortages. And the crippling of tourism, along with the halt on imports and exports, would lead to millions of deaths in the third world. Surplus food supplies would run out and the starvation of hundreds of millions would begin. The remaining columns of financial stability would collapse as businesses and individuals defaulted on loans.

Gilder's arm fell limp in his lap, and he folded his cell phone shut. His face was frozen in stone like a Pompeii citizen overrun and petrified by a river of lava.

"What is it?"

Gilder's eyes shuffled in their sockets, relaying the flurry of thoughts that plagued his mind.

"We're getting reports from the blast sights—"

He stopped in mid-sentence. Raphael prodded him.

"What about them?"

"The hospitals have been overrun by patients spitting up blood."

Raphael sank back in his seat as if he knew precisely what was happening. Even the presidential guard, usually intent and focused on their jobs, averted their eyes upon hearing the news.

"What do they think?"

"Blackpox."

Raphael hung his head and pulled his hair back from his face. Gilder kept going.

"All seven areas have been cordoned off at the perimeter, quarantined under armed force."

"Fatality rate?"

"Ninety to ninety-five percent...Communicability is close to a hundred."

Raphael plopped his hands down on his knees and drew in a deep, prolonged breath.

"It gets worse," Gilder said.

"Worse? How could it get worse?"

"China's gathering troops for an invasion of Taiwan and possibly India. North Korea is amassing a wall of soldiers at the thirty-eighth parallel, and the Arab nations are gathering for an attack on Israel. Already, the Palestinians have cornered three IDF divisions in the West Bank."

"What the hell for? At this rate, the whole world will be dead by the end of the week."

It seemed that, in a single moment, all of Western civilization crumbled and faded into ruin. The culmination of centuries and millennia of culture, knowledge, and contribution to the world drying up to disappear forever, condemned to fall away into the shadows of a new Dark Age.

*　　*　　*　　*

"Everything will be fine."

The man's voice dripped over the woman with the same comfort of the soothing damp rag he held in his hand. His brown robe flowed down to the floor, covering his feet and creating the illusion he hovered high above it, exempt from the known laws of the universe. The cloak had a hood that veiled his face in darkness and only the reflected light dancing on his bare hand was evidence of his being human at all. The soft waves of brown material trickled down his arms, ending where his wrists began. As if to emit a healing energy, his soft hands massaged her face and shoulders with delicate precision.

The woman mustered every ounce of energy possible to lift her neck and view the room around her, but she only caught a fleeting glimpse. Her face itched from a mixture of sweat and cold water, and the damp bed sheets irritated her skin as she tried to move.

"Save your strength," the voice said. "You're just outside Tel Aviv. You're very sick, but God is with you."

Inside, her heart raced forward at a torrid pace. She made an effort to speak, but fatigue wrapped its chains tight around her chest. All that came out was a heaving breath, her lungs frantically rising with each passing gasp. The man reached down and took hold of her hand.

Only a dim bronze light filtered through the room, but a spotlight seemed to sparkle on this one hand. Gurney after gurney packed the room from one wall to the next, and the quiet air paralyzed its occupants. Other than Garrison, only a lone Rabbi dared to be in the presence of the deathly ill. From the far doorway, Dr. Dolev entered the room and walked toward the woman's bed. The sharp echo of his footsteps flooded the lifeless vault as he stopped next to her. Granting her a cursory glance, he directed his attention to the man in the brown robe.

"I saw you maneuver around the IDF."

The hood nodded in acknowledgement.

"I don't think they anticipated having to keep people out," Dr. Dolev said.

The brown robe remained silent, guiding a wet sponge over the woman's arms and face. Dr. Dolev tried again.

"Aren't you afraid to come here?"

"And why are you here?" the hood asked.

"Not by choice. I was the first doctor on the scene. So far, my body has fought it off."

The robed man cradled the woman's hand in his.

"I'm not the only one," he said. "The kingdom of God is made for such people."

He pointed across the room to the Rabbi standing over several ill people, then he fanned his free hand around the room.

"Everyone of these people is no less precious than God in the flesh. To turn your back on a single one, is to turn your back on God. This is what the Lord meant when he said, 'whatsoever you do to the least of those among you, you do to me'."

Dr. Dolev studied the vague outlines beneath the hood.

"I know who you are," he said. "You're the one from the Temple Wall. Some say you're the prophet Elijah."

The man shook his head and pealed back his hood. A light fell over his face even though the room remained dim.

"I'm not a prophet. I'm a man," he said.

Dr. Dolev held out his hand and gave his name. The hooded man grabbed it and introduced himself.

"Garrison Nance," he said.

The doctor returned his attention to the woman.

"If God is with you Garrison Nance, then why can't he save this woman?"

Garrison brushed his hand across her forehead and pushed her hair out of her eyes.

"Because God has already saved her. She will be with him soon, and it will be to her benefit not to be here as a witness to the terrible things to come."

"The terrible things to come? What could be worse than this?"

Garrison's eyes didn't blink as he stared back at the doctor, a lifeless frown drooping over his face.

"You will soon see."

*　　*　　*　　*

The motorcade pulled into the mountain compound, and Raphael made note of the sign as they drove underneath. "Welcome to Assembly Hall," it read. The massive facility was a perfect bunker from which to manage the crisis. It boasted independent power and water supplies, a clean air filtration system, and the communications infrastructure by which the government could continue to operate. Passing numerous checkpoints and penetrating deep within the mountain, the procession came to a final stop. Attendants ushered him into the compound. Several cabinet members waited to greet him.

"Let's get down to business," he said. "What do we know about this mystery plague?"

One of his cabinet ministers stepped forward.

"Agents in the Agriculture Ministry obtained a sample and isolated a virus. It's a genetically modified version of smallpox with a strain of Ebola spliced into its nucleus."

"What can we do about it?" Raphael asked.

The cabinet minister hesitated as though he wished not to respond.

"Apart from a full quarantine of the area—nothing. It's a weaponized version produced in Vector during the Cold War. No one has a vaccine, and even if one's possible, by the time we create it, it'll be too late."

Silence reigned for a few brief moments, until Raphael pushed forward.

"What else?"

As they continued the discussion, a presidential guard walked into the room and whispered in Gilder's ear.

Gilder whispered back, and the guard left. A few seconds later, Lord Becton entered the room. He stared straight ahead at the president as if he could feel the impatient glare of the president's inner-circle boring into the back of his head. A look of discomfort and embarrassment burdened his shoulders as if he wasn't certain of speaking in front of anyone but the president. Raphael's mind lost track of the previous discussion.

"What? What is it?" he asked.

A stunned, but excited look gripped Becton's face.

"It happened."

Raphael returned a confused stare.

"What?"

"The assembler breakthrough."

A look of shock melted over Raphael and Gilder. The cabinet members looked around as if waiting for someone to explain what was going on. Even with a full understanding, it took a few seconds for Raphael to fully comprehend. His mind mired itself in confusion, then raced with excitement.

"When?"

"Less than twelve hours ago."

Becton held his hands locked behind his back and waited for Raphael to absorb the information. He cast a fleeting glance at the cabinet ministers, still steeped in their ignorance, then he studied the floor.

"How many do we have?" Raphael asked.

"Enough."

"Can we design something to combat this blackpox attack?"

"It's already done, Mr. President."

Becton handed him a piece of paper, an executive order with instructions for the disbursement of blackpox disassemblers.

"All we need is your signature."

"How fast can we deploy them?"

Becton was stoic and cold in his presentation.

"The threat will be gone by the end of the day, Mr. President."

The cabinet ministers looked at each other in total confusion, shaking their heads. One of them stepped forward.

"Mr. President, what is this?"

"It's our weapon," Raphael said. "The weapon that will win the war on terror."

His explanation did nothing to alter the row of blank expressions.

"Should I contact the Americans?" Gilder asked.

Raphael shook his head.

"No. The Americans are half the problem. Had they mustered the resolve to do what was necessary, we wouldn't be faced with this situation. No, we won't need American cooperation. I'm going to do what the Americans refused to do, and I'm going to name it what they would not—*Operation Infinite Justice.*"

*   *   *   *

After almost thirty-six hours at Assaf Harofeh Medical Center, Dr. Dolev neared his wits' end. He still wore the same clothes from the night of the attack, but at least he had gotten some sleep. The government had cordoned off the entire city as well as surrounding areas. Israeli Defense Forces erected temporary medical tents outside the hospital walls to care for the victims of the bio-terror plague. Dr. Dolev couldn't help but think about little Richie as he washed the sleep out of his eyes with water from the sink. He wondered if he himself would die, and he wondered if the rumor of a vaccine was true.

As he stepped into the street just outside of the trauma ward, the sun filtered back on top of him through a thin veil of plastic. The medical tents created a different world, a sterile world devoid of hope for its victims. Looking around, he saw several of his colleagues swarming around a series of boxes, tearing at their edges. He ran toward the stacked crates, and as he did, he noticed Garrison walking away in his flowing brown robes. Dr. Dolev placed his hands on Garrison's shoulders and looked him in the eye.

"Is it?" he asked. "Is it the vaccine?"

Garrison appeared decidedly unexcited and his reply had a dire finality to it.

"It has begun."

He emitted only those three words before shaking off the doctor and fleeing the hospital. Dr. Dolev raced forward and captured a glimpse of the first vials as the doctors removed them from the crate. Lifting one out, he hurried it over to the bedside of the nearest patient, a man in his early thirties. The man's body trembled continuously under the weight of the ghastly disease. Dr. Dolev wondered if the man was even aware someone stood over him. Extracting several cc's of the hazy liquid, he pierced the man's arm and injected it. Removing the syringe, he stood back and waited. Inside the patient's body, a horde of disassemblers tunneled through the bloodstream. Carrying a simple on-board computer, the micro-sized machines located and identified the blackpox virus in every part of the body. Then with blazing speed, they picked it apart, one atom after another.

Within a few seconds, the trembling convulsions began to dissipate. After five or six minutes, the man pulled himself out of bed and walked around as if this had been his normal condition for the past twenty-four hours. All throughout the former death chamber, people laughed and skipped around. Each of them gave praise to God, and thanked him for the glorious miracle.

*   *   *   *

A rumble of voices lingered over the Operations Room and the three men gathered around a small table. Raphael, Gilder, and Becton discussed United Europe's current military status. Becton directed his comments at Raphael.

"Executive Order P13 has been implemented as ordered. Within twenty-four hours, the new United Europe military will be in a state of absolute readiness, awaiting your further order, Mr. President."

As they spoke, the original prototypes constructed duplicate copies of themselves in the largest, fastest, and most potent military build-up since the dawn of creation.

"And targeting?" Raphael asked.

"Ongoing as we speak," Becton said. "All of our military objectives have been prepared. On your order, all will be simultaneously achieved."

Raphael nodded his head in a show of approval.

"That includes individual terrorists?"

Becton gave an affirmative, and Gilder entered their conversation.

"Since nine-eleven, we've been trading information with the Americans, constructing an immense genetic database of terrorist DNA. All known terrorists will be in our crosshairs."

Raphael turned back to Becton.

"What's the timetable? I want total victory."

"Less than forty-eight hours, Mr. President."

During the conversation, Gilder whispered something to an aide. Raphael shot a glare his way, and Gilder informed him of the news.

"Seventeen project engineers are unaccounted for. All of them had apartments in Paris and were on holiday leave. Four held executive positions with top secret clearance and authorization."

Gilder thumbed through a stack of papers his aide had brought in. Raphael's answer was quick and decisive.

"Until we have confirmation, I want them treated as deserters. If only one is gone, he poses a vital threat to the international order. Put Jean on it. Tell him this search takes precedent over everything, including the investigation."

Gilder agreed and left the room to execute the order.

*   *   *   *

Eduardo walked into the office with a frown stretched over his face. Raphael detected several beads of sweat on his friend's forehead as he stood to greet him. He offered Eduardo a chair. The offer was turned down.

"There's no shield. Where's the shield?"

His eyes reduced themselves to penny-size slits as he stared at Raphael, and his accusing voice was noticeably irritated. Raphael tossed a stack of papers onto a pile.

"What are you talking about?"

Eduardo bounced around on the carpet in near hysterics.

"An active shield. You know, to keep us from dying? I walk onto the platform this morning, and I find out that our thousands of exploratory engineers have been designing offensive weapons and second generation military hardware."

Raphael walked out from behind his desk.

"That's what they were employed to do."

Eduardo pointed his finger.

"In addition to construction of an active shield."

"And they've done that."

Eduardo's body language illustrated his complete descent into a state of confusion.

"Then why am I told that all our molecular manufacturing capacity is being expended on the construction of an overwhelming force?"

Raphael folded his hands calmly.

"Because that's what's happening."

"You're building up a strike force before you have an active shield?"

"That's right."

Eduardo slammed his hand on the desk.

"I agreed to this job on the stipulation that an active shield be constructed before or in tandem with the White Horse Plan, not after it."

"I know. You and Burton agreed to that. I did not."

Eduardo looked lost as if he wanted to start pacing the room or run off in one direction or another, but he couldn't move his feet from the floor.

"Do you realize the situation? An active shield is the lifeblood of liberty in this age."

"I know. And we're going to build one."

"With each day you wait, you place the security of this planet in grave jeopardy."

Before he could get any further into lambasting the world's most powerful man, Raphael picked up a glass from his desk and hurled it against the wall. It shattered into a thousand tiny fragments. His teeth clenched together as he moved forward.

"Damn you, Eduardo! You're just a bureaucrat sitting in a room drawing up ideas on paper. I have to implement them. I'm the one with the decisions to make. I'm the one with the fate of humanity saddled on his shoulders, and you don't have any idea what it's like."

He stopped shouting for only a brief moment, and let his eyes bore into Eduardo's skull. His nostrils heaved downward and his face puffed out red. No one understood. They couldn't possibly understand. Most of the world didn't yet know what an assembler was, but Raphael had the distinct honor of knowing that any wrong step on his behalf could lead to the eradication of all life on earth, or worse yet, a world-wide totalitarian regime, a Planet Taliban. How could any of them understand what he was going through? His voice grew softer and took on its usual professional tone. It was not like him to raise his voice.

"I will present the proposal for an active shield to the United Nations. Neither of us is a dictator, and a world shield isn't worth anything if we lose freedom and liberty. Perhaps someone has a better proposal. We will let the proper democratic process decide."

Eduardo calmed down. Raphael's explanation made him feel like a total jerk. Perhaps he had been arrogant in believing his proposal was the only viable answer. He was just a guy with an idea, a theoretical idea that would effect real people—billions of people, everyone on Earth.

"I'm sorry. It's been a bad week," he said.

"It has been for everyone."

Eduardo studied the expression on Raphael's face. He was an experienced leader with great political skills. He had endured the pressure of the Indian-Pakistani conflict, and he would do everything possible to avoid greater catastrophe. His actions had always been for the good of the common man, and he had never expressed a desire for anything less than the spread of goodwill and democratic principles. Eduardo's fears eased.

"When will you make this proposal?"

Raphael stared out of his window, imagining the changing world that slept outside.

"The end of this week. But first, we must secure the peace."

*   *   *   *

It was not a day to be celebrated. Xiopang took his usual morning route through the city. But today, he detected a faint trace of excitement circulating through the air. It hinted of some sort of retaliatory measure. He could sense it. The streets of Beijing gushed forth with commerce as though the New Year's Eve attacks had little bearing on the everyday life of its citizens. To Xiopang, it was merely the calm before a great storm.

Rounding the corner, he took a brief look over his shoulder before entering Lang Wu's. The store was a small, hole-in-the-wall grocery, packed with an assortment of dry goods and canned foods. It boasted only two aisles, four walls, and a sales counter. Xiopang lingered down the first aisle and studied the other customers for a few brief minutes before approaching the counter. He addressed the clerk.

"Do you have any recommendations for the discriminating reader?"

The clerk motioned to the magazine rack in front of the counter.

"We have *Time*."

"No, no," Xiopang said. "I'm looking for something different."

"How about *Rolling Stone*?"

The two of them looked at each other then looked around the store. The aisles were now empty.

"Would you like something to drink?" the clerk asked.

"I'll have a Coke and a pack of Marlboro Reds."

The clerk reached underneath the counter, and his hands reemerged with both items. Xiopang paid him with exact change and left the store. Walking down the street toward his apartment, he popped open the Coke and drained its contents. It had a strange flavor, but still tasted sweet. He thought they were strange items to pick up for a mission, but the directive had come from the top. Nothing came from that high above without a distinct purpose, and he could sense the hour of retaliation was near.

*   *   *   *

About the same moment Xiopang walked into Lang Wu's, cargo planes of the Armed Forces of United Europe encircled the globe. The majority of the planes flew over international waters, and Union soldiers pushed large white cubes out of the cargo bays and into the oceans below. They looked like giant sugar cubes splashing into the water, and they dissolved just like sugar. Thousands fell into the four oceans, the seas, and the major waterways of the world.

The dissolved particles multiplied, and along with their self-replicating offspring, they drifted in all directions, swarming the ocean depths. Like lions of the jungle, the mechanized clumps of atoms scoured the ocean floor, hunters stalking their prey.

*   *   *   *

The Operations Room of Assembly Hall reminded Raphael of pictures from his youth of NASA's Houston headquarters during the moon landing. Manned computers covered the floor of an entire area several acres in size. The far wall resembled a giant 50's drive-in movie theater with three large screens pasted on the far wall. Hundreds of smaller screens mounted themselves around larger ones, as a small contingent of engineers monitored world events in the aftermath of the most lethal terrorist attack in human history.

Raphael glided through the room escorted by Offen Gilder and General Kohl. Kohl put his assistant, Edwin Mackey, in charge of briefing the president. Mackey took the president to a small computer console with a flat screen monitor. The visual display painted a map of the world with lines flowing in every direction. Taking a seat, he traced over them with his finger.

"The yellow lines denote the routes of our planes over the last twenty-four hours."

He circled the mouse around, and a few clicks later, a revised map appeared on the screen. White dots multiplied across the monitor like falling raindrops. They covered most of the oceans and waterways of the world.

"This screen gives us a real-time snapshot of what's happening. The white dots indicate pockets of coverage permanently secured by our forces."

Raphael studied the screen. Covering land presented a greater challenge, and the closed airspace over sovereign nations would require ground operatives to covertly transport forces into those countries.

"Do we have any idea how much longer this will take?" he asked.

Mackey glowed with life as he flipped through successive screens.

"Certainly. At any time, we can view an estimated time to completion. If any new airlifts or ground deliveries take place, it automatically updates the estimate to reflect them."

Fascinated with the entire process, Raphael glued his eyes to the screen, but he didn't take the estimate at face value. Everything depended on this part of the operation executing flawlessly. The smallest mistake could result in millions of lives being lost, and the world was already bathing in blood.

"How certain are we that every one will be located?"

Mackey didn't hesitate.

"One hundred percent sir."

"Not, ninety-nine point nine or anything like that, but one hundred percent?"

Raphael wanted to make sure. If only one of the many thousands broke through, it would be one too many. The horror of India and Pakistan had left a permanent scar upon his soul.

"One hundred percent, Mr. President. If we chose to do so, we could blanket the entire solar system by week's end."

Raphael seemed content with the answer. One hundred percent. Now, all he had to worry about was time. Time was his enemy. He wished he knew the details of Price's actions. With Pakistan and India, time had run short. He would not make the same mistake twice.

"What is the current estimated time to completion?"

Mackey moved back one screen and looked up at the president.

"Less than seven hours. At the break of dawn, we await your order."

*   *   *   *

The presidential suite stood as an elaborate oasis in the middle of a utilitarian desert. The cathedral ceiling sloped at an upward angle from the doorway to the farthest wall, composed entirely of a camouflaged window. From the outside, the outer wall maintained the appearance of a jagged mountain ridge. From the inside, it gave a transparent view of the valley down below. The office itself housed a single walnut desk with a furniture suite for entertaining guests. Plasma screens flanked the walls, and Persian rugs blanketed the hardwood floor.

It was two in the morning, and the eastern edge of France was enveloped in total darkness. Raphael entered the suite by himself and turned on a lone television. It was pre-tuned to CNN, and he listened intently while he poured himself a Seagram's 7&7 from the wet bar. The journalist on location in Haifa droned on about the impending war between the Arabs and Israelis. The armies of the Arab nations were poised at the Israeli border and the expectation was they would attack in the morning if Israel did not attack first.

Raphael lit a tightly rolled Cuban cigar and pressed its leaves between his lips. The intoxicating aroma was a sweet reward to his forty-eight hour marathon. It had been the worst two days of his life, and it began to sink in, finally, in this rare moment of quiet reflection that Poyner was gone forever. As the fire billowed from his cigar, Raphael stood before the giant wall that served as his window to the outside world.

His advisors sent him away with the intention he get some sleep before the following day's activities, but he couldn't sleep. He only thought of the day ahead. His fingers inspected the thin transparent wall, and it occurred to him that a nuclear warhead could strike dead center, right in front of his nose, and it wouldn't move a hair on his head. In fact, he thought to himself, that would be quite a sight! Perhaps in the aftermath of *Operation Infinite Justice*, he could turn this room into a theme park where children could witness just such a phenomenon while their schoolteachers recounted the horrors of a bygone nuclear age.

He melted into his chair and kicked up his feet. With his cigar in one hand and his drink in the other, Raphael watched the news of the impending Middle Eastern war unfold right in front of his eyes. A headline ran across the bottom of the screen stating that a run on gasoline was underway. The price of oil had reached an all-time high. His head flooded with the concepts of Western oil dependence, OPEC, the Persian Gulf, the Shah of Iran—all the events of the past century and all predicated on the uninterrupted flow of oil.

He couldn't help but think that these Islamic radicals who had brought the West to her knees were messengers of God sent to punish the Western world for her sins in propping up the evil governments of the Middle East, ruthless dictators who imprisoned, raped, and tortured. The Western democracies paid a terrible price, but no God would allow a radical interpretation of Islam to triumph over democratic freedom. Democratic government and liberty would win. There would be no Arab-Israeli war. There would be no Chinese invasion of Taiwan, and no rekindling of the Korean War. Only the conclusion of a costly war on terror, and it would have one final victor. As he sat in his chair, puffing away on his cigar, Raphael was certain of that victor's identity. And as the smoke curled away from his cigar, it caused him to grin from ear to ear.

CHAPTER 2:

Inevitable Conquest

"I looked up and saw a white horse. Its rider carried a bow, and a crown was placed on his head. He rode out to win many battles and gain the victory."

—John
Revelation 6:2

Raphael stood before his window and watched as the breaking sun lit the room with a kaleidoscope of color as the early morning hours moved the world closer to an era dominated by assemblers. The television still focused on the impending Arab-Israeli war, only now in its first hour. Gilder opened the door and walked across the cavernous room to Raphael's desk.

"Mr. President, are you ready?"

Raphael turned to face him. He nodded without comment and made his way around to Gilder's side of the desk. With a quick flip of his wrist, he changed the picture on the television and found himself face-to-face with General Kohl.

"Good morning, Mr. President," he said. "*Operation Infinite Justice* is field compliant and awaiting your order to proceed."

"And each target is locked in?"

"Yes, sir."

Raphael looked at them both as if he was going to say something, but no words came out. He tore the document from Gilder's hand and laid it on the desk. With one long stroke of the pen, he scrawled his signature across the parchment, as bold and black as the night. Gilder picked it back up.

"Thank you, Mr. President."

He turned ninety degrees and fashioned a quick salute to General Kohl. In a brief instant, he left the room and *Operation Infinite Justice* was underway. Raphael returned to his window and wondered to himself what he would say to Thomas Price.

*   *   *   *

Seconds after Raphael signed the presidential order, a United Europe satellite constellation reigned down a series of orders to the world below. In the depths of the oceans, the signals called a mighty army of dormant warriors into action. On land, they crawled into position. With unencumbered ferocity, they lurched for their prey. A swift assault penetrated every nuclear power facility, every nuclear warhead, and every deposit of plutonium and uranium on the face of the earth.

Instantly, a spherical shell of pre-stressed diamond composite formed itself around all the world's fissile material. The spheres cast themselves in multiple redundant layers, rendering the world's nuclear weapons and nuclear power plants useless. Tiny wires constructed of carbon nanotubes branched out, relaying signals throughout the concentric layers.

The outermost layer of each sphere consisted of trillions of sensors. Any attempt to remove or puncture the outer layer would trigger a chemical chain reaction resulting in a gas of metal oxides hotter than the surface of the Sun. Burning in a fraction of a second, and confined to the core of the sphere, the reaction would raise the core temperature beyond the melting point of all known substances, thus making it impossible to salvage the dangerous weapons grade elements inside.

Phase One of *Operation Infinite Justice*, the defensive phase, completed itself. The total elapsed time from the president's given order to the mission's end was two minutes, seventeen seconds. At that moment, the Nuclear Age came to an abrupt and final conclusion. The long-standing threat of nuclear annihilation disappeared forever, nuclear warheads now a relic of the past. A new age, the Nanotechnic Age, seized the throne of power.

*   *   *   *

Jiang's transport from Zurich to Beijing had been slowed by the same attack he had helped orchestrate. International commercial flights came to a complete standstill, forcing him to make a visit to the Chinese embassy in Zurich. From there, he caught a diplomatic plane and a series of military cargo flights until he finally got back to China. It put him almost two days behind schedule.

Now, looking out of the back of his limousine's tinted windows, he couldn't help but smile. He had pulled off the mission of a lifetime. No, it was bigger than that. His story was one of legend, a story to be told for centuries on end hereafter. His gaze fell on the Time-X watch strapped onto his left wrist. Soon, he would be meeting face to face with Chairman Jintao. The glory of the Chinese Empire would be unending, and he would be one of the youngest men since the days of the emperors to wield power in the ruling class.

As the limousine rolled to a stop in front of Zhongnanhai, Jiang watched the guards approach the vehicle door. One of them pulled the handle, and they saluted as he stepped out. The driver pulled away as Jiang approached the front door of the Chairman's quarters. Once inside, he began to feel faint and light-headed. His breathing constricted, and he staggered into the foyer, falling unconscious. On the other side of the palace, Xiopang had begun his mission.

*   *   *   *

Just west of Tiananmen Square on Changan Avenue, Xiopang strolled toward Zhongnanhai, China's equivalent of the Kremlin. Large vermilion walls surrounded the rectangular complex, and two wall banners unfurled on either side of the main entrance, reading "Long Live The Great Chinese Communist Party!" and "Long Live The Invincible Mao Tse-Tung Thought!".

Looking at his watch, he could see the appointed time had arrived. By far, this was the most outrageous assignment he had ever been given. He was certain to be dead momentarily. His mind weighed the likelihood he was nothing more than a pawn to be used in a last ditch effort by the Western powers to hold onto superpower status—a kamikaze mission destined to plunge back to earth in flames. Part of him, however, held out hope some sort of secret weaponry developed by United Europe labs would burst out at the last moment and save the day. They had never steered him wrong in the past.

But Xiopang thought all of this through on the previous night. If he was going to die, so be it. Better death, than to live in a world of despotic terror. It was that level of dedication to fight for freedom that drove him to join the ranks of United Europe's intelligence service. Now was his time to pay the price.

His orders were only as follows—at five past the hour, he was to light a single cigarette, smoke it, and storm the headquarters of the Chinese government—taking Chairman Jintao and his entire entourage into custody until reinforcements arrived. He doubled-checked the orders to make sure something wasn't mistranslated or damaged in transit. They came back the same as before—carry on as ordered.

It was now five past the hour. Xiopang took a deep breath and pulled out his pack of Marlboro Reds. He held them out in the palm of his hand and studied the outer packaging. It read in bold black letters, "The Surgeon General Warns". This better be a pack of magic beanstalk bean cigarettes he thought, and he set about preparing himself mentally for impending death.

Clasping the narrow paper shaft between his fingers, Xiopang ignited a fire from his other hand, which held a Zippo engraved with his name. He inhaled on the cylinder, anticipating a last surge of nicotine before his demise. In so doing, the fire leapt upward to the end of the cigarette and set it ablaze. He let the first puff leave his lips as a cloud of black smoke, and he walked toward Zhongnanhai. Immediately, the guards took notice. Several pointed in his direction, and two left their posts to intercept him.

Unbeknownst to the guards and Xiopang, a mighty army lurked around the corner—an army the likes of which the world had never seen before. Inside the billowing stick pursed between his lips, the SPIDERS began their work. Sprung to life by the scourge of fire, they remained invisible to the human eye. Although seemingly small, the cigarette in Xiopang's mouth became the largest and most productive manufacturing facility ever devised by men. Assemblers purged the surrounding air of molecules, each moving into its appointed place. One by one, individual atoms were drawn together by universal forces. Not a single one jostled another; each moved exactly in the right place. In blind obedience to their stated purpose, they formed copies of themselves, replicating at breakneck speed and with unrelenting rapidity.

As the guards approached, bits of sullen ash fell to the ground unleashing holy terror on the evil men of the world. They forged through the physical realm, kings of the universe, exacting total control over their dominion. And no weapon could stop them.

Xiopang smiled at his captors as they seized him. In seconds, they locked his hands behind him and cuffed them at the wrists. One of the guards shoved a 5.8mm assault rifle in Xiopang's face as the other disarmed him of his .22—the weapon with which he was to seize the entire seat of Chinese government! Now, it was time to die, at least following a few days of torture and interrogation.

He considered these last moments, and the fact that his cigarette had yet to yield a single jolt of nicotine, but his life did not end. He was not tortured.

To his utter amazement, both his captors fell to the ground unconscious. Xiopang surveyed the area. Not a man was left standing in any direction. He stepped over his chained wrists and searched one of the fallen guards for a key. He quickly found one and set himself free. Liberated, he recaptured his handgun and took possession of the guard's assault rifle for extra firepower, and to his astonishment, he proceeded onward with his mission to storm the most heavily secured venue in all of China.

The access gate was locked, but easily opened with the key obtained from the guard. In stealth, Xiopang peered around the corner with his weapon drawn. He saw three men, but they too lay on the floor passed out. He tip-toed onto the grounds, letting a blueprint of the entire facility run through his thoughts. He had lived for this moment, memorizing every nook and crevice, but he never imagined he would actually set foot in the place. Entering the Chairman's quarters, he slipped through the hallway, stepping over several more downed bodies before arriving at the door to the Chairman's office.

A sudden rush of excited ecstasy poured over him. He smiled in a devilish manner as he stared at the door in front of him. Was this some sort of dream? Could he really be standing in the middle of Zhongnanhai? He charged forward and kicked the door. It burst open, and suddenly, Xiopang felt like Rambo times ten or the Terminator himself.

He looked inside. Chairman Jintao was asleep at the wheel, unconscious in his mighty chair of power. Fixed on the wall next to him was a ceremonial sword. Xiopang pulled it from the wall and charged toward the chairman's desk, waving it wildly and screaming at the top of his lungs. With his final step, he plunged the blade into the desk and laughed hysterically. Jintao sat in his chair, passed out, while the blade flittered through the air, and his advisors lay on the floor drooling. The whole scene was surreal and absurd.

The phone rang, and Xiopang looked around as if he expected someone else to answer. After a couple of rings, he picked it up.

"Yes."

"Xiopang," the voice said. "Do you have the perimeter?"

He nodded his head and grinned.

"Affirmative," he said, astonished to hear such a word glide past his lips.

*   *   *   *

In Aden, Yemen, a small apartment hummed with life. The three roommates rode a wave of success and the atmosphere was festive. Fareed stood in the kitchen, peeling through the pages of a new plan that would cause America to bleed. He shivered with each turn of the page as if he could feel the Western nations cringe. Islam would prevail. He never doubted. Allah would wreak his final vengeance on the infidel. It had been the arrogance of the Western powers, their refusal to follow Allah's ways that had led to the New Year's Eve destruction, and Fareed planned to see to it that the attacks continued until he annihilated the last vestiges of the West from the face of the earth.

In the neighboring room, Fahd and Ali studied their own parts of the plan. It was at that moment when Fareed heard their cries.

"Fareed! Fareed! Oh, Allah have mercy!"

The shrieks terrified him. A chill raced up his spine with unrequited terror. Fareed dropped his manual and flew into the adjacent room. He rubbed his eyes, believing they now deceived him. Ali writhed on the floor in fits of rage as if possessed by the devil. Fahd yelled down at him, condemning the evil spirits.

"He's filled with the devil!" Fahd shouted.

Without hesitation, he grabbed a lamp stand off the table and beat Ali with it. Fareed joined him, and the two of them mustered all of their combined strength in an attempt to beat the demons out of Ali. They bludgeoned his body, one stroke after another, as he dissolved in front of them.

Trembling in abject terror, Fahd dropped the lamp stand from his hand. Fareed froze in place and looked into his friend's wide-open eyes with a paralyzing fear. He watched Fahd's tongue dissolve in his mouth. Fahd fell to the floor as his eyes dissolved in their sockets and his arms melted to the floor.

Fareed pivoted to his right. Ali was gone—vanished without a trace. He called out for mercy in the name of Allah. Inside his own body, the SPIDERS carried out the same mission. Each one possessed a molecular computer with a thorough record of his DNA. The initial swarm withdrew samples from his tissue, double- and triple-checking his gene expression patterns so as to avoid a false positive. The quick test confirmed his identity, and the SPIDERS launched into a process of unencumbered self-replication.

With exponential speed, they burned through his internal organs, one atom after the next, using tiny assembler legs to break the chemical bonds holding his atoms together. He watched in the mirror as his own limbs began to fade away, and one by one, piece by piece, the SPIDERS plucked Fareed apart, spewing his atoms onto the floor like a combine splattering grain onto the threshing floor.

*   *   *   *

Raphael remained standing as he picked up the phone. He directed the voice on the other end to dial Thomas Price. The morning light poured through the window as he stood alone in the cavernous Presidential Suite. Price's voice arrived quickly.

"Thomas, it's me, Raphael. I assume you know why I'm calling."

He waited to see what kind of reaction he received.

"I have a fairly good idea."

He wasn't sure what Price knew, but Raphael did know American satellites still functioned properly. The US government suffered a tremendous blow, but intelligence gathering hadn't been so affected as to miss something this big.

"I hope you can understand. We had to use our advantage. Surprise was essential, and the prospect of further nuclear assaults was not something I could tolerate. United Europe no longer retains nuclear capability either."

He explained away as if his hand had been caught in the cookie jar, but Price did not attack him.

"I understand. So, what's the objective? What can you tell me?"

"European forces are poised to conquer every non-democratic nation in the world. By day's end, their leaders will be in custody. I would appreciate US support in occupying and rebuilding these territories. I don't want securing borders and restoring order to translate into the drugging of whole populations."

"I don't want it to come to that either."

"Look, I don't relish being a dictator, but for the moment, I am. I want you to know you can trust me Thomas. This won't last long. Our nations have a long-standing relationship, and we share common interests. We should work together on this, and I fully intend to share these technologies."

Price quickly changed the subject.

"What form of government do you envision for these nations?"

"The United Nations can deal with that when it reconvenes. Right now, our focus should be victory. We haven't won yet, and we need coordination between our armed forces."

Price agreed, and the wheels were put into motion for a summit meeting within the next forty-eight hours. For the interim, the American military had no choice but to follow the lead of United Europe.

*   *   *   *

Following the surprise nuclear attack on Tel Aviv, most of the Knesset was dead. The Israeli political leadership, headed by the Prime Minister, now flew high above the country. Inside the plane, the Prime Minister, his cabinet, and several top aides scurried through the cabin, their mouths speaking into cell phones.

One young aide plopped down in a window seat and sunk into the headrest. He placed his elbows on his knees and his face in his open hands and let out a deep breath. Wiping the stress from his eyes, he sat upright, straight in the seat.

He touched his hand to the glass window, meditating on God's wondrous creation. White clouds floated over the Mediterranean like pieces of torn cotton, and the rising sun burned across the sky as if God had plundered his supernatural canvas with a torrent of yellow fire. Where the sun blended with the sea, a silver line appeared and it wavered erratically as if the young man's eyes had fallen out of focus. The gray blur stretched across the sea and grew in size as the seconds passed. The young man forgot his work and squinted his eyes to try to figure out what it was he was seeing. The Foreign Minister noticed his inattentiveness.

"Moshe!"

The young man didn't respond, and the Foreign Minister's cheeks puffed out in blots of red.

"Moshe!"

His aide continued to stare out of the cabin window. The angry man rose from his seat and stormed over as if ready to deliver a swift left hook. He latched his burning eyes onto Moshe, then followed their path outside the window. The Foreign Minister swallowed, his Adam's apple dropping to the deepest part of his throat. The sun was barely visible from behind the cloud of silver. It floated through the sky like dust blown from the surface of an antique table. The swirling particles moved closer and closer until they struck the edge of the cabin.

Both men veered back in their chairs at the sight of the cloud hurtling toward them. The gray dust pelted the plane like clumps of dry sand. Gravel flakes beat against the window like tiny hailstones on a tin roof. First, a single stone or two, then a torrential downpour. The aircraft continued forward without a problem, and just like a hailstorm, the cloud passed over as quickly as it had come.

The two men rushed to the opposite side of the cabin, and everyone onboard now looked out of the windows. They watched as a silver streak moved across the landscape in tandem with the gray storm cloud.

The growing cloud of LOCUSTS, and the legion of SPIDERS that followed on the ground, descended on Israel like a Biblical plague. The sight would have made Pharaoh open his heart and Moses stand in awe as the nanomachines raced onto the battlefield.

The swarm of forces trickled over the grass like mourning dew. They hopped off of plants and trees like fleas on a mangy dog. With the soft rumbling of a heavenly legion of chariots, they spread across the earth with the roaring force of fire sweeping over a field—a mighty army moving into battle. The rank and file soldiers of *Operation Infinite Justice* were nothing more than mere atoms. With single-minded purpose, they strode ahead like Napoleonic warriors and scaled city walls like trained soldiers. They marched in lock step, never once breaking rank. Lunging through the gaps in the physical universe with graceful ease, no weapon could stand against them.

The earth quaked as they advanced, and the heavens trembled before them. They were no less than the wrath of God, and the world was at their mercy.

*   *   *   *

Aloft in the air at more than twenty thousand feet, a Syrian pilot engaged his MiG-25 in a rolling dogfight with an Israeli F-15. He had the rival jet locked in his crosshairs when his instruments went dead. Looking up from the control panel, the world outside his cockpit faced an assault from a barrage of silver pollen blowing across the sky. The pilot's face twisted in horror as the micro-sized particles latched onto the cockpit and wings of the plane. They bore their way through like salt dumped on a mollusk, eating away at the wings until nothing remained.

The pilot pounded on the ejection switch, but nothing happened. He yanked backward on the controls, but the plane continued its downward spiral. Out of options, he lifted his head. He could see the tiny particles still digging through the cockpit. They burst through and leapt onto his face. His hands ripped and tore at them, but he couldn't hold them back. Layer by layer, they chewed through his face like termites, plucking him apart and spewing his atoms in every random direction.

*   *   *   *

The wind furiously churned as the helicopters set down inside Zhongnanhai. A whole fleet arrived from a British carrier anchored off the coast of South Korea.

For a one-mile radius surrounding the seat of Chinese government, every living biological entity was under complete control. A team of special ops forces jumped out and ran toward the palace. Xiopang waited on the steps to greet them. Tiny molecular machines probed their bloodstream to communicate with any SPIDERS that tried to infiltrate their bodies. They directed the SPIDERS not to pick the oxygen molecules from their bloodstream. That kept these men standing, while their enemies lay unconscious.

Xiopang pointed into the compound, and the soldiers raced into the building. One of the soldiers remained in the foyer and knelt beside a man's body. He pulled a laptop from his duffel bag and clicked it on. Grabbing hold of the man's arm, he placed his hand on a flat device and scanned his fingerprints. The laptop flashed through thousands of profiles but came up empty.

The young operative searched the man's pockets, but they contained no form of identification. The man on the floor wore the clothes of a common peasant and a cheap Time-X watch decorated his left hand. Pulling out a pair of restraints, the soldier fastened them on Jiang's arms and legs, then pulled out a syringe. Extracting a small amount of liquid from a test tube, he injected it into Jiang's left arm. Instantly, the man's eyes opened, and the soldier interrogated him in Chinese.

"What's your name?"

Jiang didn't answer. He looked confused, and the soldier repeated himself.

"What's your name?"

As he woke from his haze, Jiang became cognizant of what had happened. He had been too late. Did they know what he had? No, of course not, they couldn't. Although he couldn't be sure how long he had been unconscious. He used his alias.

"Li Ming Hu," he said.

"And what's your title?"

Jiang didn't know how much his captor knew, so he played dumb.

"I work for the Chinese government."

"I know you work for the government. What do you do?"

At that point, Jiang realized that he had only been under for a couple of hours at the most. Obviously, United Europe had taken possession of Zhong-nanhai, and good Samaritans that the democratic Westerners were, they were trying to separate the culpable leaders from the innocent staffers.

"I'm—I'm a driver for diplomats and the Chairman's staff," Jiang said.

The man grabbed Jiang by the back of the hands and led him into another room.

"I've got another one," he said.

One of his buddies manned the door. Around twenty-five or thirty people congregated in the room, all of them cleaning crew, kitchen workers, and other staffers. They gave Jiang a strange look as he straggled in to join them, but the soldiers didn't notice.

After an hour, another man entered the room dressed in military clothing. He looked at everyone in the room, and he spoke in fluent Chinese.

"It is with great pride that I inform each of you that the People's Republic of China has been liberated. Each of you is now free. The Chairman and his political staff have been taken into custody and will face trial before the International Criminal Court. We will release you immediately, and we encourage you to spread the word to your fellow citizens that China will from now on be ruled by her citizens via democracy."

He gave them all a salute and motioned to the solider beside him to release the captives from their restraints. Jiang stood in silent disbelief, his body paralyzed. The soldier stared at him with a smile.

"You're free to go, sir."

Jiang nodded in recognition and walked out onto the street a free and liberated man.

*   *   *   *

Jean Riguad Prieur sat across from the president's desk with a manila file in his hands. Raphael peeled through a second copy.

"And how is this connected to the assassin?"

"We don't know. It may not be, and we may never know."

"Your best guess?"

"It's not likely he worked for Iran or Iraq, but it appears the state or organization he worked for wanted us to draw that conclusion."

The investigation had a great number of leads in America. All pointed back to one man, but in Europe they only hit dead-ends. Jean explained further.

"Following the attacks, the FBI uncovered a lead on a group of Arab Muslim males living in New Jersey. Co-workers of a man named Fahd Al-Shehhi grew suspicious of his excitement in the days leading up to the attack. Afterward, they contacted the FBI. A quick check of his apartment revealed a mountain of evidence linking him, his roommate, and another man to the New York bombing."

"The FBI hasn't apprehended them?"

"Not a trace of Al-Shehhi or his roommate, but the third man boarded a plane the morning of the attack."

"Who?"

"A man named Yousef Abdullah Al-Rahman. Several months before the bombing, he arrived in New York, claiming political asylum. He apparently set-up another man as a diversion to facilitate his entry into the country. Later, he threw off investigators by selling a plane ticket to a man in a DC mosque. The guy's well-trained, probably more so than the other two."

"Al-Qaeda? Foreign agent?"

Jean shook his head.

"Remains to be seen. His fingerprints match those of a Kuwaiti named Khalid Al-Oraifan under whose name he boarded the flight to Paris on the morning of the attack. His fingerprints match those on file with the Kuwaiti government."

Raphael studied Jean's face, detecting a hint of doubt.

"You don't think he's our man?"

Jean shook his head.

"Those files were compromised during Iraq's invasion of Kuwait. Al-Oraifan's friends and family say he disappeared that same month. They haven't seen him since."

Raphael scratched the side of his head, confused.

"You think this guy was an Iraqi agent?"

"I think whoever coordinated this wanted us to draw that conclusion."

*   *   *   *

Despite what he was about to do, Raphael was not the least bit nervous. In fact, it was just the opposite. For once, he felt a sense of peace. He no longer had to worry about irrational men plunging the globe into nuclear holocaust. Never again would he have to read stories of ruthless dictators hacking the limbs off innocent men. Images of starving children would no longer be a worry. It would require a great balancing act and flawless execution, but Raphael felt his whole life leading up to this point was preparation for this day. He would not squander the moment.

He gathered himself behind his desk, with his hands pressed together and his fingers neatly interlocked. He could hear the countdown and see the cameras adjust to his presence, spurring his soft-spoken voice to press forward.

"Greetings. Citizens of United Europe, friends and allies abroad, and people of the world...

I speak to you in the aftermath of a horrible time in the human experience, and at a time history will forever remember. Not one of us will forget the horror of this New Year's Eve, and I pray we never do. United Europe will hunt down those responsible and bring them to justice. To do so is all part of our continuing war on terror.

In past years, that war has pitted the civilized world against dark enemies, those who worship a culture of death. With unhindered zeal, these individuals and regimes murder the innocent and choke off freedom all in the name of a twisted interpretation of God or an unwavering political ideology. Our war on terror is against everyone and anyone who seeks to deny the world's citizens basic freedoms bestowed by God.

As I speak to you today, United Europe is moving forward to secure those freedoms for all citizens of the world community. This morning, I ordered our forces to invade the nations of China, Iran, Saudi Arabia, Syria, Libya, Sudan, North Korea, and Cuba. Through their own actions, these nations have proved their only aim is to spread oppression and destroy innocent life. These nations will soon be transformed into self-governing democratic republics. Their citizens will soon enjoy the same basic freedoms those of us in the West have long taken for granted.

But these nations are not alone. Other governments should be placed on notice that they too are subject to the same fate if they do not change their ways.

In a matter of hours, the world has been inexorably transformed. Unbeknownst to the terrorists who sought to undermine our way of life, those of us in the West harbored a secret plan of our own. For over two years, United Europe has been at work in conjunction with the United States and Japan to develop a new technology for securing world peace. This secret project has been known as the assembler project, and it has changed the world in which we all live.

It is the creation of an assembler that has given Europe the power to bring these nations to justice. By fostering the development of this new technology, humanity now has absolute power to manipulate the physical world. We now have the ability to rearrange matter with atomic precision, building things from the bottom up. This thorough and inexpensive system for controlling the structure of matter has enabled us to build fleets of nanomachines to restore justice for the people of these oppressed nations. And the implications of this technological breakthrough are far-reaching.

In the field of medicine, assemblers will quickly lead to new breakthroughs, allowing humanity to conquer forever the cruel enemy of disease. It is no longer science fiction to envision microscopic machines traveling through the circulatory system. Assemblers will be able to identify and destroy bacteria and viruses. They will be able to restore lost limbs and repair previously irreparable damage.

Our environment will become cleaner as the ability to capture, position, and change the configuration of molecules will reinvent our concepts of manufacturing, leaving behind zero byproducts, much less hazardous ones.

More importantly, assemblers will give us the ability to create material abundance for the world's population. Just a fraction of the elements found in our atmosphere alone are enough to provide everyone on earth with adequate food, clothing, and shelter. Poverty will become a nightmare of the past, and all people will be able to enjoy the fruits of life and freedom.

All these wonderful possibilities lie at our doorstep, but they do not come without a price. Although assemblers have destroyed the unconventional threats of nuclear, biological, and chemical warfare, they have become by their very nature, a threat more potent than all our previous fears combined. In the hands of deranged men, assemblers could sound the death knell for freedom and liberty, and perhaps even life itself.

It is my goal to ensure such men never have the opportunity. Such evil men still lurk in our midst, and United Europe and her allies will uproot them. The war on terror is not yet over, but its conclusion in favor of victory for freedom is a certainty. For assemblers will provide us with the means to export our greatest product to the world community—democracy.

In the coming days and weeks, United Europe extends its hand to all democratic and civilized nations. We long to stand in unity with our friends in America, our Russian neighbors, and our Japanese friends. We hold out an olive branch to the nations of Australia, Canada, Mexico, and India. Our hope is to work together with all free nations to construct a better world, one littered with freedom-loving people and democratic governments. Tomorrow will create a better day, and bring a final end to the horrible wars and destruction of our past.

In the coming months and years, the assembler breakthrough will touch every aspect of human life, from the water we drink to the air we breathe. It will be a time of celebration for the poor and oppressed. For as the Bible says,

'I was hungry, and you fed me. I was thirsty, and you gave me a drink. I was a stranger, and you invited me into your home.'

So it will be. God has triumphed.

We will do far more than visit the world's people. We will liberate them. In the coming months, the world will unite as never before. And it will unite for freedom and justice. We will leave the days of evil behind us, and forge forward in an era of everlasting peace. That is our great hope. That is our final end.

May God be with us in this quest."

The cameras rolled to a stop, and Raphael waited to make sure they were off air. Once certain, he stood up and felt a calm peace flow over him. A great amount of work remained, but a new era would come. Failure was not an option, and the world could not afford error.

CHAPTER 3:

Zoos Of Uncaged Untamed Beasts

"And another horse appeared, a red one. Its rider was given a mighty sword and the authority to remove peace from the earth. And there was war and slaughter everywhere."

—**John**
Revelation 6:4

As the usher opened the door to the presidential suite, Garrison stepped forward. Raphael's back faced the door, and he stared out of the giant window on the far wall. Bright light from the incoming sun drenched his wavy black hair, and Garrison held his breath for all the beauty of the window. Stretching from floor to ceiling across the entire width of the office, the majestic beauty of the French Alps rested outside.

Making his way to Raphael's desk, Garrison carried a small package under his left arm. As he approached, Raphael made out the traces of his friend's reflection in the window and turned to face him. At once, his face lit up. He moved forward and gave Garrison a hug.

"You've been quite busy since our last encounter," Garrison said.

Raphael let out a faint laugh as his hand tapped the desk.

"It's been interesting."

Garrison was unsure of what to say given the circumstances. Poyner was gone. That's all he could think of. That the world had gone to hell once she left—well, that was for other people to worry about. Unfortunately, Raphael was one of, if not the person who had to worry about it.

"I brought you a gift," Garrison said.

He pulled the tightly wrapped paper square from underneath his arm and held it out in his hand.

"You didn't have to do that, Garrison."

Wearing a look of surprise, Raphael took hold of the gift and tore into the paper wrapping, flinging it to the ground. Holding the unwrapped book between his hands, he smiled his first true smile in over a week. He read its title out loud.

"*If I Ran The Zoo*...by Dr. Seuss."

His eyes seemed to gaze off for a while, transporting him back in time to some unseen place. Garrison could read the thoughts weighing on his mind.

"I have complete confidence no man on earth can do a better job."

"Perhaps," Raphael said.

The trace of doubt in his voice stabbed in Garrison's heart.

"You're a good man, and your intentions are righteous."

"Intentions go wrong."

Raphael's eyes moved from the floor to Garrison, displaying a dire seriousness.

"Garrison, you're the best friend I have. Lately, it feels like you're the only friend I have."

Garrison didn't know how to respond. He could see the pressure of the job taking its toll. Could he even begin to imagine? Of course not, and he didn't want to try.

"You have Eduardo here. Your advisors. You're surrounded by lots of friends."

A brief pause cut into their conversation as Raphael turned to look out of the window once again, his back turned.

"Eduardo's part of the problem. They all are. Advisors, crowds of people—all with an agenda to push."

His voice softened to a lower tone, but quickly the life and energy surged back into it.

"But is it not worth it? I shudder to think what would have happened if some of my rivals had been appointed to this position. I'll do something for the people. This world will be better off when I leave it."

He turned back toward Garrison, the glow back in his eyes.

"You know, you're the only person I know who could walk into a place like this and not ask for a tour. Let's go," he said.

He led Garrison to the door, and he gave him the full tour of Assembly Hall.

*   *   *   *

Planted firmly in the Mediterranean, the USS Nimitz housed a few thousand people. The crew stood at attention as President Price introduced President Vicente. The media attended, along with the leaders of many nations. Jean Riguad Prieur stood firmly beside his president. Along with him, he brought an elite contingent of Europol officers, chief among them, a young man named Hans Blitner.

Born in Hamburg in the late 1970s, Hans Blitner was the son of a man who had leapt to his safety from a building window on the night the wall went up that divided East and West Germany. His father had never forgotten the coldness exhibited by the twisted barrier of iron and concrete and the soldiers who guarded it. He raised his son on stories of Soviet oppression and the greatness of democracy, especially American democracy.

Hans Blitner lived to serve his nation, to live his life in service to its people. After graduating from the University of Bonn with a degree in Political Science, the opportunity arose to join the ranks of the newly reorganized Europol. The establishment of United Europe had been a dream come true, and he plastered his college dorm room with posters of its charismatic president.

Now, he stood only a few feet from his hero. He listened to the man who fought to bring not only Europe, but the entire free world, into an era of unprecedented peace and prosperity. His friends never let him hear the end of it for his self-proclaimed status as a true believer in the "Man from Mexico".

They preferred to smoke weed and drink beer above all else, but now, they too would benefit from the revolution taking place.

As the president wrapped his fingers around the outer edges of the podium, Hans hung on every word. His eyes followed every darted glance and every jostle of hair. The dead silence in his brain between Price's introduction and Raphael's first words only served to feed his soul.

"It is with great honor that I, and other servants of United Europe, join our American brothers on this deck today. For over two centuries, our countries have been tightly bound together. It was the British Empire that gave birth to the American experiment, and it was the success of the American experiment which continues to change Europe for the better to this day. We have learned much from each other, and now, it is our duty to share this way of life with the rest of the world.

I take great pride in Europe's partnership with the United States, and we both take pride in our partnership with all democratic, freedom-loving nations. Today, this carrier will leave port for the shores of China. Once there, you will serve the interests of the United States as well as the entire world. No longer will your job be to destroy and defeat your enemies, but to protect and guide your fellow man. You will help to feed those who are hungry, and you will serve in the role of protecting and policing the new Chinese Republic, saving them from the evil grasp of common criminals and international terrorists alike.

Most important of all, you will be protecting our most cherished entity of all. An idea. For while most nations were founded by conquest and glory, America was founded on a simple idea. America taught the world that more important than life itself is the idea all men are created equal, and that governments should derive their powers from the consent of the governed. There is no more honorable goal in life, no more noble profession, than to be protectors of this idea.

And today, I commend the American military for its efforts both past and present. One day, centuries from now, historians will look back to this day, to the people on this deck, and they will say, 'They did what had to be done. Without complaint, they rose to the task at hand, and in so doing, they secured the blessings of liberty for themselves and their children for all of eternity.'

I applaud the people in this room, for the human race owes you a debt of gratitude it will never be able to repay. May God bless you, and good luck on your journey."

Being present at such a moment gave Hans the greatest high of his entire life. A surge lifted through his body from the tips of his toes to the individual hairs on his head, and the endless possibilities of such a world danced inside his brain. Not only was he honored by being present for this great moment in history, but he was now an integral part of it.

*   *   *   *

Jiang took a chair in the common space of the student center at the University of Beijing. The clock ticked off the beginning hours of the day, and the special-issue Time-X still strapped itself to his wrist. Nestling himself into a corner, his legs rested below the table as his hands unfolded the newspaper. The headlines flooded over the page, boasting of anything and everything dealing with United Europe and Raphael Vicente. It would have made him physically ill had he believed it would last. He remained convinced China would once again rise to world dominance, but this time instead of being merely among the elite, he would be the undisputed emperor.

Surprise was a vital element in the art of warfare, and Jiang held his daily intelligence briefing in his hands as if it were the bearer of all life. His fingers peeled through the pages as his mind soaked up every detail of the modern world. The operational timing was integral. He needed to strike fast, before a shield was built and his window of opportunity closed. It had to be well planned. His thoughts languished under a hundred different scenarios and the weight of them was enough to break him when he turned back to the front page and read the article.

The words pasted themselves next to a sickening picture of the smiling President Vicente. The headline jutted out in bold letters: "President Makes Sweeping Promises". There's an original. A politician making promises. Why was this news? Jiang read on. The article dealt with all of Vicente's assurances to foreign leaders that assemblers would be shared and individual rights and liberties would be respected. One issue dealt with privacy and human rights. Would United Europe use assembler-based nanotechnologies to spy on individuals? Would they infiltrate people's bodies and create a modern SS? Of course not.

Mr. Wonderful would never allow such a thing to happen. He gave his solemn oath assemblers would only be allowed to enter human bodies for the detention of prisoners and for the destruction of disease, and the latter only with the patient's consent. Vicente also made it clear his government did not seek to control people, but to liberate them. There was no reason to doubt him. If he wanted to enslave the entire human race, he could do it without lifting a finger. He didn't have to assuage fears or play politics. He was a regular old boy scout.

The dominant message of the administration concerned the protection of civil liberties. Even though assemblers could be embedded in the human circulatory system safely, and in fact, used as a deterrent to the abuse of nanotechnology, the whole idea was totally opposed by the public at large. The thought of tiny mechanized sensors probing the human body aided widespread fears of a dreadful modern day fascist regime, a common theme perpetuated by science fiction movies and doomsayers.

True or not, the Western leaders were weak. To wield and hold onto power, one had to exercise everything at his disposal, or else risk losing it. What made this concept so difficult? His thoughts traced his footsteps back to his run-ins with the idiot Claudel who wanted to provide two nations with the same horrendous weapon under the brilliant conclusion it would lead to peace, or at least some muddled concept of fairness. Throughout all of his dealings with the West, its leaders always seemed intent on self-flagellation. This time, they had succeeded magnificently, and it would be their last opportunity to do so.

Jiang refolded the newspaper and tossed it onto the table. He smiled as he considered his options. It was almost too easy.

*   *   *   *

The Mediterranean shimmered a sparkling blue and rays of sunlight swept over the cloudless sky. Hans Blitner dangled his legs from the tailgate of an Israeli cargo truck, part of a military supply line winding down the coastal highway. As the truck entered the Gaza Strip, he made note of the crumbling Palestinian ghettos sprouting out of the landscape like wild dandelions. Tin shanties pasted together with rusted nails and carpeted with dirt floors, packed themselves wall against wall for as far as he could see. The truck dug its wheels into a narrow dirt road running between rows of the tenements.

Packs of small children ran between the vehicles, playing in the dirt and mesmerized by the convoy. The truck stopped, and the engine shut off. The giggling voices of the children sprung to life, no longer muted by the roar of machines. Hans jumped off the tailgate, a mushroom of dust curling underneath his feet.

Around him, the bodies of Arab soldiers, shrapnel, and munitions littered the street. Israeli Defense Forces regulated the avenues with tanks and machine guns. Next to the truck, several members of the IDF sifted through a cache of hand grenades, assault rifles, and bomb making materials. One of the soldiers glued his eyes on Hans as he approached, but his body kept hard at work on the task at hand.

"You must be Blitner," he said.

Hans nodded. The soldier gathered a huge bundle of the confiscated weapons into his arms, tossed them into a strange container, then turned to shake hands.

"I can get you out of here as soon as we clean up this street. Place was a hotbed of vipers."

The soldier motioned to the sprawling line of war equipment spread out on the street's surface.

"Where you going again?" he asked.

"Ar-Rutbah," Hans said. "Overseeing the construction of a new detention facility."

"Well, there's plenty of people to throw in it," the soldier said.

As he spoke, he threw another arm full of weapons into the container. Hans focused his attention on the odd wastebasket and crept closer to its edge, keeping a safe distance away.

Its open mouth resembled a fountain, but no streaming waters illuminated its depths. Approximately ten feet in diameter, it emerged from the ground as a circular steel wall. Engraved on its side, large shiny letters inscribed the acronym "H.O.L.E." Hans watched while the other soldiers continuously dumped entire crates of ammunition and armaments into the cylinder, but it never filled.

"What's this?"

The soldier looked up at Hans while he strained to lift a box of hand grenades.

"That's our never ending trashcan. It's called the Hole—Harvester Of Liberated Elements."

Hans braved an extra few steps and peered over its edge. All he saw was an empty blackness as the soldier threw another box inside.

"It's a fixed location disassembler. Breaks atomic bonds instead of creating them. Atoms are sorted and collated by type, then transferred to a centralized depository until they can be reassembled into more humane objects."

Hans watched as the flurry of items crashed to the bottom, quickly melting like snowflakes on a sun-baked road. Guns, knives, bullets—every object thrown into the H.O.L.E. was eaten alive. Circling around to its opposite side, he noticed a second inscription. It read as follows, "and they shall beat their swords into plowshares, and their spears into pruning hooks—Isaiah 2:4".

CHAPTER 4:

Eternal Institution

"And I looked up and saw a black horse, and its rider was hold-ing a pair of scales in his hand. And a voice from among the four living beings said, 'A loaf of wheat bread or three loaves of barley for a day's pay. And don't hurt the olive oil or wine.'"

—John
Revelation 6:5–6

Lingering through the streets of Beijing, Jiang Yafei figured he had at least a few weeks, at most a few months, but he couldn't afford to be caught. It would take the Europeans, even with the help of American intelligence, a long time to wade through all of the documents in Beijing. And even once they did, back-up locations and secret underground bunkers would not be the highest inspection priorities on the list. Until then, he had an open win-dow to start and complete his own assembler project.

Walking through the Dongcheng District of Beijing, he finally came to the place he was searching for. He checked over his shoulder to make sure he wasn't being followed. He had no reason to suspect he was, but one never knew. In front of him, the landmark stood tall in the early morning sunlight. Dong Lai Shun was a Muslim restaurant in the heart of the city. He had eaten there years earlier. Their specialty was sliced boiled mutton, and he wondered how the Christian Westerners would like that, a Muslim restaurant taking pride in the slaughtering of lambs. The mere thought brightened his spirits.

But Jiang didn't come to this part of town to eat mutton, he came because of what was hidden behind the restaurant. The dark corridor in back of Dong Lai Shun hosted a door to a small series of rooms set up by the Chinese government. Standing before the brown steel door, Jiang inserted his identity card and the door clicked open. Inside, the lights automatically flicked on.

The room was empty, plain white with undecorated walls. Several computer terminals lined the walls. The place had originally been constructed as a bomb shelter, but was rarely used. Most of the people visiting in the last three years came only to ensure everything remained in working order. Jiang figured as a landmark of such little importance, it would be one of the last places raided for intelligence. He needed as much time as possible to get his work up and running, because he was unsure how much time it would require.

Sitting down at one of the computer terminals, he again entered his identity card, along with his password and thumbprint. The screen lit up with the Windows template, and Jiang shook his head. Again, the Americans had provided him with the tools necessary for their own destruction. Taking the Time-X watch off of his left hand, Jiang pulled off the back face. In its new state, it formed a perfect fit for the USB port on the back of the CPU. A spool of wire ran out from the back of the watch to the remaining parts, containing the dormant assembler. Peeling the glass casing off the watch face itself, Jiang held it up to the light, and he could barely notice traces of the carved out grooves. Opening the CD-ROM, he placed the glass watch face inside and closed the disk tray.

Double-clicking on the CD-ROM icon, he quickly pulled up the software for his project. It was done. He paused for a moment out of respect for Claudel and what he had been able to pull off. Roving through the screens, he marveled at the homemade software interface the man had put together. Complete with graphical icons, a child could have used it. Now, all that remained was to design a plan of action.

The newspaper rested on the desk next to his hand. He scanned the headline for at least the fifth time, "President Makes Sweeping Promises". His path was clear, and he remembered his father's words. He needed to design a fighting force capable of carrying out an overwhelming surprise attack. With total anonymity, plenty of time, and an assembler, Jiang was now, at the absolute least, the second most powerful man in the world.

*   *   *   *

Sterile and cold, the room was empty except for the modest table and two small chairs. The one-way glass window looked out into a similar room. Inside, they could see him. The old man sat alone, waiting like the old dog he was. His beard was a deathly gray, and rumors circulated that he was senile. But did any of this matter? The man spent most of his life imprisoning, murdering, and destroying the Cuban people, threatening the world on countless occasions, and now, the mighty nations of justice would put him in a country club prison for a year or two before he died of natural causes. Albert Fiennes wondered if this was what they called justice.

"Well, everyone is entitled to a defense."

His assistant looked across the table, and Albert knew she had read his mind. As deputy defense attorney for the case, he held her in high regard as a lawyer, although it was obvious their ideologies did not match up well. Albert was an idealist, and he believed in justice, but he also believed in liberty and freedom and national sovereignty. He harbored reservations and mixed emotions as he looked through the glass, his eyes trained on his newest client, Fidel Castro.

"A good one?" he asked.

It was as if he was asking her for approval to botch the whole trial and send his client to the gallows. Only the ICC didn't implement the death penalty and the worst possible outcome was a life sentence. He hated the man behind the glass, a man who ruled an island nation of people with an unrelenting iron fist and who, over forty years earlier, brought the entire world to the brink of nuclear destruction. His assistant sensed his unease.

"You know they'll nail him one way or another, so don't worry about it," she said.

Albert responded with a concurring nod.

"I know, but part of me just wants to see him take it in the rear, you know?"

She laughed.

"You aren't getting cold feet are you?"

"Of course not. So help me God, I'm going to do everything in my power to get this case thrown out. My biggest fear is that we're fighting an impossible war," he said.

Her eyes fell to the table as Albert turned to look once more at his infamous client. He had defended some of the worst vermin humanity could conjure, coming face-to-face with bloodthirsty killers, but never had he been as frightened by a case. The fate of the world, or at least everything in it that mattered, rested upon how well he performed in this trial. He couldn't let his emotions overrun reason. Not now. The rest of the world had already done that, and that's why it was in this situation. One chance. It's all he felt he had to preserve liberty and freedom before it was lost forever.

*   *   *   *

From the bell tower of Notre Dame Cathedral, Raphael viewed the entirety of Paris. The nuclear device detonated just off the bank of the Seine opposite the Eiffel Tower. The resulting ripples peeled back everything in their path for over a mile, melting the landscape into a pile of jagged glass and metal. It was as if a single drop of water crashed into a puddle, then froze solid just at the moment it touched down to Earth.

Preeminent above all else was the absence of the Eiffel Tower. Paris without the Eiffel Tower. That was like New York without the twin towers. Or Wall Street, or Times Square. All of which were now gone. Missing too was the Arc de Triomphe. A thin layer of dust still swirled over top of the battered city, and pieces of Paris still rode the currents, but the river crawled back to life. LOCUSTS hopped over the wreckage like bits of gray sand, cleansing the city of radioactive particles. Thousands of people walked through the rubble cleaning up the mess with the aid of cranes and trucks. Others coated parts of the city with a special nanotechnic paint to strengthen and preserve the older buildings on the outskirts of the city, reinforcing them from further collapse. In the center of the rubble stood a giant H.O.L.E., lifeless and immobile. Thousands of workers climbed over the pile of broken city and dropped the bits of wreckage into the wide chasm.

Gilder walked up behind the president and tapped him on the shoulder.

"It's time to go."

Raphael followed, turning to take one last look at the city, then climbed down the stairs. Outside, cameras flashed as he entered his armored SUV, and the motorcade set its course for Versailles. Raphael leaned back in his seat and clicked on the television. The commentator's voice blared through the car's cabin.

"And the UN Security Council Conference on Nanotechnology kicks off today with the world's leaders gathering at the newly renovated grounds of Versailles…"

Raphael turned down the volume and addressed Gilder.

"We need to discuss some legal matters before the day's end, matters of prosecution of non-heads-of-state. I don't want those who are guilty of crimes against humanity to evade punishment simply because of their position."

Gilder's fingers seesawed over the switch for the overhead light while he explored the limousine's interior.

"Everyone is subject to ICC jurisdiction. It's only a matter of choosing the defendants."

"Good," Raphael said. "Compose a preliminary list, and don't be afraid to put private citizens on it."

A mass of protestors gathered outside Versailles cordoned off by a line of riot police. Raphael studied them through the tinted windows of his SUV. Raging hands and arms hoisted signs with such phrases as "Save The Humans" and "Protect The Atmosphere From Assemblers". Among the discombobulated shouts and ranting, he failed to locate one face of tranquility— not a single person able to hold his emotions in check.

The police pushed against the crowd as the Explorer passed by, and Versailles emerged from the earth like a garden of crystals. The sight of its blazing ediface planted a ray of excited inspiration in his breast. Even in this new day and age, he couldn't pull his eyes away, so much history had transpired within its walls.

*   *   *   *

In the Hall of Mirrors, Jean sipped on a glass of Champagne with Derek Stevens by his side. The two of them colluded in a corner, while a consortium of powerful leaders gathered in their presence, filling the gigantic room with faces. Now chief of staff for President Price, Derek was anxious to scope out United Europe's vision for the Nanotechnic Age in advance of the official meetings set to take place the following day. Jean remained calm, enjoying the pleasurable swill of the alcohol as it gushed through his veins. He handled Derek's attention with complete ease as the liquid swirled between his fingers. His words were just as soothing.

"You have my word that President Vicente's word is as good as gold."

Derek smirked, unconvinced.

"Let me remind you that gold isn't worth what it once was. Actions speak louder than words. The president's actions will dictate whether or not we should be concerned."

Jean chuckled, and his curling index finger motioned for Derek to move in closer. His voice lowered to a whisper so no one else could hear.

"Vicente is a trustworthy man. Don't repeat this, but United Europe will announce the granting of unhindered access to limited assemblers."

"What?" Derek said. "That's it? We'll need more of a commitment than that."

Jean held up his hands as if to brace for attack.

"Hey, I don't make the policies. I'm just a bureaucrat."

"That's an understatement."

"Look, I know you're upset. But Vicente hopes this will reduce the incentive for America, Japan, and Russia to reconstitute their own assembler projects. A second nation in possession of assemblers at this stage would spark a dangerous confrontation—a nanotechnic arms race placing the world on the threshold of catastrophe."

Derek tapped his foot on the floor and nervously scanned the room with his eyes.

"Whatever. What else can you tell me?"

"The president will make sealed assembler labs plentiful by week's end. And just as in the past, patent protections will apply to all new inventions and designs."

Derek considered the proposition. Sealed assembler labs and limited assemblers would provide the backbone of the new world economy. With them, America's companies would witness exploding margins, dwindling costs, and surging profits. Limited assemblers would soon bring almost unlimited wealth to the human race and the administration's financial contributors (some of them at least) would be ecstatic, but the proposal did not address the question of national sovereignty. America and the other nations still lay at the mercy of United Europe militarily. Derek didn't keep his opinion to himself.

"Fine, but what about military technology. We still remain under your thumb, and the United States does not intend to relinquish its sovereignty."

Jean gave him a reassuring nod and put a hand on his shoulder.

"You'll just have to be patient. The president has a fear of sharing military applications and unlimited assemblers with other nations before a comprehensive active shield is in operation. And can you blame him? Until then, we're all in danger, but I assure you it's the president's intention to share these technologies in full. If not, you wouldn't be standing here today."

His last comment echoed through Derek's mind. It was altogether frightening yet comforting at the same time. After all, if President Vicente wanted a monopoly on power, he would have one.

*   *   *   *

The sound of a monotone voice filtered through the microphone and bounced off the surrounding walls of the cavernous room. The representative from Belize voiced his country's position while Raphael sat, arms folded, behind a section of table displaying the United Europe nameplate. In a foldout chair directly behind him, Eduardo peeled through the conference draft resolution. Midway through, he pounded the paper with his index finger.

"We can't agree to this rule."

"What rule?"

Eduardo pulled out a pen and drew on a section marked: "Guidelines for the Safe Deployment of Nanomachines".

"Article three, fourth guideline—no state shall create a device able to replicate in a natural, uncontrolled environment."

"So what?"

"So what? That's what you say? So what?"

"Yeah. So what? We need to protect the biosphere from an accident."

Eduardo purveyed a look of utter confusion, then infused a sarcastic tone into the backdrop of his voice.

"But that's what you build an active shield for."

Raphael reclined in his chair and unfolded his arms.

"So? We build an active shield. Why does it matter?"

"You don't understand. These types of replicators are necessary to an active shield. Without them, all you have is a network of sensors. What good is the ability to know you're under attack if you can't fight back?"

Raphael twisted his neck and issued a blank stare, his glazed eyes indicated he now understood the severity of the mandate. Eduardo pressed him further.

"It's like biological weapons treaties. They sound nice and good and humane, but only the good guys obey them. An intelligent opponent will never follow these guidelines, and that's who we need to be on guard against."

The debate from the conference proceedings amplified itself in the silence between their exchange. Raphael looked straight ahead as if he had ignored the statement, then abruptly leaned back toward Eduardo.

"This is going to make us look bad," he said.

Eduardo let out a prolonged breath.

"Would you rather look bad or be dead? Because that's what's going to happen if we agree to this. When you fight a war to the death, never place restrictions on your ability to defend yourself."

"An active shield can't solve the problem?"

Eduardo dropped his face into his cupped hands and resurfaced yanking every strand of hair on his head as if frustration rained on him from hidden clouds.

"I'm talking about an active shield. Any restrictions you agree to now will hinder the ability of the active shield to do its job. It's no different than conventional war. If you agree not to bomb civilian neighborhoods, that sounds nice. But your enemy will just hide among the civilians and strike with impunity."

Eduardo looked out over the conference room and pretended to pay attention to the debate while he whispered his arguments in Raphael's ear.

"If a terrorist launches an assault using unrestricted replicators, while our forces are constrained, we'll be dead in the water. If one army multiplies exponentially across the battlefield, while the other remains stagnant, the growing army will overwhelm the other. It's common sense."

Raphael threw his hands up.

"Okay, we'll pull it off the table."

*   *   *   *

"Does this have the potential to destroy the biosphere? Yes. But it doesn't have to, and it holds immense promise that can't be overlooked."

Raphael stood in front of the onslaught of flickering cameras, Eduardo by his side. Journalists shoved microphones into the air and shouted their questions up to the podium. The president held up his hand, and the media fell into silence. Their outstretched arms vied for his attention, and he pointed to a woman in the front row.

"Mr. President, many environmental groups live in fear that nanotechnology will lead to an exponential explosion in waste products in our oceans, our forests, and the atmosphere itself. What is the conference doing to address these concerns?"

Raphael let out a half-hearted laugh.

"Most of these fears have been blown out of proportion. Molecular assemblers will most likely lead to an exponential decrease in waste. In essence, this is a manufacturing process without byproducts, or at least byproducts that can be recycled. Regardless, United Europe has agreed to the formation of two United Nations regulatory bodies that will oversee the oceans and the atmosphere."

"What powers will they have?" the journalist asked.

Raphael shrugged his shoulders.

"They won't have enforcement powers per se, but they will have the power to measure our world's shared resources and report any irregularities."

The hands shot back into the air and hollered up at the podium once again. Raphael pointed down to the second row while flashes of light splattered around him.

"Mr. President, sources tell us the conference has yet to agree on a ban of replicators capable of operating in a natural, uncontrolled environment. Is this true? And if so, why the delay? Isn't this one of the chief fears put forward by the environmental lobby?"

"The conference hasn't been able to agree on everything. There are always details that need to be hammered out. Now, if you'll excuse me…"

He stepped away from the podium, the sounds of their shouted questions ringing in his ears, and he disappeared into the adjoining room.

*   *   *   *

Raphael stood at the window of his private office at Versailles, his eyes surveying the exotic greenery and illuminating waters of the gardens below. The sky blended into the evening now, and the formal conference agenda remained on hold until morning. He watched the reflection of his eyes recede into the descending blackness of the window's exterior and waited in silence for the arrival of his next appointment. He stood alone, relishing the moment. It was one he had anticipated since the first day of the breakthrough. Not one to gain pleasure from another man's misfortune, he was willing to make exceptions. And he planned to thoroughly enjoy the groveling certain to take place. Edmond Bernhoff, CEO of a company Raphael loathed from pre-assembler days, would be arriving momentarily.

The world leader in diamond mining, Bernhoff's family-owned company DeBray, was generations in the making. Raphael made a personal promise to unmake it. The company maintained a certified monopoly with a long track record of Mafia-type business tactics. In Sierra Leone, they initiated a bloody civil war in an effort to seize control of the country's diamond trade. Stories of whole villages being slaughtered haunted Raphael's conscience. The victorious rebels chopped off the hands of every male over the age of twelve who did not ally with their cause, and the sound of their sharpening cleavers squealed through his thoughts. The door opened.

Bernhoff walked in. He wore an Armani suit and carried a hat pressed between the fingers of both hands. Raphael glared in his direction as if ready to attack.

"Take a seat," he said.

Bernhoff acted hesitant, but then succumbed. Raphael refused to make eye contact, continuing to stare out of his window and following Bernhoff in the reflection. The room had a dim bronze lighting to it that made the man noticeably uncomfortable.

"What brings you here?"

Bernhoff crossed his legs and let his hat fall into his lap.

"I hoped we could discuss the state of the post-assembler economy."

"You did, did you?"

Raphael held the stalwart pose of a military commander, frozen with his hands locked behind his back.

"Well, I understand plans call for the protection of intellectual property rights, that copyrights and trademarks will be protected."

Raphael nodded his head.

"That is true."

"I was hoping the same consideration would be granted to DeBray as was granted to Coca-Cola. That United Europe will agree to abstain from the use of assemblers to create DeBray products."

"Of course," Raphael said.

Bernhoff smiled.

"And of course DeBray will be making generous campaign donations to the Vicente administration. We support those who defend intellectual property."

"The law is the law. If anyone uses the DeBray name without your consent, you let us know."

A smug look of disdain covered Bernhoff's face, though he tried to hide it. He let a fake laugh roll from his lips.

"Our name we can protect. What I'm asking for—"

Raphael pivoted to face him, his eyes burning with anger.

"What you're asking for is protection of your monopoly, a patent on diamonds. You might as well ask for a patent on oil, or coal, or air!"

Bernhoff shuffled in his chair, obviously uncomfortable with the statement. Raphael could see that the man wanted to lash out, but found himself in the unusual position of lesser authority.

"Sir, I never—"

Raphael cut him off again.

"Have you any idea the severity of the crimes in which your company is complicit? Have you any idea?"

He hammered the desk with both fists and raced around the desk like a mad man, eyes blazing like a fiery jack-o-lantern. He shoved his own face in front of Bernhoff's shaking frame.

"God humbles the arrogant! What are your diamonds worth now? Were they worth all the murders, the underhanded deals, the chopped off limbs and torture?"

Bernhoff shivered with fright and spun in his seat when he heard the door open behind him. Four members of the presidential guard rushed in. Raphael stepped away as they grabbed Bernhoff. Then he looked in the man's eyes.

"Edmond Bernhoff, you're under arrest for crimes against humanity."

Surprised by the accusation, Bernhoff turned hysterical, his hands and feet trembling in terror. Raphael took one last look at the piece of trash before him, then prodded him toward the door with a swift kick.

"Get this man out of my sight," he said. "He disgusts me."

*   *   *   *

Evening spilled over the garden with its abundant blackness and omnipresent void of light. Jean approached Derek from its western edge. Prickling sounds of running water gushed through the area, and the illuminated waters meandered around the well pruned rose bushes and their prickly thorns. The audible roar of the falling waters muted each footstep and Jean nearly walked up to Derek unnoticed. As the man approached, Derek kept his voice to a low whisper.

"What's all this about?"

Jean kept his hands buried in his pockets and stared downward as if counting the individual bricks in the courtyard floor. He remained close to the fountain so that the water would muffle any listening devices that could be concealed in the area.

"I think we can help each other."

"How is that?"

Jean took a step closer so that he was only inches from Derek's left ear, but facing away from him.

"The United States and its allies need to continue the independent development of an assembler. And I can help you."

Derek shook his head.

"Price shut the project down. He felt the resources were better spent elsewhere."

"He needs to restart it."

Surprised by the statement, Derek took a small step backward.

"Why? Why are you telling me this?"

"For no reason that you're not aware of. Too much power is in one man's hands. What if Vicente dies? Both our countries need to hedge our bets against such a possibility."

"Why doesn't Vicente tell us this? Why you? Why here?"

Jean leaned forward and looked around the courtyard.

"Because this is my idea, not his. I know Vicente well, and he would view a reconstitution of America's project as a personal affront to his own power. He would never allow it. He's bent on some personal quest to shape the world in his own desired image."

Derek took a deep breath.

"Let's say I could convince Price to reactivate the project. To hide that from Vicente—that's impossible."

Jean held up a correcting finger.

"Nearly impossible. All the intelligence he sees goes through me first. I'll simply delay it until you're finished."

"And you don't think this will start a nanotechnic arms race?"

Jean let out a laugh and wrapped his arm around Derek's shoulder.

"Of course not, that's just a scare tactic—an excuse for United Europe to hold a monopoly on power."

CHAPTER 5:

Defending Life

"When people are saying, 'All is well; everything is peaceful and secure,' then disaster will fall upon them as suddenly as a woman's birth pains begin when her child is about to be born. And there will be no escape."

—**Paul**
1 Thessalonians 5:3

Light filtered through the corridor. Eduardo brushed his hand over the door-knob, then removed it and stared at the door. His hand made two additional maneuvers toward the knob before finally grabbing hold and tearing the door open.

Inside, Raphael held a ceramic coffee cup in his hand, and the door's quick opening startled him as if some haunting ghost had nudged him from behind. Placing the cup on an end table, he extended a bright smile.

"Eduardo, what a pleasant surprise."

Eduardo walked right up to him and stared in the president's face.

"I don't want to hear it," he said.

Raphael slid his cup away and sat on the edge of an end table.

"What are you talking about?"

Eduardo lifted his hands in the air, then let them crash down to his sides.

"I'm talking about this conference. It's a nightmare."

"I don't understand."

"You don't understand? Don't you understand how this bureaucratic infighting has left us exposed? How long has it been? And still we haven't agreed on a single aspect of an active shield."

"Don't you think you're overreacting a bit?"

Eduardo ran his hands through his hair, clenching the last locks that shadowed his neck.

"Overreacting? Are you living in another world?"

Raphael stood up and placed a hand on Eduardo's shoulder.

"We already have a shield set up."

"No. You have a few sensors. Nothing an intelligent enemy couldn't circumvent."

Raphael rubbed his hands together and let his eyes trace over the dark carpet.

"Look, I took your advice on the replicators, didn't I? These things take time. We need to respect other nations by working together democratically."

"We don't have time. Either we start work on an active shield today or I'm walking."

His comment brought silence for what seemed like several minutes.

"You would do that? You would leave us?"

"I would."

"But you're one of our best designers. One of our best thinkers."

Amused, Eduardo shook his head.

"A lot of good it does, huh?"

"I can't believe you would leave."

He looked at Eduardo, unable to fathom his motives.

"So? Which is it?" Eduardo asked.

Raphael's fingers pressed into the wood finish as he knelt over his desk in disbelief.

"I guess you must do what you must do."

*   *   *   *

The building boasted the latest advancements in architecture, and the chamber was a sparkling white with Doric columns decoratively outlining the walls. Eighteen men perched themselves at the helm, lingering high above the rest of the room's occupants. Fidel Castro sat in the defendant's chair for the first time in his life, flanked by a large defense team headed by Albert Fiennes. The lead prosecutor salivated as the Chief Justice pounded his gavel and called the court into order. Albert stood up from behind the table and addressed the court.

"Your honor, my client enters no plea and refuses to recognize the legitimacy of this court."

The Chief Justice peered out from behind his bifocals.

"Mr. Fiennes, the International Criminal Court is a legitimate entity chartered by the United Nations. And your client is subject to its jurisdiction."

Albert walked toward the bench, appealing to the judges.

"I'm well aware of my client's career as President of Cuba, and I won't argue that he's a good man. Perhaps many of the charges directed against him are true. However, I stand before this court today not in defense of Fidel Castro, but in defense of liberty. The crimes alleged include definitions of Crimes Against Humanity and Crimes of Aggression that are inherently ambiguous."

The Chief Justice pounded his gavel.

"Mr. Fiennes, this court's legitimacy is not up for debate."

Albert turned his back on the bench and addressed the audience in the chamber. His right hand hammered down into his left.

"If you allow this court to make a ruling, then you will lose your liberty forever. In the age of assemblers, our government has the ability to drug, bug, assassinate, seize, infiltrate, and control the very world in which you live. In such a world, if liberty is lost, it is gone forever. Forever. And I'm telling you if you give legitimacy and validity to the rulings of this court—if you give that type of power to your government, you will never get it back."

The judge slammed his gavel onto the wooden surface until the room fell silent.

"Mr. Fiennes, this courtroom is not a political soapbox."

Albert turned back to the panel of judges, a red anger distributed over his face, and he raised his voice.

"Unilaterally, this court decides who it will prosecute. Unilaterally, this court decides how to interpret the crimes with which its defendants are accused. Unilaterally, it has the authority to appeal its own judgements. Unilaterally, it decides punishment and then carries it out. This court is the judge, jury, and executioner."

He angled at the judges and moved closer toward their huddle, staring each one in the eye as he walked the length of the bench. With a raised eyebrow, he pointed in their direction.

"What will you do when they come for you?" he asked.

*   *   *   *

Eduardo settled into the chair, pulling it closer to the table's edge. Across the table, a journalist from *The Daily Telegraph* clicked on a recorder and shifted some papers.

"I'll have to say, I was caught off guard when you called me out of the blue for this. I'm the envy of the newsroom," he said.

"It has to be done," Eduardo said.

"You realize this interview will be recorded in full?"

Eduardo gave a quick nod, and the journalist began the interview.

"You were heralded as one of the brightest members of President Vicente's advisory team, but last week you had a parting of ways with the administration. Why did you resign your post?"

"I felt an obligation to shed light on a problem United Europe has failed to address. Since long before the assembler breakthrough, an international team of policy advisors has tried to uncover a solution to the Terror Conundrum."

The journalist scrawled hand-written notes onto a legal pad, and Eduardo's answer caused him to lift his head from the page.

"Terror Conundrum?"

Eduardo nodded, a grim indifference pasted on his face.

"For years before the assembler breakthrough, we knew the advent of this new technology would present the world with an incredible range of new problems. The Terror Conundrum is first among them. Prior to the breakup of the Soviet Union, weapons of mass destruction were confined to the hands of nation states. At that time, terrorism presented little threat to global security. In the years following the Cold War, weapons of mass destruction proliferated and found their way into the hands of terrorist groups. This gave immense destructive powers to individuals and small groups, making terrorism the single greatest threat to international order."

The journalist nodded in agreement.

"That goes without saying."

"But the Nanotechnic Age amplifies that threat. Prior to the creation of assemblers, we practiced a policy of risk management. We tired to limit terrorist attacks as much as possible, but even catastrophic attack, although threatening to the economy, did not threaten our existence. That is no longer true," Eduardo said.

He hung his head in frustration.

"In the Nanotechnic Age, governments must practice a policy of risk avoidance. Because a terrorist attack using the full force of nanotechnology is certain to be lethal. There is wide belief within the military and scientific communities that, among comparable opponents, a first-strike force will be victorious. A free and open society that calls attention to its weaknesses will be especially vulnerable to attack."

The journalist feverishly scribbled on his notepad, soaking up every detail.

"This is a big story," he said.

Eduardo nodded, then continued with his assessment.

"Operating in such an environment, states are forced to protect themselves against individual citizens. And taking preemptive measures to head off nanotechnic terrorism will lead to ever-greater police powers being exercised by government. At some point, the citizens will find they need to protect themselves from government. And I don't know how they can do so. The right to bear arms doesn't extend to massive armies of replicating nanomachines."

The journalist sat on the edge of his seat, so entranced by the answer that he forgot about his recorder, his notes, and his next question. Following a brief silence, he shook the cobwebs from his mind and asked his follow up.

"Can't an active shield solve these problems?"

Eduardo waved his hand through the air as if to brush off the question. His candor noticeably affected the frightened journalist.

"An active shield may help, but we haven't built one yet. And we can't have one hundred percent confidence in its effectiveness. An active shield operates like an immune system, and immune systems fail. The Maginot Line was thought to be impenetrable, and it probably was, but the German army simply marched around it. Like open source code, a good active shield will be open to the public so that many minds can submit ideas for strengthening it. That also means its vulnerabilities will be public to our enemies. We have a real problem if we want to continue to live in a free and open society, because history illustrates that the only governments capable of combating terrorism with total effectiveness are totalitarian regimes."

By now, the journalist was shaking his head in disbelief.

"Why hasn't the Vicente Administration voiced these concerns?"

Eduardo shrugged.

"To avoid panic. I think they believe these problems can be overcome."

"Are you saying United Europe is lying to the rest of the world?"

Eduardo paused while he thought about the question. Then he gave a quick response.

"Yes. And to itself as well."

CHAPTER 6:

Vicente's Eternal Pax Romana

"The locusts looked like horses armed for battle. They had gold crowns on their heads, and they had human faces. Their hair was long like the hair of a woman, and their teeth were like the teeth of a lion. They wore armor made of iron, and their wings roared like an army of chariots rushing into battle. They had tails that stung like scorpions, with power to torture people. This power was given to them for five months."

—John
Revelation 9:7–10

Navigating its way from a carrier in the Mediterranean, the helicopter kicked up shoots of grass, slapping them back and forth in the field as it pulled in for a comfortable landing. Anxious crowds congregated in the rural outskirts of Tripoli hoping to catch a glimpse of United Europe's president. Raphael stepped onto the firm soil, his black locks whipping through the sheared wind of the churning blades. Bulging eyes with hysterical voices called out to him from behind the lines of security personnel, and arms and hands waved through the mob like periscopes popping up and down on a sea of people.

Against the urging of his bodyguards, he parted the line of security and entered the mob. The roar of their voices rose in a frenzy. Smiling faces jock-eyed for position and a whole mass of feet shuffled toward him like iron shav-ings drawn to a magnet. Battling hands raged against one another for the honor of touching him, and the triumphant few clawed and ripped at his gar-ments as if the mere touch of the fabric that donned his back harbored a supernatural power to heal.

With the needlepoint precision of a master tailor, he plunged through the crowd, swallowed by the mass of bodies. His security detail fought to stay with him, but the hysterical stampede drove them back. Raphael remained calm, an enraptured smile transfixed to his face. With graceful ease, he forged his way through the crowd to the place marked by the Red Crescent flag that rippled in the breeze.

A crippled woman lay on a gurney in front of him. The mob pressed up against it and fell to an eerie silence as he held up his hand. Placing his right hand on the woman's shoulder, he spoke to her.

"What's your name?"

The woman's eyes rolled at the sky because she was blind, but she grinned at the sound of his voice.

"Nadia, Mr. President."

Raphael gripped her right hand with his left, while motioning to the atten-dant doctor with his free hand.

"Please, call me Raphael."

She squeezed on his hand while the doctor positioned an eyedropper over her. A single drop fell onto each eyeball, and immediately, the invisible nano-machines began their work. At the doctor's request, she closed her eyes so they could absorb the fluid. After a few seconds, the doctor motioned to Raphael. He tightened his grip on Nadia's hand and cradled her head with his free hand, his face leaning over her. With a melodious whisper, he spoke in her ear.

"Open your eyes and see."

Her eyelids lifted up and jubilation dashed across her face.

"Raphael, I can see you!"

Tears bled down her rounded cheeks as she sat upright on the portable bed. She kissed him on the forehead.

"And you're more handsome than I imagined," she said.

Raucous laughter broke out from the ocean of cheers. She glanced down at her legs, two limp sticks that clung to her body, and she watched as the doctor injected them with a milky white fluid. Raphael pulled her toward him and stuck his face in front of hers.

"Now," he said. "Get up and walk!"

Nadia threw her legs off the bed and placed her feet flat on the ground. She took a small step forward, followed by a giant leap toward Raphael. And her leap had all the graceful motion of a wild deer. She wrapped her arms around him, and the voices screamed out.

"Long live Vicente!"

The landscape flooded with joy, a trillion voices giving praise to United Europe. The sea of bodies carved out a pathway, men and women stepping aside so the woman could walk forward. Raphael took her hand and led her through the crowd.

A makeshift stage had been set up, and as the president approached, the leaders of the new Libyan government announced his arrival through a loudspeaker. Children gushed with excitement, and from all across the open field, more and more people were drawn to the mass of villagers. As he waved to them, his smile gave off a sense of hope and peace. For the first time in their lives, the people of Libya had reason to be idealists once again. The future gave them something to look forward to with joy, rather than dread.

Within a few moments, he alone hovered above the masses. With the gentle wave of his hand and a patient demeanor, the crowd fell to a silence. The majority of Libyans spoke Arabic, and he spoke to them in their native tongue.

"With all humility, our nation seeks to follow in the footsteps of Abraham Lincoln's. With malice toward none. With charity for all. With firmness in the right, as Allah provides us the gift to see what is righteous, let us strive to finish the work of nations. Let us bind up the wounds of this world."

The cheers called up to him, and he accepted them with a humble nod.

"It is with mercy and forgiveness that the world must move forward. The war on terror is being fought, and it is being won. In places as faraway as Cuba, political prisoners are set free. Eyes that haven't seen the sun in over twenty years are liberated to the light. Once again, they will look upon the beauty of the world. Once again, they will be free among their people."

He paused and gazed at the sky before continuing.

"In places such as North Korea, people dance in the streets. Brothers and sisters, aunts and uncles, relatives who have been divided by a line of war for over half a century are once again united. Never again will they be taken away. Never again will their world be haunted by the horrible pain of fear.

And in places such as Libya, freedom rises like the tallest mountain. People move about the country as they wish, free to worship as they choose and free to live their lives as they see fit. Political tyranny has been removed, and the brutal fist of disease is gone forever. Hunger and poverty, the pollution of our land, these things too are gone. And each citizen, with all these new blessings, has a home of his own to shield him from the scorching sun.

These are a few of the benefactors of the New Pax Romana. A worldwide peace enforced not by an all-powerful emperor in Rome, but by a self-ruled people united in the principles of justice and international law. All around the world, once oppressed peoples are experiencing liberation at the hand of this wave of humanitarian justice. Citizens held captive all their lives are now experiencing for the first time the fruits of secured liberty and individual rights, rights given to them not by the whims of a government, but rights endowed by nature and not subject to the approval of any man or any government.

This is the will of Allah, that men should live free. And it should be our first priority to secure such a way of life. For those among us who still seek to destroy democracy, to wage war for another purpose, you may believe Allah's will is to destroy such forms of government, but we believe His will is to preserve, protect, and defend them."

He stepped away from the microphone to the cheers of a hysterical mob. Glamorous new clothes hung from their backs, and luxurious new houses awaited them in their villages. To this man, their adulation was unending. He took the right to be kings of the Earth, a right he could have reserved for himself alone, and he made it the birthright of all human beings.

Descending the steps of the stage, Raphael reflected on the fruits of his labor. Soon, Africa would be composed entirely of democratic nations. HIV-AIDS, a problem that just a couple of months ago had ravaged the continent, now stood on the verge of annihilation. Poverty and homelessness were under assault, and they too would be eliminated forever.

Gilder approached from the left, and quickly fell into lockstep beside the president.

"Mugabe was just taken into custody, and we'll have Taylor in a couple of hours," he said.

Raphael seemed pleased with the news. Mugabe and Taylor were two of the last world dictators to be removed from power and taken into custody. In fact, it was Taylor who had been responsible for the unending atrocities in Sierra Leone, a series of wars fought over material greed. For over a decade, Taylor fought along with DeBray to commandeer the lucrative diamond mines of that region. In the process, his marauding gangs hacked off the arms of tens of thousands of innocent people. And for what? Now his diamonds were worthless, and all of Taylor's worldly power withered along with their value.

*   *   *   *

As Jiang walked through the streets of his beloved capital, he breathed in the cool air. On every side of him, people bobbed up and down through the crowds. As he exhaled, death quickly followed. With each puff of his breath, men and women became infected with a highly contagious nanotechnic germ. It was not preprogrammed to kill them or display any overt symptoms of disease. Disguised as chicken pox, its only purpose was to lie dormant until the appointed time.

Entering a disco-tech in the lower part of the city, Jiang found a dense collection of bodies to serve his purpose. Packed shoulder to shoulder, young Chinese men and women pounded the night away to the rhythm of electronic music. With each gasp of air, they became infected with his bug. Later, they would infect their families who would then infect their neighbors.

Jiang paused for a moment and watched them. He watched the premium beer bottles stride across the floor. He watched the faces brimming with joy, and it disgusted him. How could they dance in celebration after their nation had just been humiliated? Their leaders were held captive by a foreign enemy, and they were happy! Their disrespect for the homeland pained him as they toasted the new age—the age of abundance, the age of wealth and indulgence. As they did, Jiang danced alongside of them. He also had reason to celebrate. Soon, they would all be humbled, and he would bring about the birth of a new age—the rebirth of Imperial China as the pre-eminent world power in the Nanotechic Age.

*   *   *   *

About the same time Jiang and his countrymen celebrated the new age of prosperity, Jerusalem erupted in peaceful protest. In one part of the assemblage, a man with a megaphone read excerpts from *Blood Brothers*. Rapturous applause followed each line, and excitement was present in every face. Peace signs moved along like waves over a tide of people, and the flag of United Europe blanketed the flood of faces.

In the middle of the crowd lay the crumbled remains of the Dome of the Rock mosque. For months, the UN had cordoned off the area from the public. Now, the UN peacekeeping force was all that held back the weight of the crowd. After several hours, a wave of protestors moved forward, and the peacekeepers did not resist.

Bursting forward like Olympic sprinters, several Jews, Muslims, Christians, and a few non-religious zealots caught up in the fervor of the moment, plowed through the front line. In their arms, they carried a single block of limestone. Stopping at the edge of the tattered remnants of the Dome of the Rock, they placed the stone at the corner of the ruins. The crowd cheered and surged forward in celebration. The rebuilding of the King Solomon's Temple had begun.

PART VI

▼

In The Names Of Peace And Safety

"And I looked up and saw a horse whose color was pale green like a corpse. And Death was the name of its rider, who was followed around by Hades. They were given authority over one-fourth of the earth, to kill with the sword and famine and disease and wild animals."

—**John**
Revelation 6:8

CHAPTER 1:

Inherited Wealth Of Nations

"He required everyone—great and small, rich and poor, slave and free—to be given a mark on the right hand or on the forehead. And no one could buy or sell anything without that mark, which was either the name of the beast or the number representing his name. Wisdom is needed to understand this. Let the one who has understanding solve the number of the beast, for it is the number of humanity. His number is 666."

—John
Revelation 13:16–18

A hundred images of swastikas and pentagrams covered the walls. Hand drawn copies of the number "666" fluttered from the ceiling like strings of tiny baseball pennants, and articles headlining Europe's new president plastered every crooked angle of the apartment like planks of peeling wallpaper. Raphael Vicente held the photographs in his trembling hands. The file on

Paul Lindsay lay open on his desk. Part of a Christian extremist group convinced he was the antichrist, Lindsay botched Raphael's assassination and killed Poyner instead. *Blood Brothers* added fuel to the fire of his hatred, much as it had for Daniel Heron and his group, The Temple Seven. A profile picture of the man attached itself to the dossier by paperclip. It displayed a smug face, a dead face—the face of the man who had killed his wife and might as well have killed him.

Was it mere coincidence this man attempted to murder him on the same night seven nuclear warheads nearly devastated human civilization? And on the same night nuclear disaster was averted in the same city? Some greater power brought him into the picture, supplying him with intelligence and training.

Nevertheless, officers shot Lindsay on the spot, and he died two days later before they could find out. Officials investigated his apartment in the days that followed. A flurry of protestors and crazies scurried out of the woodwork following his appointment, but never did he realize how much some of them truly hated him. Their religious fanaticism remained a foreign concept, but their intense hatred did not. He hated them just as much, if not more, than they could possibly hate him. Religious zealots were a cancer on free society.

He paid careful attention to the television as it threaded its images into the silence. The ICC sentenced ten additional men from the Temple Seven Group. All to life. The Court also convicted several Muslims for plotting suicide attacks against Israel. Christians, Muslims, Jews—it didn't matter. Extremists from every nation and religion filled his world, hiding and plotting around every corner. How did such people evolve? And how did they arrive at the demented conclusion that God wanted them to kill in his name? God is God. If he wanted someone murdered, he would do it himself. Wouldn't he? Wasn't that the point of being omnipotent?

The door opened, and Jean entered the room. In his hand, he held a folded newspaper that he quickly tossed on Raphael's desk. The headline jumped off the page in bold typeface: "ORTIZ BASHES TERROR POLICY".

"He's insinuating that your policies will lead to a dictatorship, or worse, an end to all life," Jean said.

"Eduardo's entitled to his own opinion."

Jean placed the palms of his hands flat on the president's desk and leaned forward.

"And I think his opinion is valid. In a world of assemblers, individuals are more dangerous than ever. We can no longer afford to wait for the terrorists among them to announce themselves."

"What should we do?"

"The same thing America did to Iraq. We have an obligation to take preemptive measures against prospective terrorists."

Raphael reclined in his chair, folding his fingers together.

"But people have rights."

"People have the right to life and liberty. The people have a right to be protected from harm. They chose democracy and a pluralistic society. Anyone who opposes that form of government is incompatible with the rest of us, and they must be dealt with."

Raphael nodded his head. He loathed the intolerant, the arrogant religious fanatics, and anyone harboring exclusionist, hard-line views. One by one, he was determined to round them up. One day, he would wipe all terrorists, religious fanatics, and extremists from the face of the earth. And that day would be a great day of victory, a day of rest for the whole world.

*   *   *   *

The hard limestone cast a giant shadow over the courtyard as it obstructed the sun's rays in all their glory. Garrison sat on the ground surrounded by a number of Jewish and Christian followers. They turned their heads in wonder.

"Isn't this Temple magnificent?"

Garrison's face grew long.

"Haven't you learned your lesson yet?" he asked.

"What do you mean?" they said.

"Why do you waste your time with this building, when not one stone will be left on another. You can not love the things of this world and still serve God. God does not want your sacrifices. God does not want material objects or buildings. He wants you to be merciful. He wants you to love each other."

Garrison stood up and spoke in a loud voice that resonated high above the surrounding crowd.

"God has issued this warning to his people—Repent! For the kingdom of heaven is near! That great and vengeful day of the Lord is coming, and this is what the Sovereign Lord says: A mighty force will rise against you, and it is I who send this great destroying army. In that day, you will know that I alone am the Lord your God!"

With a great shout, his voice carried over the crowd like a sonic wave passing through their bodies. Outside the Temple Gate, an angry mob of protestors burst through the wall of peacekeepers, weapons in hand. They surged inward, clubbing Jews and screaming out to the heavens.

"Death to the Zionist enemy!"

"Death to the Temple!"

Incoherent rants muddied the air and their sounds were interrupted only by the violent slashes of fists and sticks. Rocks rained down from the sky like snowflakes. One of them smacked Garrison in the forehead and hurled him to the ground. And blood poured out from his head while feet and legs trampled over his body.

*   *   *   *

The chain of Jeeps plowed down the dirt road on the outskirts of Harare, Zimbabwe. As the procession traveled past, herds of people numbering in the thousands chased after it like kids chasing an ice cream truck in the early months of summer. Off in the distance, a sprawling village folded over the rolling landscape. Raphael stood in the passenger seat, his left arm locked on top of the windshield, and he waved to the crowds as the vehicle bumped along the pebbles encrusted in the mud road. The parade of Jeeps pulled into the village and parked in a circle as though they were covered wagons in the Old West.

Men, women, and children emptied out of their dwellings and bolted toward the procession. Raphael looked over his shoulder. In the back seat, Edna Machinga, the de-facto president of Zimbabwe, presented him with a smile.

"Will you do the honors?" she asked.

In her arms, she held a silver basket that spanned the length of her arms. She handed it to him. He planted the basket on the ground next to the Jeep.

Below his feet, a force of nanomachines soaked into the ground and started to construct a network of carbon nanotubes deep within the earth like the roots of a giant oak tree. Specially rendered machines excavated the soil in search of potassium, calcium, magnesium and other useful elements. One-by-one, the nest of nanomachines individually crammed the elements up through the nanotubes and into the silver basket, where a regimen of assemblers patterned them to form bread and fish.

Raphael seized the first plank of bread and offered it up to a deluge of battling hands. He turned to President Machinga as she passed out the bread and fish to the excited crowds, his face painted with sadness.

"There are so many children," he said.

"AIDS has devastated our country. Most of our population is orphaned children. Until you arrived, we stood on the brink of disaster."

He reminded himself of the horror of the New Year's Eve attacks. For these people, the terror was just now subsiding. With their trade partners decimated and no means to produce their own food, many third world nations found themselves relegated to starvation.

He observed the landscape. Around the caravan of Jeeps, lines hundreds of people deep stretched to the far corners of the village. Lifting up the back seat, he pulled out a long pole and lodged it into the ground like a giant war spear. It was five feet tall with a spigot jutting out of its side. He twisted the cap off its top.

In an instant, what felt like a weak vacuum steadily sucked pockets of surrounding air down into the shaft. Inside, nanomachines sorted out the elements, breaking chemical bonds and molecular structures. A legion of assemblers pulled together hydrogen and oxygen atoms and molded them into a new composition. From the mouth of the spigot, a steady stream of water gushed forth. Raphael loosened the cap a little bit more, and the pressure increased, spraying a flume of water onto the ground below.

The mob of people fought to get in front of the fountain, opening their mouths to let the sweet liquid dance off the tips of their tongues, jockeying for position so they could fill up jugs and buckets. The baskets and fountains churned forth a never-ending stream of sustenance, and by the end of the day, over five thousand people were fed in that village alone. Around the world, Raphael put similar programs into place, and the New Year's famine and all famines ended forever.

*   *   *   *

Placing his hands on the brass handles, Raphael parted the French doors and let the breeze surge forth from the fifth floor balcony. The swirling air nurtured the seeds of unrest with a crisp smoky tinge, the smell of gunpowder and burnt metal. Outside, the streets of Jerusalem crackled with sporadic gunfire. He closed the doors and latched them shut, content to watch the world from inside his room. What was wrong with these people? Had he not liberated them? Rather than accept the best of what this world had to offer, they only redoubled their commitment to achieving destruction and to the task of enforcing a perverted view of God onto the rest of the world.

The jiggling doorknob behind him shattered his train of thought, and he turned in time to see Gilder open the door and gravitate across the carpet. His steps were methodically soft so as to avoid waking the president's guest. Across the room, in a bed butted up against the far wall, Garrison lay silent, passed out with a wet rag draped over his forehead. Gilder crept over to Raphael and whispered in his ear.

"We erected a temporary wall around the Temple. The construction won't be damaged."

Raphael squeezed his hands around the leather belt strapped to his waist. His gaze fixed itself on the world outside as though locked in a daydream.

"What's wrong with them? They still think they can win?"

Gilder walked over to the bar and picked up a crystal bottle filled with bourbon.

"We're dealing with religious fanatics, fascists worse than the Nazis."

"Whatever their problem is, I want them removed."

Gilder placed two ice cubes in a Collins glass, looked up to make sure the clanging of the cubes hadn't disturbed Garrison, then poured several shots of bourbon over top. He used a straw to mix in a trace of water.

"We got rid of the Nazis," he said. "By eliminating Hitler and conquering the German nation. How do you suppose we deal with the Muslims? In this case, we have hundreds of millions of potential Hitlers dispersed into the farthest corners of the world."

He lifted the glass to his lips and waited for Raphael's answer.

"We'll deal with them one at a time," he said.

His determination was outwardly apparent from the hard look gripping his face. He looked over his shoulder to make sure the conversation hadn't awakened Garrison, and then he continued, his voice still in a whispering tone.

"We need to reeducate these people. Most of them have spent their whole lives bombarded with propaganda. I would hate Jews and infidels too."

Gilder gave a slight tilt to his head, then took another swig.

"It may not work."

"Perhaps. But we must try. Just like mental patients, these people need to be separated from the rest of the population—for their own safety as well as that of others."

Gilder paused for a moment while he considered the proposal.

"A wall?"

"No."

Raphael shook his head, considering other options. Gilder spit out ideas in a brainstorm.

"Segregation? An independent nation?"

"No. No. Something more…results oriented. If we're going to recreate the Garden of Eden, first we must weed the garden."

Gilder drained the remaining contents of the glass, smacked it down on the counter and threw his hands up.

"So what do you want?"

The sound of the glass striking the countertop caused Garrison's body to rustle back to life. Raphael turned and trained his eyes on the bed while still whispering to Gilder.

"We'll round up every Muslim. We'll detain and question them, one at a time, until we've had time to weed out every terrorist among them."

"Without any evidence, how do we determine who is and isn't a terrorist?"

Raphael rested his palm on the side of his cheek while he thought through the possibilities.

"The law says beyond a reasonable doubt."

"But by who? We can't have jury trials for that many people. It would take forever."

Raphael flipped his hand through the air.

"Then we'll turn it around, and make them prove their innocence."

Gilder let out a laugh and shook his head as though it were the silliest idea he had ever heard.

"I don't know. You think the people will stand for that?"

A light smile built itself on Raphael's face as he watched Garrison roll over on the bed and place his feet on the floor.

"For peace and safety, the people will submit to any measure."

*   *   *   *

In Ramallah, two Palestinian boys chased each other through the street. Through the window of their makeshift apartment, their mother kept her eyes glued to them as she wiped off a sink of wet dishes.

"Look, mama!"

The young woman peered out of her window. Tiny dancing objects like millions of falling balloons descended from the sky. The woman fixed her eyes on them, her hands frozen on the old dishrag and steel pot. Frozen faces grazed the streets like old New England lampposts, their eyes locked onto the falling balloons in all their hypnotic motion.

Ten thousand feet in the air, the balloons cracked open like eggshells, and every eye on the street blinked, every spine shuddered. Like a piñata bursting into a ticker tape parade, a hailstorm of glittering dust floated down to the earth. As it landed on the rooftops, the pavement, and the passing cars, every ear in the vicinity heard the powerful buzz of their engines. The dust attacked them in swarms. Within minutes, all of the frozen figures from the street looked as if they had been tarred and feathered with model glue and tinsel. The metallic dust mites bored under their victims' skin and probed for oxygen molecules. Several minutes later, the entire West Bank fell into a peaceful slumber.

CHAPTER 2:

A Humane Shield

"I will demolish your cities and make you desolate, and then you will know that I am the Lord. Your continual hatred for the people of Israel led you to butcher them when they were helpless, when I had already punished them for all their sins. As surely as I live, says the Sovereign Lord, since you show no distaste for blood, I will give you a bloodbath of your own. Your turn has come!"

—Ezekiel
Ezekiel 35:4–6

The Jewish Temple emitted a brilliant glimmer of mid-day light as Raphael arrived for the opening ceremony. The area inside the Temple as well as within overflowed with people from all nations of the earth. Outside of the towering gates, satellite dishes dotted the streets so the major media outlets could carry the event live. A procession of Jewish elders escorted Raphael through the Golden Gate and into the Court of the Gentiles.

The Dome of the Rock, rebuilt in less than a few months, towered high above the raging mob, its golden minaret bathing in the sunlight. Raphael took the time to shake hands and sign autographs, while being carried along by the mass of flailing hands and elbows like a piece of driftwood in the pounding surf. Wall to wall people clamored around him, and they cheered as he entered their presence. He bowed with humility while climbing the steps of the Great Gate into the Court of the Israelites. The Temple Alter burned in front of him with the same sense of sacred duty as exhibited by the Olympic Torch every four years. Humanity united together for this day and all days to come, but not under the auspices of a series of athletic events, but under the intent of creating eternal peace on earth.

Raphael circled the Temple Alter, and the mass erupted at his appearance. Not until he had safely climbed the steps of the porch leading to the Holy Place did the courtyard finally grow silent. He stood in one place, stout and erect, with a legion of LOCUSTS encircling his body like the Holy Ghost. A podium stood mid-center, awaiting his remarks. Each ear angled itself to the heavens, hoping to capture a brief fraction of the moment's glory. For the occasion, he paraphrased a single verse from the Old Testament.

"The spirit of the Lord is upon us, for he has appointed us to preach good news to the poor. He has sent us to proclaim that political prisoners will be released, that the blind will see, that the downtrodden will be granted freedom from their oppressors, and that the time of the Lord's favor has come."

As he stepped down from the porch leading to the Holy Place, the crowd let out a magnificent roar. Each body in the ocean of humanity hurled itself in his direction. Starting in a soft whisper, and then escalating, the chants filled the Temple with a deafening cadence.

"Messiah! Messiah!"

He pushed his way through the crowd, smiling and patting babies on the head and reaching through the mass to touch the extended hands vying for his attention. A young woman pushed through the crowd, plowing over everyone in her path to get to him. She arrived face-to-face with him and shoved a microphone in his face.

"Mr. President," she said. "You've worked so hard to see these holy structures rebuilt. What does this day mean to you?"

The smashing faces and flailing arms jostled him as he spoke. The billions of cheers forced him to raise his voice to a shout, but still his words were barely audible.

"For centuries on end, mankind has dreamed of a world without war. A world without poverty and hunger and fear. Today, we build that world. The rebuilding of the Jewish Temple, the Dome of the Rock, and the al-Aksa Mosque under the unified efforts of men and women from diverse races and religions is a symbol of the new era of peace the world now enters. For we have overcome the world of the past, a world of death and disease, a world of poverty and hunger, a world of illiteracy and violence. The world we create is nothing less than heaven on earth."

The drunken mob of bodies maimed the journalist, trampling her underfoot, and they plowed forward screaming their hypnotic chants for all to hear.

"Messiah! Messiah!"

*   *   *   *

Baking waves of sunlight saturated the desert platform as Hans Blitner waited for the people to arrive. Flying grains of sand traveled in thin layers an inch or two from the ground, the rocky pigments jabbing at his skin like a thousand prickly cactus needles. He paced along the platform, the massive windowless prisons looming over the desert hills around him. From the far left, a man approached and saluted his superior. Hans returned the salute, and the man spoke in a disciplined cadence.

"At the risk of sounding incompetent sir, what is it I'm supposed to do with this mass of people?"

Jean pulled out a cigarette and lit the end.

"You're supposed to weed the terrorists from among them."

The man twitched in his uniform as though uncomfortable.

"And how do I do that sir?"

Hans smiled, letting a puff of smoke leave his lips, then grabbed the man by the shoulder.

"Now that the world is filled with democratic republics, it becomes necessary to ensure its individual citizens remain loyal to the legitimacy of their government. Any attempts to undermine the authority of that government must be considered conspiratorial acts of terrorism."

"But isn't this more of a cultural problem, sir?"

"This is more than a cultural problem. Our current government is the agreed upon way of life, chosen by a majority of humanity. Those who refuse to recognize its preeminence are a threat and must be dealt with before they carry out their horrendous acts of terror."

The man swallowed hard, still standing at attention.

"Shall I make them take a vow of allegiance to the state, sir?"

"Whatever it takes. It's for their own good."

Hans tossed his cigarette butt on the platform and squashed it with his shoe. He sent the man away and reflected on the massive undertaking of reeducating so many people.

In complete silence, the noiseless train shuttled into the station, and the spinning grains of sand that hugged his ankles reversed direction. Without the clang of an engine, and absent the puff of a hydraulic fuel pump, the railcar slowed to a sleeping position.

Hans raised his hand and a number of uniformed men stationed along the platform stepped toward the train. A conveyor belt, parallel to the railway, spun into motion, snaking along like a rolling bucket of coal only to disappear into the mineshaft that was the prison system of Ar-Rutbah. In the dead silence, the doors on the railcars slid open and the uniformed men stepped inside.

From floor to ceiling, the bodies of Middle-Eastern men, women, and children were stacked like frozen dinners. Lifeless and stiff, those in uniform peeled them off like planks of dead bark on a dying tree and tossed them onto the conveyor. Hans oversaw the passing bodies with his hands locked behind his back as if he were the proud recipient of some grand medallion yet to be pinned on his chest. An arm fell over the edge of the conveyor, and he nudged it back with the tip of his shoe. Browsing through the jumble of bodies, something caught his attention. It wasn't a concentrated attention, but more on the order of a raised eyebrow or a wrinkled nose as if a fly had granted him the displeasure of landing on his face.

He called out to the nearest uniformed man, and the conveyor stopped at once. He pointed down at it.

"Here. This one. And the children."

The uniformed man lifted the body of a woman along with three children from the conveyor and placed them on the platform. Once off, the conveyor reanimated itself. The man knelt over the bodies with a syringe, and filling it with a strange fluid, he plugged it into the woman and then into the children. Within seconds, the woman's eyes jutted open and every muscle in her body tensed at the sight of the strange men. She fell back on her hands and stumbled over her legs, but Hans caught her with his comforting words, speaking in fluent Arabic.

"You have no need to be afraid. We are here to help you."

The woman eyed the conveyor as it moved forward, horrified by the pile of bodies. Hans squatted down beside her.

"They're not dead," he said. "They're only asleep. Soon, almost all of them will be set free."

"Why have you done this?" she asked.

"It's only temporary. Your people have been subject to lies and propaganda, and the world needs to weed out those who pose a threat to the safety and security of innocent people."

He didn't think of Ar-Rutbah so much as a prison, but more like a laundromat for the mind, a place to cleanse the brain of incorrect ideas. He held out his hand, and she took hold of it. He lifted her from the platform and onto her feet.

"In the morning," he said. "You will be free. Everything is going to be all right. I promise."

*   *   *   *

Raphael looked out over the landscape from the balcony of his room. The completed structure of the Jewish Temple hung high above the city. The limestone edifice, constructed wholly of superior nanotechnic materials, glistened in the morning sun like a well-cut diamond. Seeing the Temple rebuilt gave him great pleasure. He was embarrassed, and somewhat alarmed, by the expanding number of people who believed him to be the Jewish Messiah, but he didn't let it bother him. Why would someone believe Jesus was a regular man, but he, Raphael Vicente, was the long awaited Messiah? Religious fanaticism permeated every facet of his world, but at least these fanatics were peaceful. And so what if they thought he was the Messiah? Did it hurt them to think that?

What mattered most was an end to the slaughter, an end to the violent conflict. Christians, Jews, and Muslims living together in peace, and if that meant being their Messiah, he would play the role. Seeing them work together rebuilding the Jewish Temple, the Dome of the Rock, and the al-Aksa Mosque, and knowing he played an integral role in bringing it about, gave him a sense of spiritual pride. If only Poyner could see it. She believed in his grand dreams, and she never judged him.

The rusty creak of a door opening forced him to turn around. Dozens of advisors and bodyguards already filled the hotel suite to capacity, but somehow this new person felt there was room for one more. Jean walked in, burned a straight line through the carpet and stopped in front of Raphael. His look was beyond serious. It was despondent. He walked over to the balcony and closed the doors without speaking. Then, he told everyone in the room to get off the phone. As they gathered around, he revealed the news.

"They found Henri Claudel in the rubble in Paris this morning."

Raphael waited, expecting something more. Then he shrugged his shoulders.

"So? Claudel was among the missing. We expected as much."

Jean did not share his apathy.

"He was found with a bullet in his head. Did you expect that?"

Raphael cocked his head in surprise, his teeth noticeably clenched together from the news.

"We searched his residence months ago, but when we returned, a more thorough search uncovered a laptop we were unaware of. Three days before the attack, Claudel created a crude software program on it. A program for activating an assembler. His daily planner made mention of the area where his body was found with a single dictation to himself: 'Deliver Device'."

Raphael slowly shook his head, unwilling to admit the truth.

"We don't have any missing assemblers," he said.

Jean pounded his finger in the air.

"We have to face the possibility—somehow he got one or created one of his own, but it's a possibility we can't ignore."

The room stayed silent for close to a minute while the news soaked in. Raphael turned to look out the window, his thoughts focused on solving the problem. No one had to explain the implications. They had to assume Claudel had an assembler, and whoever shot him now held it. They also had to assume that person or persons made it out of the city to safety. But why hadn't they attacked? Perhaps they were dead or in detention. But perhaps they were lying in wait, preparing for an overwhelming worldwide assault. Current United Europe defenses were ill prepared for such an attack. Raphael broke the silence.

"What are our options?"

Gilder spoke up.

"We have to begin building a comprehensive active shield now. And we need to do everything in our power to hunt down this assembler," he said.

What terrified Raphael most was that whoever this last terrorist was, he could have assemblers now roaming the earth side-by-side with those of United Europe. They had never built tracking devices or watermarks to differentiate their assemblers from someone else's. There hadn't been the need. He had, until now, focused all of his attention on state abuse. He had already set up basic shields and sensors to detect an attack. He hadn't been completely negligent, but he also hadn't anticipated a threat emerging this quickly. Now, a delayed response of only a few minutes could mean the end of his world, all that he had worked so hard to create. For all he knew, this opponent maintained a secret overwhelming force capable of seizing the world at this very moment.

Wasting time was not an option. He slapped his hand down on an end table.

"Gather all the engineers from Project Mercury and begin designing an impenetrable active shield now."

Gilder paced the room. In mid-step he delivered a glare of abject horror.

"If we're going to build an active shield, we need to do it in secret. If this man knows what we're doing, it could trigger a preemptive strike we're unprepared for."

Raphael held his arm up to his forehead. The shield needed to be constructed in secret, but an undertaking requiring so many atoms would be nearly impossible to conceal. He couldn't tell the international community without the last terrorist finding out, and he couldn't use atmospheric atoms without the international community taking notice. After all, he had voluntarily given them jurisdiction to regulate the air. The same was true of the oceans.

Using plant life remained an option, but satellites would make that difficult to conceal. It was an unwinnable scenario. He knew something like this was bound to happen when the New Year's Eve attacks forced him to move so quickly. It didn't give him adequate time to develop the proper policies for creating a new international order.

His train of thought shattered when Jean spoke out.

"Mr. President, we also need an effective offense to compliment our defensive efforts. If we destroy the last terrorist, then a shield will be unnecessary."

Raphael looked confused.

"What do you mean?"

Jean spoke out.

"We can listen for him."

Raphael stared at Jean, his eyebrow raised, waiting for further explanation. Jean provided it.

"Mr. President, we can listen for this last terrorist. We can listen to all the world, and he will have nowhere to hide."

Nowhere to hide. Somehow it had sounded infinitely more noble when he heard President Burton repeat the same phrase long ago. Now, Raphael felt as though he had entered an episode of *The Twilight Zone*. Jean sang out the words like some vitriolic sales pitch he had memorized for just this moment.

"With replicating assemblers, we can saturate the earth's environment with miniature surveillance devices. Bugs can be as plentiful as dust mites and as impossible to avoid. With the aid of speech-translating and speech-understanding AI systems, we can filter out incriminating words and listen in on every conversation on the face of the earth. Effectively, we can spy on everyone without having to employ anyone."

The offer tempted Raphael, but frightened him. He only needed to locate one man, but spying on the world would open a Pandora's Box of police state measures. What sort of precedent would he set? The next man to hold his office might not be as well intentioned.

Jean's expressionless face stared back at Raphael, its eyes unblinking. Raphael had no choice. Either he protected United Europe, or he would have no successor.

"We must do what needs to be done," he said.

The Frenchman responded with a smile that reminded Raphael of the toothy grin flashed around by the Cheshire cat in *Alice In Wonderland*.

"You made the right decision, Mr. President."

Gilder jumped back into the fray, his eyes bulging from their sockets and his face reddened with blood. He threw his hands in the air then slapped them to his sides in despair.

"Suppose we do catch him, our problems don't end. Not if he's built a decisive force in secret."

He was right. Even if the listening devices locate and identify the last terrorist, if he's already constructed a decisive force, he can attack and win. They still faced the complex problem of building an active shield, perhaps a massive force of offensive weapons as well.

"We can't build such a force without tipping our hand. It would consume too many inputs to go unnoticed," Gilder said.

Jean waved his hand around.

"Not necessarily."

Every eye in the room focused in on him. If he held the answer, they all wanted to hear it. He paused for effect, until he had the undivided attention of everyone.

"We need an abundance of elements, especially carbon. Right?"

Everyone agreed.

"And the most abundant source of carbon is life."

Gilder threaded his hands through his hair and shook his head in frustration.

"But we can't use plant life or vegetation without calling attention to ourselves. We might as well wave a white flag. Satellites will pick that up, and we must assume he's watching. In fact, he may be listening right now."

A sudden paranoia swept over the group, holding the room in a gripping silence. Only Jean seemed unaffected by the possibility, and he wasn't pleased at being cut off in mid-sentence. Nevertheless, he kept his response calm and directed.

"I'm not talking about plants."

"Then what are you talking about?" Gilder asked.

Like a tree snake sunning on a budding limb, Jean remained poised in his delivery.

"I'm talking about Ar-Rutbah."

Raphael dropped his head, but Gilder never flinched. Immediately, he lashed out.

"What! You want to use humans?"

Jean kept his emotions in check. Showing no expression, he accepted the verbal onslaught. It was obvious only one man's opinion mattered, and Raphael did not overtly dismiss the proposal.

"No," Jean said. "I want to use terrorists. Those are the only things at Ar-Rutbah—dictators, terrorists, and violent religious fanatics. It's about time we put their lives to use for the common good, for a decent purpose."

Gilder pointed his finger at Jean and slashed at the air.

"Capital punishment is illegal in United Europe, and the prisoners at Ar-Rutbah were sentenced under those guidelines. They're entitled to due process under the law. If you want to change that sentence…"

Jean heaved his chest outward and waved his fist under Gilder's chin.

"For God's sake, Offen, we're in a war! We're in a fight for the survival of the human race. If we lose, there's no such thing as due process or maybe even life! This is our only option, and it's our obligation to protect this nation."

The whole room broke out into raucous verbal infighting. Only Raphael remained outside of the argument. He strolled about as if he were the ghost of Christmas past floating through the room with only a passing curiosity in the outcome.

Staring through the window, he noticed the sparkling reflection of the Temple Mount and the golden minaret of the Dome of the Rock as it lifted skyward. He visualized Jews and Arabs walking side-by-side in the streets below. He envisioned the world in his mind's eye. A world of peaceful co-existence. A world of tolerance, prosperity, liberty, and freedom. It was a world good men fought and died for.

He gave his only son in its defense and sacrificed the only woman he loved. On the alter of freedom, he laid his career, his possessions, and any sense of a normal life—his only mission to serve others. One outcome, and one outcome alone, justified the sleepless nights, and from the window, he saw it all within his grasp.

He spun around and silenced the bickering chatter with his raised hand.

"Many years ago, Harry Truman faced this same problem. He could do nothing and watch hundreds of thousands of Americans and Japanese die. Or, he could drop a single horrible bomb and end it all for good."

The men in the room hung on his words as if he were about to pronounce eternal judgement on each and every one of their souls. With unapologetic authority, the words floated from his lips with the razor edge tenacity of the Grim Reaper's sickle.

"We will drop a single bomb."

*   *   *   *

In the blue skies spread out over the Pacific, an old C-17 Globemaster III from the RAF hummed with a low purr that would put most people to sleep. It was a dry hum like the hum of a car motor rolling down the interstate, one that would hypnotize the driver and slowly make the yellow lines merge into one and blend the flanking trees into a giant green wall. The cargo bay stood open, and in the back, two men cracked open a pair of wooden crates with an iron crowbar. White and silver sand leaked from the cracks. They dumped it on the floor, and it vibrated as if filled with a special magic.

"What the hell is this?"

The second man shook his head.

"Probably some sort of ocean chlorine or marine filter to appease the enviro wackos."

With long-handled brooms, they swept the powdered sands into the sky and forgot all about them. In the ice-cold chill of the sky, the sun's warm rays were enough to spring the flecks of shiny sand to life.

Like tiny fruit flies, their wings started to buzz and they roved off in billions of different directions to populate the earth. Ordaining dust particles as their prey, they replicated across the earth, taking the place of all dust. The sparkling glitter settled into the corners of office buildings and onto tabletops in homes. It floated in bedrooms and airports and restaurants. It was ear dust, not the yellow kind that builds up in ears and turns into wax, but dust with ears of its own. Ears like the ears of God. Ears that listened to every word of every utterance of every human being on Earth.

CHAPTER 3:

Listening Ear

"And with all the miracles he was allowed to perform on behalf of the first beast, he deceived all the people who belong to this world. He ordered the people of the world to make a great statue of the first beast, who was fatally wounded and then came back to life. He was permitted to give life to this statue so that it could speak. Then the statue commanded that anyone refusing to worship it must die."

—John
Revelation 13:14–15

"In here, Mr. Nance."

One of the president's aides led Garrison to an open lobby area across the hall from the Presidential Suite. A series of chairs arranged themselves around a glass table covered with newspapers and periodicals. Hans Blitner sat in one of the chairs, his legs crossed while he scanned through a copy of Jewish World Review. Garrison took a seat across the table from Hans. The man lifted his eyes from the lettered pages and repositioned them on Garrison. Tossing the magazine back on the table, he sat up straight in his chair.

"You're the president's friend, Garrison Nance."

Garrison nodded, and Hans extended his hand and introduced himself. He pointed to the magazine's cover, a panorama of the Temple Mount.

"What did you think of the Temple ceremonies?"

Garrison shook his head.

"I didn't go."

The man appeared noticeably surprised, borderline offended.

"Oh…Well, President Vicente delivered an address that electrified the audience."

His eyes focused on the ceiling like those of a young boy trapped in a daydream, and his hands swayed through the air as if some hypnotic power forced them to be drunk while the remainder of his body kept sober.

"It was a marvel to be there, to witness the splendor and glory of that historical moment. A feeling of—"

Garrison interrupted him.

"Do you really think it matters?"

"What matters?"

Garrison rolled his eyes and looked around the room.

"Any of it."

"Of course! President Vicente has brought an end to the fighting in the Middle East. Jews and Muslims and Christians worked together to rebuild the Temple Mount. Who would have dreamed of that a year ago? And so much more has been brought by his leadership. War is a part of our past now."

Garrison concealed the frown on his face with his open hand, and sitting in the chair, his pose bore a striking resemblance to Rodin's famous sculpture.

"You have a lot of faith in the abilities of government and government officials to overcome these problems that have plagued humanity since the dawn of time."

Hans nodded his head with confidence.

"And why shouldn't I? Look at all that's been accomplished so far. All the nations have been liberated and the world is at peace. Assemblers will yield nearly unlimited prosperity. I would say I have faith. You don't?"

"I don't place my faith in men, because I know what's in the heart of a man."

Hans smiled and bobbed his head, knowing a lot about the man he was talking to.

"Jesus was a great man and his teachings were virtuous, but what have they done for us in the last two thousand years? The world remained an awful place until President Vicente brought assemblers into it. Look at all the fruits of his labor—the end of disease, the end of poverty, the end of hunger, and the end of war. Jesus didn't bring any of these things."

Garrison nodded in agreement, seemingly unconcerned that his belief system was under assault.

"You're right. What Jesus gave the world is greater than all of those things. Why is it so difficult for the world to recognize the Trojan Horse that the devil has delivered? For it was this generation of which the Lord spoke when he said, 'You say: I am rich. I have everything I want. I don't need a thing! And yet you don't realize that you are wretched and miserable and poor and blind and naked.'"

Hans laughed at the comment.

"But we are rich. We've conquered the physical universe and unraveled its secrets."

"So it appears. But man will not be able to conquer war. Because war is the result of man's own selfish nature, his own jealous desires. No technology can change human nature. For all of mankind's advances in science, art, business, and culture, if we want to end war, we must change the hearts of men."

Hans retreated backward, leaning into his chair.

"I agree that the world is not perfect, but that doesn't mean war is a permanent part of our nature. Most wars have been fought over oil, mineral resources, and territorial resources. Assemblers make material wealth abundant, eliminating the reasons for anyone to fight over them."

"But the sad reality is that no matter how much wealth or power man obtains, he is never satisfied. The place inside us where God should be is transformed into a vacuum that can never be filled with anything else. The frustration of trying to fill that void is what drives men to fight and war with each other. God is the only one capable of providing man with the true fulfillment for which he was created."

Hans shrugged and waved off the comments.

"Whatever. We just have a simple disagreement, a difference of opinion. That's all."

"You're correct. But nevertheless, one of us is right, and the other is wrong. And I'm telling you that the truth is your government has already betrayed you. And soon you will find out for yourself."

* * * *

Jean swaggered into the presidential suite with a handful of CDs. Raphael scribbled his signature across a pile of papers as the man's figure cast a long shadow over the room, one that covered the documents on Raphael's desk. Looking up, he stood from his chair and moved forward to greet him.

"You found him?"

Jean's face indicated otherwise.

"No. But we've blanketed the planet. If so much as a mouse farts, you'll know about it."

"If that's true, then how come we don't have him?"

Raphael clenched his fists behind his back, and a dark purple vein protruded from the skin beneath his hairline. Jean diverted his attention for a brief moment before looking his president in the face.

"Many reasons. Maybe we've heard him, but he hasn't yet said anything incriminating. The best case scenario is that he's dead—died on the night of the attack. Regardless, it's been less than forty-eight hours, and he probably doesn't know we're looking for him."

Raphael relaxed the muscles in his body and stopped gritting his teeth.

"And you're sure he'll pop up?"

Jean maintained the same cold expression.

"These people did."

He plopped the stack of CDs on Raphael's desk.

"What's this?"

"Recordings. Hundreds of them. I guess you could call them the unintended consequences of our search."

Raphael picked up the top case and opened it. He pulled out the CD. No label was on it.

"What's on them?"

"Sedition. Racism. Religious intolerance. Hate speech in general."

Raphael tossed the CD back onto the pile.

"And what am I supposed to do with them?"

"Well, they may not pose the lethal threat of a nanotechnic terrorist, but they still pose a grave threat to stability and order. They're capable of—"

Raphael held his hand up.

"No. I mean what am I supposed to do with them? I've got enough on my desk already."

He hooked his thumb onto a stack of papers and flipped through them.

"If people are committing crimes," he said. "Then arrest them and put them on trial. That's your job. Don't bother me with it."

"So you finally approve of preemptive measures against individual terrorists?"

"No. I approve of you enforcing the laws of United Europe and the United Nations. Xenophobia and racism are high crimes, and religious intolerance breeds these types of terrorist activities. Just because one terrorist may have an assembler doesn't mean he's the only one, or that others won't come along in the future."

"So what you're saying is that the threat of nanotechnic terror should apply to individuals as well as states. I agree, Mr. President."

"Terrorists are like mosquitoes, Jean. We need to eliminate the conditions that allow them to breed. We need to ensure they have no place to hide and stop them from being born."

*   *   *   *

Garrison's comments echoed through Hans Blitner's mind as each passing second brought him closer to the Ar-Rutbah Prison Center. He was determined to prove the man wrong. United Europe did not exercise unchecked power over the world and it certainly didn't mistreat prisoners. He oversaw the construction of the initial buildings himself. Nevertheless, the Middle East now loomed as a vacant wasteland.

Pulling into the stone courtyard, he parked his jeep alongside one of the prison centers and stepped out. Outdoor speakers fastened to the building brushed waves of Bach into the alleyways, and patches of perfectly manicured lawn grew out for several feet from around the buildings. The prisons themselves resembled long windowless ovals, warehouses of terrorists and hardened criminals.

Hans walked to the nearest building, its front entrance decorated with fragrant petunias. He was shocked to find no one manning the door. In fact, now that he thought about it, he experienced a strange feeling from the moment he entered town. The abandoned compound rested on its foundation, absent the sound of a single voice or the sight of a single person anywhere. Only the constant flood of classical music playing over the courtyard speakers sparked any memory of civilization.

He placed his hand on the knob of the door, and it clicked open. Stepping inside, he gave his eyes time to adjust to the darkness. With each step forward, his shoes tapped an echo in the grand hallway as he inspected the empty prison cells. Several floors above him, the cells stacked themselves like crates, all as empty as the others. The sharp clack of his heels remained the only sound breaking through the silence as he tried to unravel the mystery.

Did they move the prison? But where? Why? Perhaps this had been converted to a holding area for Muslims prior to their release. A thousand or more questions rushed through his mind. Still, his feet hammered those constant echoes onto the tile floors and his eyes still attached themselves to the empty cells when he came to its rounded edge.

It was at least fifty feet in diameter, and it looked as if the marble floor had decided to rot away in this one place, only not by accident. The void extruding from the floor was dark and endless.

Hans fell to his knees, his face suspended over its edge. Deep within himself, he felt something tear apart—something like his soul or where his soul should have been, but for its absence. It was as if poisonous venom leeched onto his veins and fed on his entire body. Hans clenched his stomach and lurched forward, hurling a line of vomit into the open mouth of the H.O.L.E. His lunch continued to spew forth, one drove after another, and as he heaved into the pit, he watched the sterile void pick it apart, each atom stored away in its depths for future use befitting of a better, more noble purpose.

*   *   *   *

The powdered sands of the French Riviera washed over each other with each passing brush of the small waves that died in a vain attempt to climb just one inch closer to the land. With each failure, the receding folds of water dropkicked the tiny rocks as though they were miniature footballs so that beneath the surface they sprinkled the water with random bits of confetti shot from a canon.

On the shore, a stretch of palms cooled a quaint bungalow with lighted windows, and inside, Albert Fiennes sat in the floor of his living room, stacking wooden blocks one on top of another with his three-year-old daughter. As the stack grew taller, it wobbled on its foundation, a children's book they had just finished reading, and Albert laughed along with his daughter as they waited for the structure to collapse. The blocks had letters of the alphabet painted on the sides, but they weren't trying to spell anything in particular, just build the largest tower they could.

The force from the front door bursting open felled the tower like an earthquake, and Albert's daughter cried. Four armed policemen stormed into the living room, guns drawn. Albert jumped to his feet.

"What is this?"

He demanded an answer, but they only stared ahead like mind-numbed robots.

"Are you Albert Fiennes?" they asked.

"Yes."

He provided them a look more curious than accusing, but they trained their guns on his temple. One of them spoke above the others.

"You're under arrest for conspiracy to commit terror and crimes of aggression."

Albert relayed his shock.

"What? Under what pretense?"

The men didn't answer. They simply cuffed his hands behind his back, while Albert struggled against them. The more he pushed, the more he felt restrained as though he were sinking in quicksand.

"You can't do this," he said. "I'll call the authorities."

A voice ripped at his soul from inside the hollow doorframe.

"We are the authorities, Mr. Fiennes."

Jean stood in the doorway. A thin jacket hung from his shoulders like the flowing robes of a royal prince, and the dark shadow formed by his person fled from the doorframe as if the devil himself decided to model an emperor's robe. Fiennes struggled with his constraints and shouted back.

"You can't do this!"

Jean stepped over the fallen blocks, a small recording device in his hand, and he pressed a button. Fiennes heard his own words flood back to him.

"Where'd you get that?" he asked. "That was a private conversation."

Jean smirked, the curls of his smile rolling up to his ears, where the jagged spears of hair twisted over his skull.

"I don't think you're in a position to ask such questions, Mr. Fiennes."

Albert shook his head, near hysterical from the chains tied around his wrists.

"So what? What's wrong with it? I have a right to free speech."

"The things you've said make you guilty of sedition against United Europe."

The man's jaw bit down in anger, and he shouted louder than ever before.

"I have rights! I have rights under the UN Charter!"

Jean wagged his index finger as if to discipline a small child.

"Yes, and article twenty-nine of the Universal Declaration of Human Rights clearly states that rights and freedoms may in no case be exercised contrary to the purposes and principles of the United Nations. And, of course, we are the United Nations."

He waved his arm and pointed toward the door.

"Take him away."

The armed men dragged Fiennes out of his home kicking and screaming. Jean stepped forward to follow them and almost tripped over the book. Reaching down, he lifted it from the floor. It had a simple cover that read, *The Sneetches & Other Stories* by Dr. Seuss. He broke open the cover and flipped through the pages. Plain-belly, Star-belly sneetches...South-going, North-going Zaxes...

He let his best sarcastic smirk fly free, then tossed the book back onto the floor with a thump. It wasn't until it hit the carpet that he noticed the three-year-old girl still lying on the floor. Her thumb was lodged in her mouth, her eyes all watery. Jean pointed to the book and walked to the door.

"I advise you to read more non-fiction," he said. "It will better prepare you for the real world."

*   *   *   *

Raphael smudged his feet into the carpet of the presidential suite, a glass of scotch in hand. He studied the rolling mountains outside his window, while Gilder entered the room. He could make out shades of the man's smoky gray reflection in the tinted windowpane.

Raphael sipped from the edge of his glass.

"What is it?"

Gilder walked only as far as the desk and spoke to the back of the president's head.

"The shield is making progress. We have hundreds of engineers on it. Their combined efforts will allow it to adapt and respond to any threat that any man can dream up."

Raphael jiggled the ice in his glass, took one last tall swig, then turned to face Gilder.

"We're prepared for any attack?"

Gilder looked at the floor, slow to answer.

"Almost."

Raphael crossed his arms and turned back to the window, his swirling hand still rustling the ice against the sides of the glass.

"Let me know when we are."

Gilder accepted the order and prepared to leave. Behind him, Jean flung the door open. His hurried walk pounded a path through the carpet straight to the president's desk, where he held out a digital recorder in the palm of his hand. He placed it on Raphael's desk.

"We found him."

A wellspring of life entered Raphael's face.

"Where?"

"Jerusalem."

Jean pressed a button on the outer edge of the device and the recorded conversation flowed into the room. Two unknown voices invaded Raphael's head.

"Allah has given me power, Jahil. Remember when Saeed wrote to me? He said the glory of Palestine would once again rest in the hands of Allah. Look..."

A few seconds of silence passed before the second voice spoke.

"What is it?"

"An assembler, just like the one the infidels have. With this power we can spread Islam to the ends of the earth. Truly this is Allah's will."

"How did you get it?"

"A friend of Saeed's dropped it off. Saeed stole it and made him promise to give it to me, but it doesn't matter. What matters is that we have it, and it will give us power equal to that of the West..."

Jean clicked the recorder off.

"The man's name is Tamil Al-Shehhi. His brother Saeed orchestrated the New Year's Eve attack on New York City. It's quite possible his group was linked to Claudel's killing and stole the assembler on the night of the attack. We have no reason to believe this man has a overwhelming force."

Raphael assessed the situation.

"If this conversation is genuine, and what you say is true, then he's not a threat to be concerned with. You have him in custody?"

Jean piddled with his fingers as though Chinese handcuffs latched them together.

"No."

"No? Why not?"

"He hasn't been back to his apartment since we picked up his conversation, but we still have bugs everywhere and voice recognition software that will hunt him down the moment he speaks."

"Very well. You can go."

Jean didn't move, and Raphael issued a concerned glance.

"What?"

"I have more."

"More?"

"Yes, and you won't like it."

He reached down and pressed a second button on the recorder. The sounds of three voices stretched across the room. Raphael recognized one of them as Derek Stevens.

"Vicente is too powerful. Didn't he promise to share unlimited assemblers with other nations? Then where are they? This is our only option."

Another voice came in.

"And Price is on board with this?"

"I don't say a word except on behalf of President Price."

Jean clicked off the recorder and floated a stern look in Raphael's direction. Pure horror writhed on his face.

"The other two voices belong to Mr. Stevens's Russian and Japanese counterparts. The three nations have reconstituted their assembler projects, and as we speak, they plot to overthrow our rule."

CHAPTER 4:

Only For Safety

"As I was looking at the horns, suddenly another small horn appeared among them. Three of the first horns were wrenched out, roots and all, to make room for it. This little horn had eyes like human eyes and a mouth that was boasting arrogantly."

—Daniel
Daniel 7:8

Outside of Jerusalem, Garrison stood at the foot of a mountain ridge helping to disperse bread and wine to a large crowd. Treetops brushed across the sky like stilted paintbrushes, separating the outskirts of Jerusalem from the barren wilderness of the mountains. Eduardo navigated through the crowd, twisting his head side to side in search of his friend. Once he saw him, he bolted in Garrison's direction. Grabbing his arm, he pulled him aside.

"I've been looking everywhere for you."

Garrison nodded, while Eduardo marveled at the size of the crowd, appearing to lose his train of thought.

"Who are all these people?" he asked.

Garrison directed his gaze at the hillside, surveying a crowd of more than one hundred thousand.

"These are they who have been persecuted because of the Lord."

A look of astonishment covered Eduardo's face until he gathered his composure.

"Then you know why I'm here. You have to speak to Raphael."

"I know."

"You're the only one he trusts and listens to. This terror campaign is out of control. He's made faith in a god other than democracy and tolerance a crime against the state."

"That's why everyone has come here. God is protecting them."

Eduardo continued to marvel at the crowd's size.

"People are disappearing. Raphael's moral crusade is leading the world into a police state, one that will be permanent. It's like the Salem Witch Trails."

Garrison placed his hand on Eduardo's shoulder.

"I agree, but his intentions are not for himself. He's doing everything he can to fight a losing battle."

"I don't doubt his intentions, but his policies—"

He folded his hand over his forehead and exhaled a long held breath.

"Who am I kidding? There's nothing we can do. From the very beginning, this is what I feared most. It's time I accept the fact that assemblers are inherently incompatible with a free and open society."

Garrison gave a somber nod, his eyes closed as though he were grieving.

"What you've said is true. There's no way to avoid what must happen. God chose Raphael for this purpose, so that his frustrations will be a witness to the glory of God. Raphael will teach mankind not to put its faith in the things of this world. For all the things of this world will soon melt away, but God will stand forever. Mankind strives to find an earthly answer to this human problem, and they will fail."

Eduardo looked into the eyes of his friend, then turned to study the crowd again.

"I've heard the things that you've said, things that no human could know. Tell me the truth. Who are you?"

And Garrison said to him.

"I am one of two witnesses sent by the Lord to prepare the world for his coming."

Eduardo held his breath, knowing all he did about the course of world events and that everything Garrison had said in the past was true.

"Who is the second witness?"

Garrison looked him straight in the face.

"You are."

*   *   *   *

"All our technological advancements, and we still can't get rid of this dust."

With a broad stroke, Derek wiped a sheet of gray dust from the surface of the table. It shot off the edge in a giant puff that mushroomed into the air before slowly settling into the place and falling to the floor. Price let out a chuckle.

"What's the old saying? They can put a man on the moon, but..."

Derek shook his head while he brushed his hands together to rid them of the dust that stuck like double-sided tape to his palms. His face and hands froze in place and his eyelids squinted at Price.

"What's that?" he asked.

"What's what?"

"Something just passed behind you."

Price twisted his head and looked around his body as though he was searching for some buzzing fly to swat away.

"What?"

"I don't know. It looked like dust floating in the air, but a light reflected off of it. It moved."

"It moved?"

"Yeah, it moved. Like a spirit."

Price's pudgy frame bobbed up and down. He pointed at Derek with a bony finger.

"The spirit of the Lord has come to smite you."

He kept laughing, but behind him, the dust wove its way through the air with precision artistry. The colorful particles patterned together and circled his body. Derek's mouth fell open as he watched the tiny granules replicate throughout the room. They moved in a hypnotic river, slow and meticulous. The fluidic swirl was like watching traces of motor oil meander through a puddle of water, and he couldn't detach his eyes it was so unreal.

"What?" Price asked.

Derek's chin trembled and his mouth fidgeted as he tried to muster a coherent series of words into a complete thought.

"Th—there's something in the air, spinning around you."

Price hinged his head downward and started smacking at his own arms and chest as if he were covered with millions of marching red ants. Derek took a series of slow backward steps away from the man, but as he did, a wave of silver dust bolted into the room from underneath the door. It spread across the room like fire, bursting in from cracks in the walls and burrowing out from every crevice. The air around them swirled like a vicious whirlpool, and the whole room transformed into a Van Gogh painting, with swirling pigments coming to life and filling the world around him. Price screamed across the room.

"What's happening?"

Derek didn't respond. He figured the question was rhetorical.

As they stood with their hands locked behind their backs and their legs paralyzed, a separate cloud of dust materialized in front of them, growing thicker and thicker. Slowly, a figure emerged from its depths and spoke to them. Raphael's image appeared in the middle like a miniature hologram.

An expression of horror overtook Price's face as the image came to life.

"Big Brother's been watching you," it said. "And more disappointed I could not be."

*   *   *   *

"What are you doing?" Price shouted.

His cheeks disheveled in anger, he fought back against the guards hemming him in from every side. They pushed him through the door of the Presidential Suite and hurled his body to the floor. Raphael squatted next to the fallen man and curled his eyebrows with a confused and twisted sarcasm.

"I'm surprised you would ask a question like that. Especially after you've plotted against me and committed treason."

"What are you talking about?"

Raphael pressed the button on the device Jean had given him and played back the recording. Price's face swelled in shades of red, but still he shrugged his shoulders.

"So we reconstituted our assembler project. We're a sovereign nation. I have a right to protect my country. Am I supposed to hope you never die and leave absolute power in the hands of an unknown successor? That's Russian roulette."

Price appeared to feel justified by his answer, and that infuriated Raphael all the more.

"And why don't you sympathize with my position? I'm working around the clock to build a world that protects its citizens and safeguards liberty. Now, one of my most trusted allies decides that it would be a good idea to plunge the world into the destructive abyss of a nanotechnic arms race."

"No. I would never launch an arms race against you. America's interest in an assembler is strictly precautionary."

"Not America's interest, Thomas. Your interest. You would never do that, and I believe you. But try to understand my position."

He pounded his own chest with a poking finger, seemingly on the verge of violent outburst.

"What about me, Thomas? Am I supposed to hope you never die and leave your power in the hands of another? How do you know that person won't plunge the world into war?"

Price lowered his shoulders, and his body sunk into a fetal position. His eyes were glazed over by the revelation of what he had done, and he could only mutter out a whimpering string of words.

"I'm sorry. I didn't think—"

Raphael cut him off, gently whispering in his ear as if to comfort him.

"I know Thomas. That's why you've been removed from power."

He rose to his feet, an element of pity shining from his eyes, then he turned his back to the man on the floor. He spoke into the open air, and Price watched him from the floor, unsure as to whether or not he was an object of personal address or merely the witness of a deluded man's ravings.

"All of my life, I've sacrificed for a dream that one day the people of this earth could live under freedom, liberty, and democracy, and now I find myself on the verge of realizing that dream. And no one will stop me, Thomas. Not you. Not America. No one."

*   *   *   *

"Their irresponsible actions placed the future of world security, stability, and peace in serious jeopardy."

Flashing cameras flickered through the room, and arms holding microphones lunged upward at the podium in request of Raphael's comments. Like bumper cars at a summer amusement park, they collided into each other, vying to have the president's finger point in their direction. Raphael singled one of them out, and the room grew silent as she posed her question.

"Around the world, men and women have been rounded up and detained for questioning. The overwhelming majority being Christians, Muslims, Jews, and Hindus. Isn't this religious persecution? What can you tell us about these detentions?"

"Those men and women have been detained as part of a zero tolerance policy concerning hate crime and hate speech. They are accused of seditious acts and terrorist activities, and they will be afforded all due process and placed on trial before the International Criminal Court."

The instant the last word left his mouth, the raucous mob of reporters once again shouted a barrage of questions in his direction. He pointed out the next member of the press.

"Mr. President, is all this extra precaution necessary? There hasn't been a major terrorist attack since the New Year's Eve horror, and with the advent of assemblers, hunting terrorists down has become easier. Some call this an abuse of power."

"The terrorist threat remains grave. The war is not over, as some would have you believe. In fact, the arrests of these three national leaders exemplify the threat we all still face from nanotechnic war and terrorists with assemblers. The recent spate of arrests and detentions is the result of an ongoing United Europe policy to carry out its obligations to protect the world and secure the peace."

Another hand waved in his face, the words of its owner rising above the crowd.

"Already people fear speaking in their own homes. What would you say to those people?"

"There is a price to be paid for security and protection. We're dealing with threats the best way we know how, and we ask citizens to behave as the eyes and ears of law enforcement."

"But some people, your former advisor Eduardo Ortiz would be one, say these measures inevitably lead to the creation of a police state. Is it possible to defend against the threat of nanoterrorism and still have a free and open society? The widespread fear is that United Europe is setting up a dictatorial administration. What is your reaction?"

The question caused his tone to spoil with anger.

"If our intentions were anything less than noble, we wouldn't be holding this press conference."

*   *   *   *

Raphael rushed down the hallway into the Operations Room. Every screen in the chamber focused on Jerusalem. General Kohl stood behind his assistant Edwin Mackey who was seated at one of the computer terminals. Raphael approached them from behind.

"Where is he?"

Kohl pointed to the wall of screens. A young Middle-Eastern male dressed in off-white khakis with a blue shirt and tie strolled along the sidewalk. In his left hand, he carried a silver briefcase. His steps were smooth and directed, and the wall of digital monitors studied his appearance from every angle.

"Jerusalem," Kohl said. "We have reason to believe he's headed for the Temple Mount."

"Well, are we going to hit him?" Raphael asked.

"We have to proceed with caution. He probably doesn't know we're watching, and we don't yet know what his force capability is. An ill-planned attack could trigger a massive counter strike."

Kohl put his hand on Mackey's shoulder and leaned over to study his screen in detail.

"Run a comprehensive inspection of the atmosphere within five kilometers of the target and his briefcase."

Mackey entered several commands into the terminal and Kohl scurried throughout the room relaying commands to the other officials. Raphael watched the screens with lip-biting intensity.

Worshippers, locals, and tourists littered the streets leading up to the Temple Mount, and Tamil Al-Shehhi walked among them. As he passed by a dark alleyway, a cloud of silver glitter peeked around the corner then followed at his heels. On the sidewalk beneath his feet, a herd of silver particles raced along the mortar and cobblestone hungry for his ankles. He continued to step forward, one foot in front of another, unaware of the army chasing him down.

SPIDERS climbed from the sidewalk up the back of his legs, onto his body, and onto the briefcase in his left hand. A cloud of glittering LOCUSTS orbited his moving body, probing and sampling the air for foreign replicators and nanomachines with military applications. Through radio signals, they relayed their information back to the Operations Room.

"What'd we get?" Kohl asked.

Mackey sifted through the data on screen, scrolling through charts of readings.

"He's clean. The assembler's in the briefcase."

"And the air around him?"

"Nothing."

Kohl gave Mackey a pat on the back and turned to Raphael.

"We await your order, Mr. President."

Raphael stared at the screen with his arms crossed.

"By all means, please," he said.

Kohl picked up a phone from a nearby table and spoke into the receiver. Raphael locked onto the visual image of the terrorist as he moved closer and closer to his target. Within seconds of his order, the operation went into effect.

Inside the silver briefcase, the SPIDERS replicated and quickly raced to isolate the assembler. The cloud of glittering LOCUSTS started to whirl around Tamil like a small tornado. The man stopped dead in his tracks, and his hands batted at them as though they were gnats or mosquitoes. He dropped the briefcase and covered his head with his hands as the LOCUSTS multiplied and attacked his body like a pack of salivating wolves. With unimpeded barbarity, they asserted their absolute mastery over the elemental compounds of his body.

On the sidewalk around him, men and women cringed in horror as they watched a man dissolve right in front of their eyes. Raphael looked at Kohl.

"Now he can be reconstituted to serve a more noble purpose."

As the words left his tongue, an explosion burst forth in the sky over the Temple Mount. Tamil had vanished, his silver briefcase alone on the sidewalk with a swarm of replicators crawling over it. From one of the perspective angles offered up by the millions of nanotechnic cameras present on the scene, Raphael caught a glimpse of the massive burst in the sky several yards from where Tamil once stood.

"Jesus! What the hell was that?" Kohl said.

Mackey pounded away at the keyboard frantically. Scrolls of data spewed from the top of his screen to the bottom.

"Foreign replicators are attacking the Temple Mount."

"What? Do we have shields in the area?" Raphael asked.

The room erupted in chatter and shouting as a cloud of fire and destruction expanded over the Temple Mount. Mackey uttered series after series of expletives underneath his breath while Raphael's disposition exploded into hysteria along with the rest of the room.

"What's going on?"

He demanded an answer, but everyone ignored him. Kohl was running his mouth into a phone that led to God knows where, but the general just lodged his hand in the president's face and continued to holler into the receiver.

Raphael glared at the man, then ran over and plopped his face in front of Mackey's computer monitor.

"What's going on?"

Mackey keyed away in front of the screen, running his eyes left to right and quivering in fear as if death shone its headlights straight in his face.

"Wild replicators. Swarms of them. Legions of them!"

He pounded away on the keys, a frightened craze pouring from the depths of his soul, revealing itself through the expanding and contracting pupils of his eyes. With the stroke of a key, the screen summoned a visual blueprint with specifications numbered in the margins. Mackey traced it with his finger.

"I've never seen this design before. This isn't one of ours. Look at the complexity."

Around him, the whole room stammered in chaos. Two men and a woman ran through the aisles, and one official slammed his headset down in frustration. Raphael felt the desperation drench his body.

"What are we doing?"

Mackey threw his hands up.

"We're fighting it! We're fighting it! Just calm down!"

Raphael ran his fingers down the back of his neck, his elbow resting on his head like a hat, and with his free hand, he gnawed on his fingernails. By now, a thick cloud encapsulated the Temple Mount, and something changed the mood of the room. Mackey scurried through the screens on his computer. He slapped his hands together.

"Yes! Yes!"

"What? What?" Raphael asked.

"We're winning. We pushed past the tipping point. We've got him."

Throughout the room, cheers rushed to the ceiling. Raised thumbs lifted into the air, relaying the message of final victory from person to person. A joy of relief swept through the chamber as everyone patted each other on the back. Exasperated, Raphael's mouth hung open.

"What the hell just happened?"

Mackey looked up, his hands tired from the repetitive motion.

"The first nanotechnic war, Mr. President."

*   *   *   *

The far wall of the presidential suite flickered with color as screen after screen relayed the news of the day. The topic of central interest that continually flashed across the screens was the arrest of "The Big Three"—the President of the United States, the President of Russia, and the Prime Minister of Japan. All charged with crimes against humanity. The all news stations made a passing reference to the unexplained incident at the Temple Mount. Raphael leaned against his desk immersed in the news when the doorknob twisted open and Garrison stepped into the doorway.

Raphael stood up straight, his body all at once brimming with life. Garrison observed his friend, standing tall in the magnificent room. He breathed in the air. It was perfectly clean, not a single flake of dust floating within. Through the great window, the light of the sun fell down on Raphael, appearing as if it had doused him with a bucket of rays and set his body ablaze. Around him, a glittering cloud of foreign particles swirled in slow revolutions like tiny galaxies, making him literally bulletproof.

Outside the window, a cloud blocked the angle of the light, and the LOCUSTS disappeared, causing Raphael to once again resemble a normal human. Garrison approached him.

"How are you?"

Raphael returned a broad smile that traveled from ear to ear.

"Great. Just great."

He displayed a noticeable twitch, a tremor in his arms and hands as if his blood pressure boiled a stew of frustrated nerves. Then he shifted his body and paced the floor.

"Actually, I'm not great at all."

He threw himself into the chair behind his desk, his shoulders knotting up in bundles. Garrison looked down on his friend.

"What's wrong?"

The knots in Raphael's shoulders unraveled like spools of thread, and he plopped his hands flat on the desk.

"I had the world at my feet. I promised myself liberty and democracy would spread to every corner of the earth. No matter what, I would never let freedom slip away. Now…I don't know."

It looked as if his mind was wandering, as if he believed all his dreams had ended in failure. Garrison leaned on the corner of the desk.

"What's going on?"

Raphael looked at him in a way he hadn't since the death of Juan Diego.

"I don't know what to do. Sometime ago, we discovered the existence of a terrorist in possession of a stolen assembler."

Garrison angled his eyes side to side, aware of the incident at the Temple Mount.

"The man in Jerusalem?"

"His name was Tamil Al-Shehhi. Brother of a man involved in the New Year's Eve attacks."

"But you stopped him."

Raphael didn't respond. He seemed lost in a daydream. Garrison tapped on the desk.

"You stopped him, right?"

"Yeah," he said, his voice waning in strength. "We stopped him. But it's more complicated than that."

"Why?"

Raphael strummed his fingers on the wooden desk like miniature drumsticks, and his body rocked back and forth in the chair in a methodic rhythm. Without warning, his eyes began to glow.

"Do you remember the time when we fixed the water bucket over Eduardo's door, and it came splashing down?"

His hands drew an invisible picture of the doorway, and he laughed by himself at the thought. Garrison didn't crack a smile.

"What's going on?"

Raphael's once animated hands now cowered on the table, the victim of nervous tremors. He shifted in his chair, bouncing his leg on the floor, unable to sit still. But his head froze, and his eyeballs shifted at Garrison.

"The world is in grave and imminent danger. Things are drifting out of my control, and I don't know what to do."

"God will help you."

Raphael seemed to consider the possibility for a brief moment, then he placed his hand on Garrison's.

"Even God can't help me now."

"Of course he can."

Raphael shook his head.

"Maybe someone else, but not me Garrison."

"That's ridiculous. God can help anyone, no matter how dire the circumstances."

"Not me, Garrison. Remember the detention facility in Ar-Rutbah?"

"Yes."

"We transported Muslims from all over the world to that facility."

"You can't live in this world and not know that."

Raphael's tongue hesitated as if it wanted to form a series of words, but couldn't quite get them to come out and his eyes turned to stone, unblinking with eyelids painted open. His head shook side to side like a meadow of weeping willows swaying in the open breeze. Finally, the words crept out.

"They're dead. All of them."

His hands held his face, and his elbows were stacked on the table like a tripod.

"Every last one of them," he said.

A silence blared through the room.

"And do you know how many there were?" he asked.

Garrison shook his head.

"I don't want to know."

"One billion. One billion, two hundred sixty-five thousand twenty-one."

A hollow chill spiked into Garrison's body, emptying his arms and legs and feet of all blood flow. He stood up straight from his seat on the edge of the desk.

"Why?"

He could see the rolling streams of water slipping off of Raphael's arms and onto the desk, his face still buried in his hands. A broken voice escaped from the hands.

"I had no choice. An assembler was loose. We had no active shield. No way to build one without welcoming an attack. We needed carbon, and there was no alternative."

Garrison opened his mouth, but he couldn't speak. He placed his hand above his friend's head, then laid it on top. His heart wept for those who perished, and his soul bled in sorrow for the one before him. In a flash, Raphael leapt to his feet. He wiped his face clean and dragged his hands over his clothes like they were covered in filth.

"But I had to do it. I had no choice. Who knows what this last terrorist is like? To not act would've placed the world at the mercy of a regime like the Taliban, an eternal planet Taliban."

His eyes glowed like some strange nocturnal creature. He stared at Garrison locked in pure fantasy as if placed in another world far removed. Garrison didn't speak, but noticed the fidgeting hands as his friend paced the room.

"I'm not proud of what I was forced to do, but I will not let them die in vain. Freedom and liberty will not wither away on my watch. They had to die, and their blood will be the cornerstone of an eternal democratic world government."

Garrison returned to his seat on the corner of the desk.

"You have to consider that this problem may not have a solution."

"No. I will not give up. Giving up is not an option."

"I'm not talking about giving up. I'm talking about letting go of this dream and realizing there is something greater than the things of this world."

Raphael's neck swelled, his head turned red like an apple, and his face transfixed itself on some far off landscape outside his window. With unwavering passion, his right hand beat down into the palm of his left.

"No! Nothing is more important than the things of this world. If the world is headed toward destruction, so be it. But I'm going down fighting for it. No man will stand in my way. No religion, no group, no nation—no government will stand against me. With God as my witness, I will not let freedom slip away."

*   *   *   *

Garrison had left and Raphael stood in his office reflecting on the course of recent events when Jean entered. He took a seat just across from Raphael's desk.

"I've been thinking about our friend Tamil."

"And I've been thinking the same thing," Raphael said.

It was so clear he didn't understand why it wasn't his first suspicion from the day they located him.

"So what do you think?"

"The last terrorist gave Tamil an assembler with a bogus story about his brother."

Raphael scratched his forehead, studying the individual fibers in the rug beneath his feet.

"I agree. It's a theory we must consider seriously."

"Oh, it's not a theory."

Raphael lifted his gaze from the floor.

"Excuse me?"

Jean handed over a sheet of paper covered with numbers and letters.

"Following my instincts, I ran a check. Three of our own satellites were used to gather floods of data from the Temple Mount at that very hour."

Raphael clenched his jaw, his lips curling together.

"He used our own satellites?"

"He knows everything. The weaknesses in our designs. Our swarm capabilities. All of it."

Raphael picked a pencil up from his desk and clamped it between his teeth, gnawing his tooth marks into the wooden stick.

"At least we know what happened, even if we're not certain how. I assume our buddy was Saeed's long lost friend."

"Most likely, but one thing's certain. He's still out there. And he's someone to be reckoned with."

*   *   *   *

Jean stretched out his bony frame and leaned against the hardened wall of his office. His lips drew downward like those of a small woodland creature sipping from a pond, eyes erect and ever watchful, while the rim of the coffee cup caused a wave of hot steam to collect underneath his chin. Behind him, a ventilation grate piped out a steady stream of warm air that twisted through his yellow locks like the blades of a lawnmower on fields of crabgrass. He let a smile escape as Gilder walked through the door.

"I'm surprised to see you," he said.

Gilder hesitated in his reply and walked over to within inches of Jean's face. His voice spoke in a low whisper that harbored a twinge of anger.

"I should turn you in for treason. Or conspiracy."

Jean ripped off a swaggering smile and lifted the cup to his lips.

"Spare me. If you really felt that way, you wouldn't be here."

"I'm beginning to wonder why I am here."

Jean swallowed his coffee and placed the empty cup on an end table.

"We're here for the same reason. The man is incompetent and weak. He claims to fight terrorism while refusing to arrest his friends and their legions of followers."

"Maybe if we approached him—"

"Oh, come on, Offen! It's too late for that. Either he has the desire to combat religious fanaticism or he does not. We need decisive leadership at the helm. The world is still in grave danger."

"And who do we put in his place?"

"Myself, you, and other cabinet members. We'll govern by quorum. We can't risk another man having this much authority. Look at what it's done to Raphael. The man's drunk with power. He's become a modern day Caesar."

Gilder ran both his hands through his wavy hair, then used them to rub his neck. Jean moved into his face.

"This power belongs to Parliament, just as it belonged to the Senate in Rome."

Gilder lifted his head.

"What do we do first?"

"First, I'll take care of Garrison and Eduardo. It should have been done a long time ago."

"And what's my role?" Gilder asked.

Jean studied the man's face and smiled in his devilish toothy grin.

*   *   *   *

The tremendous crowd moved in lockstep like a slow moving river channeling its way between the homes of Palestinians, Jews, and the people of all nations. From one direction, angry fists hammered in hatred; from the other, gentle hands reached out in reverence. Garrison waded his way through the jungle of souls, Eduardo by his side, and listened to the stirring noise of love and hate as the two emotions melted into one voice.

"Rot in hell, you intolerant fascists!"

"We love you Garrison!"

"Go back to where you came from, Nazi pig!"

"If you don't like Vicente's government, leave!"

"Praise Jesus!"

Half the crowd heaped insults like grains of rice on a wedding party, while the other half poured out praise in heaping buckets. In the middle, arms and bodies and legs interlocked in conflict. Feet kicked, and elbows battled. Garrison drifted forward, unconcerned by the pushing and prodding of the herd. The slow moving river of faces continued to the end of the street, then stopped. A brief silence rippled through the masses, followed by a large number of people fleeing the street like scattering roaches caught by the kitchen light.

A giant opening formed itself in the wall of people, a tunnel rolling out like a long red carpet from Garrison's feet to those of Jean Riguad Prieur who now stood less than forty feet away. Garrison studied the man's bloodshot eyes. A cloud of LOCUSTS surrounded him, flying all around his body like an annoying flock of gnats. He stood, frozen in that position, like a gunslinger poised for a high noon showdown. Garrison stepped forward and approached him.

"Is there something you seek?" he asked.

"Yes," Jean said. "Your arrest."

Eduardo slung his arm into Garrison's stomach to protect him.

"On what charge?"

Jean gave an angry look.

"Religious intolerance. And you, Eduardo, will be arrested for sedition."

Eduardo charged forward, but Garrison grabbed him by the belt and pulled him back. Jean laughed in amusement.

"You're a smart man, Garrison."

"I have no fear of you. God is with us. What man can stand against us?"

"I can," Jean said.

He commanded the guards to arrest them. They grabbed Garrison and Eduardo and dragged them over to his feet. He knelt down and whispered in their ear.

"Bow down and worship this nation. Swear allegiance to United Europe, then we'll believe you aren't terrorists," he said.

Both remained silent, and Jean addressed the crowd.

"These men will not swear allegiance to their government! What kind of men are they?"

The mob convulsed with hateful epithets.

"Terrorists!"

"Intolerant bigots!"

"Nazi terrorists!"

Jean held up his hand to quiet the crowd.

"What shall I do with them?"

Then a mighty roar arose from the crowd, and with one voice they shouted, "Release them to us"! Jean pretended to be undecided, and the mob chanted in the street.

"Release them! Release them! Release them!"

Again, Jean held up his hand and silenced the mob.

"Very well," he said. "I will release them to be judged by their own people. Let their fate be a lesson to all those who oppose freedom and liberty."

He motioned to his entourage, and the guards threw Garrison and Eduardo into the crowd. The mob pounced on them and trampled their bodies into the cold gravel of the street. The elated celebration of captured prey consumed the street as the mob kicked and beat the two men, growing louder as the blood of the victims trickled into the rocks and mud.

The mob circled around the bodies like wild hyenas. Pockets of spit showered down on them, along with hateful curses. Jean turned to his guards.

"Make sure their bodies remain in the street—undisturbed," he said. "Let them be a message to those who will dare to oppose the preeminence of United Europe."

The guards placed signs on the two bodies which read, "Intolerant" and "Seditious". And the whole world rejoiced at the death of these two men who had tormented their beloved society.

*   *   *   *

The door of the presidential suite kicked open on its hinges and a swarm of LOCUSTS and SPIDERS barged through the entrance. Raphael sat on the edge of his desk with one leg dangling in the air and a wide open book resting in his lap. He turned only his head, the page still twisting in his hand, and he watched as several members of the presidential guard walked into the room. Jean followed behind them with Gilder in tow.

Raphael closed the book and placed it on his desk. He remained seated in the same position, and his leg lingered in the air as if swayed by a gentle breeze.

"What's the meaning of this?"

Jean stepped in front of the pack, and Gilder shuffled to his side.

"We're placing you under arrest," Jean said.

Raphael gently placed both feet on the floor and walked over to confront the group.

"On what charge?"

Jean took a slow stroll around Raphael, tracing a circle in the carpet as he stared at his boss.

"Weakness," he said. "Just plain old-fashioned weakness."

"What are you talking about?"

Jean returned to the pack of conspirators. His hands rested in his pockets and his back faced Raphael.

"Your leadership," he said. "This world faces the prospect of an eternal world-wide totalitarian regime because you are too weak to apprehend its terrorists. The religious intolerants especially. You know, your two friends?"

Raphael kept silent.

"Yes. Eduardo and Garrison," Jean said. "They've done nothing but stir up trouble since the day of the breakthrough. But they won't be causing anymore disturbances."

"Why do you say that?"

"Because they're dead."

A smile spread across his face as he gazed at Raphael who bit his lower lip, but restrained himself from physical or verbal anger. Jean shook his head.

"And you won't even show remorse for your dead friends, or defend their honor."

Jean pulled one of his hands from a pocket and swept his whole arm through the air.

"Arrest him."

No one moved. Only the faint buzz of LOCUSTS could be heard in the ensuing silence. Gilder stood expressionless and the presidential guard stood at attention like stone statues. Jean gnashed his teeth together, his face now red.

"I said, arrest him!"

The guards didn't flinch and the nanomachines held their position. Gilder turned, looked Jean in the eye, and then slowly walked over to Raphael's side and placed his hand on Raphael's shoulder. Raphael's flagrant stare blazed like a boring hot iron into his betrayer's body. He stepped forward, never letting the man out of his sight.

"You must've thought me weak if you believed for one second I would turn my back on you. Price—I'll have to admit—Price surprised me. But you? The only way you could've surprised me is if you hadn't tried to stab me in the back."

Jean now trembled under the weight of Raphael's glaring stare. A trickle of urine ran down his pant leg and formed into a puddle on the carpet. But even the puddle didn't divert Raphael's concentration.

"There is no moral authority in either strength or weakness," he said. "Moral authority comes from righteousness. But since you believe we should penalize weakness, we will judge you by your own standard."

He walked up to Jean and circled him as he spoke, retracing the steps of the condescending stride Jean had subjected him to moments earlier. Jean's hands trembled in fear and his eyes watered at their edges.

"You were weak for believing these men would follow you. You were weak for believing I would trust you, and you were weak for following your own selfish ambition rather than the good of humanity. Therefore, United Europe condemns you."

He tapped him on the head and walked away. Placing his hand on Gilder's shoulder, he whispered in a low voice.

"Where are Garrison and Eduardo?"

"Lying in a street in Jerusalem," Gilder said.

"What can we do?"

"Their bodies haven't decayed. It seems reasonable to believe they can be reanimated."

The idea gravitated through Raphael's mind. If only he had possessed the means to resurrect Poyner after her death.

"Do it. Go retrieve the bodies now."

All the time he spoke with Gilder, he nearly forgot Jean was still in the room. Turning around, he gave a flick of his wrist to the guards.

"Jean. I forgot you were still here," he said. "Dip him in the hole. And make it slow so he can watch what happens to his body."

Chapter 5:

Valley Of Har-Megiddo

"Blow the trumpet in Jerusalem! Sound the alarm on my holy mountain! Let everyone tremble in fear because the day of the Lord is upon us. It is a day of darkness and gloom, a day of thick clouds and deep blackness. Suddenly, like dawn spreading across the mountains, a mighty army appears! How great and powerful they are! The likes of them have not been seen before and never will be seen again."

—Joel
Joel 2:1–2

No other place on earth shrouded itself in such mystery. A man-made earthen mound built up by centuries of war, a handful of palm trees speckled the green plateau in the Jezreel Valley of Israel known as Mount Megiddo. In ancient times, Megiddo served as a fortified stronghold envied by kings. It controlled the flow of trade, and more importantly of armies, between the eastern and western parts of the known world, between Egypt and Mesopotamia. Each time the city fortress was ransacked and burned, the incoming conqueror rebuilt it. Each passing year, it traded hands and added new foundations on top of old ones to create an ancient landfill, a trash heap of history.

For centuries Megiddo lay in ruins, until today, when the power of nations resurrected the old city for one last purpose. Satellite up-links circled the base of the plateau, and moving columns of people inundated its surface like ants on a giant hill, while microphones swayed above their heads like thousands of tiny bobbing ostrich heads. Elated talk of a new era of human glory saturated the air. Standing in the middle of it all, Raphael approached his chief-of-staff.

"Did you get them?"

Gilder seemed uncomfortable with the question, squirming in his standing position.

"They aren't there."

"What? What do you mean they aren't there?"

Gilder kept his eyes on the ground, his shoulders low.

"Witnesses say they woke up, stood up in the place where their bodies lay, and flew off into the sky."

Raphael raised his hands into the air.

"Glory hallelujah, it's a miracle!"

He laughed out loud before chastising his advisor.

"Come on, you know Garrison had many followers. They probably stole his body so they could claim he rose from the dead, that he's the Messiah returned."

"Mr. President, we have the event on tape. It happened."

Impatience exhibited itself on Raphael's face, and a red color swelled around his eyes.

"Dead bodies don't rise from the dead and fly off to heaven. I lost my wife and my son. I will not lose my friends as well. Continue the search and don't stop until you find them."

Gilder consented, and Raphael climbed the edge of the stage. The crowd watched from their seats as the figure approached the podium, his hair floating through the breeze and his eyes fixed on the clouds.

"For centuries on end, the city of Megiddo was a home for war. And in the centuries since, it has enjoyed a reputation of horror and mystery. For the place where we now stand, the Hill of Megiddo, is bathed in legend. In Greek, the name Har-Megiddo translates into Armageddon, and the prophet

John singled it out as the place of final conflict between good and evil. In the Book of Revelation, John writes, 'And they gathered all the rulers and their armies to a place called Armageddon'."

He lifted his eyes from the prepared speech and let them glaze over the crowd. The hundreds and thousands of cameras bathed him in flashes of light.

"Today, the leaders of the world gather not as conquerors bent on destruction, but as men committed to peace. The last of the world's terrorist threats has been removed. The evil delusions of men like Tamil Al-Shehhi, men who seek to subjugate the will of free men to an authoritarian ideology—the evil dreams of such men have been eradicated. Only the bold dreams of a new generation remain, the threat of war no longer a possibility. For humanity has overcome war."

Each face in the congregation focused on the striking figure behind the podium, entranced by the glorious dust that encircled his body and the power it gave them to live like kings.

"The freedom-loving democratic nations of the world have banded together to destroy forever those false idols, those false systems of governance which led to previously unimagined slaughter and bloodshed. Together, we have exacted a resounding rebuke of war. We took on the great menace of our day, the greatest threat ever experienced in our history…the horrors of unconventional warfare—chemical, biological, and nuclear weapons. Together, we ended their threat and the dark shadow of the evil men who planned to use them. Together, we have fed a starving world and given refuge to the world's homeless. Realizing the dreams of prior generations, we have eliminated poverty, hunger, and disease."

Shoving his hands high in the air, he lifted his voice.

"What could one possibly add to the lists of accomplishments meted out by this generation? What generation could ever repay its debt to a people charged with ushering the human race from the edge of annihilation to this exalted plateau of everlasting life and prosperity? Could any age in history possibly compare?"

He looked out over the sea of faces—elated, intoxicated by the grand dreams of the future.

"But history demands much more of us than this. Although much has been done, much remains. To whisk humanity into the cradle of the stars, to take charge of our destiny as the rightful inheritors of the vast wonders of the

Milky Way. To feed the human mind with new discoveries and yet unknown galaxies. To educate every human life, to spread the benefits of assembler-based technologies, to build an international active shield protecting all men against the future threat of nanotechnic aggression. These are the tasks as yet unfinished."

He pounded his fist on the podium's frame, and jutted his chest outward like a strutting beast.

"But humanity is up to this challenge. Humanity will not fail. For we have overcome obstacles in the past, and we will be victorious once again. The great threats that once plagued our past are now relics of that past, but the great triumphs of the age rest at our fingertips. What idea can change our destiny? What army can stop us? What god can thwart our plans? For we will overcome them all!"

From the base of the hill to the top of its surface, body after body rose from its seat in rapturous applause. The crowd believed every word, but alone among them, Raphael knew the world still faced a grave and imminent danger—a single terrorist who still roamed the earth. He smiled at them and waved his hand through the air as they called out his name.

"Long live Vicente! Long live Vicente!"

The whole of the crowd fell into a rhythmic chant, unaware that their leader had gathered them together as bait for that final terrorist. Raphael blushed at the adulation of the crowd, knowing them to be a target so tempting the last terrorist would have to stick his head out, and when that moment arrived, he was determined to cut it off.

*   *   *   *

Using the same satellites of the enemies he sought to crush, Jiang Yafei watched the gathering at Armageddon with heightened interest. He studied the democratically elected leader of China who joined in the applause, and the clanking echo of his fat hands drove Jiang's blood pressure higher and higher. What a vile, malicious traitor! As a youth, he learned to fear the foreign progenitor, the enemy from abroad. Never in his wildest dreams, did he surmise a scenario where his own countrymen would align with Western enemies. That they could allow the nation's sovereignty to be trampled, its culture subdued, and its values replaced by a rekindled form of European colonialism.

He was forced to watch as United Europe snatched the glory of his Chinese Empire at the final moment, carrying its leaders away in chains. For all these many months, he prepared—plotting his future attack with meticulous precision and infinite patience. The time for action had arrived.

The Chinese people remained superior beings, and this total victory over the world's other nations would confirm and record this fact for all of eternity. Trained from birth to restore the glory of Imperial China, Jiang had succeeded beyond his father's wildest expectations. With little fanfare, and only himself with whom to celebrate, he put in motion his plan of conquest.

*   *   *   *

In a small church several blocks from Jiang Yafei, a bride and groom stood next to each other in the presence of their wedding guests. As they accepted their vows, horrible sores broke out on the bodies of all the guests, causing everyone to stand up from their seats and bat at their own skin, cursing the sores.

Inside their bodies, mechanically engineered strains of chicken pox, long dormant, erupted into action and attacked their internal organs. Feeding off their hosts, the machines continuously churned out copies of a series of self-sustaining replicators, capable of surviving in nature and unrestrained in their ability to multiply.

Never letting his eyes leave the face of his bride, the groom screamed out as her face dissolved in front of him as if eaten away like a carcass covered with flies. Her gown fell to the floor, but quickly disintegrated as the flies descended on it like moths feasting on a box of ragged clothes. The groom lunged forward as his own body decayed in mid-movement.

Throughout the wedding party, guests turned to dust, their bodies rusting away like burnt cigarette butts—the leftover ash blowing away as the fluffy rods of a dandelion in the springtime breeze. The room filled with a rising tide of voracious replicators, piling up to the ceiling and sweeping in every direction.

Bent only on destruction, they pecked away at the structure of the physical world surrounding them, tearing apart the remaining guests and bursting through the sides of the building. Outside, the light of the sun grew dark as a black cloud of replicators eclipsed the sky and surged westward like waves of churning ocean.

Cars crashed into walls and embankments as their drivers whittled away. Airplanes bumped through the air and spiraled to the ground, their engines caught in the mass of tiny machines and their pilots eaten alive. Yet before they crashed to the ground, they were overtaken by the violent tide of angry replicators.

In the oceans, fish, mammals, and plant life broke into pieces, flooding the depths of the seas with armies of replicating nanomachines. Sensors deployed by United Europe detected the threat and unleashed a counterassault of their own to halt the advance. The surface of the oceans turned red with blood as replicators shredded every living creature and conscripted atoms into the mightiest fighting force ever assembled. The oceans dwindled in size as if someone had opened a drain and poured them out, and as the water level receded, a giant wall of black and gray goo rose to the heavens in a towering tsunami of nanomachines.

*   *   *   *

On Mount Megiddo, Raphael waved to the cameras and his fellow leaders as he met with his staff. Gilder approached him, shaking his head. It was obvious something was underway. Gilder handed him a secured phone, and Raphael lifted it to his head.

"Did it work?"

General Kohl's voice spoke from the other end.

"He struck less than one minute ago, Mr. President."

"Have you isolated his position?"

"Yes, sir. We believe he's in Beijing. The enemy forces have been launched from mainland China."

A tide of emotion steam-rolled Raphael as he finally got his answer to the torturing question. China. Could it be true that the People's Republic had been responsible for the New Year's Eve attacks, Tamil's test run, and now, the world's final act of terror? It made more sense than the alternatives. But that was part of the past. For the moment, Raphael only cared about winning.

"What's the status?"

"A mass of replicators is moving westward, encompassing most of the Eastern Hemisphere. But our counter forces are ready for them."

"What will be the outcome?"

"He obviously underestimated our preparedness, Mr. President. Most all of the designs he's using are from his test operation at the Temple Mount."

A smile formed in the corners of Raphael's mouth, but the voice continued.

"However, he's incorporated some new designs into his forces, designs more potent than originally anticipated."

"What's that supposed to mean?"

"Only that it will be tougher than we thought."

"We'll still win. Won't we?"

Flush patches of red climbed up the back of Raphael's neck, and sweat beaded up on his forehead. His voice fumbled at the prospect of anything less than the absolute victory he sought. Kohl's voice hesitated—for only a fraction of a second, and this made the blood spill even further over Raphael's face. He repeated himself.

"We'll win, won't we?"

This time, Kohl gave the answer his boss wanted.

"Victory is ours, Mr. President. We won before it began."

*　　*　　*　　*

Following his prediction of imminent victory, General Kohl gazed over the shoulder of Edwin Mackey with a dour frown resting on his chin. Complete panic overtook the Operations Room with people racing through the aisles of computers and pounding away at their keyboards. Mackey remained still behind his monitor, no visible emotions present, but more of a shocked surprise at what was happening.

"He's just turning earth into gray goo...Intentionally!"

Kohl didn't respond to the statement, but watched the wall of images as they relayed the horror. It was a simple scorched earth policy. Maybe the weapons of war had changed, but the tactics remained the same. The battle plan was genius. Whoever this guy was, he would destroy every square inch of the earth except the place where he stood then he would rebuild it from scratch with god-like authority. Kohl shook his head.

"Respond in kind."

Mackey turned in his chair.

"What?"

"You heard me. Respond in kind. It's our only option. You fight fire with fire. Get our AI systems working on competing designs superior to his and turn over every decision on strategy to AI. We need to do whatever we can to overwhelm his forces."

Mackey hesitated, his mouth lurched open. Kohl shoved him in the back. "Do it now. That's an order."

With reluctance, Mackey moved forward with the plan while Kohl issued the order to everyone. It was the only option, and at that moment, the war accelerated.

In the brief seconds after the war was put on autopilot, the outer atmosphere of the earth deteriorated. Atom-hungry replicators picked out all the available elements, clamoring to seal final victory for United Europe. Those in the Western Hemisphere, as of yet spared the wrath of Jiang's chicken pox, witnessed a sudden thinning of cloud cover and the disappearance of the ozone layer. The sun's raw energy rained down, pelting the earth's surface with waves of blistering heat. Most of the victims died from direct contact, but those who lived cursed the earth and everyone on it as well as the heavens and everyone in them.

The ocean waters, long turned into a towering tsunami of destruction, swept forward, eating away at the land and gathering in strength and height like a rolling ball of ice tumbling down a snow covered mountain. The eastern wall of water hoisted itself to the heavens while transforming the landscape into an army of complex replicating military machines, small but capable of infinite destruction. They pounced on the Euphrates River, sucking it dry as they passed over. The leftover bits and pieces of two hundred million Chinese citizens swirling in their ranks as the tsunami of replicators headed for Megiddo.

From the west and north, a towering wall of equal power hurled toward Megiddo. It bled the Nile dry and destroyed every object in its path. It crushed the pieces as small as chaff on a threshing floor, and the wind blew them all away without a trace.

*   *   *   *

On Megiddo, the lush plateau teeming with the world's leaders transformed in an instant. Raphael fell to his knees in horror as he saw people eaten alive in front of him, and the air thinned under the burden of a nanotechnic war. People panicked and scattered from the lawn like roaches. His dreams of a utopia, everything he had worked for his entire adult life, shattered to pieces right in front of him. He had given his wife's life, his child's life, his own life, and the lives of others in a desperate effort to preserve hope, liberty, and freedom for future generations. But it was all in vain.

As the gathering at Armageddon fell into disarray, the sky returned as a blanket of black clouds. Darkness enveloped the area, and thunder crashed and rolled overhead. The earth began to shake uncontrollably, escalating into a massive earthquake that tore the earth asunder.

Across the world, the mustered forces of United Europe and Red China swept away entire cities, transforming them into heaps of moving dust. The oceans disappeared, the islands in them disappeared, and every mountain on the earth flattened as the armed forces of the world's two final superpowers conscripted all available matter into the conflict. The swift and massive changes to the atmosphere caused hail to fall down onto what was left of a dying world. Out of the small remnant of humanity still alive, several found themselves crushed by hailstones weighing hundreds of pounds or more.

Voracious machines loosed every atom within grasp, breaking chemical bonds, the very fabric of the physical universe tearing like a brittle curtain. From his knees, Raphael looked to the heavens, and he could see a ray of hope riding in on the clouds. The figure of someone who looked like a man dominated the sky, clothed in beauty and splendor. From his knees, Raphael's mouth fell open long enough to ask his question.

"Who are you Lord?"

A spark of life entered his brain, trickling down through his body as if to cleanse his soul, then a gentle voice declared within him.

"I am Jesus."

Raphael hung his head. The anger fled his body, and a sense of peace poured over him. He gave little thought to his utopian visions and grand dreams. They had all come to nothing. All he could think of now was *her*.

How he wanted so much to see her again, to touch the soft blade of her shoulder, to stand in the warmth of her smile. How he wanted the pain to end forever, because even with all his worldly power, he could never relinquish the pain. He could never rid himself of the void that burdened his soul.

CHAPTER 6:

Effervescent Dreams Of Places

"Now learn a lesson from the fig tree. When its buds become tender and its leaves begin to sprout, you know without being told that summer is near. Just so, when you see the events I've described beginning to happen, you can know his return is very near, right at the door. I assure you, this generation will not pass from the scene before all these things take place. Heaven and earth will disappear, but my words will remain forever."

—Jesus Christ
Matthew 24:32–35

Sliding through the wind like bits of paper, the multicolored leaves cascaded downward, nudged along by the icy-cool breeze that lazily drove its way past. Riding the mountains like a rolling carpet, these leaves of every shape, color, and size dotted the walls of the figure's world. Their pastel colors melted into the receding skyline, creating a luminescent stage for the unavoidable drop.

They were crisp and ripe and tumbling in the wind, most likely unaware that their lives were about to be cut short, snuffed out forever. For each leaf had to fall, whether it acknowledged so or not. Soon, thousands and millions and billions of them would foolishly stumble back and forth upon the frozen turf with no particular destination in mind, and the trees would all be bare and the mountains would be carpeted by the biting frost of early November.

The wind picked up as they scattered across the lawn, and the shadows succeeded in overtaking all but the last reflected rays of light as the mountains met and dissolved with the setting sun. It was the time of year when the summer became the fall, when the warmth of the sun and the bitter cold breeze pecked at your cheeks and bore into your arms with a slow swarm of prickling needles from one of Poe's horrendous and imaginative creations.

Sputtering over the hilltops, it was these last remaining rays of light that excited the figure. The change of seasons mitigated one of those moments when everything seemed to unite together in just the right combination, with everything falling into place in such a way that forced his spirit to scream out with life. The air seasoned itself with sprinkles of a biting frost that burned his nose and throat just slightly enough to remind him that he was alive and free and brimming with life and the anticipation of all that was good. The sky rendered the illusion that a giant paint brush had plundered its canvas for only his eyes, and the fallen leaves, with their crisp bodies and smoldering aroma—those he could almost taste! Figures live for such moments, and for all his good intentions and grand dreams and generous longing—this figure remained no different from any other. He breathed in the moment and relished its flavor like a fine and aged wine. It swirled around, untainted and complete with the incense of the season and the strands of copper-golden hair that belonged to *her*.

The warm cradle of her breath…the electrifying touch of her hand…it all poured over him, drowning the void that pierced his soul and rescuing it from certain death in the lonely desert in which he now resided. With unblemished temerity, her touch emitted an aesthetic sensation, steam-rolling his fear and crushing his anxiety. It was the spark that ignited his reason for being—*her*.

Detached from the world, in one arm he held *the Book of Life*. In the other, he held her. And, as if by some unknown physical law that compelled him, the figure orbited her. From the depth of his being, he was drawn to her, and his entire life emanated from her. All of his magnificent illusions and charitable deeds were dust—a mere pittance—when placed in contrast to his dream of dreams, his well of life—*her!*

A series of automatic lamps snapped on, engulfing the lawn and flooding the darkness with light, especially the exterior of the Rotunda building high atop its majestic spreading steps. Still, it was barely enough light by which to read, and the book neared its climatic conclusion. The rising chill in the air drove Poyner Vicente closer into the arms of her husband as it pierced and singed her cheeks, and amid the icy chill, the two turned the pages of the good doctor's new and exciting book.

"I want to finish the last chapter!" she said.

She tore the book from his hands, and he only half-heartedly fought back.

"But this book is like five pages, there are no chapters!"

She smiled in her usual playful manner and looked into his eyes as she brought the book before her, and amused, he willingly submitted himself to her pleasure as she completed their book and added her own words and plot twists to the good doctor's story—a story of triumph, a story of human will, a story of dreams and places…*the Book of Life!* And as the starry-eyed skyline surrounded its victims, she read him those last words.

"And will you succeed? YES! Yes, you will indeed! 98 Percent and three-fourths guaranteed. KID, YOU'LL MOVE MOUNTAINS! So…be your name Buxbaum or Bixby or Bray, or Mordecai Ali Van Allen O'Shea, you're off to Great Places! Today is your day! Your mountain is waiting. So…*get on your way!* And, oh, oh indeed, my sweet Mr. Vicente! The places you will go!" she giggled.

"Oh," she whispered in the frigid cold of the darkness, "Oh, the places you will go…"

AUTHOR'S NOTE

"States at war fight like beasts, but using citizens as their bones, brains, and muscle. The coming breakthroughs will confront states with new pressures and opportunities, encouraging sharp changes in how states behave. This naturally gives cause for concern. States have, historically, excelled at slaughter and oppression."

—**K. Eric Drexler,**
Engines of Creation

The characters in *Conquest of Paradise* are complete works of fiction; the ongoing international race to build an assembler is not. September 11th raised the stakes and provided a necessary incentive for the Western democracies to accelerate the day of the assembler breakthrough. By the close of this decade, assemblers will be a reality of our world, and no issue could be considered of greater importance to our current national security debate.

The creation of assemblers will provide the leading force with an unprecedented concentration of absolute power over the material world. And the prospect of deliberate abuse of that power threatens to destroy human liberty or perhaps life itself. In an environment such as this, we must remain on guard against the pitfalls of mob rule and demagoguery. The perpetuation of bad ideas will complicate an atmosphere in which our leaders will have little room for error.

The horrors of September 11th opened many eyes to the awful reality of the post-Cold War world. We now live in an era when a single individual or a small group can transform the foreign policy of the world's lone superpower. America faces her greatest crisis since the Civil War, and the first real threat to her shores since the War of 1812. The proliferation of nuclear, chemical, and biological weapons provides terrorists with an almost infinite number of options for attacking the global economic system. The financial and logistical impossibility of guarding against every possible attack necessitates the construction of assemblers to defend our way of life. Just as December 7th catapulted the world into the Nuclear Age, September 11th will plunge it into the Nanotechnic Age.

Ironically, the assembler breakthrough will lead the Western democracies to certain and total victory over radical Islamic terrorism, but in its place, a greater threat will emerge—the threat of assembler abuse itself. Because of the accelerated development of molecular nanotechnology (MNT), assemblers will be unleashed on a world ill prepared to handle them. Efforts in the field of exploratory engineering will likely be expended creating new weapons to win the war, rather than focusing on the groundwork for a non-partisan active shield. The war on terror has increased the probability assemblers will strike an eternal deathblow to human life and liberty by leading to the premature birth of MNT.

Over centuries of development, the industrial revolution spawned Nazi fascism, Soviet and Chinese communism, sweat factories, genocide, and countless other horrors and atrocities. We should expect similar growing pains during the nanotechnic revolution, although we will not be afforded the same luxury of time. The industrial revolution unfolded at a relatively slow pace. In the few months following the assembler breakthrough, humanity will experience a greater level of technological advancement than has been experienced from the dawn of time until the publication of this book.

I encourage everyone to learn as much as possible about MNT. By preparing ourselves before the assembler breakthrough, we can avoid the most dangerous pitfalls. The primary organization seeking to create universal guidelines for the safe development of MNT is the Foresight Institute. Anyone wishing to learn more should visit their website as well as read the book *Engines of Creation* by its founder, Dr. K. Eric Drexler. Also, visit the US government's website at nano.gov.

Whether used for ill or not, assembler-based nanotechnology is imminent. It will come upon most of the world swiftly and without warning. I hope *Conquest of Paradise* will help bring these issues to the forefront of public debate. By working together and preparing in advance, we have the opportunity to ensure a new era for the human race, one of material abundance with liberty and freedom for all.

Britt Gillette
20 December, 2002

www.nano.gov

www.foresight.org

www.brittgillette.com

About the Author

Britt Gillette is a member of the Foresight Institute and a fervent advocate of mass public education on the benefits and dangers of the coming era of molecular nanotechnology. He currently resides in Chesapeake, Virginia. To learn more about the author, please visit his website...

www.brittgillette.com

0-595-26454-9